MW01223729

LIGHTLAND

LIGHTLAND

KENNY KEMP

Alta Films
PRESS
SAN DIEGO

LIGHTLAND
Copyright © 2008 Kemp Enterprises, Inc.

This is a work of fiction. Name, characters, places and incidents are
either the product of the author's imagination or are used fictitiously,
and any resemblances to actual persons, living or dead, business
establishments, events, or locales is entirely coincidental.

Cover and author photo by Douglas Page.
Photos copyright © 2008 Kemp Enterprises, Inc.

Library of Congress Cataloging-in-Publication Data

Kemp, Kenny.
Lightland : a supernatural thriller / by Kenny Kemp.
p. cm.
ISBN 978-1-892442-39-0 (trade pbk.)
1. Viruses—Fiction. 2. Human cloning—Fiction.
3. Future life—Fiction. I. Title.
PS3561.E39922L54 2007
813'.54—dc22   2007032695

02 03 04 05

PRINTED IN U.S.A.

www.kennykemp.com

Alta Films
PRESS

LIGHTLAND

PART ONE

_____

EASTERN AFRICAN SAVANNA

4000 B.C.

THE OTHER WORLD

A twig snapped underfoot. K'tanu froze, gripping his spear, afraid to breathe. Talon, awakened from his light slumber, raised his massive head and scanned the tall grass. K'tanu struggled not to cry out when the lion's shaggy head turned in his direction and stopped.

He was well-protected by the thick reeds; the lion could not possibly see him. He was downwind; the lion could not possibly smell him. But Talon was looking directly at the place where K'tanu crouched, and he knew the lion could definitely *feel* him.

Suddenly, Talon got to his feet and coiled himself. K'tanu hurled himself backward, trying to find his feet. In one great leap, Talon was where K'tanu had been a second before, and in another, he'd have the young hunter by the throat. K'tanu raced to his left, knowing it would take the cat a moment to hear where he'd gone. But that moment had already passed between one leaping footfall and another, and Talon knew his quarry's course. He came charging through the brush, letting out a blood-curdling roar.

K'tanu lost his footing at the edge of the springs and went down, slamming his knee against a sharp rock. Pain radiated up his leg, but he dared not slow. The thunderous footfalls behind him betrayed no hesitation. He could almost feel the animal's hot breath on his neck.

K'tanu broke through the head-high grass and was momentarily disoriented. Instead of the wooded savanna of the rolling caldera floor stretching out before him, he was high above on the collapsed volcano's rim, only a few paces from the precipitous edge. Without thinking, he sprinted toward it. Before he had taken three steps, Talon burst from the tall grass behind him, yellow eyes squinted with effort, silver ropes of saliva trailing from massive jaws. In two more steps the lion would have him, and K'tanu would die.

But not in your jaws, he thought, throwing himself off the cliff.

Behind him, Talon ground to a stop, paws on the edge of the abyss, chest heaving, golden eyes focused on the dark abyss below, ears pricked with the sound of K'tanu's trailing cry.

THE WAKING WORLD

K'tanu cried out and awoke, his fists clenched. He blinked in the darkness. A moment before, the lion had chased him off the cliff, and yet here he was, alive, in his own hut. He had almost perished in the Other World. The diviners said that when you died in the Waking World, your Other World life ended as well. The reverse, said the old diviner Antram, must also be true. But not this time. Splaying his fingers, K'tanu forced himself to stop shaking. He whispered his gratitude to Mother Moon for sparing him. She had brought him back alive to the Waking World.

He glanced down at his injured knee that moments before had been gushing blood. He felt his kneecap for sticky wetness, but there was none. Another grateful prayer and then he turned to Maya, fully expecting to see her awake and startled at his cries.

But she slept, breathing shallowly, her lips and eyes and hands puffy from the Sickness. Over the last few days she had slept rarely, even though she was exhausted. But the blue-black bruises on her face could not overshadow her beauty. Even approaching death, she was striking: high cheekbones, full lips, and a narrow chin that went almost to a point. K'tanu gently stroked the rows of scars under her eyes. She stirred and turned away, wandering in her own Other World.

Beyond her was the baby, a tiny girl only twenty days old. When she was born, the entire village was elated that she had been spared the Sickness—no other baby had. But joy turned to anguish when the first bruises on her tiny arms and belly began to appear, and her clear eyes soon turned red with blood. She cried weakly, her stomach bloated, her hands and feet cracked and bleeding, and on her tiny dark face an expression of painful wonder at the misery of her newly-entered Waking World.

K'tanu uttered another thankful prayer to Mother Moon that his return had not awakened Maya or the child. He kissed Maya on the forehead, then kissed his forefinger and touched it to the sleeping baby's lips. He picked up his spear and shield and crept out of the hut. Just before leaving, he turned back, reaching under the woven sleeping mat and retrieving the tiny ivory carving from the depression in the dirt floor.

Outside, Mother Moon was turning away and only a sliver of her gown could be seen. Father Sun was still hours from birth. Though the Sickness had caused great sorrow in the village, this time of month was always the happiest—if happiness were still allowed—because for a few short days, Father Sun would race across the sky, chasing Mother Moon, who would still be visible all morning until she disappeared behind the western mountains shortly after midday. On most days, as he followed his teasing wife through the sky, he rarely saw her; but for three or four days a month, Father Sun would be blessed with the sight of her increasingly slender image, laughing and turning away, moving steadily toward the far horizon.

Once, when K'tanu was a child, Father Sun actually caught his wife in a twist of roles that only married people understood. That day, Mother Moon arose shortly after he did, and that afternoon she came and stood in front of him. D'ranja, K'tanu's mother, said Father Sun was kissing his wife, and though the gray shadow covering the land terrified the little boy, D'ranja hugged him, turning him away. "They want privacy, K'tanu. Just like your father and I."

"Will they ever stop kissing?

"Yes," she said. "In a few minutes, Mother Moon will laugh and tug Father Sun's beard. Then she will flee and he will chase her again."

She did just that, and when the shadowed world returned to brightness and Mother Moon disappeared behind the glory of her husband, little K'tanu breathed a sigh of relief.

Now, under the starry arc of heaven, he looked up at Mother Moon. "Watch over my family," he whispered. "And the others," he said, nodding at the circular mud and dung huts in the village. "Turn away your wrath." He bowed, facing east, hands held out, palms up, and then stood. He knew what he had to do. Picking up his lance and shield, he skirted the fire pit and stopped at Antram's hut. He whistled his low, unique greeting. There was stirring inside and soon Antram's bald head emerged. He pulled a leopard skin around him and squinted up at K'tanu.

"Are you ready to go?" asked K'tanu.

"I'll bless you," said Antram, getting slowly to his feet. He touched K'tanu's neck amulet, a ropy bend of human-shaped silver on a leather thong. He closed his eyes, lifting his chin. "Care for K'tanu on his quest. Give him success, that he might prove our worthiness." He opened his eyes and smiled up at K'tanu, then suddenly coughed—a long, racking cough that brought up bloody red spittle. K'tanu helped the old man sit on a nearby stone, and only then did he see the diviner's chest. K'tanu pulled back in horror. Now he knew why Antram was not coming with him. Antram saw K'tanu's look and pulled his leopard-skin cloak tighter around him, hiding the bloody pustules and bruises.

"And now you," whispered K'tanu, horrified.

The old man nodded. "No one knows, only you."

"Then we are all doomed," said K'tanu bleakly.

"Not if you are successful. I wish I could go with you. I truly wanted to."

"Besides me, you were the only one healthy enough to help."

"At my age, I wouldn't have been much help even if I were not sick. Perhaps I could have acted as the bait, but I doubt I could have done much more," said Antram, smiling weakly.

"In the Other World, just moments ago, Talon stalked and killed me."

"Obviously not, for here you are," said Antram. "That is the Other World, not this one."

K'tanu nodded doubtfully. "But sometimes they collide."

"Yes," said Antram, fingering his own silver amulet thoughtfully, "they do." In the distance, a jackal howled, and a moment later, another answered. "The Waking World goes on," said Antram. "We are but a small part of it. Our flesh feeds the hyenas and our bones feed the earth."

"I have been thinking about the Valley of Bones."

"You will not hunt there, I hope," said Antram, clutching K'tanu's arm.

"No. It is too far, beyond the crater. But it is a powerful place—a place of answers, I think."

"And questions," said Antram. "In that gorge, the Other World spills into ours. But you can learn nothing there that will help us here; it is a place of darkness, not light."

K'tanu nodded, even as he thought about the leather pouch at his waist. It contained a mandible he had found in the Valley of Bones during his vision quest years before. As he walked down the rocky defile on a stifling hot afternoon, the jawbone had called out in a weak, anguished voice, and he had turned. All along the valley walls, rocks and bones and teeth of animals and men protruded— strange, unknown animal skeletons with immense curved tusks, and curious, ape-like skulls. The sobbing jawbone jutted forcefully from the hillside as if to say, "Hear me!" K'tanu had followed the voice, and on the other side of a large boulder he saw the mandible, half exposed. He dug it free from the shale wall, brushed the sand and dirt from it, and thereafter kept it in a soft leather pouch tied to his waist cinch.

Once in a great while the mandible would speak—so quietly that only K'tanu could hear—and he would open the pouch and hold the yellowed bone up to his ear. It would whisper strange and confusing things, but occasionally it would also tell K'tanu when a storm was coming or where the white-tailed antelope were grazing or if Maya was thinking of him.

And long before anyone fell ill, the jawbone told K'tanu about the Bleeding Sickness. So when a child came down with a fever and malaise and others believed it was the Sleeping Sickness, K'tanu knew they were mistaken. Within days the whites of the child's eyes had turned a bright red, and his little face took on a drooping, masklike expression as he lay in his family's hut. His stools were bloody and large blue-black bruises covered his body. He vomited a chunky black liquid. He became delirious, and many villagers suspected demons and hid from the sound of his cries. Soon the little boy was bleeding from the ears, nose, and mouth, and even his pores oozed blood. His distraught mother sat with him, horrified, wiping away the blood, clutching her own silver amulet and weeping.

Antram prayed for the child, but the bleeding did not stop. After a week, the exhausted child finally fell asleep and never woke up. And when the villagers lifted him from the bed, the skin on his bloated stomach tore open and a torrent of stinking black tissue gushed out. His organs had liquified, and his bones floated in a thick, bloody stew. They couldn't even bury him in the cliff tombs in nearby Ngoro caldera as was their custom, for there was nothing left to treat and wrap. Soon after, his mother fell ill and died. Within a month, nearly half the village was dead.

That was just six weeks ago, and this night, with the slender Mother Moon overhead and Antram's bruised chest revealed, K'tanu realized he was the last able-bodied man in the village and the only one with the strength to curb the gods' anger.

THREE

THE CALDERA

K'tanu opened the wooden gate and stepped outside the village. Just beyond the perimeter, a ring of protective thorn bushes surrounded the bodies of twenty-three of his fellow clansmen who had died. Their bodies were waiting to be purified, stuffed with natron, wrapped in linen, covered with bitumen tar, and carried to the caldera. There they would be buried facing west, the scarab amulet placed under hands crossed across their chests, their hearts removed from their bodies and sealed in white stone jars to await the call of Father Sun, who would receive them in Lightland to follow him on his journeys across the sky forever and ever.

Under Antram's direction, K'tanu had prepared many of the dead for burial. But if Antram died, then everyone's soul was in jeopardy. K'tanu was not a diviner; he did not know the spells and prayers; he was unsure about certain steps of the mummification ritual. Without Antram's crucial knowledge, the dead would not be able to navigate their way across the broad, black River of Death and they would never find Lightland.

As he walked along the path toward the caldera, K'tanu scanned himself for traces of the Sickness. He ran a hand over his forearm, but felt no tenderness. He touched his bushy stubble of hair, but felt no sores. He had not vomited, his stools had been firm, and his dark eyes were clear of blood. He was still healthy, and had counted on helping Antram prepare Maya and the baby for burial. What would he do if Antram died before they did? How would he make certain that his family could find the light?

The path turned at the crater rim, plunging down the wall in steep switchbacks to the caldera floor two thousand feet below. As K'tanu cleared the forest, which gave out a few feet from the rim, he stopped, trying to see where he had burst from the swamp in the Other World, chased by the lion Talon. But, of course, there was no swamp anywhere on the caldera rim. The thicket existed only at Nokitok Springs far below on the crater floor, on this side of the veil of sleep—more evidence that while the Other World was similar to this one, different rules applied there. For instance, in that world, one could fly. And one might swim underwater for hours without taking a single breath. And one might die there as well. His mother had died in the Other World, and when they went to her hut in the morning, her spirit had fled. That was two years ago, and her body had been buried in a carved-out tomb on the caldera wall.

Just then a distant explosion turned K'tanu around. In the black predawn eastern sky, K'lii spit fire, turning the low clouds surrounding the summit a dusky red. The rumblings echoed past Ngoro caldera, passed the Valley of Bones, rolled across the grassy savanna, and finally slipped quietly into the waters of the Great Sea, many days' walk to the west.

K'tanu's people did not go to K'lii, for it was Father Sun's birthplace and was sacred. Two years ago, when someone suggested that Father Sun didn't actually rise from K'lii, Antram just shook his head. "K'lii is his birthplace, but he doesn't begin his journey there. He is born, then he searches for his wife. When he spies her, he begins the chase across the sky."

Antram told them the story. The Ngoro caldera was Mother Moon's birthplace, and it was once a volcano bigger than K'lii. In ancient days, she did not traverse the night sky as she did now, but accompanied Father Sun on his daily journey, invisible behind his brightness. And each evening, when Father Sun would grow old and die in orange fire on the western horizon, Mother Moon would cry, fearing her beloved husband would not be reborn the next day. Her fear made her wakeful, and she began to travel the darkness of night, tracing his daytime journey, watching over him. When K'lii ignited Father Sun's fire at dawn, she ran happily ahead, and he would chase her across the daytime sky. Sometimes she would trick him, slipping in front of him, eclipsing his light, as she had when K'tanu was a child. Theirs was a joyful marriage, built upon duty and passion—a love to emulate.

Ngoro volcano, abandoned by Mother Moon as she took to the sky, collapsed, leaving only the tall, jagged walls as a reminder of its ancient purpose. When Father Sun learned of his wife's nightly devotions, he gave her a generous gift. He placed animals in the crater for her enjoyment: ponderous gray elephants, browsing giraffes, numberless square-jawed wildebeests, glistening black rhinos in the muddy spring waters, chittering chimps in the pot-bellied baobab trees, stealthy spotted cheetahs and leopards, slinking caracals and golden jackals, and a dozen types of gazelle and antelope. He also placed several prides of lions, one of which lived in Nokitok Springs, on the crater floor directly below where K'tanu stood. This was the very spot he had leapt off, screaming, in the Other World. He turned and peered into the forest, but he did not see Talon's glowing eyes, nor did he hear his heavy, rasping breath.

As he picked his way down the steep slope, K'tanu envisioned the first rays of Father Sun, which would slant across the shadow-filled caldera bowl. As he rose, Father Sun's rays would awaken the animals he'd given to Mother Moon. Starlings would flit through the fever trees and thousands of flamingos would gracefully take to the sky on their way to the Great Sea, five walks to the west. Lions would loll on granite outcrops, yawning and stretching, welcoming the light.

The Waking World near Ngoro was a beautiful place. There was ample game. Most of the nearby clans were peaceful. And yet the Bleeding Sickness had come, and the people feared they had angered Father Sun and Mother Moon. Perhaps an incorrect prayer; a lapse in morning oblations; a failure to prepare the dead properly; a lack of gratitude after a successful hunt. But were any of these sins sufficient to merit the slaughter of young and old, healthy and sick, good and evil? Antram had killed a hyena and examined its entrails for clues, but he could not discern what sins the people had committed or how to appease the gods.

Just last week a stranger came to the village, begging for help. His face was a bruised mask and he coughed blood. Antram listened to his tale of death in his own village, and held the man's head when the death rattle came. He was buried in the clan's tombs in the crater wall. Day after day, K'tanu had helped Antram and the last two healthy women prepare bodies for burial; but when bloody bruises appeared on both women's necks and breasts, they took to their huts. He had not seen them since yesterday. He did not want to go into their mud shelters, for he knew what lay within.

And now it appeared only he and Antram were left to prepare the dead for their journey. But with Antram ill, there would be no burials at all, except for what K'tanu could do before he himself died; and the unprepared and unburied dead would sleep in darkness forever, with no hope of reunion with their loved ones in Lightland. The thought made him shudder in despair.

K'tanu trotted down on the sloping path. He must hurry and finish his errand and get back to the village. He prayed Maya and the baby would still be alive when he returned. If Antram died, he would have to prepare their bodies by himself. He shook his head; he knew so little about the afterlife. He hoped the gods would forgive his ignorance and accept Maya and the baby anyway.

But there would be no one left to prepare his body and bury him. He decided that when the Sickness overtook him, he would roll the stone aside, crawl into the cave, and lie down next to his beloved Maya and their children. He would die with his wife in his embrace, and if he were denied passage across the River and entry into Lightland, at least he would be holding her when eternal sleep came. It would be enough, that memory, to endure the endless darkness.

⌃⌃⌃

Even in the dark, the path was familiar because K'tanu had trodden it so many times in the last two weeks, carrying bodies to the cliff tombs. He counted the turns, and when he arrived at three, he left the main path. Mother Moon's light fell upon the boulder marking his family tomb. K'tanu set his lance and shield down, placed his hands against the black stone, and put his back into it. After a couple of grunting pushes, it rolled aside enough for him to slip into the small cave. He had no fire, so he crawled, feeling his way. He grazed his head on a protruding stone, absently wiping the blood away. He reached, touched something, and recoiled. With a trembling hand, he touched it again, feeling the sticky tar-encrusted cloth. Tears filled his eyes. "Son."

He'd touched N'kala's feet, then moved his hands up the body. The head was little more than a small, featureless sphere—the same head he had held so many times in his hands, looking into those dark, mischievous eyes. In the darkness, he could almost see N'kala's face and the tiny scar under each eye. One scar was given at birth, another would be added when he became a young man, and another when he completed his vision quest and became a warrior. Forever after he would bear the three scars on his cheekbones, as K'tanu did. K'tanu touched his own cheek. "My son," he said quietly. "My son."

K'tanu touched the bulge over the boy's chest. Under yards of cloth wrappings, N'kala's tiny hands were crossed over his chest. Under them, a carved green serpentine scarab lay in a ring of gold, a reminder that the heart was not in the body. Beyond the boy's head, leaning against the sloping cave wall, was a small white stone jar. It held N'kala's heart, the seat of conscience and intelligence, goodness and virtue. At the final judgment, N'kala would present his heart to Father Sun to be weighed against his actions, and if it balanced—a measure of happiness against a measure of sadness; a measure of joy against that of pain; goodness against frailty; kindness to others against self-love—then he would dwell forever in Lightland.

K'tanu opened the leather pouch at his waist and withdrew the ivory figurine. It was Mother Moon, large-breasted and full-bellied, indicating fertility. He had finished it only last night. He was hopeful that the boy's spirit might still be near; that he would find the carving and take it with him on his journey. K'tanu tucked it into the dressing in the crook of N'kala's right arm. "May we one day hunt together in Lightland," he whispered.

He slipped out of the tomb and rolled the black stone back into place, then picked up his spear and shield. Looking up, he could barely make out the jagged crater rim. Father Sun would be born soon. Mother Moon was passing through the twinkling river of stars overhead. He strode back to the trail and moved quickly down the path toward the caldera floor.

THE HUNT

K'tanu approached Nokitok Springs from the north. They bubbled from the ground in several places, spreading out to form a shallow swamp, filled with rushes and reeds. Surrounding the springs stood several stands of tall, stately, silver-leafed trees, which overhung several *koppie*s, granite rock formations bursting from the black volcanic soil of the crater floor.

The Nokitok lion pride was ruled by Talon, a large male. There were three younger males in the pride—actually his sons—but they steered clear of him, and because of his dominance of the females, they avoided their own mothers as well.

K'tanu climbed atop a rounded koppie and lay flat. From the glow on the horizon, Father Sun would rise above the rim in less than a half hour. He must be in position by then.

K'tanu's people had hunted lion for centuries, but never for sport. To them, the lion's mane, tail, and especially the heart were sacred totems, rarely taken. True, a youth on the cusp of manhood was required to kill a lion, but this was often the only lion he would ever kill. Ngoro was literally full of prey, and the warm climate meant that K'tanu's people did not need to eat much meat anyway. Wild cereals made delicious bread, and roasted termites were a candy savored by all ages.

So when they did hunt lion, it was not undertaken lightly. The hunters knew all the lions by name and watched them from a distance. When all were accounted for, the hunters would signal each other with birdcalls, pointing toward the intended target, always an older male. Females were never killed, for they gave birth to the young. If an older, dominant male were taken, there would be a younger, aggressive male left in his place, and the balance would continue.

K'tanu absently fingered his silver amulet, waiting for the light. Some distance away were the three koppies arranged in a loose triangle where this lion pride lived. Talon, the dominant male with the raking scar on his left shoulder; three females; three younger, challenging males; and five cubs, born just last spring.

It had been debated by firelight many times whether they should take Talon. He was a powerful force in this part of the crater, and he even hunted, a rarity for males. Once, K'tanu and his father had seen Talon kill a gazelle and then turn away without even taking so much as a haunch. Seeing the surprise in his son's eyes, M'uano said, "He knows we are here."

"How does he know?" whispered K'tanu, who was no more than eight at the time.

"He killed that antelope for us."

"Does he always do that?"

"He does when a drought is coming. There will be little rain this season." M'uano climbed down off the koppie, helping K'tanu down. "We must tell the others."

"What about the meat?"

"It was symbolic—meant only to speak to us."

"The meat is not symbolic," said K'tanu, licking his lips.

"No," said M'uano. "If we respect his message, there will be others. In a while, other animals will come to feed off the gazelle. They, too, must eat."

"But what about us?"

"Do not be greedy, my son. Talon has given us something more important than a meal. He has given us knowledge. Let's share it with the others."

M'uano was right about other hungry animals. Before he and K'tanu had retreated far, black-billed vultures had begun to circle, and the yips of jackals were heard. As they climbed up the crater wall on the way home, K'tanu looked back and saw several animals devouring the carcass, fighting among themselves and howling.

Now, lying on his belly, K'tanu strained to see the three koppies in the darkness. Though cheetahs and leopards were nocturnal hunters, lionesses preferred to hunt by day, returning hours later, their chops glistening blood. They would then lead their cubs to the kill, a feast in the offing.

Squinting in the fading darkness, K'tanu noted Kiana, one of the females, suckling her cubs under a granite outcropping. She scanned the horizon for threats, for at no time was she in greater danger than at this moment. Danger did not come from leopards or hyenas; it came from Banda, a cubless female that had recently been ejected from the pride because she had killed one of Kiana's cubs. There was a big battle between them that Talon had watched placidly, and in the end, Banda was driven from the pride by the other females.

There was a shifting of dark shapes and K'tanu finally made out Talon lying on top of the nearest koppie. He'd raised his head and was looking around. Even at this safe distance, the lion raised the hackles on K'tanu's neck, for he knew how quickly Talon could erase the flat ground between them. The lion's eyes glinted in the darkness, and K'tanu was suddenly reminded of the Other World, where Talon had chased him off the crater rim.

K'tanu gripped his spear and slipped backward off the boulder. A stand of bushy trees lay to his right, and K'tanu trotted silently toward them, bent low to the ground. The air was cool, and a mist arose here and there from the springs, fooling K'tanu's eyes into thinking a tree was a boulder, or a mound of earth a grazing wildebeest. He stepped carefully, remembering the betrayal of the twig in the Other World. He was near the edge of the springs. The grass was tall and he could hear the burp of frogs.

In an opening between two trees, K'tanu could make out the three koppies, much closer now, and from another angle. The lions were invisible beyond the rise of the closest and biggest koppie. He moved quietly forward, his leather shield held tightly in his left hand, his spear clutched in his right. As he moved, the gap between the koppies began to open up. He ducked behind an immense baobab with a trunk wide enough to hide a dozen hunters and watched through the leaves as the first rays of light struck the western crater wall.

He scanned the koppies. In the increasing light, bumps he'd taken for the lions turned out to be stone. K'tanu inhaled sharply, his stomach clenching. The lions were gone. He looked around in alarm. From his first vantage point, he had counted five lions. Now there were none. They must have sensed him coming. He sniffed the air. The breeze blew gently in his face—the reason he'd come from the north.

But they knew he was here. His heart pounded. He was only a dozen paces from the pride's stronghold. Under those rocks were dugouts where the lions might be hiding, waiting for him. Not seeing a single lion was terrifying. Lions were like beads on a string: if you saw one, there would be another one close by. But if you saw no lions at all, they might be right behind you, quietly changing you from hunter to prey.

K'tanu took a few steps back from the baobab, hoping to get a better perspective. The tops of the koppies were barren. Where was Talon? And where had Kiana and her cubs gone?

Then he heard it. A low, sonorous growl, not so different from K'lii's distant rumble. He slowly turned right where a wall of reeds swayed in the morning breeze. K'tanu raised his spear and took a step back, and he saw them: two large yellow eyes. The rumbling ceased, and for an instant, there was complete silence. Then Talon erupted from the grass, roaring, his teeth flashing.

K'tanu rolled away, raising his shield. A claw tore through it, raking him from shoulder to elbow. Talon tumbled through the grass, then got to his feet, roaring, saliva dripping from his fangs. K'tanu grabbed his spear with both hands and let out a short, percussive shout. Talon cocked his head and then made two quick circles, sizing up his opponent. K'tanu screamed again, a guttural burst that sounded like a dying wildebeest, intended to draw the lion to him.

Talon paced, wondering why an animal making that sound was not writhing on the ground. K'tanu brandished his spear and took a step forward. Talon jumped up on a rock outcrop and bellowed.

K'tanu knew this moment was inevitable. Talon had nearly killed him in the Other World. Now he must kill the lion in the Waking World, or die himself. "Huh!" he yelled. "Huh! Huh!"

Talon leapt into the air and K'tanu hurled the spear into his gaping jaws. The beast landed on him, choking, his paws clawing at the air, pinning K'tanu to the ground as he thrashed. For a long moment, the lion heaved and shuddered, his breath hot on K'tanu's face, and then he gave way, a gurgling followed by a hot, musty exhale, and collapsed on K'tanu, knocking the breath out of the hunter. The giant head lay right next to K'tanu's, the eyes open but lifeless.

K'tanu wriggled out from under the lion's body, bathed in blood. He rolled Talon over onto his back. Kneeling down, he placed his hands on the coarse stomach fur. "We, who all our lives have watched each other from a distance, finally meet." He touched the wet snout of the great cat. "I know the greatness of your heart, which is why I came to you today."

K'tanu picked up his spear and stood. He ran his hands down the shaft, sluicing off the blood. Grasping it firmly, he thrust it between Talon's ribs and thought he saw the lion's soul take to the heavens like an ibis, neck stretched out, white wings extended, ascending toward Father Sun.

K'tanu sawed the spearhead through muscle and ligaments. He began to get light-headed, both from the exertion and the loss of his own blood from the raking he'd received down his arm. He pulled a ropy length of tendon free and used it to bind a broad, waxy croton leaf around his left arm, stanching the blood flow. Then he returned to his labors.

Only when the giant, gory heart filled his trembling hands did K'tanu's own heartbeat slow. Antram would sacrifice the lion's heart to Father Sun, and by nightfall they would have the gods' blessing. Surely their anger would be placated.

K'tanu closed his eyes in gratitude, holding the heart up so Father Sun could look upon it. The sun was just peeking over the caldera rim. It was then that K'tanu heard her familiar growl. He opened his eyes and turned slowly. Up on the rock Talon had leapt from moments ago, was his prime mate, the lioness Kiana.

K'tanu looked around slowly. His spear lay on the ground just out of reach. If the lioness meant to have him, she would. But her attention was on the body of her mate, and she barely noticed K'tanu, who slowly inched away, Talon's bloody heart held in the crook of his injured arm, blindly searching the ground for his spear with his other hand, never taking his eyes off the lioness. When his fingers found the shaft, he lifted it slowly, leaning back on his haunches, raising the tip. Kiana was still looking at Talon, her head tilted in what looked like wonder. K'tanu slowly stood. "I am sorry," he whispered.

Kiana let out a throaty, heart-stopping roar. K'tanu felt her hot breath on his face and steeled himself for her attack. But she simply turned away and, in another second, was gone.

K'tanu knew he had little time. Now that the lioness had left, hyenas and jackals would soon arrive. And they would scarcely distinguish between a dead lion and a badly injured human.

FIVE

THE END OF THE WORLD

By the time K'tanu reached the rim, the sun had filled the caldera, banishing the morning mist. Clouds scuttled across the cerulean sky. In the middle of the Blue-Eyed Sea in the center of the caldera, thousands of flamingo made a giant pink dot. And high above Nokitok Springs vultures circled, awaiting their turn at Talon's carcass.

K'tanu barely slowed when the trail turned back on itself, and the stone that fronted the family tomb came into view. K'tanu's head throbbed, his shoulder and arm felt like he had thrust them into a fire, and his fingertips were numb and dead. He would probably lose the arm. He almost laughed. He would die, like all the others, and one arm or two wouldn't matter then. Using his spear as a staff, he limped toward the village, carrying the lion's heart bundled in lobelia leaves. Blood leaked from it, running down his side, staining his leopard skin loincloth. The sun dappled the leaf-carpeted ground, and drying perspiration cooled his forehead. But a song was in his heart. Surely Father Sun and Mother Moon would reward his courage.

Then he smelled something and looked up. Above the trees, black smoke roiled. He heard screams and shouting. He gripped his spear tightly and broke into a hobbling trot.

As he burst into the bright village clearing, he saw in horror that the thorn barricade protecting the bodies was a giant torch belching flames into the sky. The acrid smell of burning flesh filled the air, and he saw a piece of red fabric carried aloft on the hot updraft.

The village gate stood open. Most of the huts inside the surround were on fire. Several warriors of the *Ukula* clan, distinguishable by their ear loops and ocher-painted faces, were dragging people from their huts. A man dashed the brains of a child out with a large stone. K'tanu ran toward him, stabbing him as he passed. He fell to the ground with a grunt. The boy's mother lay nearby, already dead, blood pouring from her abdomen.

Another Ukula emerged from Antram's hut, prodding the old man with a long flint knife. Antram's ceremonial scars had been sliced many times in an effort to shame him. Antram stumbled and fell. The Ukula raised his spear and kicked at Antram to turn him over. At that moment, K'tanu, in a full run, released his spear. It struck the warrior in the chest and he stumbled backward, tumbling into the fire pit.

Ignoring the commotion around him, the screams and whoosh and crackle of fire, K'tanu knelt by Antram and turned him over. His face was bloody and one eye had been gouged out. A gurgling sound came from his throat, and K'tanu feared the old man was about to die. But Antram smiled up at K'tanu. "How did you fare?" asked the old man.

"I did it." K'tanu carried Antram inside his hut and lay him gently on his mat.

"Where is it?"

K'tanu ducked outside and retrieved the lion's heart. He placed it on the ground near Antram. "Lie still. I'll be right back."

"Wait," said Antram, grabbing K'tanu's wrist. "If you do not return, I will prepare you and your family to meet Father Sun." He coughed and spit blood on the ground. "It will go slow, with only one eye." He smiled toothlessly up at K'tanu.

K'tanu's heart was filled with love for the old man. "I will return." He ran out of the hut, scooping up his spear and angling toward his own hut, his heart racing. Ahead of him, two Ukula warriors were entering a hut. He screamed and they turned. What they saw was a bloody and frenzied specter careening toward them. They dropped their spears and fled in panic.

Rounding the hut, he finally saw his own home, and through the low doorway, a man inside. K'tanu bent and charged, landing on the man in a cloud of smoke and dust. The man threw him off and turned. He held a long curved antler knife in one hand and the baby in the other. Beyond him, Maya lay stunned, blood flowing from her temple.

K'tanu swept the antler blade from the man's hand and thrust it into his stomach, pulling the baby from his grasp at the same instant. The warrior, who was covered with pustules and bruises from the Bleeding Sickness, sunk to his knees and coughed a spray of blood onto K'tanu's feet, then looked up, smiling. "We go together."

Before K'tanu could turn, he felt a sudden, hard jolt and looked down. A bloody spearhead was protruding from his chest. He looked up and saw Maya, whose eyes were wide with shock and horror. She pressed her hands against her mouth, stifling a scream.

K'tanu's bloody hands still held the baby, who mewled weakly. The spear had miraculously missed her. He held her out to Maya and she took her from him, her eyes never leaving his.

In Maya's ears, the Waking World receded to a soundless void, vaguely visible through tears and smoke. She lay the baby down and took K'tanu's hands in hers, holding them tightly, her eyes searching his. "We will walk together in Lightland," she whispered, tears in her eyes.

K'tanu was very tired. He seemed surrounded by the mists of the River of Death. "Lion heart," he gasped. "I . . . I brought it." He gripped her hands with all his strength. Then his eyes closed and he settled against her.

She buried her face in his neck. "Lightland," she repeated. "Meet me there."

PART TWO

NEW YORK CITY

2029 A.D.

MODERN TIMES

Christopher Tempest took the D train uptown and got off at 81st Street. It was a perfect summer morning. He headed across Central Park where, for the next twenty minutes, he didn't have to think about the Age. No modifier like the Stone Age, the Space Age, or the Dark Ages; just the "Age."

Actually, the "Plague Age" would be more appropriate, but in these short-attention-span times, it had quickly become known simply as the *Age*. For Americans, the Age began in 2024, when reports started coming out of central east Africa—Tanzania, mostly—about a new form of hemorrhagic fever, the latest in a long line of viral killers. The virus was hosted by an unknown natural reservoir and was one hundred percent lethal. In the last five years, scores of millions of Africans had died of this mysterious illness.

Americans, as they always do, shook their heads, dug into their collective deep pockets, and sent literally mountains of food and medicine to Africa, little of which reached the victims because of the uniquely African system that had developed over the last century—a system designed to siphon off large portions of charitable aid to the warehouses of petty dictators and warlords.

When the epidemic continued for so long that the Satellite News Network decided to update the theme music, news editorial boards across the country agreed that enough air time had been devoted to a crisis halfway around the world. After 2027, the plague had become just another item in the news, like hurricanes in the Caribbean, Islamic terror in Europe, and nuclear accidents in former Russian satellite countries.

So in March 2028 when the World Health Organization finally upgraded the epidemic to a *pandemic*, it barely raised an eyebrow. It was just one more thing to be afraid of. Everything you could eat, touch, or breathe was caustic, toxic, or carcinogenic. No wonder people pulled back, cocooning themselves in their homes and waving distantly to neighbors across a fence, if at all.

Fear-mongering, long a growth-industry in environmental and personal health areas, spilled over into interpersonal relationships as well. The AIDS scare of the 2010s, when the syndrome abruptly spilled into the heterosexual population in large numbers, resulted in a practical moratorium on male-female interaction. Protective parents passed single-sex school initiatives nationwide. Along with anti-drug and bike-helmet campaigns, the "Don't Touch, Don't Die" slogans sunk into young minds, and an entire generation of kids grew up with little more than a passing acquaintance with the opposite sex. Experts decried the overreaction to their own hysterical warnings, forecasting plummeting birth rates. For once, they were right. By 2019 the United States had surpassed Greece as the country with the world's lowest birth rate.

People, schooled in fear, had reacted predictably. Not only did sex decline among teenagers, it declined across the board. People simply opted out of human interaction, preferring instead the new generation of Internet holosex programs, which were touted to be as real as the real thing, but far less dangerous. By 2022, cybersex had become the single largest Internet business and made up an estimated twenty percent of the country's GNP.

So when the virus—called "Cobalt" because of the bluish-purple bruises it produced on the skin—cropped up in Europe and Asia, Americans rightfully believed that the government, so worried about their cholesterol levels, would cinch up the borders and protect them. The Department of Homeland Security, long engaged in the struggle against Fundamentalist Islamic Fascism (FIF in these acronym-rich times), had mechanisms in place to do just that, but Abu Ishmael Mohammed stood in the way.

Mohammed was an American Islamic cleric who was convicted of bombing the Holocaust Museum in Washington, D.C., reducing one whole wing to rubble. But Mohammed's conviction was overturned because the Supreme Court found that after the bombing, the cleric was singled out while waiting to board a plane at Dulles airport for Saudi Arabia, simply because he was an Arab. At his trial, the prosecution presented three key bits of evidence: (1) Mohammed carried a Sudanese passport. The man who had driven the explosives-laden U-Haul truck to the museum was also an Arab and had been traced to Sudan; (2) the homicide bomber's accomplice, also a Sudanese, was found shot in the head in his Maryland apartment with the same caliber gun that Mohammed's body guards used; and (3) a cache of C-4 explosive, like that used in the bombing, was found in the very mosque over which Mohammed presided in Virginia.

No matter, said the Supreme Court: it was racial profiling and was prohibited under the Equal Protection Clause of the Fourteenth Amendment. The Court ruled that, "in these troubled times, where the color of one's skin can be interpreted as a license for negative innuendo, hate speech, physical abuse, and even murder, no profiling based solely upon racial characteristics is permissible under the Constitution."

Therefore, by extension, a black person with a Tanzanian passport could not be refused entry into the United States, even though Tanzania was considered Cobalt Ground Zero. After initial exposure, Cobalt had a five- to seven-day period in which no symptoms were apparent. When the ruling became public, conservatives howled, the ACLU rejoiced, and America's borders remained open, even as Cobalt began to rage across Europe with a devastation not seen since the Black Plague in the Middle Ages.

By 2028, Tanzania was ninety percent depopulated. Its neighbors to the north, Uganda and Kenya, were equally decimated. United Nations experts began to hope that historic tribal divisions would somehow slow Cobalt's advance. Ironically, they were thwarted by their own hubris. In the early 1970s, the U.N. recommended the construction of the Trans-African Highway stretching from Nigeria on the west coast to Ethiopia on the eastern shore. The TAH was designed to do for Africa what the transcontinental railroad did for the United States: bring it into the modern world by making communication and trade easier, faster, and cheaper.

What the planners didn't realize was that they had built a road not only for goods and people, but for viruses as well. In much the same way stowaway rats brought the hantavirus to the United States in the 1980s by climbing down mooring ropes and disappearing into American sea front cities, forty years later, long-secluded rainforest viruses hitched rides on the TAH and soon infected an entire continent. Before the Highway, an outbreak in a secluded region might decimate a tribe; but without more victims, it would recede into the green background, hiding in its unknown natural animal host, awaiting another opportunity to break out, which sometimes wouldn't happen for years.

But now the viruses were freed from their geographic gulags. Truckers on long hauls purchased tainted monkey meat—a delicacy prized by the African pallet—and took it home to share with their families. Diseases that hadn't traveled a hundred miles in a millennia now traveled a thousand miles in a week. The Trans-African Highway, once called the "Wonder of Africa," now received a succession of more appropriate monikers: the "AIDS Artery" in the 1980s, the "Ebola Expressway" in the 1990s, and now the "Cobalt Corridor" in the late 2020s.

With advances in transportation, scientists figured that no one on earth was more than fifteen hours removed from anyone else. And if Cobalt could be transferred by aerosol—tiny micro-particles expelled when a person sneezes or speaks—then no one on earth was safe.

Like everyone else, at the beginning of the Age, Chris Tempest spent hundreds of dollars on high-tech ultra-low particulate air (ULPA) filtration masks, with micropores so small that not even viruses could pass through them. Instead of tightening borders, thereby reducing the risk of an infected person coming to America, the government spent billions developing a ULPA mask impregnated with microscopic organic NanoBots (NBs) that surrounded foreign objects and encapsulated them in a harmless silicon shell. Unfortunately, the dense masks also created a near epidemic of people passing out, increased instances of asthma, and brought about a strange increase in the number of cold and flu cases nationwide.

By late 2028, Cobalt was raging across Indonesia and India, with outbreaks in Europe, Russia, and northern China, but not a single case of Cobalt had been verified in the United States. And then, in February 2029, the inevitable happened. A Michigan woman died from a mysterious viral infection. The Centers for Disease Control (CDC) in Atlanta stated emphatically that it was a flu-related death, not Cobalt.

When he heard this, in his tiny Tribeca apartment, Chris pulled the dusty box of ULPA masks from under his bed and wondered. Then in March, five people died under mysterious circumstances in Miami. News holos said they had been in Cuba on an illegal gambling trip. Rafael Castro's government was not forthcoming with any information. The CDC would not confirm Cobalt in this case, either.

The Michigan and Miami Cobalt cases—if that was what they really were—subsided into the background noise of a busy world, with one small change. Human contact, already in short supply, fell off even more precipitously. Few people rode the subway or buses. Restaurants, live theater, and sporting events suffered from low attendance. It seemed that instead of instilling panic in the public, Cobalt had merely pushed them further inside their private safe zones. You didn't need to run home if you never left it in the first place.

Chris had shoved the box of masks back under his bed, determined to not succumb to alarmism. But on his subway ride uptown this morning, he noted that most of the people in the stuffy car were wearing masks. He was not. Something had changed, and he'd missed the news. He wasn't a fool—he was just as afraid of Cobalt as the next guy—but he'd dodged a bullet a few years back and that had made him, if not foolhardy, at least not easily spooked. For three days in the summer of 2025, he was lost in the Sudanese desert, five days north of Khartoum and still two days from Jebel Barkal, an immense sandstone mesa where archeologists were excavating a predynastic Egyptian cemetery. That hot August afternoon, his Hummer was rolling across the featureless desert, the temp well beyond forty degrees centigrade, trying to keep to the almost invisible camel trail. The H^{10} struck a rock, poking a hole in the oil pan. Within minutes the engine seized. The GPS unit had been stolen months before and not replaced, and the SatPhone battery had corroded in the desert heat. Chris sat in the stifling cab, cupping the useless SatPhone in his hands, his heart racing. He had never been this isolated in his life, and for few minutes panic clawed at his reason. He had no provisions except a packet of trail mix and a liter of water.

But when evening came and the sun perched on the western horizon, a calm settled on him, and he realized he had never experienced such a total absence of noise in his life. There was no wind, no bird calls, no rustling of palm leaves, not even the subliminal whine of unheard radio frequencies. Just himself sitting on the Hummer tailgate listening to the blood pumping in his ears. He watched the sky fill with pink, orange, and red. Venus glowed in the west. The air finally cooled and Chris pulled on a jacket, wondering how long it would be before he was missed. Strangely, he didn't really care. He told himself that, if he survived, this might be one of the best moments in his life, and if it ended in heatstroke tomorrow, he wouldn't feel cheated. There was nothing better than being an archeologist, even one who was going to die in the desert.

As the night progressed and the calm voice faded, panic returned, and Chris fought back with reason. What did it matter? You live, you die; all is dross, as the poets say. Whether you were a mad prophet squinting into the sun and calling it God or an astronomer peering through a telescope at the M13 globular cluster and calling *that* God, it was the same—neither answer was definitive. But at least now, sitting out here in the silent darkness under the Milky Way, Chris finally knew what both prophet and astrophysicist meant when they talked about heaven.

When he was picked up two days later by a camel caravan, parched and delirious, Chris just smiled: being rescued by a camel drover was heaven too.

So is this place, thought Chris as he walked past Belvedere Lake in Central Park. Ahead, through the trees, he saw the rear of the Metropolitan Museum of Art. He rounded the south side of the immense granite building and strode up the broad steps facing Fifth Avenue. As always, he noted the giant stone blocks sitting atop the façade, placed there by an angry architect when the trustees refused to fund the Winged Victory sculptures he'd designed for that location.

Most people failed to notice the gray blocks, but Chris keyed on them the first time he stood at the foot of the steps leading to the museum's two-story copper doors. He'd learned about noticing small things during a summer he spent in Kenya working for famed archeologist Richard Leakey. Richard was the son of Louis and Mary Leakey, discovers of *Homo habilis* ("Handy Man") at Olduvai Gorge in Tanzania. *Habilis* was thought to be the first human to leave Africa.

Richard was digging several hundred miles north of Olduvai near Lake Turkana in western Kenya. There he discovered *Homo rudolfensis*, a hominid that coexisted with *Homo habilis*. In the years to follow, Richard's tireless work made him as famous as his literally ground-breaking parents. But he had been confined to a wheelchair because of an airplane crash many years before.

One day Chris was pushing Leakey down a dirt path when, suddenly, Richard asked him to stop and turn him around. Chris had been studying the ground as they walked, listening as Richard talked. Like all young archeologists, Chris hoped to add his own discoveries to the evolutionary puzzle. But he'd missed something this morning. He turned the wheelchair around and pushed it forward. "Stop," said Richard. "See it?" Chris scanned the ground. Shale and loose rock, little else. "See it?" repeated Richard. Chris had to shake his head. "Over there, next to the flat stone. See it?"

Finally, he did. Chris bent and pushed dirt away, revealing a molar. He looked up. "Human?"

"Let's see," said Richard, and Chris handed him the tooth. "Definitely. See the cusps here? Hominids have five on each tooth; apes only four." He handed the tooth to Chris. "Your first find."

"*Your* find," he said, disappointed at missing something he could have literally stepped on.

Richard patted his arm. "The day is long, and yours has just begun. Pace yourself."

Since that day at Lake Turkana, he had kept his eyes open but had not yet found anything of note. He knew that most discoveries were made early in one's career. He was almost thirty-five. If he was going to make his contribution, it had better be soon, because it wouldn't be too long before some grad student would be pushing *him* around in a wheelchair.

ELECTRIFYING NEWS

At the museum entrance, Chris took his turn in the SmellScan, wondering if it knew the difference between *Homme* and *Old Spice*. The scanner sought molecules of bomb manufacture: traces of gunpowder, TNT, C-4, or even methane, a byproduct of the ammonium nitrate/racing-car fuel incendiary device favored by American separationist militias.

Finding none, the green light went on, the Lucite door opened, and Chris was admitted to the museum. He held up his ID lanyard and was waved through. He turned right toward the Egyptian wing. Just beyond the vaulted entrance (designed to look like the Karnak pylons) was the predynastic collection focusing on the tribes that inhabited the Nile before Menes united the northern Nile delta with the southern river lands five thousand years ago. The collection was meager. No great temples or immense statues had been found from this period. Stone Age cultures left little evidence beyond pottery shards, antler-carved figurines, and flint cutting tools; yet it was this very scarcity of evidence that drew Chris to this area of study early on. The thirty Egyptian dynasties, stretching from Menes to the Roman occupation three thousand years later, were well documented, mostly because the pharaohs themselves kept such good records. All Egyptologists really did was dig up the evidence and catalog it. When

French archeologist Champollion deciphered the Rosetta Stone in 1822, it finally became possible to read hieroglyphics, and the secrets of one of the world's oldest civilizations were revealed, including a cosmology that made Masonry look like the invention of a bored bricklayer on a Sunday afternoon.

But what attracted Chris to Egyptian belief was its origin, or rather, the lack thereof. In short, the Egyptian religion seemed to emerge fully formed around 3100 B.C. Up until his last year at Columbia, Chris had been focusing on the origins of man, studying bones that were at least a million years old. Then a stop in Cairo on his way to Kenya had changed his life. He walked into the dirty, crowded Egyptian National Museum and was overwhelmed at the immediacy of the mummies, carved reliefs, and stone sarcophagi filling every corner of the massive building. He gaped in wonder at Tutankhamun's gilded face mask, was fittingly impressed by the complexity of the Book of the Dead burial rituals, and was completely blown away three days later as he stood at the foot of the four immense seated statues of Rameses II at Abu Simbel on the shore of Lake Nasser.

From Cairo, Chris caught a plane to Lake Turkana in Kenya to work on Richard Leakey's dig, but his heart was no longer in it. He listened listlessly to the debate around the dinner table about whether *Homo habilis* really did coexist with *Australopithecus africanus*. Suddenly, all he could think about was Egypt, an isolated nation that developed an entire culture devoted to death, and yet what full, remarkable lives they lived!

At the end of the summer, Chris stopped back in Egypt before returning to New York. He spent a week walking through the ruins of Thebes, Egypt's capital for thousands of years. The Karnak Temple, with its immense eighty-foot columns resembling papyrus plants, raised his eyes to the sky and pulled him entirely out of the volcanic rubble of Lake Turkana. He'd lost faith in the origin of man. What captured his heart now was the origin of man's *beliefs*: a fascination with a culture that was a mere eye-blink in time from his own, but so compelling he couldn't blink it away.

Back at Columbia in September, Chris told his graduate committee he was rethinking his dissertation. Expecting a subtle shift from Achelean flint-knapping techniques in western Kenya to Achelean flint-knapping techniques in southern Kenya, the committee was stunned when he declared he was scrapping knapping all together, opting instead for a study of the origins of the ancient Egyptians.

"You'll have to start over," said a startled committee member.

Chris nodded.

"You'll never finish at this rate," said another.

Chris nodded.

"You were so close," said Dr. Barton, his faculty advisor.

"I know," said Chris, "but I just don't care about flint-knapping any more." To a room of archeologists, that was stupendous heresy. The committee exchanged dark looks and a stony silence fell upon the room. "I'm going to find out where the Egyptians came from," added Chris.

"Why, Libya, of course," said the startled committee member.

"Nonsense! It was Mesopotamia," said another.

"Everyone knows it was the Sahel, maybe even the Congo," said another.

Dr. Barton smiled, understanding. He extended his hand. "Good luck finding the answer, Chris."

Chris left that day, excited and scared. Dr. Barton helped Chris make the switch, hooking him up with Dr. Chandara of the University of Chicago, which had a dig at Qustul, near Abu Simbel, the same site that had so captured Chris's imagination earlier that summer.

In the 1960s, when Lake Nasser rose behind the Aswan dam, burying some of the most ancient and least-studied temples ever found, archeologists were panic-stricken. Abu Simbel was saved, along with the Dendur Temple, which Egypt gave the United States in return for its help. The Dendur Temple now stood in an east-facing, glass-walled gallery in the Met, and Chris passed it daily on his way downstairs to his office.

Dr. Chandara's mentor, Dr. Phillips, had worked at Qustul long before the Aswan dam was built, and Chandara continued on after the lake buried the site under two hundred feet of water. Chris was readily accepted onto Chandara's team because of his scuba-diving experience, and he manned one of the small submersibles that moved slowly along the dark floor, disturbing the mud with its articulating claws. All that summer Chris worked with Chandara and his team, and it never ceased to amaze him, after emerging from the sub after six hours under water, to see the orange sun setting over brown desert hills, not a shred of vegetation visible, only endless desert on either side of the blue lake waters.

The following summer Chris moved further south to the knee of the Nile, in the Sudan, and worked on the Nubian temple at Jebel Barkal, excavating a royal cemetery founded by the Nubian kings who ruled Egypt around 700 B.C.

Working his way further south each season, Chris then found himself in Khartoum, the capital of Sudan, where the Nile tributaries met. What an awesome sight it was to stand on the balcony of the Hotel Sudan and watch the aptly-named Blue Nile meet the silt-laden White Nile, the waters commingling, eventually turning a light brown—the world's longest river and the life-giving artery of the world's most intriguing civilization.

And still Chris's questions about Egyptian origins remained unanswered. Scores of theories fought for precedence in the journals. The so-called "Black Mummy" of a small boy argued for Libyan provenance, but a Mesopotamian connection seemed the most likely. The fertile area between the Tigris and Euphrates rivers (Mesopotamia, after all, means *between the rivers)* in the modern-day Democratic Republic of Iraq was the indisputable cradle of civilization, and the people who lived there invented farming, animal husbandry, irrigation, writing, mathematics, and a highly-evolved religion. But the Mesopotamian religion was as distinct from the Egyptian religion as evangelical Christianity was from Shinto. Nothing in Mesopotamia could explain the Book of the Dead—the complex rituals and spells required of the deceased to pass the tests in the Underworld. As a result, Chris remained unconvinced of a Mesopotamian-Egyptian connection.

Year by year, Chris's attention was pulled ever further south. Since he was familiar with Kenya from his earlier graduate studies, he wondered if the answers lay in that direction. The Blue Nile headwaters were in the Ethiopian highlands, but no ruins of importance had ever been found in those wet, misty mountains. The White Nile's source was fifteen-hundred kilometers to the southwest, in the Congo-Ugandan highlands at the very center of the continent. The highlands formed the western ridge of the Great Rift Valley, an immense oval running from Kenya and Uganda in the north to Tanzania and Zambia, a thousand kilometers to the south. The Rift was not volcanic in origin, as one might think after seeing its highest peak, Kilimanjaro, but merely volcanic in result. It began forming millions of years ago when eastern Africa began pulling away from the rest of the continent. Eventually, the tectonic forces will create an ocean where Lake Victoria now sits, and Ethiopia, Somalia, Kenya, Tanzania, and Mozambique will form a continent of their own, drifting toward India. In the meantime, the tension has resulted in some of the most fantastic geology on earth, including a multitude of incredibly deep lakes on the Rift's western rim, including lakes Albert, Edward, Kivu, Tanganyika, and Malawi, and steps on the eastern rim, where a series of active volcanos continue to boil forth lava.

In the Rift's great cauldron, humanity apparently began its long journey. The oldest human bones ever found were discovered in Olduvai Gorge near the eastern Rift rim. The world's greatest collection of animal life exists just twenty miles east of Olduvai, in Ngorongoro crater. And directly west of Olduvai is the Serengeti Plain, where a million wildebeests make their annual migration north to Kenya in a display of animal movement unrivaled anywhere else on earth. Beyond the Serengeti is immense Lake Victoria, the largest freshwater lake in Africa.

Looking at all of these varied elements packed so tightly into such a small area, it seemed to Chris that the origin of *all* things might very well have been in the Great Rift Valley—perhaps even the Egyptian culture itself. He couldn't help but feel that questions he had posed along the Nile from the delta to Khartoum might be answered somewhere even farther south, in the Rift. Last summer, Chris and his team excavated a cemetery in the desert near the Sudd swamp, five hundred miles south of Khartoum, where the White Nile spreads out in a shallow vascular system for a hundred miles before narrowing once again to a main artery. But they had no sooner pitched their tents near the swamp when the world's longest civil war, the battle between Sudan's northern slave-trading Muslims and its free southern black tribes, flared up again, and the team had to leave the country. They were lucky. In the year since, over 50,000 people had died in that conflict, and with the Cobalt ravages, Sudan was on the verge of complete depopulation.

Though their small collection of finds were limited to bits of broken pottery, the shards were remarkable: the black, ripple-etched pieces were similar to stoneware found at Al-Badari in Egypt, more than a thousand miles to the north. Burial sites near the Sudd swamp contained rings of stones surrounding desiccated bodies lying on their sides, facing west. Like the Badarians (and the Egyptians to follow them), the bodies were buried with food, amulets, tools, and weapons.

But the most unique Egyptian theological elements— mummification and stone jars bearing lungs, liver, stomach, and intestines—were absent. Still, it was the furthest south any Egyptian-like finds had ever been uncovered, and Chris published papers in *American Archeologist* and *Paleontology Today*, which were widely read and commented upon. His stock rose sharply, and he was made Assistant Curator of Predynastic Egyptian Collections at the Met. He now had two research assistants, and they were making a dent in the dusty shelves of labeled but not catalogued finds. But his thoughts constantly returned to the Great Rift Valley, another two hundred miles south of the Sudd swamp. The answers were there, of that he was certain.

Leaving the light-filled Dendur Temple gallery, Chris took the broad stairway downstairs, passed a security guard, pressed his ID card against the door plate, and entered the wing offices.

Since the Met had been under constant construction for the last 150 years, it had begun to resemble the museums of Europe with its confusing hallways, galleries, and subbasements. His own section was small. He had an office and his assistants worked on tables in a windowless room, surrounded by steel shelves groaning with the weight of pottery shards, bones, and even flint spearheads and handaxes. It seemed he hadn't gotten away from flint-knapping after all, even though his focus jumped from four million years ago to just under ten thousand years ago. After all, the Stone Age continued right up until copper and tin were smelted to form bronze in 3500 B.C.

Chris sat down behind his cluttered desk. Often chided by others for the mess, he would smile blandly, then usher them out, shut the door behind them, and leave things as they were. Besides, in looking through the detritus, his mind had time to concentrate on matters more important than finding a particular paper. It was often during these times that answers to the "big questions" came. It was here he'd determined where he would lead his next expedition: the Ruwenzori Range, an eighty-mile long section of the western Rift rim west of Lake Victoria. When the ever-present clouds dissipate, revealing the Ruwenzori's stark, jagged, snow-capped majesty, one can understand why the Greek geographer Ptolemy called them the "Mountains of the Moon."

Recently, a colleague, Dr. Patrick Connelly of the British Museum, had phoned Chris to tell him of a rumor he'd heard while he was in Uganda a few months before about a mummy the local Banyoro tribe had found in a cave high on the eastern flank of the Ruwenzoris. Connelly hadn't seen the mummy, but the natives' description of it pointed to Egyptian similarities. "Sounded predynastic, which I believe is your specialty this week," said Connelly, smiling out of the VidPhone holo.

"Where exactly is it?"

"That's the difficulty," said Connelly. "Some of the tribe were afraid of the thing, so they stole the mummy and hid it. The others were angry but relieved, you know, because they were a trifle worried themselves about violating a burial site. We couldn't get anyone to tell us where it was. But maybe you can find it."

"I'll think about it," said Chris. "Thanks, Pat." He switched off.

He didn't have to think long. Imagine, a mummy just three hundred miles west of Olduvai Gorge, the birthplace of humanity! What if man's first instinct, once he'd mastered tool-making and hunting, was to create religion? And what if that religion became the Egyptian cosmology? Then Chris would be out of this cold basement office forever, and his name would appear right alongside Petrie, Champollion, Leakey, and Johansen. Not bad company, that.

Chris had barely sat down at his desk when the VidPhone rang. He heard the familiar voice before he could find the phone and see the face. Pushing a stack of magazines out of the way, Albert McFadden's ruddy face came into view, remarkably clear for a satellite call. "Chris, you there?" asked McFadden, his eyes searching the room. "Chris?"

"Just a moment," said Chris, pushing the magazines aside, revealing the phone screen.

"Ah!" said McFadden, seeing Chris. "Up to your ears, are ye?" His strong Scottish brogue, tailored to an even more sonorous level for American ears, filled the room. "Not too early, am I? Almost midnight here."

"Al? Al McFadden?" Chris hadn't seen McFadden since they were graduate students working at Lake Turkana. "Where are you?"

"Tanzania, near Olduvai. You remember Olduvai, don't you, son?"

Chris smiled. He was two years older than McFadden, but Al called everyone "son." His red beard and sunburned face made McFadden look older than he really was. Being called "son" by Al now wasn't as aggravating as it was when they'd last seen each other, ten years before.

"How's it going there? Find China yet?"

Al laughed. "I said we're *near* Olduvai, son, not *at* Olduvai. Found something that might interest you. A mummy."

"A mummy? How old?"

"*Old*. But the mummy isn't the main event. It's what we found *with* it."

"Tools? Amulets? Weapons?"

McFadden smiled. "Knew I was calling the right fellow. All that stuff, and *more*."

"Dammit, Al, tell me!"

McFadden shook his head. "Can't say over the Vid. You think about it and you'll suss out what I'm talking about. In the meantime, get over here."

"You mean Tanzania?"

"You worried about Cobalt?"

"Isn't it bad there?"

McFadden held up his own blue ULPA respirator, grimy with dirt. "This place is Ground Zero, son, what do *you* think?"

"How many dead?"

McFadden's face went hard. "All of 'em."

"You're nuts, Al! Get out of there!"

"I'm not leaving before I know what we've found," said Al. "That's why I need you."

"But you said everyone's dead!"

"Dammit, Chris, are you coming or not? I can always call somebody else."

"It's *that* important?"

McFadden's pale blue eyes held Chris intently. "I'd rather Cobalt made me a bag of bloody mush than leave this behind. I want you on a plane today. Understand, son? Today!"

The holo dissolved. Chris's mind raced. What had they found besides the mummy, tools, and weapons? What was so important that Al wouldn't even mention it on the phone? Chris steepled his fingers, letting his eyes wander across the mountains of paper on his desk. Suddenly, he jumped up. "Canopic jars!" he shouted to the empty room. "They found canopic jars!"

BIO-SAFETY LEVEL 4

Cate Seagram held the vial up. The bottom third was opaque goo, a rabid culture apparent by its sickly yellowish color. A trickle of sweat ran down her nose. She could not brush it away because she was wearing a Blue Suit, standard issue in BSL4 labs, her gloved hands thrust into the even bulkier gloves built into the wall of the sterile Plexiglas laminar flow box in front of her.

The Centers for Disease Control, located in a leafy suburb of Atlanta near Emory University, had a number of Bio-Safety Level 1, 2, and 3 labs scattered around the facility. But it had just one BSL4 section, and it was buried deep underground, with four-foot thick concrete walls, its own air-filtration system, and negative pressure so that if a leak ever occurred, air from outside would be sucked in and not the reverse.

This was because Level 4 agents were the most deadly viruses on earth. Though workers were gloved and suited and plugged into separate air sources, they were not vaccinated, for no vaccines existed for these viruses. If you were exposed, you died.

Cate had been working in Level 4 for two years, a good deal longer than most of the others in the section. Burnout in this stressful environment was common and expected, where the discovery of a tiny tear in a suit or a needle prick meant isolation in the Slammer and study through thick glass windows as doctors waited to see if you developed any of the symptoms of Ebola, Marburg, Lassa, or any of a dozen other deadly viruses handled there.

Or Cobalt, which was what Cate was handling today. The drop of sweat stopped at the end of Cate's nose. She ignored it; life was in the balance and she had to get this sample in the containment pouch for transport to the centrifuge.

Even transporting a sample twenty feet involved a great deal of procedure. So far, Cate was on step 7 of 15. When she completed the placement of the sample in the soft pouch, she could relax a little. She would then open the box and remove the pouch, and everyone else in the room—Ron Ashby, Brad Palmer, and Teresa Paolo—would step aside as she carried it to the centrifuge room.

"Transport," said Cate, removing the soft pouch from the box. Her co-workers, their faces vague behind thick glass face plates, stopped what they were doing and turned to face her, making the required eye contact. She took three steps to the doorway and placed the pouch on a table, then clumsily pressed her ID card against the door plate. The door opened and Cate picked up the sample.

"Cate?"

Startled, Cate dropped the sample. The intake of breath of her co-workers came like a sudden roar. Ron Ashby, who had been standing behind Cate, reached for her. "I was going to open the door for you," he said, his voice muffled over the roar of pressurized air.

"Dammit, Ron," said Brad.

They all looked at the dark blue pouch on the floor.

"Sorry," said Ron, stepping back.

"It's okay," said Cate, bending down. *I hope.* She picked up the pouch gingerly. If she opened it now, they'd all have to spend the night in the Slammer. She turned back to the laminar flow box and placed the pouch inside, closing the door. The others gathered around, peering through the Plexiglas. Cate put her hands into the manipulating gloves and unzipped the pouch. "Let's see if anything is broken."

"Why do we use glass?" asked Brad. "It breaks!" His eyes were fearful behind his faceplate.

"Because, stupid, Plexi sheds molecules," said Teresa.

Cate opened the pouch. The stoppered vial of Cobalt was apparently intact. Everyone heaved a sigh of relief. "Okay," said Cate, zipping it closed again and withdrawing her hands from the thick black gloves. "Let's try it again."

"I'll get the door," said Ron.

Cate wanted to say *no*, but Ron obviously felt so bad about the mishap that he needed to do something to make up for it. Cate knew all her co-workers well, but Ron was a special case: he had a crush on her, and though they worked together for more than six months before he said anything, she knew it from the start. When he told her about his feelings in the CDC cafeteria one day at lunch, Cate had said little, just mumbling something about a boyfriend in New York.

"What's his name?" asked Ron, dejected. His crew cut and loose jowls made him look a little like a boxer puppy, and Cate's heart went out to the poor guy.

"Chris. He's an archeologist at the Met."

"He sings opera?" asked Ron, amazed.

"Archeologist. The Metropolitan Museum of Art."

"Oh," was all Ron said.

Since that time, Ron's adoring looks had shifted toward sadness. He kept asking her about the opera-singer boyfriend, trying to be funny, but Cate heard the disappointment in his voice.

Ron opened the door, sweeping it wide before Cate had even turned from the glove box. Terry cursed quietly; it was a violation for anyone else to perform a step on a safety list. Even opening the door should be Cate's job, and Ron was interfering.

Cate gave Terry a strained *I know* smile as she passed, and entered the centrifuge room. The door shut behind her, six inches of stainless steel. Ron, Brad, and Terry watched through the triple-paned window. The centrifuge sat in the middle of the room on a pedestal. Cate opened the pouch and placed the vial in a swing, counterbalancing it with a similar vial of distilled water. The same key card that opened the door had to be swiped once the door was shut again and the card owner had to be outside of the room before the centrifuge would turn on—another safety precaution.

All this because there had been breakages in the past. There was another door in the centrifuge room which opened into a hallway leading to the isolation chamber, the Slammer. All six BSL4 labs were arranged around the Slammer, hallways connecting to it like spokes.

Since there was no cure for any bio agent in Level 4, anyone who was exposed—and there had been a few over the years—would die and had died. When the architects designed the building, there was discussion as to what to do with someone who *did* die. Was it safe to burn the body? Could it be safely buried? If so, under what circumstances? The planners opted for a hybrid solution: encapsulation of the body in an elastomeric silicon gel and then incineration at one thousand degrees Celsius, hot enough to melt the hardest metals, let alone kill a viral agent. They *hoped.*

They used the Center's incinerator four times in the last five years, for just this purpose. Each time, however, there were public health concerns. Dr. Marlowe, head of the CDC, made a ghastly suggestion: Why not put victims in Yucca Mountain, the same underground Nevada site where nuclear waste was stored? When Cate heard about the suggestion, she wondered which was more dangerous: biohazards or radiation? After all, plutonium had a half-life of thousands of years, but as far as they knew, BSL4 viruses had no half-life at all—they conceivably stayed virulent forever.

When the first outbreak in BSL4 lab Foxtrot happened in 2025, Cate was in BSL3, where she dealt with viruses for which there were vaccinations. During a discussion about what to do with Roy Albertson's body (Roy had pricked himself with a needle contaminated with Ebola-Calcutta and died ten days later in the Slammer), the encapsulation idea had first been floated. Roy's body was incinerated one night when there was no wind, but Marlowe still worried. A virus so small it could only be seen under an electron microscope might evade even the cleansing of fire. A better solution was called for.

Cate was given the assignment of learning more about encapsulating a body permanently so whatever had killed the person could be completely contained. On the Internet, she stumbled across the holosite of the Disciples of Osiris, a religion that had gained popularity over the last ten years, boasting over a million members worldwide. The Disciples practiced the ancient Egyptian religion, complete with festivals, holidays, and burial rituals, including mummification.

She inquired of the Disciples about mummification and they suggested she speak with the man who had advised them on this ancient burial practice. He was out of the country, but his secretary gave her the number of a scientist at the Metropolitan Museum of Art in New York. Dr. Christopher Tempest was at first puzzled, then amused, then pleased to help. He didn't ask any really difficult questions, and Cate called him from home, so her connection to the CDC couldn't be traced.

They agreed to meet in Washington the day before Thanksgiving. Dr. Tempest said he was going to be in the capital to see friends. Cate's parents lived in Virginia, so they arranged to meet at Union Station in D.C., and just as he promised, Chris was projecting a carnation holo on his lapel. They both had a good laugh at the corniness of the tiny battery-powered holo, and Cate liked the tall, lanky, light-haired archeologist immediately. They seemed to be near the same age, but these days it was hard to tell, so many people had had PS. As they sat down at the station café, Cate scanned Chris's neck, ears, and eyes for tell-tale signs of plastic surgery. Finding none, she liked him even more. His freckles, brought out by many summers in Africa, were not unattractive, and Cate searched her memory for anyone else who allowed a freckle to appear on what was now the vogue for skin: no matter what color—the deepest, almost purple black or milky white or the increasingly ubiquitous cocoa—no imperfections were allowed. Cate had never met anyone with acne, which was routinely flagged in prenatal genetic tests and removed, along with club feet and gapped teeth.

Chris's eyes were hazel with flecks of yellow, surrounded by a ring of brown, a most unusual combination. She wanted to ask him how his parents dialed up that color scheme, but their meeting was formal, and with the recent Supreme Court decision that no one may make a personal-appearance comment to another person without permission, it was out of the question anyway.

She wasn't even allowed to tell him he looked nice. And he couldn't say the same to her, although she *did* look nice. She was wearing a tan skirt and jacket combination, cut just below her knees, considered quite racy in these days of "look but don't touch" male-female interaction.

Chris wore a dark nonchameleon syn-silk suit. That, too was rare. These days, professionals had one suit that could be programmed to change color according to the occasion. But Chris's suit was mono'd deep gray with thin white lines. Very *beyond*, but also a bit dated.

Oh, who cares? Everything is either dated or beyond these days, thought Cate, chiding herself.

Chris seemed just right, sitting there at the café in his ponderous black boots and gray suit, a fedora on his lap, looking both debonair and at the same time ready to go camping.

After their meal, Chris placed a small, oval disk on the table between them. He had created a short visual of the mummification ritual, featuring SynthActor Charlton Heston, who played the deceased Pharaoh being prepared for burial, and a pale, intense Laurence Olivier, who played the jackal-mask-wearing high priest, Anubis.

Cate watched Chris's eyes as he narrated the holo. His excitement was contagious, and by the end of the presentation, Cate wanted to be mummified herself, so long as Chris did the honors. She chuckled at the thought, and Chris, thinking she was laughing at him, abruptly passed his hand over the projector, pausing the image. "Something funny?" he asked, apparently perturbed.

"No," said Cate. The image of Chris gently winding the long linens around her body stuck in her mind. "Just thinking about whether I'd like to be mummified."

"I would," said Chris immediately. "Absolutely."

Cate smiled. "I'll bet you would." She paused. "Do you believe in the afterlife, Dr. Tempest?"

Chris leaned forward to see if she was serious. She wished she were as undefiled as he appeared, but she had made a number of changes: a straighter nose, higher cheekbones. She smiled, revealing a set of teeth so perfect that fifty years ago, people would have mistaken her for a movie star. But nowadays every third woman looked like an ingenue straight from central casting. As it was, Chris noticed her pale blue eyes, apparently not manipulated. "I don't believe in religion."

"I didn't ask about *religion*, Dr. Tempest. I asked whether you believed in the afterlife."

"Do you?"

"Of course not. Who does?"

"Well, you thought *I* might."

"Well, I thought that since you spent so much time in the past, it might rub off on you. I was hoping I'd met a genuine mystic, an acolyte of the ancient mysteries, a conjurer of esoteric spells."

"Nope. Just a kid from Montana who thinks mummies are cool."

After lunch, they were about to part when Cate asked Chris what he was doing for Thanksgiving the next day. "No plans," said Chris, stepping outside the train station into the biting wind.

"Aren't you spending Thanksgiving with friends?"

"What?" asked Chris, caught in the lie. "Oh, yeah. I am. With friends."

Since they barely knew each other, it was not permitted under federal and state law to touch unless they first agreed. "May I?" she asked, touching the elbow of his gray suit.

Chris looked down at her hand on his sleeve. Her touch felt good. "Yes?"

"Pardon me, but you're lying."

"First you touch me, then you call me a liar," said Chris. "I smell a lawsuit."

"I'm sorry, but you are."

Chris smiled. It was a perfect moment, standing in the afternoon gloom of a chilly November day, looking down at a beautiful woman whose face was framed in tight blonde curls. He didn't want it to end. "I do have plans," said Chris. "But no friends in town."

Cate smiled up at him. "That's a lie too. I'm your friend."

They ate Thanksgiving dinner at Cate's sister Abigail's house in Maryland. Her other sister Dana and their parents came over from western Virginia. Her parents had been together forty years. Chris had never met anyone married for forty years. Cate's father said, "Well, you wouldn't. Not in New York."

"But I'm from Montana," said Chris.

Cate's dad was about to say something when her mom said, "He's a guest, Don."

"We'll be married for forty years," said Abigail, nudging her husband David and smiling.

"You betcha, Sweetie," said David. "Even if it kills me," he added, laughing.

Back at Union Station, Chris held out his hand. "I still don't know where you work."

"A pharmaceutical firm."

"A pharmaceutical firm interested in mummifying the people who die from the side effects of its drugs?"

Instead of answering, Cate removed her gloves and took his bare hand, a gesture as intimate as a kiss. "I hope we see each other again."

"Me too," said Chris. With his fedora pulled low, he looked like a detective in an old holo.

"Thank you for the introduction to Egyptology. It was fascinating."

"So was the introduction to your family," said Chris. "They're quite a bunch."

"You liked them?"

"I like *you*," he said touching the brim of his hat, his hazel eyes holding hers.

Suddenly, all the old holos about train stations were proven right. They *were* romantic places, with the noise and bustle and comings and goings. Cate finally understood how it felt to stay behind when someone you cared about was leaving. Her heart raced, but unlike those old movies, this was the Age, and social distance was the rule. "Goodbye, Dr. Tempest," she said, and the monorail, as if on cue, started moving.

"Call me Chris," said Chris from the doorway.

"We'll see," said Cate, smiling.

That was a year and a half ago, and they'd seen each other nine or ten times since then, though their regular VidPhone calls were long and involved. Every Sunday night, they'd talk for an hour or more. Last spring, Chris told Cate he'd be in Georgia to present a paper at an archeology seminar in Augusta. Would she like to get together?

Cate was in a bind. They were working night and day on Cobalt, with no results. The first stateside cases in Michigan and Miami had not broken yet, so there was no panic, but everyone knew an outbreak on American soil was inevitable. She managed to get Saturday afternoon off and volunteered to meet Chris in Augusta, a couple of hours drive east. They met for dinner at *Chez Nous*, where she finally came clean about the CDC over dessert.

Chris almost jumped from his chair. "Aren't you the guys who *invented* Cobalt?"

"We didn't *invent* Cobalt, Chris. We're trying to eradicate it."

"But you guys invented SchleraSim."

"A rogue element in the CDC invented it, but that was ten years ago. They're all in jail now."

Chris was looking at her like *she* was General Cartwright, the man who'd unleashed SchleraSim in Malaysia, killing not only the five thousand terrorist targets, but another twenty thousand civilians as well, virtually emptying out Kuala Lumpur. Papers called the tongue-twisting plague the "Second Hiroshima" because it had done as Cartwright believed: it had ended the sectarian Islamic war the insurgents had been waging, but it had also engendered a dozen other FIF groups worldwide. Chris fidgeted in his chair. "So why the interest in mummies?"

Cate sighed. "Who's getting the check?" Chris frowned at her. "Okay. Here it is: I work in a Bio-Safety Level 4 lab, where we study Ebola, Marburg, and Cobalt—mostly Cobalt these days. I handle the virus, Chris. Scary enough for you?"

"But you wear those suits, though, right?"

"Yes. Big, thick, rubber suits. And gloves and face masks and boots. We take every precaution. Now, let me ask *you* a question: Do you really think I would be working in a place where they *created* deadly viruses?"

Chris looked down at his hands, which trembled on his lap. To think, tonight he'd planned on *kissing* her! His throat went dry. He looked up. Cate's face was impassive, but her breathing betrayed anger. He had only a few seconds before she would storm out. He put his hands on the table. "It's just a surprise, that's all. And the lies don't help."

Cate knew he was right on both counts. She reached across the table. He pulled his hands back, but she kept her hands on the table, inches from his. "Chris," she said. "Chris, look at me."

"I am looking at you."

"No. I mean *look* at me. My whole life is dedicated to saving lives. And I believe so much in what we're doing that I'm willing to risk my own."

Chris couldn't help it, it slipped out. "And mine?"

Cate pulled her hands back. "Don't you know me at all by now?" Her own hands were shaking, whether with rage or fear, Chris couldn't tell. Her mouth was set firmly, not a good sign, but her eyes were pleading. And eyes told the story, Chris believed. He reached out and this time she pulled *her* hands back. Chris reached further and took her hands in his. He took a deep breath.

"We've held hands before," said Cate.

"Not knowing what I know now."

"What do you know now?"

"That you work in the most dangerous environment on earth; that every day you risk your life studying a virus that could kill everyone on the planet. And every Sunday, we chat about sports and music and you never say a thing about *your* life, which has got to be terrifying!"

"I didn't want you to react the way you're reacting now."

"What I mean," said Chris, "is that you kept it inside, to protect me. I know you wouldn't risk infecting me if there were the slightest chance. I'm sorry. I was just . . . surprised, you know?"

"And scared."

Chris nodded and let go of her hands, but before he could withdraw, she grabbed his again.

"I would never take a chance of hurting you, Chris. Please tell me you know that."

Chris nodded. "I was just acting like the coward I am. Sorry."

Cate patted his hands. "Where I work, there are no cowards, just people with wisdom. We are cautious . . . kind of like you are when it comes to me."

"Not after tonight," said Chris. "You're gonna get a kiss that is guaranteed to infect you with the Love Bug, and with any luck—and no interference from the CDC—there will be no cure."

Cate felt a chill go up her spine. "I forgot my biosuit. Is it safe?"

"Not on your life. But it's worth the risk."

LONG DISTANCE

Cate unzipped the biosuit and stepped out of it, then hung it on the hook below her nameplate. She took a long, slow breath. The air was fresh, possibly the most pure air any human had ever breathed, but so many chemicals went into making it that way that even if you couldn't actually taste them on the tongue, you imagined them anyway. It was always a relief to breathe regular, microbe-infested air again. Ron got out of his own suit. "Sorry," he said, looking hang-dog. "Sorry I made you drop the sample."

"Ron, you've got to remember the rules."

"Right, I know. I just wanted to help."

"You can help us all if you follow procedures, Ron. In the lab, chivalry is a liability."

Ron smiled, looking even more like a puppy. "So what are you doing this weekend?"

"Ron," said Cate. "Please."

Ron raised his hands. "I know. It's against the law. I was just wondering."

"Ron, I appreciate your interest, but it's uncomfortable. And if anyone else heard . . . "

"I could get into trouble. I know. But you wouldn't tell anyone, would you?"

Cate looked down at Ron's arm, a sign she was going to touch him. "Not if you behave." She touched his forearm. "Help me out, here, Ron. Our job is tough enough without complicating it. Isn't it?"

Ron nodded, electrified by her touch—on his *bare* arm! He stared at her hand in amazement. Their first touch, and it was everything he'd ever imagined it would be.

"Ron?"

Ron looked up.

"You do understand, don't you?"

Ron nodded. "Sure. Sorry. I'll do better."

"Okay." She started out the door, then turned back. "And just between you and me, I have no plans this weekend, okay? Just hanging out with friends."

Ron nodded. "No opera singer?"

Cate shook her head. "See you Monday, Ron." The door silently sealed behind her.

Ron raised his forearm to his nose and inhaled. There it was: the slightest trace of her perfume, still lingering. His heart was racing. Looking around furtively and seeing only the security cam in an upper corner, Ron turned his back to it and gently pressed his lips to the place where she'd touched him, just above his wrist, closing his eyes and inhaling her scent. Cate.

Cate returned to her office and saw a message icon blinking on the computer module. She punched in Chris's number at the Met. The phone rang three times before the screen came up from black, revealing a stack of papers. "Yeah?" came a voice.

"Chris? It's Cate."

The papers were swept off the desk. Chris was grinning. "Cate! Oh, I have great news!"

Cate had listened to Chris ramble on about cartouches and rituals for hours and, honestly, couldn't see what was so interesting about any of that stuff, but she loved watching him as he talked about it. "What news? You guys find a new mummy or something?"

"How did you know?"

"Just guessing. They find those all the time, don't they?"

"Have you heard anything? On the news holos?"

"It was a lucky guess. What happened?"

"They found something in Africa—Tanzania. Egyptian. Predynastic, maybe."

Cate froze. "Africa?"

"Yeah. A mummy, and other things with it. Canopic jars, I think. Can you imagine? Canopic jars—in Tanzania!"

"Africa?"

Chris missed the note of concern in her voice. "I'm going there to check it out. It might be the find of a lifetime!" He brought his fist down on the table, startling Cate. "Dammit! It should have been *me! I* should have found it! I was planning to go to the Ruwenzoris next summer to look for a mummy there, and then Al McFadden calls me and says they already found one in Tanzania. And it might be Egyptian! The biggest thing since *Australopithecus boisei*—maybe bigger!" He was breathing heavily, his eyes glistening with excitement. On the monitor behind him was a familiar blue and white swirl in the shape of a globe—an airline reservations site.

"You're not thinking of going over there, are you?" asked Cate, her stomach churning.

"Yeah, that's why I called. I'm gonna see what they found!"

"Chris, you can't!"

"It will be expensive, but I've been planning for the last hour how I'll finagle the money from Dr. Hansen—once he hears about what they've found, he'll *have* to let me go and stake a claim for the museum. We must be financing *something* over there."

"Chris!" shouted Cate.

Chris looked fully into the screen for the first time, meeting Cate's eyes. "What?"

"You *can't* go!"

"Why not?"

Cate took a deep breath. "You just can't. Trust me."

"Why can't I?"

"It's . . . it's unsafe," said Cate, trying to be vague.

"You mean because it's Cobalt Ground Zero?"

No, that's not what she meant, but it would do. "Yes, because of that."

Chris laughed. "Hell, Cate, Al McFadden has been there for a year. He's not infected."

"But millions have died over there."

"I'll be careful. I won't go near the natives. Won't eat the food. Won't even touch the ground!" He laughed. "Doubt I even could!"

Cate shook her head. "Chris, listen to me! You can't go." Then, quietly, "Don't go. Please."

Chris leaned back and folded his arms. "Why?"

Cate leaned toward the screen, lowering her voice. "You might not get back in."

"Back in where? The U.S.?"

Cate nodded.

She had his attention now. "What's going to happen, Cate?"

"They're going to embargo Africa."

"Oh, that's bullshit. The ACLU will freak out. And you can't embargo an entire continent anyway. People come and go from there all the time."

"Not after this week they don't. We've got an outbreak in San Diego; no one outside the CDC knows about it. I just heard about it this morning. I'm going there tomorrow."

"Hell, Cate, that's clear across the country! How will that affect the East Coast? Besides, I'll just be a few days, get over there, pick up the goodies, and get back home. What's the problem?"

"I can't say, Chris. You have to believe me. Don't go."

"Sorry, Cate."

"Chris! Please! Okay, okay, I'll tell you, but this is top secret, understand?" Chris nodded, but his eyes remained doubtful. "The Director is going to recommend to the President that we seal the borders," said Cate. "Finally. The outbreak in San Diego is confirmed, but we have a half-dozen others scattered all over the country that aren't confirmed yet. But they probably will be."

"I'll be back before the curtain drops."

"No, you won't," said Cate. "Six months ago, they put an emergency plan into place. It can be up and running in forty-eight hours. Then even the lettuce pickers from Tijuana won't get in."

"Nonsense. They've never sealed the borders. Never could."

"This time they'll do it, Chris. They will. Don't go."

"Have to, babe. I'll only be a few days—a week, tops. Don't worry."

"But Chris!"

"Listen, Cate. I'll get back into the country if I have to hire a *coyote* in Calexico to sneak me across the border."

Cate was crying. "Chris, please."

"Sorry, babe, gotta go. Tell you all about it when I get back. And don't worry!"

The screen went blank. Cate pressed the heels of her hands into her eyes. She hadn't told him half of what she knew. They *would* close the border. And it wasn't a half-dozen outbreaks scattered across the country. It was a hundred.

Chris leaned back into the cushioned leather chair. His hands were shaking. He hated to lie to Cate, but couldn't she see how important this was? It meant his career! *Besides*, he thought, *they're always putting us on red alert—all my life they've been warning me about smoking and cholesterol and terrorists and climate change and nuclear waste and AIDS and now Cobalt. What's new? I'll get back in before they know it.*

"Sure," he whispered, taking a deep, calming breath, "I'll get back in. No problem."

INTO AFRICA

When the McDonnell-Boeing 797 came out of near orbit, and gravity once again pulled Chris down into his seat, he felt like he was still floating. Not only had Dr. Hansen, head of Egyptian antiquities at the Met, approved the trip, he'd put Chris in first-class on a nonstop flight to Dar es Salaam. Chris didn't even want to think about how expensive *that* was.

"Just get the damned thing," said Hansen, his eyes boring into Chris. "If this is for real, we're going to get a museum of our own!"

The sun was just rising over India as the supersonic descended through one hundred thousand feet. Chris could see the curve of the earth. The emerald green of Africa stretched out below him. There were rumors at JFK that this might be the last sonic flight to Africa. He wasn't surprised; there were only about fifteen people on the flight.

He heard a rumbling and glanced out the window. The swept-back wings were returning to their forward position. The sun shone brilliantly through the window, reflecting off a sea of clouds over the Indian Ocean. As the jet began its spiral descent, Chris got a look at Tanzania, far below. Located on the equator, the country was green with spring. About the size of California, it once had a population to match. Now, Tanzania was returning to a preindustrial population.

Dar es Salaam, located on the coast opposite Zanzibar island, was a glittering jewel against the darkness of the sea, though there were too few lights for a major city. He saw the same to the north in Nairobi, Kenya. He realized with a jolt that Cobalt was real; the lights all over the continent were going out.

Chris hadn't been in Tanzania in ten years, and fully expected dramatic changes, some by nature and some by man. At the turn of the century, Tanzania finally gave up on *ujamaa*, or "familyhood," an anti-industrialist socialism based on a return to agriculture and small kinship villages. It had been a failure, and Tanzania, for most of the last century and well into the current one, remained one of the ten poorest countries in the world, though it needn't have been. It had great natural reserves of gold, diamonds, and, of course, incredible game preserves, including the world-famous Serengeti Plain, where thousands of Westerners paid up to twenty thousand dollars for the privilege of watching a million wildebeests migrate north to Kenya. But tourist dollars, like the wildebeest themselves, only visited Tanzania. They soon moved on, back into the pockets of international hoteliers, restaurateurs, and safari companies. The Tanzanians remained poor as ever.

And when Cobalt erupted, the tourists stopped coming and the economy collapsed. At first, Cobalt almost did Tanzania a service. With few foreign dollars being extracted from the bulging pockets of safari vacationers, for the first time in seventy years, Tanzanians had to truly do for themselves. They left the filthy, crime-ridden cities and went back to their villages, picked up their hoes, and began to till the earth again. Almost immediately, there was more food in village markets than there had been in years. People started wearing traditional clothing again. But because of the Trans-African Highway, Cobalt did not distinguish between remote village and big city, and millions died in the ensuing outbreaks.

As the jet settled onto the tarmac at Dar, Chris noticed something else. There were only three airliners on the field, and none of them was at the boarding gates. All were parked out on the taxiway, far from the terminal. Chris's plane did the same, and the flight attendant walked down the aisle with a tray of white surgical masks. Everyone took one, and silence filled the plane. Chris had three in his luggage already.

The short flight to Arusha was as Chris remembered it: bumpy and scary, flying at tree-top level over lush montaine forest. He chose a seat on the right side so he could see Kilimanjaro. It was the tallest peak in Africa and its summit was once covered with snow and ice, but on Friday, March 13, 2020, it erupted, literally blowing its stack and vaporizing the glaciers that had for so long crowned it. Within two weeks, lava filled the volcano's mouth to the brim, and another great explosion, a 6.7 Richter-scale quake, tore a large gash in the southwestern face, releasing a torrent of magma that melted thousands of acres of forest reserve and displaced almost two hundred thousand people. Doomsayers, noting that the Cobalt outbreak had erupted just a few months earlier in 2019, predicted dire catastrophes for 2021, which was confirmed—at least in New York—when the Mets lost the 2021 World Series to the Rio de Janeiro Raptors, 3 games to 4.

As the small twin-engine Aztec skimmed along the southern edge of the Pare Mountains, Chris strained to spot Kili; and suddenly, there it was, a great cloud of black smoke rising from the decimated summit. The lurid-red lava river flowed down its flanks, spreading out on the plain to the south, reducing to smoking ash an area the size of Vermont.

Fifty miles west, Kili's sister volcano, Mount Meru, had also awoken. The entire Rift Valley was ringed by volcanos, and after Kilimanjaro's eruption, volcanos in Burundi and Rwanda were rumbling, and Uganda had an active volcano, if a only small one. Two months after Kili exploded, Meru belched, showering the nearby city of Arusha with fist-sized rocks and driving the population mad with fear. No flames lit Meru's summit, but constant earthquakes sent thousands of Arushans fleeing into the countryside, never to return.

The plane banked into a short final for Arusha International Airport, magnificently named, but really little more than single asphalt strip outside of town. Chris's plane was the largest present; a couple of old single-engine Cessnas were in tie-down, and one other twin, a Seneca, was waiting to take to the air. There were few cars in the parking lot and only one taxi at the curb. It was muggy, and thunderclouds were building up around the Meru summit in the early afternoon heat. Chris hoisted his bag over his shoulder and hoped McFadden had gotten the e-mail he'd sent from Dar.

Exiting the ghost-town terminal, Chris stood at the curb for almost an hour before an old silver Toyota Marauder roared into view, tires screaming. It screeched to a stop inches from him, nearly making him dive for cover. Its windows were opaque with dirt. The fenders were dented, and a large stone lay on the hood. The driver's door opened and a ruddy man got out, dressed in bush shorts and a garish Hawaiian shirt. A respirator covered his face, but Chris recognized his old friend's blue eyes and red hair. "Son of a bitch! You made it!" shouted the man.

"You drive like a maniac, Al," said Chris. McFadden motioned him to the rear of the vehicle. Broken window glass was scattered across the cargo area. Chris threw his backpack inside. "What happened?"

"Hell, son, *everything.*"

Chris opened the passenger door and noticed a sawed off shotgun on the seat. McFadden got in and tucked the gun between his own seat and the transmission console. He reached in the back for another respirator, this one a dirty olive color, handing it to Chris.

"Some kind of war?" asked Chris, putting the thing on. It smelled like a jock.

"Some kind, son," yelled Al, stomping on the gas pedal.

As they rumbled down the airport road toward Arusha, Chris held on for dear life. The normally laid-back McFadden was doing seventy down a road designed for half that, gripping the steering wheel like the neck of an enemy. The shotgun pointed up between them like an angry middle finger. Chris felt around for a seat belt; there was none. Instead, he hung onto the panic loop on the door pillar. "Since when do you own a shotgun?" yelled Chris.

"It's not mine," barked McFadden. "Goes with the truck. We take it when we leave the lodge."

"Why?"

McFadden just gestured at the road before them. It was empty except for the usual broken-down vehicles along the shoulder. They roared past palm-thatch roadside stalls where once a busy tourist trade sold carved masks and ebony figurines to sunburned American tourists.

Entering Arusha, they careened through a roundabout where a dust-covered statue celebrated the town's location halfway between Cairo and Cape Town. They saw no other moving vehicles. Tanzania had always held a grudge against technology. Cars wouldn't start. Roads threw up boulders and opened up ruts big enough to hide a black rhino in.

The downtown, once the site of a flourishing safari trade, was abandoned. Buildings were either boarded up or reduced to piles of rubble from nearby Meru's earthquakes. Far away, above the rooftops, smoke billowed. Part of the town was on fire. "Everybody went home," said Al. "Home to die."

Leaving Arusha, they continued west and soon found themselves in desolate, rolling hills dotted with stands of wilting fever-trees. Here and there Chris saw abandoned tin-roofed cinder block huts. The news holos were right; the country had been emptied out. Maybe Cate was right. This was looking like a mistake—a big mistake. His breathing notched up and he began to fidget with the respirator straps.

McFadden saw the anxiety building in Chris's eyes and stopped the car. "Right now you're wondering what you got yourself into. Listen, we wear the masks *only* when we leave the compound. I don't think there's any real danger out here and I'll prove it." He pulled his respirator off and took a deep, full breath, nodding for Chris to do the same.

After a moment's hesitation, Chris pulled his own mask down. The air smelled like smoked, spoiled milk and compost—the familiar Tanzania smell.

"Like it always did, right, son? "Al patted him on the shoulder. "Just pull her up when you meet a local, all right?"

Chris pulled his mask up.

"Guess you're right," said Al. "To you, *I'm* a local." He put the truck into gear. "Hell of a world, son. Hell of a world." A rooster tail of dust flew up as they bounded down the road.

On their drive west, Chris saw few animals. Dogs were rare anyway in Tanzania. Hyenas saw to that. But cattle, the indigenous Maasai tribe's prime economic engine, were missing as well. Al said most of the surviving Maasai had returned to the bush, taking their cattle with them. Yet, here and there, Chris saw stands of long, green grass. He wondered out loud how many of those bunches surrounded human remains. Al shook his head. "Too many."

At the village of Makuyuni, they turned left and headed towardTanzania's famous tourist attractions: Ngorongoro Crater, Olduvai Gorge, and the Serengeti Plain. The pavement ended and the road turned into a washboard trail. It took four hours to travel thirty miles. They passed Lake Manyara, a shallow soda lake, and entered the Maasai homeland. They were nearing Ngorongoro Crater. The land sloped upward, culminating in eroded red walls surrounding the immense crater, which encompassed a hundred square miles of pristine animal habitat—the world's largest zoo.

A few more bone-jarring miles and they turned off the main road. A bullet-riddled sign came into view, a long Maasai staff protruding from one of the support posts. Dangling from the lance was a tuft of what looked like human hair, encrusted with blood.

Al saw Chris's slack-jawed stare. "Don't know if it is, son. You wanna get out and check?"

Chris shook his head. To his right, Chris saw a small cattle herd and the familiar Scots-tartan wrap of a Maasai herdsman, who turned as they passed. Chris saw that along with his traditional quarter staff he wore a bandolier. "Hunker down, son," said Al. "Might get nasty here."

Chris scrunched down in his seat. "What's going on?"

"Just hold on and we'll get through the beggars as quickly as possible."

Suddenly, a rock bounced off the Marauder windshield, sending Al careening off the road. He swerved back onto the washboard, cursing and reached for his shotgun. "Roll your window down." Chris made a four-inch space and Al cocked the shotgun. "Cover your ears," he said, and before Chris could do so, he squeezed the trigger.

The blast dazed Chris. Acrid blue smoke filled the cabin, and Al pulled the gun back inside. "Let the boys at Sopa know we're coming. We might need the cavalry, as you Yanks would say." Chris heard another, distant rifle shot answering Al's.

Another stone hit the truck, then another. Before them, three Maasai youths trotted out of the trees. Two brandished the typical Maasai walking stick; the third, a rolled black umbrella. They hurled stones at the Marauder as it passed, and Al laughed as they outdistanced the rocks.

"What's so funny?" asked Chris. The stones hitting the side of the truck still rang in his ears.

"Welcoming committee," said Al. "We'll see more." Behind them, the three teenagers stood in the road, still throwing rocks. "Keep the gun handy, son," said Al.

Chris nodded and gingerly took the gun. More stones flew through the air, hurled from the safety of the forest bounding the road. As they rounded a curve, a group of Maasai men appeared, blocking their way. Most appeared in their twenties, and all appeared ill, their dark skin mottled with purple bruises. Al braked to a stop. "I heard a Maasai had an AK. Looks like this crew only has sticks." He nodded at the shotgun. "Let these boys see our friend."

"I'm not gonna shoot anybody!" said Chris.

"*They* don't know that. Let them see it." Al let the brakes off and the vehicle started moving slowly forward.

Chris rolled his window down a bit and stuck the gun barrel out. The men saw the shotgun, shuffled indecisively for a moment, then reformed. They wore typical Maasai beaded necklaces and ostrich feather headdresses. As the Marauder rolled toward the group, its wheels crunching the gravel, the men stepped aside, but their stern expressions indicated they were ready to fight. Al whispered to Chris, "Remember, we're friends. All three of us," he said, nodding at the gun.

When the men would not part, Al stopped the truck. One of the warriors walked to the driver's side window. "McFadden, where you been?" he asked.

"Picking up my friend at the airport. Another archeologist."

"What about doctor?"

"Not here yet, Jetaa. Soon, very soon."

Jetaa harumphed. "He is not doctor?"

"Not that kind," said McFadden.

None of the warriors wore antiviral masks. Chris felt both ridiculous and pathetic wearing a respirator. He began to pull his mask down and Al caught his arm. "Makes them feel powerful to know we're afraid of Cobalt—even though it's *they* who are dying. Go figure." He inched the truck forward. "Very soon. Doctor's coming. Very soon."

Jetaa leaned in. "You lie, McFadden," he said. His eyes were red, a Cobalt precursor. The man had maybe a couple of weeks to live. Chris wondered if he knew that.

"He's coming," repeated Al.

Jetaa peered at Chris. "You will die too. Ngai hates *iloredaa enjekat.*" He coughed. Clearly, the speech was difficult for him; he was weak, the virus moving through his blood, turning his eyes red, blue-black bruises blooming on his face and neck. He stepped aside and Al let off the brake, moving them slowly ahead. Jetaa made a gesture, and the men blocking their way reluctantly parted. The Marauder passed them and Chris gulped. He'd never seen such icy hate as he saw in the sick men's eyes.

"Who's coming?" asked Chris, suddenly aware of how much he'd been sweating.

"A doctor from Dar. I talked to him three days ago. Haven't heard back, and I can't raise him on the wireless." McFadden upshifted, leaving the nine black men, dressed in their ritual finery, in a cloud of dust. "Won't come anyway. He's not stupid."

Chris looked back over his shoulder. The men, so tall and proud when they surrounded the truck, shuffled off the road, their lances now supporting them like canes.

"What was that he called us?" asked Chris. "Iloredaa . . ."

"*Iloredaa enjekat.* It's Swahili for 'those who confine their farts by clothing.'" He laughed. "If you ate nothing but milk and blood, you'd have indigestion too."

Chris stuffed the shotgun back between the seats. "Al, what the hell is going on here?"

Al adjusted his mask. "The end of the world, son."

NGORONGORO CRATER

The narrow dirt road wound up the volcanic slope through a dense jungle hung with thick, ropy vines. The sun cast long shadows. Chris wondered aloud why Al didn't turn on the Marauder's headlights. "Don't want to give them too much notice," said Al, peering through the dappled shade. Suddenly, the forest opened up and there they were on the southern rim of the crater, where the road split. The left branch went to the park headquarters and the economy tourist lodges. The right fork ran along the rim to Sopa Lodge, a high-end tourist hotel located on the eastern edge of the caldera.

"Hold up," said Chris, and Al stopped the SUV. Chris got out, walked to the rim, and focused his binoculars on Ngorongoro Crater. Ten miles across, it was the largest collapsed volcano in the world, with sheer, two-thousand foot, heavily forested walls. In the middle, like a great blue eye, lay Lake Magadi, home to tens of thousands of flamingos, storks, and herons. Panning across the rolling plains surrounding the lake, Chris saw great herds of wildebeests and zebras. North of the lake, trees shook as elephants stripped bark off their trunks. Eland and waterbuck browsed the low hedges of the Lerai Forest near the southwest wall, and several prides of lions lazed in koppies by Ngoitoktok Springs, just below him. Hyenas, eagles, and buzzards cleaned up after predators, and the sky was full of starlings, plovers, and finches.

Chris was overwhelmed. The sun perched on the western crater wall, turning the sky pink. Shadows began to fill the caldera bowl. He turned to Al, shaking his head, speechless. Al shrugged. "Yeah, it's awesome. But we'd best get moving. Light's failing."

Chris got back into the Marauder. It made perfect sense that they'd found something primordial here; if there ever were a place on earth that deserved to be called Eden, this was it.

They traveled along the eastern crater rim, which dropped precipitously off to their left. To their right, the densely wooded land sloped gently away. After about ten minutes, Al slowed, but did not stop, for off to the left, near the rim, they saw campfires and figures hunkered down next to them. Al still hadn't turned on the headlights. There was still a little light in the sky, but not much. When they quietly rolled past the camp, the people jumped to their feet and began running toward them, yelling. Al stomped on the gas.

"Who are they?" asked Chris.

"That's our excavation. That's where we found him."

"The mummy?"

"There's an entire cemetery carved into the crater wall just beyond the rim there. It was covered with foliage, and no one, not even the Masaai that are guarding it now, knew it existed a month ago. They claim it's theirs, even though the Masaai have only lived here for three hundred years. What we found is from a culture we estimate to be six thousand years old."

"How did you find it?"

"You know how they found the Dead Sea Scrolls?" asked Al.

Chris nodded.

"Like that. A Masaai kid went down there to retrieve a stray cow. He saw a strange-looking stone covered with vegetation. He pulled the vines aside. The stone was almost a perfect circle. He told his mum. She knew one of our workers, and she told him. He went down there and rolled the stone aside. He described a pan-burial grave, like you see in Egypt, near al Badari."

"But they didn't bury in caves."

"No, but they have the same contents: rock rings, burial goodies, and the like."

"And canopic jars," said Chris.

Al nodded, pleased. "Head of his class."

"Are they Egyptian?"

"That's for you to confirm. Strange writing, not hieroglyphic or cuneiform, but almost cursive. Quite beautiful."

"What about the jars?"

"We've only pulled one out, but . . . well, you've got to see it. Unbelievable."

It was dark now and the road was barely visible. "Why can't we turn on the lights?" asked Chris. "I don't want to drive off a cliff."

"Worse things, son," said Al. "Look."

And there, lining both sides of the road ahead, were probably a hundred people. Al pressed down on the gas. "Fire a couple of shells into the air."

Chris grabbed the shotgun, poked the barrel out the window, and squeezed the trigger. People scattered. Al leaned on the horn and switched on the headlights. A scene of pandemonium appeared. Colorfully dressed Masaai were running everywhere. Al swerved to avoid a woman and almost hit a young boy standing on the road shoulder.

"Al!" screamed Chris. "Look out!"

Al missed the boy by an inch, but someone else glanced off the truck's right front fender, making a sickening *thudding* sound.

"Again!" shouted Al.

Chris fired again. Another shot answered, and then a bullet came through the windshield. Chris dropped the gun, shouting, "I'm shot!"

"Hang on!" yelled Al, weaving in and out of running people. A barrage of bullets tore through the driver's side of the SUV. "Holy hell! They got a machine gun!" He hit the gas, not caring anymore who was in the way. Chris felt a bullet whiz past his ear. The passenger window lay in pieces in his lap. He yanked off the respirator and pulled his tee shirt up to his face, which was streaming blood.

The truck hit something and Chris looked back. A cow was spinning on the road behind them like a plaster lawn ornament. Spears arced through the air toward them. One bounced off the roof. Another flew in through the rear window and rammed into the back of Al's seat. Al lurched forward, eyes popping in surprise. Chris grabbed the wheel, but he could barely see for the blood in his eyes. Al was saying, "Hell, son, the Injuns got me!" But his foot was still on the gas and the road ran straight for awhile.

By the time Al let up on the gas they were out of range and all Chris could see in the red tail-light-lit darkness behind them was dust. He turned on the dome light. Al was slumped against the wheel. The spear had penetrated the seat, but only a couple of inches. The back of Al's shirt was red with blood, though, and he was babbling something about General Custer.

Chris jumped out of the SUV, ran around the front, hauled Al out, and dragged him to the rear of the vehicle, pushing him inside, over the tailgate, all the time expecting to be impaled by a spear. He then jumped in the driver's seat and hit the gas. Gunshots continued. He turned off the headlights to make less of a target. In the back, Al moaned, and Chris leaned forward, avoiding the spear head still protruding from the driver's seat.

He drove this way for a good ten minutes and then he saw it: a bank of headlights before them. Three black Marauders were parked in the road, blocking the way. Chris skidded to a stop.

"Hands up!" yelled someone.

"Al McFadden's been shot!" yelled Chris. "I mean, stabbed! Hit with a spear! Oh shit, help!"

Suddenly, the Marauder was surrounded by a dozen black men wearing khaki work pants and boots, naked to the waist, pointing laser-sighted rifles at him. "Al's been hit," he squeaked.

Someone opened the rear hatch. "He's bleeding," said a voice.

"Get out," said another in clipped, accented English.

Chris got out, his hands raised. "I'm Chris Tempest."

"We were expecting you," said a rich, syrupy voice. A tall black man strode through the guards, gently pushing down the gun barrels as he passed. "I am John N'garra, Dr. McFadden's second in command." He extended his hand to Chris, then, noting Chris's face, reached into a pocket, removed a handkerchief, and began dabbing at Chris's bloody right eye.

"I've been hit!" said Chris.

"No," said N'garra. "They hit the windshield. Your eyebrow was cut by flying glass. Your eye is perfectly fine." He folded the hankie into a compress and raised Chris's hand to hold it in place, then whistled to the men surrounding the SUV, speaking to them in Swahili. They trotted off into the darkness, the red laser dots of their rifle sights bouncing before them.

N'garra led Chris toward the SUV barricade. As he eased Chris into one of the Marauders, he smiled. "Welcome to Tanzania, Doctor Tempest."

THE FIND

Chris didn't remember much of the rest of the ride to Sopa Lodge; his left eye was aching, the blood wouldn't clot—he wondered wildly if he already had Cobalt—and he was thoroughly shaken up. This was not archeology as he knew it.

When they arrived at the lodge, he expected a camp with foul-smelling latrines, musty tents, and open campfires. Instead, they drove beneath a tall, arched stone entryway and entered a large, well-appointed compound that once boasted manicured lawns, swimming pools, two bars, and a twenty-four-hour spa.

N'garra drove up the gravel drive and stopped under the looming cantilevered porch. A dozen concrete steps led up to six immense glass doors. The lodge itself consisted of three cylindrical buildings with tall, conical roofs, designed to mimic traditional Masaai mud-and-dung huts. Beyond the empty swimming pool were a dozen smaller guest cottages of the same design. N'garra led Chris into the lobby, which was lit by propane lanterns. The curving western wall was floor-to-ceiling windows, weakly reflecting the yellow lantern glow. N'garra led him to the bar at the far end of the lobby. "I imagine you could use a drink," said N'garra, seating Chris in a plush red leather chair. "Sorry, but we have only warm beer."

"Good enough for me," said Chris. "By the way, your English is excellent."

N'garra nodded at another man, who left and soon returned with two beers. N'garra opened them and handed one to Chris. "I was raised in Kenya," said N'garra, "but educated in Georgia. If you can speak suth-un, you can speak enna-thang." He smiled.

"How's Al?" asked Chris, sipping the beer.

"Getting stitches," said N'garra. "He'll be okay."

"What are the Maasai so heated up about?"

"The find," said N'garra. "They think they own everything around here. Their god Ngai not only gave them all the cattle in the world, but apparently he also gave them all the land to graze them on. Ruthless capitalists, like you Americans."

"I'm not ruthless," said Chris. "I'm not even a capitalist."

N'garra laughed. "Of course not! You're pure! A scientist! You're only here to *look*, isn't that right? Not take?"

Chris shrugged. "Al asked me to identify the find. Can I see it?"

"When Al gets fixed up." N'garra leaned forward in his chair. "Did he tell you about the jar?"

"He was about to. We got interrupted by the war. What's so special about it?"

"Nothing," said N'garra. "What's special is *inside*."

He must have dozed off, for he was being shaken awake. "Chris, wake up!"

Chris blinked. Al stood before him, still wearing the bloody shirt, which was open, revealing a cotton wrapping around his chest. "Not exciting enough for you?"

Chris got to his feet. He felt groggy. The adrenaline aftermath: sleep. "You okay?"

"Close one, that was," said Al. "It's getting dicey to leave the lodge. And we're gonna have to, soon—we can't stay here much longer. Another worker got ill this morning; we put him in one of the guest cottages where we're keeping the sick ones."

"How many are sick?"

"A dozen or so. Only ten of us are still well. Time's running out and so must we; so, if you're not too tired, let's go see what you risked life and limb to see." He held up a propane lantern and nodded toward the dark doorway. Chris followed him out of the bar. N'garra stood near the reception desk. Al led them up a winding stone staircase to the second floor, N'garra following them. They entered a large room, one side of which was all windows. The darkness outside made the windows into mirrors, and Chris watched the three of them walk to the center, where a number of folding tables were set up. They were loaded with scientific equipment: microscopes, analyzers, and portable computers.

"We need juice, John," said Al, walking over to another table, where an aluminum steamer trunk sat. He spun the combination and opened the lock. N'garra went to a window, opened it, whistled, then made a whirling motion with his finger. Chris heard a generator outside cough to life. The lights in the room began to come up. Al, still bent over the box, said, "Chris, would you turn off the lights? Don't want anybody taking potshots at us, do we?"

Chris went to the switch and threw the room into darkness again, except for the blinking equipment lights. Al's module booted up. John folded the sides of another box down, revealing a large black donut about two feet tall with a hole in the center about twelve inches in diameter.

"CAT scanner?" asked Chris

"Yes," said Al, turning toward them, holding a football-sized object in his hands, draped in a white towel. "Our computing power is limited, but we still got an interesting image." He set the object on the platform extending out of the donut hole and removed the coverlet.

Chris leaned forward. It was a canopic jar all right. "Alabaster?"

Al nodded.

"All the way down here." He turned to N'garra. "Ever heard of that stone in these parts?"

"It isn't local," said N'garra, "but it can be found beyond Lake Vic, in the Ruwenzoris. Around here, rock is granite or volcanic."

"Bring the lantern over," said Chris, and Al held it close to the jar, which was urn-shaped, ten inches tall, and had an orb-shaped stopper. It had the strange cursive script Al had described just below its midsection, but no hieroglyphics, just three wavy lines around the jar's waist, reminding Chris of the way kids sometimes draw the ocean. When cleaned, the jar's surface would gleam a brilliant, speckled white, but it was dirty now, and strangely blackened toward the top. "I don't see Duamutef, Hapi, Qebehsenuf, or Imsety," said Chris, peering at it closely.

"Who?" asked Al.

"The four sons of Horus. Duamutef, the jackal, topped the jar with the stomach in it. Hapi, the baboon, guarded the lungs. Qebehsenuf, the falcon, contained the intestines, and Imsety, the human, held the liver."

"So what does the orb on top mean?" asked N'garra.

"It might be the Sun," said Chris. "The Black Sun. Strange."

"Why?" asked Al.

"Because the whole point of the Egyptian burial ritual was to sustain life—to enable the deceased's soul to live on, to cross the River of Souls, pass the trials, be judged, then live for eternity in Lightland. The Black Sun denotes death—the end of everything. Eternal coma."

"What about the wavy lines?" asked N'garra.

"Looks Badarian or earlier," said Chris, running his finger across the lines. "They indicate the river." He straightened and faced Al. "The Nile River."

Al's face broke into a huge grin. "You're sure?"

"More than likely," said Chris. "Beyond the jar itself, it's the one element that's clearly Egyptian. Nilotic peoples have always used those three lines to represent the river." He touched the stopper, hoping to remove it.

"Don't!" exclaimed Al.

Chris stopped, surprised.

"That's part of the mystery," said Al, gently taking the jar from Chris and setting it on the scanner platform. He touched a button on the module and the screen came to life. The platform moved silently through the donut hole. Al tapped a series of buttons and a sound like tiny marbles rolling around in a metal cup was heard. On the top of the module, the crystal lens glowed, and in a moment, a three-dimensional holo of the jar appeared floating in the air.

Chris' mouth dropped open. "What is that inside?"

Al folded his arms, grimacing with pain as he did so. "We think it's the heart."

"No," countered Chris. "The Egyptians didn't remove the heart during mummification. They left it in the body. The Book of the Dead absolutely prohibits its removal."

"Maybe so, but *these* folks removed it."

"Unprecedented," said Chris, leaning closer. "It looks so *healthy*. Why," he said, turning to Al, "it almost looks *bloody.*"

Al nodded. "That's what we thought too. The blood looks bright red with oxygen."

"Why haven't you opened it?"

Al gestured around the room. "In this environment, using this equipment? We didn't dare. The heart might be destroyed the moment we let air into the jar."

"Probably right," said Chris. "How about the owner of this extraordinary organ?"

"Over here," said John, picking up the lantern and leading the way toward the dark floor-to-ceiling windows. On a folding table pushed against the windows was a heavy vinyl body bag. N'garra set the lantern down and unzipped the bag. They all crowded in close, straining their eyes in the dim light.

The mummy lay on its side, arms folded across the chest and legs drawn up. It was wrapped in narrow strips of cloth, painted with tar, and covered with a thick, yellow layer of tree resin. It was an adult, and the proportions indicated that it was male. In the flickering lantern light, Chris saw something glimmering, peeking out from underneath the hands crossed over the chest as if in prayer. He pulled a pen out of his pocket and gently pried loose a small oval shape. It was a scarab beetle, exquisitely carved in green serpentine, lying on a field of beaten gold. He looked up. "My God. The Heart Scarab."

"Looks like a beetle," said Al.

"A dung beetle," said Chris, turning the amulet over in his hands. "The early Egyptians watched this beetle rolling a ball of dung along, and then, miraculously, tiny beetles would emerge from the ball. They didn't know about larvae; they thought the beetle was magically regenerating itself—a resurrection, if you will."

"But why over the heart? What significance was it to them?"

"They believed the mind was located in the heart. At the final judgment, before Osiris, King of the Dead, the supplicant—our friend here—had to present his heart to be weighed on a scale, to see if he was worthy to enter heaven. Lightland, they called it."

"Looks like he didn't make it," said N'garra.

Al slowly zipped the bag closed. "Or maybe he did."

OUTBREAK

Cate emerged from the CDU and leaned against the wall. Sweat poured down her face, even though the Racal suit's battery-powered filters were set on high. She felt light-headed. For a moment there, in that room with the dying man, she thought she might vomit, which would have been a major problem in a biocontainment suit. Sally Cloudburst, Cate's supervisor, followed her out the door. She put a hand on Cate's shoulder. "You okay, Seagram?"

"I've never seen anyone crash and bleed out before."

Cloudburst nodded. "I've only seen it once, back in Gallup, in '15, when I was just starting out. It was Hanta, and they'd had trouble with it in the four corners area for twenty years."

"Because of the rats," said Cate, trying to slow her breathing and think of something besides that poor man in the next room who had aspirated bloody vomit a moment before, spraying the interior of his clear bubble. He scrabbled at the plastic, smearing the blood. A moment later he started bucking with convulsions. At that point, Cate was elbowed out of the way by the CDU staff, who held the man down as he thrashed, kicked, and finally died.

"Yes, the rats," said Cloudburst. "Rats are everywhere in the southwest. They're the natural reservoir for the Hanta virus; it cycles in them, doing them no harm. But the virus contaminated their urine and feces, and when humans inhaled the dust, well . . . " She shook her head. "Seven hundred twenty-four dead."

Cate looked up sharply. "And we had a vaccination for Hanta! But what have we got for Cobalt? Nothing!"

Down the hall, on the other side of the sliding glass door separating the Contagious Disease Unit from the rest of the hospital, were several people, including reporters, watching Cloudburst and Cate talk, though they could not possibly hear them through the thick glass. Cloudburst, acutely aware of the potential for panic, not only inside Scripps Hospital but everywhere in San Diego, pulled Cate further down the corridor, turning her away from the journalists' cameras. "Seagram!" she hissed. "Get a hold of yourself!"

"He was third-spacing, bleeding under the skin," groaned Cate. "Now I know why they call it Cobalt!" She looked up at Cloudburst, eyes wide with fear. "He looked like someone had taken a baseball bat to his entire body—one big purple bruise! You couldn't even feel his organs anymore—they'd turned to sludge! *Sally, we're all going to die!*"

Cloudburst gripped Cate's shoulders with both hands. "Not if you and I do our work. We came here to draw antiserum and get back home. We can't save that man, but we *can* save others!"

"Antiserum? There *is* no antiserum, Sally! We drew his blood, but *no one's* body makes Cobalt antiserum! Once you're infected, it's over. No antibodies means no vaccinations, which means no cure. Someone sneezes on you and you've got three weeks, tops. And who knows how many people that poor man in there infected before he bled out!"

Cloudburst was not angry at the exchange; she was actually pleased. A moment before, Cate had been close to panic. She was angry now, and in this case, rage was a good thing. It kept the mind focused, and Cate would forget the terrifying feeling of watching the dead Asian seaman in the CDU. "We quarantined the seaport," said Cloudburst. "He was put in a bubble stretcher before he even left the ship. Besides the EMTs, only five people—including you and me— have been near him. It's not an outbreak, Cate. It's an incident."

Cate laughed hoarsely, shaking her head. Her blonde hair was matted against her forehead. "An incident? The hospitals all up the corridor to Santa Barbara are reporting increased admissions of people with headaches, along with backaches and joint aches. That's Day One! By Day Five, they'll be experiencing fever and nausea, diarrhea, flu-like symptoms. And within two weeks, they'll be third-spacing! Then it's all over." She pointed at the room they just left. "That man was coherent when they took him off the cargo ship. Look at him now! He's dead, and that was only three days ago! How can we stop this?"

Cloudburst held up the vial of blood Cate had drawn. "With this. We take this home and analyze the shit out of it. We've cornered four of the six proteins making up Cobalt's shell. The fifth protein may manifest in this sample. We're gonna number-crunch this little bastard into submission!"

Cate was feeling a little better now; the nausea had passed. Her suit still dripped from the envirochem they'd sprayed on themselves before leaving the CDU. Standing there, wearing her orange bio suit, the green disinfectant pooling around her booted feet, made Cate feel like a deep sea diver just emerging from the abyss. She looked up at Cloudburst's broad, brown face, the dark eyes calm amidst the flat Navajo features. "Okay. We'll do our best, I guess. But this thing is smarter than we are. I've seen it mutate when exposed to ultraviolet. No virus can survive ultraviolet light! But Cobalt seems to know what's coming and it changes, protecting itself, shielding itself. And the RNA strand is millions of nucleotides long! There are infinite protein combinations. It's a hopeless tangle of possibilities."

Cloudburst nodded. "And our job is to examine every one of those possibilities and determine if it is the answer, and if it isn't, then move on to the next one. We'll beat this virus, Cate. We have the technology. The entire NSA computer system is working on this. It's only a matter of time."

"Maybe," said Cate. "But when the computer finally spits out the answer, will there be anyone left alive to read it?"

ᨆᨆᨆ

They sat side by side on the plane. Now that it was over, Cate felt foolish about her outburst at Scripps. She touched the plasma screen on the seat back and it went black. She was tired of reading. She looked out the window. It was night, and the 787 raced eastward, the waxing quarter moon casting its silver light on the clouds below. She wondered how Chris was. Would she ever see him again? He would be at the archeological site by now, deep inside Tanzania. She shook her head. *He's as crazy as I am*, she thought. *Going into a hot zone. Hell—he's crazier than I am! At least I went in wearing a biosuit! He went to a place where everything he sees might be Cobalt's natural reservoir!* Her shoulders slumped and her eyes teared up. *I'll never see him again.*

"Cate?" Cloudburst gently touched her shoulder.

Cate wiped her eyes and turned.

"Are you all right? You want another stress tab?"

"No. I'm okay. Still a little shaken, that's all. Worried about someone."

"The opera singer?"

"Right. He's a tenor, with a stomach out to here." She made a barrel shape with her arms, laughing at the thought of Chris with a potbelly. It made her want to cry, and she broke down.

Cloudburst patted her arm. "What is it?"

"They found a mummy or something in Tanzania and he went to check it out. Can you believe that? Ground Zero!"

Cloudburst was horrified. "When did he go?"

"The day before we went to San Diego."

"Have you heard from him?"

"No. There are no uplinks there. The whole country's gone Neolithic. Ninety percent of the population dead, Cobalt probably cycling in some organism, and Chris walking right into it!" She broke down again.

Cloudburst put her arm around Cate's shoulder. "He'll be okay, Cate."

"How do you know?" sniffled Cate.

"He's in love with you, right? So he must be *smart*. He'll take precautions. You'll see."

Cate tried to imagine herself waiting at JFK, watching the disembarking passengers coming through the terror- and bio-gates, Chris, tanned and smiling, holding his backpack high, waving at her. But all she could picture were two white-suited attendants wheeling a gurney with an olive-colored body bag on it, and somehow she knew Chris was inside that bag.

She looked bleakly out of the window across the sea of darkness.

NINE

OUT OF AFRICA

Al McFadden shut the Marauder tailgate. "Everybody ready?" he asked, looking around at the men. Inside the SUV was a coffin, crudely-fashioned out of wooden fence slats. Inside the coffin was the mummy, wrapped in cotton batting and zipped in its vinyl body bag.

The faces of the shirtless workmen holding M-35 pulse rifles were grim. They had begun work a few months ago at the crater as diggers; now suddenly they were a provisional army. Having spent two summers at digs Tanzania, Chris knew the natives well enough to read their faces. They were scared to death.

"You okay, son?" asked McFadden.

Chris nodded. "Got it right here." He held up his bullet-ridden backpack.

"You sure you want to risk it? We can put it back in the shipping trunk."

"That trunk's no more bulletproof than I am. At least this way, I'll have it with me, in case . . ." He didn't finish; everyone knew what he meant.

Over the last four hours, they'd repelled two incursions. Just after midnight, three rocket-propelled grenades had landed in the compound, one in the empty swimming pool. When it went off, the entire front of the lodge was showered in white plaster dust. Another grenade hit the lawn surrounding the pool, rolled toward the crater rim, and detonated as it fell off the cliff. A third hit the stone-paved driveway and rolled under a vehicle. The explosion killed three men, and outraged the others so completely that five of them ran out into the darkness armed only with sidearms and a single rifle. Gunfire ensued for a time, and then silence. None of the five returned.

While they were getting ready to leave, Chris donned his respirator and walked toward the small, cylindrical, conical-roofed guest cottages ringing the compound. He peered into a couple of windows and saw people lying motionless in beds in the dark. In one room, a delirious man thrashed around. Chris was about to open the door when someone grabbed his shoulder. "It is too late," said John N'garra.

"He's dying!"

"Yes. He is," said N'garra, leading him away.

Now N'garra spoke to the workers. "You all have your weapons and ammunition?"

The men nodded. They kept looking at the wooden coffin in the back of Al's shot-up Marauder.

"We should leave this thing here. It is bad luck," whispered one worker to another.

"What?" barked N'garra. "That's superstition! Foolishness!"

The workers shuffled uncertainly, looking at the ground. N'garra closed the distance between them, looking each man in the eye. "We must leave; the Masaai will kill us if we stay any longer. And your brethren, who died protecting this find, will call you cowards from the Other Side!"

This seemed to straighten the spines of the men, and several nodded.

Chris looked at Al, who had been watching the conversation. He'd put on a new shirt, but the bandage around his torso still made a bulge.

Al coughed and said, "Okay. Saddle up!"

Everyone got in the Marauders. N'garra and three guards in the first one; Al and Chris in the second SUV with the coffin; the rest of the men in the third vehicle. One of the men went to the roll-top door and began tugging on the chain to raise it. It was about half-way up when the familiar *pop* of an RPG launcher was heard. *Tink! Tink! Tink!* A grenade bounced past Chris's vehicle and rolled toward petrol barrels at the rear of the garage.

"Al!" he yelled. "Go! Go! Now!"

Al was still buckling in, but hit the gas anyway. N'garra's truck was already rolling, and Al slammed into its rear end, tires boiling black smoke. The driver of the third SUV was struggling with the keys, while everybody in his vehicle was screaming, "Go! Go! GO!"

Al was only half-way out of the garage when the grenade went off, exploding several 50-gallon fuel barrels. Chris felt a rush of heat. The rear of his vehicle was lifted off the ground. Turning, he saw a fireball envelope the third Marauder. The men inside were frozen in fiery silhouette.

"Goddammit!" yelled Al, downshifting. In front of them, N'garra's SUV had rolled off to the side of the driveway. Al nudged past the vehicle and Chris heard the sound of tearing metal. "Let's go!" yelled Al as they passed. "John! Let's go!"

Another RPG bounced off their hood and exploded in the air behind the two SUVs. Chris turned around and saw N'garra grab his steering wheel, lurching after Al's vehicle, which had taken the lead. "Sons of bitches!" shouted Al.

"Where are they?" shouted Chris. He held the backpack firmly between his knees.

"Everywhere!" yelled Al. From trees inside the compound came the flash of small-arms fire. Two shells hit their truck. Al stood on the gas pedal. "Goddamned hybrids! Gutless!"

Chris looked back. The men in N'garra's Marauder were firing into the trees on either side of the driveway. Al roared around the rear of the lodge and up the incline to meet the main loop. The iron lodge-entrance gates stood ajar. Al downshifted, the tires squealed, and they hit the heavy gates at full speed, throwing Chris forward. The backpack was thrown onto the floor. Chris reached for it.

"Forget that thing!" yelled Al. "Grab the gun!"

Chris pulled the shotgun out. They crested a rise and roared down the road. They were driving without headlights; Chris could barely see the road. He wondered if Al was driving by memory. Suddenly, gunfire erupted from the jungle on both sides of the road. Chris squeezed the trigger twice before Al shouted, "For Chrissakes! Shoot at something you can *see*!"

Chris took his finger off the trigger. The problem was, he couldn't see *anything*. He heard a crash and turned. N'garra's SUV bounded through the compound entrance, rolling over the flattened metal gate, which caught on the truck's undercarriage, raising sparks. The SUV veered off the road into a shallow ditch. Within seconds the vehicle was at the center of a fireworks display of discharging weaponry.

"Stop!" yelled Chris. "John's in trouble!"

"Aren't we all," said Al, still staring ahead.

Chris looked at him, dumbfounded.

Al glanced in his direction. "What can *we* do?"

"We can help!" shouted Chris, still turned around in his seat.

Suddenly, there was a bright flash, and just before the SUV disappeared behind a curve, Chris saw an RPG arc through the air and land on the vehicle. It exploded, a fireball rising into the sky.

"Shit!" yelled Al, seeing the explosion in the rearview. "Damned Masaai!"

Chris focused on the road. They were near the excavation site where they'd run the gauntlet earlier that evening. He recognized it because the cow they hit was still lying in the middle of the road. He saw campfires through the trees. Suddenly, Al shouted. "There!" He pointed at a figure standing by the side of the road. Chris put his finger on the shotgun trigger. "Shoot!" screamed Al.

Chris squinted. It was only a boy. The SUV roared by so close Chris could have clubbed him with the shotgun. As it was, he met the boy's blank stare. Each saw the same expression on the other's face: stunned incredulity.

∧∧∧

Once they cleared the crater, they didn't see another person the rest of the night. Al drove as fast as he could, headlights on, not caring if anyone saw them or not. As dawn began to lighten the sky and their road turned east, toward Arusha, Chris finally stowed the shotgun and picked up the backpack. He unzipped it, removing the bath towel from around the alabaster jar. It was undamaged. They exchanged relieved looks.

"Hell of a way to get famous, son," said Al.

Chris looked at the empty road behind them, the dawn turning the rising dust red. "You think anybody else made it out?"

Al just stared ahead, his jaw set.

"You're right," said Chris, turning the jar over in his hands. "A hell of a way to get famous."

They arrived in Arusha by mid-morning. The town, sitting empty at the foot of grumbling Mt. Meru, seemed even scarier than yesterday when Chris had first entered it. Was it only yesterday? He reached for the shotgun again. He was beginning to feel naked without it in his hands. It *was* just yesterday, and then he'd been horrified at the idea of holding a firearm. And yet in just twenty four hours, he had fired that gun twenty times, probably killing any number of people.

His stomach lurched as they hit a bump, but it did so because of the revelation. He'd killed people, and for what? A mummy and an alabaster jar? The world had turned upside down! Suddenly, the shotgun seemed as infectious as smallpox. He handed it to Al, who asked, "What is it?"

"Nothing," said Chris. What was there to say? He'd done the unspeakable and he was forever changed. He had killed people, stolen archeological artifacts, and put himself in a place where everyone was dying of Cobalt. And for what?

As they passed the roundabout near the half-way monument, Al said, "Son, you drive."

As the Marauder slowed, Chris looked at Al closely for the first time. He was horrified. McFadden's eyes were red, there was blood at the corners of his mouth, and blotchy bruises mottled his neck. He had a glazed expression and his face muscles didn't seem to work. He looked sixty. His hands trembled on the wheel. "Get your mask on. Now." The Marauder stopped. Chris put on his mask and jumped out, running around to Al's side and helping him out, leading him to the passenger side. As Chris closed the door, Al said, "Get me my mask."

Chris fitted Al's ULPA respirator on him and got into the driver's seat. He couldn't think of a single thing to say; they both knew what was happening. Chris drove to the airport in shock. Beside him, Al sat quietly, his head resting on the door post, his hands clasped limply in his lap. Occasionally he would cough, but mostly he sat there, wincing at each bump in the road, not saying anything, his bloody eyes closed.

When they arrived at the abandoned airport, Chris saw a chain-link fence with a sliding gate just past the terminal. Using the Marauder bumper, he pushed it off its track and drove out onto the tarmac. "When did the pilot say he'd be here?" asked Chris, but Al was asleep.

There were only two planes on the apron. One was an old Seneca twin, the engines cannibalized. The other was a Cessna, not big enough to carry the coffin and both of them. Besides, Chris was no pilot, and even if Al was, he was in no condition to command an aircraft. Just then Chris heard a rumble and looked up. A plane crossed overhead. Chris said, "I hope they're coming for us."

"They're coming for *you*, son," said Al, his eyes mere slits. The bruises on his neck were worse, and his fair skin had taken on a shiny, sunburned appearance. Tiny droplets of blood were standing on the back of his left hand—he was bleeding from the pores.

"Jesus Christ," said Chris, staring at Al's hand.

Al smiled weakly. "Stigmata. I'm saved, son. Nick of time." He began coughing and reached to pull his mask off. Chris reflexively pulled back, falling out of the open door onto the asphalt and scrabbling away from the vehicle. Al coughed wetly, spraying the interior of the SUV with gory bits of bloody mucus. When the fit passed, he settled back in his seat, exhausted.

Chris stood and slowly approached the vehicle. "Al, you okay?"

Al raised a bloody hand. "Right as rain, son. Your ride's here." He pointed.

The twin had landed and was taxiing toward them. It stopped a few yards away, engines pulled back to idle. Chris started toward the truck. "We'll get you to a hospital in Dar. They can help you."

Al shook his head, waving him away. "Remember, when you write this up, 'M' comes before 'T'." He spit bloody phlegm out the passenger window.

"God, Al," said Chris. "What can I do?"

"Go home, son, and don't forget: McFadden, *then* Tempest."

"Al," said Chris. "Oh, God. Al."

Al looked at Chris, shaking his head ruefully. "Africa. What a fucking nightmare."

The pilot of the twin was an old friend of Al's, and he came prepared. As Chris stood on the tarmac, watching Al die, two men descended from the King Air wearing bright blue biosuits. They pulled Al from the vehicle and carried him under the corrugated terminal porch. When they returned, they stripped Chris naked and sprayed him with a green liquid and brushed him down hard. Then they put him in a blue biosuit, fitted him with a new, bright blue respirator, and loaded him and the coffin into the aircraft.

Exhausted, Chris soon fell asleep. He awoke at the Dar airport sitting in a wheelchair, still wearing the respirator, but dressed in regular clothes. One of the men who'd come to Arusha sat nearby. "Doctor Mobali," said the man, pointing to himself. "Dr. McFadden asked me to come to Ngorongoro to treat his men. It took me some time to get things together, and by the time I was ready, I got his call about you folks leaving in a hurry."

"Is Al dead?"

"Yes," said Mobali. "But you are not. You have no Cobalt symptoms."

Chris shook his head. "I will. I was with him, riding in the same SUV, for hours."

"Perhaps this virus travels through the air," said Mobali. "Perhaps not. We must wait and see." He went back to reading his magazine.

When the jet finally arrived, it disgorged just three passengers. Chris was placed alone in First Class. The crew and other passengers wore respirators and surgical gloves. His gloves had been taped to the long sleeves of his plaid flannel shirt with duct tape. His pant legs were taped to the oversized sneakers he wore. He had on a light blue paper surgical head covering and goggles. The get-up wasn't protecting him—it was protecting everyone else *from* him.

Once aloft, Chris looked out the dark window and listened to the low whine of the turbines. The moon shone on an unbroken sea of clouds far below. Polaris twinkled in the distant, cold north. Chris leaned back in his seat and wondered when the headache would begin.

BIO-CURTAIN

He awoke with a start, startled by gunfire. Sweating black men with blood-red eyes came out of the darkness, firing at him. Chris blinked. Then it was day and he was alone, sitting by a window, looking down at an uninterrupted expanse of sparkling blue water. He looked around and saw no one, then touched the screen on the seat back. A woman's face appeared. "Yes?" She wore a maroon respirator with the airline insignia embossed on the side.

"Where are we?"

"Eleven hundred nautical miles off the U.S. coast. We'll be home in a couple of hours."

Suddenly, Chris remembered. He undid his belt and stood. "Where is it?"

"Where is what?" asked the attendant.

"My backpack!"

"Sir!" said the attendant. "Please sit down. The captain has activated the seat belt—"

"Dammit!" howled Chris. "Where is it?" He started opening overhead bins. Nothing but blankets and pillows. He checked the storage closet near the exit. He pounded on the bolted cockpit door, and immediately a klaxon sounded and a voice commanded, "Stand clear! Stand clear!"

Then, behind him, he heard a bolt slide back. The door to coach opened and the flight attendant appeared in person. "Please. Sit down. Sit down."

"Where is it?" he shouted hoarsely.

"Where is *what*?

Chris, bent over a seat, searching, then heard a gruff voice say, "Sir, sit down. Now."

Chris looked up. A beefy air marshal had edged past the attendant. He aimed a pulse pistol at Chris. Pulse guns fired charged plasma bulbs that disrupted the nervous system, initiating a *grand mal* seizure. A taser strike was, in comparison, like being pinched. Chris sat down. The marshal moved forward, his gun still aimed at Chris, wearing his own black respirator. "Seat belt, sir." Chris clicked his seat belt. Then he felt something by his foot and bent forward. "Sir!" shouted the marshal. "Don't move!"

But Chris already had his hand on the nylon surface, lifting it. "My backpack."

The marshal dived, slamming Chris into the bulkhead, tearing the backpack away and hurling it across the cabin. In another instant the pulse pistol was pressed against Chris's temple. Chris gulped back fear and said, "It's harmless. Check it out."

The marshal nodded at the attendant, who picked up the bag, opening it. "Looks like a rock."

"I'm an archeologist," said Chris. "It's a stone jar—a relic."

She gingerly handed the backpack to Chris and backed away. The marshal scowled, holstered his weapon, and left the cabin. The attendant smiled weakly. "Sorry," she said, closing the door behind her. Chris heard the latch slide shut. He held the jar to his chest and heaved a sigh of relief.

Because jet aircraft had been proven to be one of the most lethal weapons of mass destruction several times over the last two decades, they had been secured. No phones, no computers, no outside communications whatsoever. Chris didn't know what he would tell

Cate even if he *could* contact her. "Hi," he'd say. "Great trip. Hey, listen, just in case I've got Cobalt . . ."

Good conversation that would be.

He leaned his head back against the seat, closed his eyes, and tried to remember what day it was. Al had called him on Friday. He left New York on Saturday, arriving in Dar early Sunday morning. Then the flight to Arusha, arriving around noon. The ride to the crater, arriving after dark. The mummy examination took until midnight. Then the escape and arriving in Arusha early Monday morning. Back in Dar sometime Monday afternoon. No telling how long he was there; he'd slept for quite a while. But unless he'd slept an entire day, it was now Tuesday, and from the looks of the sun, late afternoon. He'd been gone just four days.

A lifetime.

The stack-up on final to JFK was the worst Chris had ever seen. There were at least twenty heavies in the holding pattern, awaiting their turn to land. Chris watched the beautiful New York night skyline slowly pass his window seven times as the plane circled. When they did land, a sense of *déjà vu* gripped him. The aircraft stopped out on the tarmac, a hundred yards from any gate. It was met by a phalanx of black airport-authority vehicles and passenger vans, blue lights flashing. A stairway truck backed up to the aircraft, and Chris felt the fuselage decompress.

A dozen men wearing blue biosuits exited the vehicles surrounding the jet. A tall man walked toward the aircraft, looking like an astronaut in a white biosuit with a large fishbowl helmet. Chris picked up the backpack. The air marshal stood in the doorway to coach, glowering at him above his respirator. As he stepped into the aisle, Chris looked back. There were about fifteen other people in the very back of the aircraft, each wearing a respirator and latex gloves, all watching him closely. No one spoke. Chris exited and descended the stairs. When he was five steps from the bottom, the tall man said, "Please get inside," pointing at a black step van. Chris stepped onto the tarmac. The man stepped back, giving him a wide berth.

"What about my luggage?" asked Chris.

"Please get in the van, sir." The sodium lights illuminating the tarmac reflected off the tall man's helmet. Chris could not see his face, but was certain the man was *not* smiling.

Chris walked toward the van. As he got in, he looked back at the airliner. No one else had deplaned. He sat on a metal bench. The rear doors slammed shut and the van began to move. Chris settled back, holding the backpack on his lap.

Chris found himself in a small, secured room, apparently many stories beneath JFK airport. They must have converted customs detainment rooms into quarantine cells. There was a single bed and a bathroom cubicle in the featureless room. A holo projector hung from the wall. Nothing else. He pulled off his respirator and untaped his wrists and ankles, removing his gloves and the oversized shoes.

"Holo," he said. The HP popped on and the JFK logo appeared, then ANS came on. The Airport News anchor was talking about a Paris riot, where a nightclub owner ejected two blacks because they were African. A riot ensued, the nightclub was burned, and the owner beaten severely.

The next story was from Pakistan. Mysterious circumstances surrounded the crash of a Nigerian airliner en route to Islamabad. Satellite images showed a wing sheared off the wreckage, indicating the possibility that the aircraft may have been shot down. Neither Afghanistan nor Pakistan would admit to firing on the aircraft, but traffic controllers confirmed rapid course and altitude changes just before the crash. There were no survivors.

The news shifted to El Paso, Texas. Fifteen Mexican laborers were killed by a group of self-appointed militia men as they waded across the Rio Grande. Autopsies revealed no Cobalt infection in the illegals. Thus far, none of the murderers had been apprehended.

Chris was about to switch off when the news moved to California. The female reporter stood before Scripps Memorial Hospital in the upscale community of La Jolla. It was night, and police guarded the floodlit entry. A number of sailors from an Asian cargo ship had been admitted to the hospital. Their condition was unknown. The reporter wore a surgical mask and her voice was muffled and shrill. Chris shook his head. "If that's all the protection you got, sweetheart, it's already over."

He switched off the HP and went into the bathroom. Cate was probably in that very hospital right now. He looked in the mirror, saw his red eyes, and his heart skipped a beat. He hoped they were just bloodshot. He examined his neck for bruises and opened his mouth to see if his gums were bleeding. He thought of Al dying on the sun-glazed Arusha tarmac. Just three days before, when he picked him up at that same airport, Al didn't look sick. Chris studied his own face closely so he would know the moment the first bruises began to appear.

Twenty senior researchers sat around the conference table. The holomap of the United States still hung in the air. Blood-red splotches dotted the coasts. Dr. William Sandusky, head of the Special Pathogens Branch of the CDC, leaned on the table, an exasperated look on his face. "Somebody give me some *good* news. Dr. Cloudburst? Any sunshine in our forecast?"

An old joke; Cloudburst was used to it. "We're testing the blood sera. Prelims indicate Cobalt, but it's a different strain from Cobalt-Detroit or Cobalt-Miami. We don't know if it's airborne or not."

"Of course it's airborne," said Sandusky, pointing at Cloudburst through the holo. "Explain the rapid transmission any other way."

Cloudburst said nothing.

"You'd think you folks would have something—hell, you've been cracking hemorrhagic fevers for fifty years."

"Cobalt is not a VHF," said Cloudburst.

"Goddammit!" exploded Sandusky. "I know that! What I'm saying is that you've decoded RNA viruses before. And you've had five years to crack this one, but you've failed. Why?"

"It's the Uncertainty Principle," interjected Cate.

Sandusky shook his head in disgust. "That's bullshit."

"No, really," said Cate. "Heisenberg said that when you measured an electron, for example, the energy in the measuring device—usually short-wavelength light—changed the particle's momentum. But if you used a longer wavelength light, you could measure momentum, but then the electron's position would be inaccurate."

"You have a point?" asked Sandusky.

"Cobalt has its own version of the Uncertainty Principle. A hundred times we've reconfigured the protein RNA in Cobalt that switches off the victim cell's immunological response. Then we infect a test animal with the corrected protein and it kills the animal like always. We draw serum and examine the virus, and it's still there, ready to do it again. We can't figure it out. It's like . . . "

"Yes?"

"Like it *knows* what we're trying to do and it mutates away from our change."

Cloudburst shook her head. She'd never believed in Cate's theory; she just thought Cobalt was one tough little bug. Enough time and they'd crack it. She had confidence in their ability to map its RNA and zero in on the virus's weaknesses. Eventually.

Sandusky ran his hands through his thinning white hair. "Well, I've got a *Certainty* Principle for you folks: This virus has killed three hundred million people worldwide. That, in case you've had your noses buried in textbooks, is nearly the population of these United States. The President is about to drop the biocurtain around the U.S., but it might already be too late—we've got these outbreaks . . ." He gestured angrily at the holo. "Shut that damn thing off!"

Cloudburst killed the holo. The room got very dark, except for the table, which fluoresced a pale green. Sandusky glared at the researchers. "I'll be damned if I'm going to preside over the CDC while this country crashes and bleeds out from this friggin' . . . *microbe!*"

He hit a button and the HP sprang to life again. But this time, an image that looked like a human made of Chinese crispy noodles hung in the air. It had a shepherd's crook head and two

outstretched arms above a slender stalk of a body. The caption read:
Virus Magnification: 50,000 Times.

Cate had studied the virus under an electron microscope and it
had always looked to her like the ancient Egyptian symbol for life:
the *ankh*.

Now *that* was irony.

PRESCIENCE

President Burrows looked into the camera and dropped the other shoe. A Cobalt outbreak had occurred in San Diego. The entire crew of the Japanese container freighter *Ichihara* was infected; five had died, the rest were dying. There were outbreaks in Seattle and San Francisco. Galveston had twenty reported cases. Burrows frowned and ordered the closure of all borders, both land and sea. Africa was embargoed, as well as Indonesia and India.

"These are temporary measures," said the President to the camera. "We have the finest scientists working to find a cure. Like the Jihadist wars, we must be firm in our resolve and unflinching in our commitment. We will eradicate this disease from the earth. May God bless you, and may God bless America." She turned and left the podium.

Just then the door to Chris's room opened. The man he'd come to know as Mr. Tall stood in the doorway. He was not wearing a respirator. "Tests are complete, Mr. Tempest. You're clean."

Chris turned off the HP. "You're sure?"

"You're very lucky. What possessed you to go to Ground Zero, anyway?"

Chris turned the canopic jar over in his hands. "Insanity, I guess."

Mr. Tall watched as Chris gently wrapped the jar in a towel and zipped it in his bullet-torn backpack. "Well," said Mr. Tall, "it's an insane world. They'll probably make you king."

The mummy had been scanned and released to the Met. Chris called Dr. Hansen, head of antiquities, confirmed the mummy's arrival at the museum, and said he'd be there in the morning and to not touch it. Hansen said no one wanted to touch it anyway. They had placed it in the Met basement freezers.

Chris took the train to Manhattan, then got a taxi to Tribeca. His walk-up on Hubert Street was cold and drafty in the winter and sizzling in the summer, but the location was ideal. There were good jazz clubs within a ten-minute walk, and the subway was just a block away.

He palmed the doorplate and entered the apartment. It hadn't even been a week, but it seemed like he'd been gone a year. He set the backpack on the dining table and tapped a terminal key. In the air above the HP, his e-mail scrolled: 357 messages, sorted by importance. Only the top three mattered to him—they were all from Cate. "Call Cate," he said. The AT&T logo popped up in a hologram mist.

"Which number?" asked the VidPhone.

"Work."

There was a pause as the number dialed and the phone rung.

"Cate Seagram."

"Cate?"

"Chris! Chris, is that you?" The image popped on. Cate had on the surgical scrubs they wore under the rubber suits in BSL4. She looked tired. Her blonde hair wilted around her face.

"Hey. I'm back," Chris said, striving to be nonchalant.

"Oh, Chris!" said Cate. "I was so worried! How did you get through the biocurtain?"

"Just slipped beneath it, I guess," said Chris. "I just got in from JFK."

"How did it go?"

"You mean, 'Did I bring the mummy back?' or 'Am I sick?'"

"Both!"

"I got it—not Cobalt, but the mummy," amended Chris. "It might be six thousand years old. It has a bunch of Egyptian indicators; it's an amazing find. But more than that: they found a canopic jar with it, and it contains the heart."

"I thought Egyptians left the heart in the body."

"So, you *have* been listening to me all this time," said Chris, smiling. "Thank you."

"I like listening to you talk about your work. You know that."

"*I* don't even like listening to me talk about my work. Anyway, this thing," he held up the alabaster jar, "contains a heart that looks like the guy just croaked yesterday."

"What do you mean?"

"I mean," said Chris, holding the jar closer to the VidPhone, "it's still bloody."

Cate's mouth dropped open. "You're kidding."

"I never kid about predynastic Egypt, Cate. You know that."

Cate nodded. "And how."

"Anyway, we're gonna check it out. We'll start tests first thing in the morning."

"Chris," said Cate, turning very serious. "You're not going to stay in New York, are you?"

"Listen, Cate, I get it now. I saw some hairy stuff in Tanzania, but I dodged a bullet—"

"What bullet?"

Shit! thought Chris. "I mean, I got out without getting sick."

"Are you sure? Have you been tested?"

"When I landed. Clean as a whistle."

Cate looked doubtful. "Don't take any chances. Avoid crowds. And get out of New York."

"Wait a minute," said Chris. "I just got *back* to New York. They closed the borders, just like you said they would. They'll control the outbreaks."

Cate just looked at him.

"They will, won't they?"

"Chris, get out of the city."

"Why?"

Cate leaned toward the camera and lowered her voice. "They're going to quarantine Manhattan. You've got to get out of there."

Chris shook his head. "I will, but I want to scan this thing first, then I'll met you in D.C. Okay? I missed you, babe."

"I missed you too, Chris. Hurry. And get out of the city."

"What aren't you telling me?" asked Chris.

"Almost everything," said Cate, and she switched off.

TWELVE

HEART OF THE MATTER

When Chris trotted up the subway stairs at 81st Street, he was relieved to be out in the fresh air again, even wearing his ULPA mask. He jogged east, through the park. Nearing a cluster of basketball courts, he saw a pick-up game going on. Black kids were charging the goal, fouling, cursing, and laughing. They wore surgical masks, but even from a distance, Chris sensed a difference between them and the silent, worried people he'd shared the subway car with coming uptown.

As he got closer, he saw the distinction. Each kid had painted his mask in a black parody of Halloween. Bloody fangs adorned one mask, a giant gold tooth in an open mouth graced another. The boys yelled, shoved, and laughed, unafraid of Cobalt.

Of all the things he'd seen, the kids' masks troubled Chris the most. Right now, Cobalt was still a joke to them—a distant, unreal threat, like the bogeyman. But when they started bleeding out of their ears and mouths, vomiting blood, and their bodies were reduced to bags of bloody sludge, they would be afraid, but by then it would be too late.

Chris hurried on his way. Cate was right. He had to get out of the city.

∧∧∧

Chris signed in at the guard station, pressed his palm against the door plate, and keyed his password. The immense steel door opened, and he entered the cavernous underground storage room. Row after row of tall shelving marched into the dim distance, and an automated forklift moved down an aisle, guided by a magnetic strip set into the floor. The lift stopped, raised its tines, and removed a steel container from an upper shelf. Then it continued down the aisle, yellow hazard light rotating.

Chris walked down an aisle and pushed open a door labeled COLD STORAGE. Inside, the lights were on and his breath smoked. Before him were dozens of rows of tall cabinets with stainless-steel drawers, the world's largest morgue. He heard voices, and as he rounded a corner, he saw two people talking. They turned as they heard his footsteps. "Chris!" said Dr. Hansen, Egyptian section head. He had on a blue ULPA mask and did not extend his hand in greeting.

"Hi, Dr. Tempest," said Roshni Kampuur. She also wore a respirator.

"We were just about to look at the find," said Hansen. "Where's your mask?"

"Here," said Chris, showing them. He'd taken it off once he was inside the Met. Hansen and Roshni looked at him like he was the bravest man they'd ever seen—or the dumbest. Now he knew how the Maasai warriors felt when they stopped them on the road to Sopa Lodge. Chris shrugged. "I don't think he's catching. Where is he?"

Hansen indicated a drawer. A digital counter above the metal handle read 10° C. "We're keeping him just under room temperature," said Hansen.

"I don't think it matters," said Chris. "He's been at room temperature for six thousand years."

He pulled the drawer open, revealing the crude wooden coffin. Roshni handed him latex gloves and donned a pair herself. Hansen took a step back, thrusting his hands in his suit coat pockets. Roshni gave Chris a crowbar and he pried the box open. He unzipped the body bag and pulled out the tufts of cotton batting surrounding the corpse. They all gazed on the mummy silently.

"He's lying on his side," said Hansen. "Which direction was he facing?"

"West," said Chris.

"West," repeated Hansen. "Of course."

"Is this really bitumen?" asked Roshni, pointing at the blackened cloth wrappings.

Chris nodded.

"And he was in Tanzania," said Hansen. "Incredible."

Chris glanced at his backpack on the floor by his feet. "You ain't seen nothing yet."

The Met's access to technology was unparalleled. Many a forgery had been discovered as the scanners had digitally and noninvasively removed layer after layer of paint, digging down to the artist's first charcoal outlines on a Renaissance-era canvas.

Two respirator-clad guards took the mummy upstairs to the labs on a stainless-steel gurney. The maddingly slow MRI scan took more than three hours to complete, and the resulting data file was over ten thousand terabytes. Chris demanded the highest resolution possible—he didn't want to miss a thing.

Once the computer finished processing the data—another excruciatingly slow hour—the holographic image finally floated in the air before them. The body had been wrapped in hundreds of feet of tar-soaked cloth windings, and a protective coating of tree resin had sealed everything in a hard, yellow shell. The technician at the console tapped the computer joystick and the wrappings in the holo vanished, revealing a naked male, early 20s, lying on his side, head bowed. He wore an amulet around his neck on a leather thong.

Hansen leaned toward the hologram, squinting. "It looks like . . . well, I don't believe it."

Roshni nodded, her dark eyes bright with excitement. "He's wearing an ankh icon around his neck."

The amulet, which appeared to be made of silver, did indeed look like an ankh. It had an oval head atop a slender body, no leg differentiation, and two outstretched arms.

"A full thousand years before unification," said Hansen, awed.

"Something's missing," said Roshni, pointing. "Pull back."

The tech moved the joystick and the image retreated to the surface windings. "Look here," said Roshni, touching the holo where the hands lay crossed over the chest. "Something was there. Go deeper. Stop. There. He had something under his hands, but it's been removed." She turned to Chris.

The green scarab suddenly felt very large in Chris's suit coat pocket. He had violated the first rule of archeology: Keep the find intact. He wondered why he didn't just produce the amulet and say, "I thought it might get lost." All would be forgiven. But he didn't. Instead, he merely made a perplexed face and grunted.

Roshni asked, "The men who found the mummy, did they say they found anything else?"

Chris shook his head. "It *does* look like there was something there." *Keep digging*, he thought. *You'll bury yourself.*

"See these tears in the wrappings?" said Roshni. "Something was removed after they found the mummy." She looked at Chris. "You had grave robbers working on your site, Dr. Tempest."

Chris shrugged. "It wasn't my site. I just brought it back."

"There's something more," said Hansen. "Look. It looks like an incision. Magnify."

The wrappings disappeared again and the man's bare chest was revealed. Hansen snorted. "See there, just below the left forearm? Torn tissue, broken bone." He pursed his lips, thinking. "This man was murdered. Run through from behind. A spear, probably."

Chris's heart finally stopped pounding. The wound had pulled Roshni's interest from the missing amulet. From this moment on, it would be harder and harder to admit he had it, and the consequences would grow more and more severe. But the green scarab beetle amulet was a secret Chris wanted to keep to himself. He didn't know why.

"Doctor?" asked Roshni. "Dr. Tempest?"

Chris came back to the present. "Yes?"

"I think I see it."

"See what?"

Roshni took the joystick, guiding the digital probe. "There's something under the hands."

That got Chris's attention. He'd assumed the scarab amulet was all there was under the layered hands, but Roshni had just discovered something else. "What is it?" he asked.

Roshni fussed with the joystick. "There. You know what that is?"

Hansen and Chris looked at the object, about four inches long, an arc of white, dotted with smaller objects along one side. Hansen and Chris both shrugged.

"It's a jawbone," said Roshni.

"A jawbone?" asked Chris. "Is it his?"

Roshni laughed. "No. But it's human."

"Why does he have it?"

Roshni shrugged. "Superstition? Cannibalism? Who knows?"

"You said you had something else to scan?" asked Hansen, gesturing at Chris's backpack.

A perfect copy of the canopic jar floated in the air before them. "I thought the mummy was the real find," said Hansen, shaking his head. "But this . . ."

The tech pushed in and the stone jar dissolved. A perfectly formed, vividly bloody heart rotated in the air before them.

"Can you determine if there's any . . . cellular activity?" asked Chris.

"You can't be serious," said Hansen.

"It's impossible," said Roshni.

"I don't know," said the technician. "It's possible."

They all looked at him.

"I used to run MRIs at Lenox Hill Hospital," he said. "This looks just like a living heart."

Roshni and Hansen were skeptical.

"Wait," said the tech, hitting keys. "I have a program. Not much use for it here because everything's inert. But the scanner doesn't know that. It just reads information. Instant-to-instant information."

"Meaning?" asked Chris.

"Real-time scanning, with the resolution you demanded, means we can go as deep as the cellular level."

"Really?" asked Chris.

"Hey," said the tech, "you're the one who wanted ten thousand terabytes. Here goes."

They watched as layer after layer of the heart dissolved, the view passing through muscles and ventricles, finding and centering on a single blood cell. The tech hit another key and the image breached the cell membrane and entered the cytoplasm, the liquid in which the cell machinery floats: the mitochondria (tiny power plants that combine food and oxygen to release energy), golgi complexes (protein storage warehouses), and the dark-colored nucleus, the cell control center.

"Is that movement?" asked Hansen, stunned.

The tech pushed inside the nucleus, which was a honeycomb of cells. "Let's look at this one," he said and centered on one pink cell. They passed through the cell wall and were suddenly engulfed in a madhouse ball of string.

"What's that?" asked Chris.

"Chromosomes," said Roshni.

"I thought they were little Xs and Ys," said Chris.

"They are when a cell is about to divide," said Roshni.

They pushed inside a chromosome strand. "I'm about as deep as I can go, but I think it will be enough," said the tech. And then they saw it, the tightly wound double helix of DNA.

"My God," said Roshni.

"I don't believe it," said Chris. "It's intact."

"What does that mean?" asked Hansen.

"It means," said Chris, "that our friend here hasn't been dead for six thousand years."

"He hasn't?"

"No. He's still very much alive."

∧∧∧

"No, he isn't really alive," said Chris, seeing Cate's expression on the VidPhone. "But his DNA is intact. You're the medical expert—you know what that means."

"It's impossible," said Cate. "No tissue can survive that long."

"What about the mummy?"

"That's different," said Cate. "Okay, I misspoke. Tissue can survive; life cannot. The cell structure, kept in the right conditions—extremely dry or cold—*can* survive for thousands of years. But even under those conditions, DNA starts to fall apart as soon as the current is switched off. The light goes out. It's been the single biggest barrier to creating life from dead organisms. Mother Nature draws the line at DNA—she never leaves that switch on. "

"I saw what I saw, Cate. The DNA is intact. His light was still very much *on*."

"You can't scan that deep anyway," said Cate. "You'd need national security clearance to use that much memory."

"We got it. The file was ten thousand terabytes."

"Well," said Cate, intrigued. "I'd like to see it."

"Okay," said Chris. "Why don't you come up this weekend? See for yourself."

"Come to New York?"

"This from someone working in BSL4? Hell, *you're* the one who's probably infected."

"Chris, don't joke about that," said Cate. "You know we take the utmost precau—"

"I know," said Chris. "I was joking."

"Besides, I've got a ton of work to do."

"Come on."

"Why don't you give me access to the file here? I'll look at it and tell you what I think."

"I can't do that," said Chris. "It's against the law. I'd get my ass sued off or wind up in jail. Or both. You've got to come up here."

"I'm not coming to New York," said Cate flatly. "Cobalt is a slate wiper and you're in the largest city in the country. Think, Chris! If you want me to see this data, get a synopsis for me. I don't need to see the whole thing. You can bring it down to D.C."

"I don't know," said Chris.

"Hey," said Cate, "have you done a blood work-up yet?"

"We haven't even opened the jar. We're afraid the heart will dissolve when air hits it."

"A blood test is an easy way to check your scanner data."

It was a good idea. Chris kicked himself for not thinking of it. "Okay, I'll get a blood work-up and you meet me in D.C. on Saturday."

"Okay. Union Station. I'll get a train after work. Meet you there, say, at eleven?"

"Your gonna eat my hat, you know," said Chris, smiling.

"Why *your* hat?"

"Because you don't wear one," said Chris. "See you then."

THIRTEEN

LIGHTLAND

K'tanu stood on the crater rim. The far walls were dark green, and the mountains beyond were a faint purple, their peaks reaching into a perfectly blue sky. The pink birds on the Blue-Eyed Sea were individually distinguishable, even though the lake was a half day's walk from here.

"Looking again?"

He turned. Maya walked toward him, smiling, the baby on her hip. He dared not blink, afraid she would disappear. On the path behind her, little N'kala stalked an imaginary lion with a stick for a spear. His eyes shone with excitement, and K'tanu smiled.

Maya held the baby out to K'tanu. "We still have not named her."

K'tanu cradled the child in his arms. Was this the same child that only yesterday was dying of the Bleeding Sickness? He studied the baby's face in wonder. "Are we really here?" he whispered. "All of us? Together?"

Maya rested her cheek against his arm. He was having trouble accepting the truth. Every day she had to remind him that there was no Bleeding Sickness, no death, and no attacking enemies here. The baby looked up into K'tanu's face, recognizing it. Light filled her eyes and she laughed. "She is Anja," he said.

"Ah," said Maya. "Light-bringer. Good, K'tanu. Good." She took the child and nestled her against her breast. The baby began to suckle. "Nothing has changed," she said. "We are home."

"This is not our home."

"It is the best of that place."

"It is not the Waking World."

"No, it is not."

"It is not the Other World."

"No."

"Then what is it?"

Maya looked up at her husband: tall, muscled, perfectly proportioned, sure-footed and strong, the three wavy scars under each eye. He was the most beautiful thing in the world, more beautiful even than the child at her breast, for he had given her the child and would give her more, and she was content.

"Look," said K'tanu, pointing to a long ragged scar on his chest. "We were attacked. I ran to the hut. There was a man inside."

"Shh," whispered Maya. She also bore the memory, but did not want to talk about it.

"He was hurting you," said K'tanu. "Anja was there, dying of the Sickness."

"K'tanu, no."

"And then there was blood. My blood, pouring out of me, all over you."

Just then N'kala burst from the trees, his little spear held high, chasing his invisible lion, shouting. He disappeared into the forest again.

K'tanu turned back to Maya. "N'kala died," he said. "I carried his body to the tomb."

Maya said nothing. It was best to let him speak.

"Do you smell the flowers?" asked K'tanu, turning back to the caldera. "I can smell every flower—*every* flower! The one here, right next to us, and the one on the far caldera rim. I can see an eagle soaring above the mountains beyond the plains, a month's walk from here. I can see into his *eye*! I can see what his eye sees! Where *are* we?"

"We are in Lightland."

He shook his head, doubtful. Suddenly a shattering pain hit him. He fell to his knees, clutching at his chest. His eyes were bright with painful tears. Maya set the baby down and knelt, taking K'tanu in her arms. "K'tanu!" she cried, holding him close. His eyes were full of shock and his hands scrabbled at his chest as if he might tear his own heart out. He opened his mouth, but nothing came out. His eyes were wide with fear and anguish, tears filling them from the excruciating pain.

N'kala ran toward them. "Father!" he cried.

Maya looked heavenward. "Father Sun! Take the pain from him!"

K'tanu began to convulse. Maya held him, but he was too strong; he would overpower her. She was suddenly filled with dread. What if he threw himself over the caldera rim in his fit?

"Hold on to your father," she said to N'kala. "Hold him tight." The boy fastened both hands on K'tanu's arm. "Gods!" cried Maya. "Do not separate us!"

Then K'tanu fell back into her arms, unconscious. "K'tanu," whispered Maya, tears streaming down her face. "Stay with us. Stay with us." She closed her eyes and prayed: "Do not separate us, please. Please."

"Re-attach the electrode," said Roshni. "It came off."

Chris's hands were inside the rubber gloves extending into the sterile Plexiglass box where the mummy's heart lay in a ceramic pan, blood pooling around it. He picked up the alligator clip with the wire trailing from it. "Same place?"

"Yes," said Roshni. "The last time we got quite a surge."

"Okay," said Chris, attaching the clip to the muscle. "On the ventricle, right?"

"Right," said Roshni. "The left ventricle."

"Left facing me?"

"Your right. His left," said Roshni.

"Don't say it like that," said Chris. He attached the clip to the muscle. "Why don't we put it inside the heart? Isn't that where the enriched blood cells are?"

"You wanted a noninvasive procedure. It's saturated with epinephrine anyway."

"I know," said Chris. "Last time, it practically hopped off the table."

"Now you're making *me* sick," said Roshni.

"Sorry. At least you're not here looking at it. It seems so . . . *alive*."

Roshni tapped some keys. "It's not, but I'm getting some interesting readings."

Chris withdrew his arms from the gloves and walked over to her. "What's interesting?" he asked, looking over Roshni's shoulder at the computer screen.

"I downloaded a set of healthy heart EKGs from the NMC," said Roshni. "I'm comparing them with the real-time data we're pulling from the mummy's heart. Look."

There were two windows open on the screen. The top one was labeled NATMEDCTR, with the subheading AFRICAN MALE, MID-20S. In the window was a graph with a line running along the horizontal axis spiking at regular intervals. The window below it read METMUSART, with its subheading AFRICAN MALE, MID-20S. It, too, bumped regularly, in sync with the upper graph.

"They're almost identical," said Chris.

"Yes," said Roshni. "We're subjecting the mummy's heart to the kind of stress a living heart experiences. Rushes of blood, contractions of muscles, the surge of adrenaline. And you know what? I think this heart could be transplanted into someone and it would function perfectly."

"But that's impossible, isn't it?"

"A six-thousand-year-old mummy is impossible. A heart in a canopic jar is impossible. And this," she said, gesturing at the identical graph lines, "is also impossible."

Chris walked over and looked at the heart beating in the laminar-flow box. "Somehow, it seems wrong to be shocking it like this," he said, thrusting his hands back into the rubber gloves.

"It's just tissue," said Roshni. "It moves the way a frog's leg moves when you touch an electrode to it. Remember high school biology?"

Chris lifted the heart gently. It beat strongly in his hands. "But it's warm."

"That's from the electricity—like cooking a steak. We're almost done, then lunch, okay?"

Chris looked at the blood dripping from the aorta. "I don't think I'm hungry."

The guards wheeled the gurney away. The heart had been placed in a liquid-nitrogen deep freeze a few aisles over. Chris stood by the open drawer, the body bag lying on the slab. He unzipped the bag and looked down at the mummy, remembering the man's face from the deep scan. A straight and noble nose. Deep-set eyes, a firm brow, high cheekbones. Three wavy scars below the eyes, like the Nile hieroglyphic. A proud chin and a complete set of perfect teeth. A handsome young man.

A man who had died in battle, run through from behind. Why? What kind of world did he live in? Was it all violence and suffering? Did he have a family? Parents? Friends?

Chris placed his hand on the mummy's head. Al never said what else they found in the tomb, and in the excitement, Chris hadn't thought to ask. Were there other mummies, or was this man special? Perhaps he was a shaman, or even a king. Chris ran his hand along the cracked yellow resin surface. Did his people fear death, or did they welcome it as a release from misery? What did they imagine the stars were? The sun? The moon? Did they gaze into the night sky with fear or hope?

Chris looked around. He was alone. He reached into his pocket and took out the scarab amulet, intending to return it to its rightful owner, but something stopped him. The green serpentine stone glinted richly in the dim light. "You don't need this anymore," he whispered, running his fingers over the beetle's back, "but I might." He placed it back in his coat pocket and slowly closed the drawer.

FOURTEEN

TROJAN HORSE

Cate yawned. It was well after the dinner hour, and on a Friday night to boot. They'd been at it all day. She called up the file and turned to Dr. Cloudburst, who sat next to her. "This is the last of today's batch. And then another twenty-five tomorrow? We'll never get through this."

"It's the only way," said Cloudburst. "Try every gene recombination and test it on a cell. Hour by hour, day by day, we're closing in on it. It can't hide forever."

"What about the Uncertainty Principle?"

"Doesn't apply. Newton's Third Law of Motion does: For every action, there is an equal and opposite reaction. Cobalt is the action. We're the reaction."

"Maybe, but I'm not sure we're equal, Doctor."

"Chin up," said Cloudburst. "One at a time. Let's see the results of this batch."

Cate keyed the computer and an image popped up into the air before them. It was titled TEST DATA 05162029-22-CS. It showed a healthy cell floating in a clear solution, like a life raft bobbing on the ocean. The dark nucleus could vaguely be seen through the cell membrane.

"Here goes," said Cate, pressing a key. A stopwatch ticker on the holo began counting up from zero. A dark, bumpy-looking glob of virus was introduced into the saline solution, and soon several little *ankh*-shaped virus threads separated themselves from the glob, floating in the water. First one, then another, and finally a dozen or more attached themselves to the cell.

"This is the genius of viruses," said Cate, watching the clock. Just a few minutes had passed. "They use the cell's own defense mechanism against it."

And sure enough, the cell began folding itself around the viruses, drawing them inside.

"Trojan horses," said Cloudburst. "The cell thinks it's going to destroy the virus, like it does any foreign body." Cloudburst had seen the process a hundred times, but she was still fascinated. "For all the cell knows, the virus is dead. It doesn't have any properties of life. It doesn't eat, grow, age, or die. It can live outside an organism indefinitely. That crystallized Ebola virus they found at Kittum Cave in Kenya? They placed it in an empty vial for two years and then introduced live cells. Within twenty-four hours, the virus had destroyed all the cells."

"Like this one is doing now," said Cate.

Inside the single cell, Cobalt viruses encircled the dark, bumpy mitochondria organelles, the tiny cell power plants. Soon the hijacked organelles were pumping out identical copies of the virus. "I get chills every time I see this," said Cloudburst.

Cate looked at her, surprised.

"Hey," said Cloudburst, "it's not illegal to appreciate one's opponent."

"That sounded more like admiration than appreciation," said Cate.

"Whatever you call it, I can't help it."

The replicated viruses had clumped together, forming inclusion bodies. They began to fill the cytoplasm, the clear liquid inside the cell, squeezing the nucleus and other cell bodies over to one side. And still the mitochondria churned out more and more of them.

"This thing's a molecular shark," said Cate. "A motive without a mind. All it does is copy itself. Nothing more. No disease, no effect whatsoever upon the host except one thing. That." She nodded at the cell. The black virus clumps entirely filled the liquid cell center, forming what looked like little bricks, which pushed against the cell wall, stretching it. Virus particles detached themselves from the bricks and began worming their way through the cell membrane, appearing on the surface of the cell like grass on a newly-seeded lawn. Cate fast-forwarded the simulation. Within a few hours on the clock, the cell wall had burst and the contents dumped out. The virus blocks floated in the saline solution, along with the dead-cell contents. A life had ended.

"It uses up the host's material, then goes back to sleep." Cate shivered. "And what's worse is it keeps changing its shell, using another combination of proteins to gain access to the next cell it encounters. How many different combinations have we charted so far?"

Cloudburst looked at her clipboard. "This makes 24,208."

"How many possible did we calculate?"

"Well over a million. Maybe two."

Cate looked down at the counter. "That's just over ninety-six hours. I think it's moving faster. What's the origin of this batch?"

"New York."

Cate looked up sharply. "There's an outbreak there?"

"Contained. Manhattan only. None of the other boroughs have reported anything."

"Where in Manhattan?"

"Harlem, I think," said Cloudburst. She looked up and saw Cate's expression. "I said it's been contained."

"It can't be contained, " said Cate, frowning. "You know that."

Cloudburst pursed her lips. "Cate. The entire country is about to crash and burn. Millions are going to die. Maybe tens of millions. You and I will probably die too. All we can do is our best: examine every protein combination, track every possibility."

"We won't have time," said Cate. The truth froze her heart.

Cloudburst considered Cate for a long moment. Then, "I'm transferring you out of BSL4."

"What? Why?"

"Because you constantly question our methodology. You don't believe in a cure. You're becoming a liability."

"Why? Because I'm worried about my loved ones?"

"I have loved ones too," snapped Cloudburst. "That's why I work as hard as I do—to save their lives."

"But we're not even sure we're on the right track!"

"You're right," said Cloudburst. "We're not sure. We *can't* be sure. That's why we try everything. And if you'd put more energy into coming up with options and less energy into fretting, you might be more help than you have been." She stood and walked away.

Cate looked back at the computer screen, which had paused at the end of its timeline. The bricks of Cobalt virus floated in the saline, waiting for their next victim. Her mouth was dry. She was in trouble. Everyone was in trouble.

Cate took a break, going to her cubicle to check her e-mail. Earlier, she had sent Chris a cryptic, "Are you still there? Get out of town!" message. Now, there was a response, the icon blinking. "Play Chris's message," she said. The holo popped up and there was Chris's face before her. He was smiling.

"I guess you're still in the dungeon," he said cheerfully. "Listen, you're not going to believe this." He held up a sheaf of papers. "I can't believe it myself. The blood tests, like you suggested. Smart girl." He paused for dramatic effect. "Our friend, our very *old* friend, is about to become *very* famous. I sent a blood sample out for a work-up. I didn't tell them where it came from." He shook the sheaf of papers. "'Normal,' they say, and then they start asking questions. 'Whose blood is it?' 'Where is he from?' And I say, 'Why does that matter?' And they tell me they've never seen blood like this—it's the cleanest, most pristine sample they've ever tested. No environmental toxins, no radiation effects, no negative genetic markers. Nothing." Chris shook his head. "And then, because they were intrigued, they did a full-spectrum immunology scan on their own dime, and guess what?" He paused again for dramatic effect. "They think he might be immune to Cobalt."

Cate's jaw dropped.

FIFTEEN

THE END OF THE WORLD, REDUX

On Saturday morning, Chris was awakened by the sounds of sirens. He went to the window and touched the opaque glass. It became clear. Above the rooftops to the north, thick black smoke rose. He turned on the HP. A reporter stood in front of an upscale apartment building. Red canvas awning, granite façade. "The Upper East Side is being evacuated," said the reporter, his voice muffled by his respirator. "The fires began on Third Avenue, in Harlem."

The camera tilted up and Chris recognized the building. The Essex House, on 59th Street. Sirens wailed in the background. The camera panned left, then tilted down again. The park came into view. Huge clouds of black smoke boiled above the trees. "Sixteen people have died from viral infections in the last twenty-four hours at Harlem's Sydenham Clinic. Police have closed the hospital to new arrivals, turning away hundreds of frantic people. New York Health Authority has quarantined Sydenham in an attempt to slow the spread of what most people believe is Cobalt, the first outbreak of the deadly virus in the city."

Chris slumped down on the couch, shaking his head. He was getting tired of Cate always being right. "Late last night," continued the reporter, "crowds stormed Sydenham, but when they were turned away, they began breaking windows and overturning cars. Hundreds were arrested. During the night, more fearful, sick people and their families came down to Mt. Sinai Medical Center on 98th Street."

Chris stopped breathing. Mt. Sinai was only a dozen blocks north of the Met.

The reporter continued. "When this mostly ethnic population was turned away from Mt. Sinai as well, more reports of broken windows and overturned cars initiated a police response. A riot ensued, and a nearby apartment building was set on fire." The reporter nodded at the cameraman, who tilted up again and zoomed in to the smoke above the park. "I understand my colleague Julia McDermott is now atop Essex House, and can give us a better view of events. Julia?"

The scene shifted. Julia McDermott, a tall, slender blonde, stood in the rooftop garden. "Thanks, Kevin. As you can see," she said, "the wind is not helping things much." The camera pushed past her, zooming up Fifth Avenue. Chris couldn't see much except for a smoky haze. "There are buildings on fire as far south as 90th Street, where—" She looked distracted, touched her earpiece, then said, "We have a breaking report from WABC's Mark Watson at La Guardia. Mark?"

Watson stood in a concrete parking structure. "Julia, Kevin, this might be where it all began. Witnesses say people awaiting family members arriving from Germany were outraged when their relatives were not allowed to disembark. Though the flight originated in Berlin, those denied entrance hailed from Kenya. A scuffle ensued and several people were arrested. A man reportedly opened fire on passengers waiting on line for screening. Police have closed down the terminal."

A series of shouts was heard, followed by an earth-jolting *thud*. Watson looked up. "People are overturning cars on the level above us. We'd better get going. Back to you, Julia."

High atop Essex House, Julia stood with her back to the stone balustrade. "Another report came in while Mark was speaking. A city bus has apparently been hijacked and rammed into Mt. Sinai Hospital, killing at least three people. The hospital is now confirmed to be on fire."

During the reports, Chris had been dressing. He switched off the HP and went into the bathroom. He examined himself in the mirror, looking for bruises. His eyes were tired, but the whites were still clear. He checked his gums for bleeding. There was none. He was still alive. For now.

Chris had a hybrid scooter he used to get around town when he didn't want to ride the subway. He had no choice this morning anyway; the trains weren't running. The streets were clogged with ambulances and police cars. At Lafayette, which a few blocks north turned into Park Avenue, he watched a retinue of twenty military vehicles tool past. Grim-faced soldiers sat in the rear of each one, outfitted in orange Racal suits and holding what looked like plasma rifles.

It was eighty blocks uptown, and before he'd gone ten, Chris had to turn off Park to avoid the roadblocks. Before long, he had gone far enough north that smoke from the fires started burning his eyes. Twice cops reached out for him as he passed, but he easily swerved away from them. Turned constantly away from Fifth Avenue, at one point he went east as far as First, where the traffic still moved sluggishly north and south. When he hit 90th Street, he turned west again. The Met was on 82nd. At one turn he saw the Guggenheim Museum, just six blocks north of the Met. It was wreathed in smoke.

Ash had begun falling, covering everything with a layer of gray dust. The sun was hazy overhead and everything took on a strange twilight cast. He was still three blocks east of Fifth, where he could see a streaming river of police, military, and ambulance vehicles heading north toward Mt. Sinai. Crowds pressing close for a view were kept at bay by police in respirators, holding Plexiglas riot shields.

Chris made his way to Madison Avenue, just one block east of Fifth. He turned left to avoid a crowd pressing against the barricade at the intersection and zipped down an alley, emerging just a stone's throw from Fifth Avenue. The crowds were thick here, and there was as great a deal of jostling. He pushed his way through and eased the bike out into Fifth Avenue. On his right, the Guggenheim's conch shell swirls billowed smoke. Further north, Mt. Sinai Hospital was ringed with fire trucks and green military vehicles. The sound of gunfire echoed off the tall buildings. A long line of policemen with clear plastic shields trotted past Chris toward the hospital.

Chris leaned his bike against a building and turned around. His stomach flipped in horror. The Met was belching flames from several upper-story windows. Fire licked up the front façade. The street was a maze of fire trucks, criss-crossed fire hoses, firemen, and police, who ducked objects thrown by people from balconies in the tall apartment building across the street, which was also on fire. Cops opened fire on a balcony far above, where a man was holding a holo projector overhead, preparing to throw it. He was hit and stumbled, and the HP fell fifteen stories, impacting a police cruiser squarely on the hood, sending shards of glass flying and knocking a dozen bystanders to the ground.

At that point, someone began shooting at the police. Everyone dove for cover. The crowd around Chris swirled, people screaming. He was shoved against his bike, toppling it. An armored troop carrier disgorged a dozen S.W.A.T. cops who stormed the apartment-building doors. The policemen who had been guarding the intersection near Chris turned and trotted toward the apartment building facing the Met.

Chris took a couple of steps into the street for a better view. The apartment building was being riddled with bullets. The fusillade was deafening. He took another step and when no one stopped him, he sprinted across the street, diving into a wall of shrubbery. He burst out the other side, saw that no one was chasing him, and ran down the grassy slope toward the Loop, which ran past the rear of the museum.

He stopped. There were a number of police cars parked on the Loop, but the cops were all turned toward the noise on Fifth. Chris ducked behind a tree. The north side of the museum was the Egyptian wing, and the Dendur Temple stood behind a great wall of glass. There was a small door just north of the glass wall, set into an alcove. It was his best option, and he raced up the lawn toward the building, hoping the cops wouldn't turn and see him. They didn't. In fact, they were running toward the front of the museum, their guns now drawn.

He ran into the alcove, skidding to a stop in front of a glass door. He cupped his hands around his eyes and squinted through the tinted glass. The Dendur Temple, a squarish collection of eroded tan sandstone, filled the room. He grabbed the door handle. Locked. He looked around. A river stone the size of a volley ball sat at his feet. The museum guards often used it to prop the door open when they ate lunch outside. He hefted the rock overhead, shut his eyes, and slammed it against the glass door.

The rock went through the door, taking him with it. He tumbled over the panic bar, rolling across the carpet. He got to his feet, dazed, his nostrils flaring. He looked up. Tendrils of blue smoke curled across the ceiling. In breaking the door, he'd caused a rush of air, further fanning the flames in the museum. Suddenly, the fire sprinklers sputtered to life, momentarily blinding him with ice-cold water.

He trotted through the gallery doorway. To his right, far down the corridor, through a floor-to-ceiling wire-mesh security gate, he saw firemen battling flames. The air was thick with smoke. It would be only a matter of minutes before the entire wing was in flames. He turned to his left, rounded the corner, and took the broad stairway down three steps at a time. At the bottom, the double metal doors were ajar. The firemen must have overridden the security system, opening the interior security doors. Before him was a bank of elevators, the doors standing open, inoperable. He raced toward the corner stairwell.

Three stories down, he burst into his offices, looking around. Nothing here mattered. All of his data files were in the museum's secure computer, protected from just this event. Whatever else remained would be sodden ash in a few hours anyway. There was only one thing he needed to save.

The stairwell was dark, the dim emergency lights offering little illumination. Chris held onto the slippery handrail as he descended. He'd fallen twice already. He took another step and was ankle-deep in water. Another, then another, and he found the landing. The water was above his knees. He had no idea the sprinklers had been on that long. He hauled the metal door open and stepped into the lowest museum subbasement. Far down the long, dark corridor, fluorescent lights flickered weakly. Overhead, exposed water pipes groaned. Water coursed down the walls, sprayed from air ducts, and dripped from light fixtures. Chris waded down the hallway.

He finally found himself in front of two huge stage doors stenciled STORAGE. Like the doors upstairs, they were slightly ajar, the security pad glowing a faint green. Chris squeezed into the dark, cavernous room. The emergency lighting was out; sparks shorted from fixtures high overhead. The only illumination was the thin slice of red emergency light from the corridor. The water had risen to his thighs. As the lowest part in the museum, this room would soon be a giant swimming pool.

Chris squeezed back through the doors, which were being pushed closed by the water flooding the basement. If they shut when he was inside, he'd have a tough time getting out. He went to the guard station. After searching several drawers, he found a flashlight, flicking the button. It was dead. Disgusted, he tossed it aside.

Reaching deep inside the same drawer, he felt something, and withdrew it. A pack of cigarettes. Cigarettes had been illegal in New York for fifteen years. He reached into the drawer again and his fingers grazed a flattened cylinder. He pulled it out. A lighter. It took him several tries before the tiny flame ignited. Breathing thanks to the guard who didn't believe in cancer, he pushed his way back into the storage area, slogging down the darkened aisles, the lighter held high. A number of boxes had dislodged from lower storage shelves and were floating in the cold, rising water. He pushed them aside and pressed forward. A large object blocked his way, a robot lift, frozen in place when the power failed, its forks held high.

He slid by the lift and made his way to the end of the aisle. Turning right, he came to another door labeled COLD STORAGE. His heart sank. It was shut tightly. He stowed the lighter and pulled on the handle with both hands, cracking the door slightly. In total darkness, he felt water rushing past his legs, pouring into the cold-storage room. He managed to pry it open enough to slip into the room. The water pressure slammed the door shut behind him. He found himself in only knee-deep water; it was getting into the room in other ways.

He pushed past row after row of tall stainless-steel cabinets, noting that none of the drawer diodes shone green. The power was completely out down here. Flicking the lighter and raising it high overhead, he finally found the right aisle and stopped before the drawer containing the alabaster jar. He put the lighter in his pocket, grasped the handle, and pulled. It slid slowly open.

He groped around inside the drawer, finding the lozenge-shaped cryogenic container, which stood on one flattened end. The regulator was covered with a layer of frost. He felt for the clasps that secured the lozenge halves together. They were undone. He lifted the top off, his heart hammering. He produced and flicked the lighter. The container was empty. The canopic jar, along with its precious cargo, was gone.

Chris started toward the next aisle, where the mummy was stored. The lighter flickered, nearly out of fuel. As he turned the corner, something large hunched in the middle of the aisle, just beyond the reach of the light. Chris stopped "Who is it?" he called. The shape did not move. "What are you doing here?" he asked, voice trembling.

It took every ounce of courage he possessed to take a step forward. When he did, the dark form resolved into an extended drawer. Water lapped at its sides, making it look like it was floating. As he approached it, he noticed the number. B-36. It was the vault he'd been looking for. He held the lighter up and peered into the drawer.

It was empty.

SIXTEEN

FRONTIER

Chris was well across the park when he heard the explosion. A fireball rose above the Met. He had no idea what could have caused such a conflagration. At Columbus Circle, he found a phone and dialed Cate. All lines were busy. He trotted toward the Lincoln Tunnel. No one would pick him up, but traffic stood still on the ramp and he hopped on the back of a truck hauling old rusty refrigerators. Finally, the traffic began to move and the truck entered the tunnel as sirens echoed in the humid darkness. When the truck stopped at a gas station in New Jersey, he jumped off.

He got a ride with a long-distance trucker and made it to Pennsylvania by the next morning, the precise moment when all hell broke loose in Manhattan and the mayor appeared on holo, looking blotchy and tired. For three days, Chris hid in a culvert outside Allentown, afraid to go through Philadelphia. When he got the courage to take to the road again, it was as if he'd missed an air strike. There were wrecks everywhere. Traffic streamed west, weaving between pileups. No one would pick him up. He trudged along the road wearing yellow dishwashing gloves and carrying bottles of bleach he'd found in a service station, a handkerchief tied across his nose and mouth. After searching a half dozen drugstores in as many towns, he finally found an unopened case of ULPA masks on a loading dock.

A Toyota Land Cruiser sat nearby, windows rolled up in the stifling heat, a man in the driver's seat, his head a gory explosion of black blood, and a carpet of flies—also dead of Cobalt—peppering the dashboard. On the dock, Chris opened the cardboard box and shed tears of relief at finding the masks.

At first, the roads were full of emergency vehicles, blue and white lights flashing, sirens wailing. But within just a few days, the Interstate became eerily empty. The power grid failed next, the maintenance engineers dead of Cobalt. Occasionally, he saw great fires raging in the distance, a power pole down, throwing sparks, igniting fields and houses, and no one around to put it out.

He found a motorcycle in a ditch, the owner's bloody body lying nearby. He hadn't died of Cobalt, but Chris doused the cycle with bleach anyway before touching it. He siphoned gas from cars and traveled mostly at night, and though he saw campfires, he did not approach them. He saw others traveling west, as he did, on foot, by bicycle, on motorcycle, and even on horseback, but he didn't speak to them, nor they to him. People wouldn't let anyone get closer than shouting distance anyway. Apparently, the first Cobalt casualty was human interaction. He rode alone, ate alone out of cans scavenged from convenience-store shelves, and camped alone under red, smoke-filled autumn skies.

In Lincoln, Nebraska, in a looted REI store, he found a solar-powered radio, which had fallen off a shelf and been kicked under the rack. He took it outside and placed it in the sun, tuning the dial. A couple of guys were talking on the shortwave band. Fires were burning from NYC to D.C. Miami was empty. Toronto was silent. Denver did not respond.

Three weeks out of Manhattan, Chris saw the Black Hills on the horizon. They were the first real mountains he'd seen on his trip, and for some reason, he felt safer once he reached them. That night he camped on the top level of the parking structure at Mount Rushmore. He leaned on the railing and looked out across the forested hills. The sky was red with smoke from a hundred fires on the horizon. He listened to the motorcycle engine ticking as it cooled and allowed himself to think about the future.

For all his roughing it on digs in the Sudan and at Olduvai, he knew next to nothing about survival in a world without electricity. Cars were a mystery; he opened a hood and saw a battery attached to a gearbox. The guy who *did* know how things worked was either dead or holed up in his basement, eyes on the ceiling, listening for zombies, his finger on the shotgun trigger, eating Spam, and slowly going crazy.

He turned toward the monument. High up on the mountain, the faces of Washington, Jefferson, Roosevelt, and Lincoln stared into the dusky, smoky distance, accusing looks on their solemn faces. The America they envisioned was over; the shining city on a hill was on fire.

Chris looked west. The sun had set; the horizon was deep blue with a strip of pink above it, fading as he watched. He thought about his mother in Montana. He wondered if he'd make it that far before Cobalt got him.

A month later he found his mother with her sister Karen near Whitefish Lake, north of Kalispell. He stood in Aunt Karen's front yard as his mother, covered with mottled purple Cobalt bruises, waved goodbye, seated on the wooden porch in a rocker.

Later that day he heard Karen crying and knew the end was near. Shortly after, Karen hobbled out onto the porch with a shotgun. "I know you want to say goodbye," she said, raising the gun with trembling hands, "but it's too dangerous." She tugged on her house dress, revealing bruises on her own neck. "I've got it too."

Chris stood in the shade of the cottonwood in the front yard, not knowing what to say.

Karen lowered the gun barrel and wiped tears from her eyes. "Come back in a month and get us in the ground, Chris."

Chris stayed at the nearby Whitefish campground, riding his motorcycle into town for provisions. When a month had passed, he went back to Aunt Karen's home and pried the windows open from the outside. That night he camped in her yard as the house aired out.

The next morning he donned the ULPA mask, pulled on surgical gloves, and opened two shower-curtain packs he scavenged from the Kalispell Wal-Mart. He shook one out on the floor of the master bedroom, where his mother lay on her bed. Her body came apart at his touch, and he was sobbing by the time he finally got her—most of her—onto the curtain and covered up. Lesson learned, he rolled Aunt Karen in the bed sheet she was lying on and placed the bundle on the other shower curtain, finishing the task. He then stumbled outside into the painfully bright day and vomited.

The night before, unable to sleep with the images of the next day's horrific chore on his mind, he'd set to work digging the graves by lamp light. He placed his mother and Aunt Karen in the ground and covered them up, then carved their names on fence slats, pounding them at the head of the graves. Then he collapsed in exhaustion under the cottonwood tree and slept.

His original plan was to come to Montana, see about his mother, then go to Atlanta and find out what happened to Cate. But the trip west and the condition of people's bodies who died from Cobalt convinced him no one could survive the plague—Atlanta would be just as empty as Kalispell was.

But he couldn't be sure and stewed about going or not. Then he remembered the solar radio and the amateur radio band. It wasn't powerful enough to pull in much, so he began a systematic search of the homes along the Whitefish river for a ham radio, a generator, and fuel.

Three miles south he found Marcia and Bob Allen's home, a rambler with an attached garage and a full basement where Bob had a ham radio set and Marcia had laid up hundreds of bottles of peaches, pears, raspberries, blueberries, you name it. The Flathead ran swiftly past the rear of the property, so he had water. Bob had stacked three cords of firewood against the garage wall. Now all Chris had to find was a generator and gas.

He rode a bicycle into town. The hardware store had been cleaned out. He'd seen a few people about, so he was not surprised. He noticed a radio tower and approached the cinder block station. It, too, had been ransacked. If he was going to find a generator, it would be at someone's house.

Chris hated going into residences. Even though the owners were dead, he felt like he was trespassing. In addition, many had died at home, and he encountered more than a few maggot-eaten corpses. He pulled his mask tight, secured his gloves to his shirt with duct tape, pulled on a yellow slicker, and doused himself with bleach before venturing inside. The pictures in hallways of smiling children and grandchildren, of photo albums open on coffee tables, of knickknack collections of bells or spoons or thimbles or whatever, depressed him. All those people, all dead. And him, scavenging their belongings, disrespecting what little they'd left behind.

Then one day he stopped a couple miles south of the Allen home in front of a large river-stone home with green metal roofing. He'd passed the driveway before, but the trees along the main road hid the house. A front-door placard read "Seidel." He went around the side of the house and saw a large, triple-door garage. He pried the side door open. Inside was an ATV, a Jeep, and a generator sitting next to a couple of plastic five-gallon gas cans, both full.

That night, Chris fired up the generator in the Allen garage and began what became a nightly ritual: listening to ham radio. The stories he heard over the crackling ether varied in particulars, but recounted essentially the same events: Cobalt had ravaged their state, their county, their town, their block, and their family. Survivors were isolated, afraid, and paranoid. They discussed survival: how to find gasoline, how to dig a well, how to purify water, how to get a solar panel working again.

When he'd learned the protocol, Chris squeezed the mike button and put in his two cents' worth. Cate was on his mind. After days of trying, he got a hold of someone in Roswell, an Atlanta suburb. "Area 51" was the guy's handle, and he said the CDC was torched just two weeks after the outbreak. Chris asked him if anybody made it out alive. Area 51 didn't know. "But I can leave a note at the PlanEx office. People post stuff there."

Chris gave Area 51 Cate's name and description, but few details. As he'd listened night after night, he'd detected a deep-seated bitterness at the government in general and the CDC in particular for the outbreak. SchleraSim came up often, the deadly virus created by renegade CDC researchers years ago. Most people believed Cobalt had the same provenance. Other, more bizarre theories concerning the outbreak spread through the midnight air: aliens had released it to cleanse the earth of humans before beginning their invasion; FIFs from Indonesia had detonated a bio bomb in Washington; Jesus Christ had returned in clouds of glory and had smitten the wicked. The fellow who said that claimed to have seen the Savior carrying a canned ham out of a grocery store in Dallas.

Chris even shared his own theory one night while chatting with a woman in Nogales, Mexico. "It's nature getting revenge," he said. "We invaded the rain forests and unleashed the apocalypse." It was a term Chris knew well by now. After the outbreak, the term "Plague Age" had been modified. Everyone called it the "Apocalyptic Age," and Chris had to admit that it had a catchy alliterative ring to it.

"Apocalypse?" asked the woman, whose handle was "Siempre Viva." Her English was iffy.

"End of the world," said Chris. "We opened Pandora's Box."

In the fall, Chris harvested the vegetables Bob and Marcia had planted in the spring. He snared fish in the river, barbecuing them over Bob's propane grill. When the propane tank emptied, he went down to the Seidel home for more. After loading two tanks onto the Seidel's ATV, Chris stood at the back door of the main house, debating whether he should enter. He finally decided he might as well; it was only a matter of time before someone else did, anyway.

He pried the door open and smelled the air. It was musty and close, but there was no smell of death. He walked into a two-story great room. To his right were floor-to-ceiling windows, looking out across the Flathead to the Rockies, tall and blue in the hazy distance.

The wall facing him boasted an immense stone fireplace, and on either side of it hung dozens of animal trophy heads: caribou, elk, cougar, moose. Chris turned and jumped, startled. An immense grizzly on its hind legs, paws raised, fangs bared, loomed over him.

Next to the fireplace was an ornate wooden gun cabinet containing a single high-powered Winchester rifle. Seidel must have used this gun to bag his trophies. Chris picked up a Remington bronze statue and broke the cabinet glass, removing the rifle and a box of shells. "It's for hunting, Chuck," he said, "just like you, you sonuvabitch."

SEVENTEEN

Ghosts in the Machine

Cate was at a staff meeting in the conference room that Saturday morning when Manhattan went Code Red. For the third time in thirty years, New York was Ground Zero, and yet seventeen planes still got off the ground at JFK before the embargo halted all flights. The President's containment scheme did nothing to stop the pandemic. Simulations predicted complete, nationwide Cobalt saturation within ninety-six hours.

Cloudburst dialed up the external security cameras. A crowd had formed outside the chain-link fence surrounding the CDC compound. Some were family, concerned about relatives working inside; others believed the CDC might be the safest place during the outbreak; and still others shouted that everyone inside was probably dead already. The guards locked the gates and retreated deeper inside the compound, their guns at the ready.

Having seen enough, Ron Ashby jumped up and headed for the door. Dr. Cloudburst stepped in his path. "Where are you going?"

"I'm getting out."

"We have work to do."

"*You* have work to do, Doc. I quit."

Another researcher, a burly man named Deke Carlton, joined Cloudburst, blocking the door. "Calm down, Ron."

"News flash!" shouted Ashby. "It's over!"

"You're panicking," said Cloudburst.

"I am not gonna die in this fucking rat hole! Let me by!"

Carlton shoved Ron, who fell backward over a chair. Carlton loomed over him. Ashby scrambled to his feet, putting the conference table between himself and Carlton. "Look," he said, trying to sound reasonable. "Don't you want to see your families? Aren't you worried about them?"

"Shut up," said Carlton.

"You moron," said Ron. "You're already dead as Nixon and you don't even know it."

"Ron, sit down," said Cloudburst flatly, "and shut up."

Ron looked around, saw he was alone, and sat down.

Within twelve hours, SNN was reporting Cobalt outbreaks in every state. There was widespread looting in Manhattan. Mt. Sinai Hospital, the Guggenheim museum, and the Metropolitan Museum of Art were reportedly on fire. Cate ran down the hall to Cloudburst's office. "I have to leave."

"You know you can't. We're in lock-down."

"I just saw a news holo," said Cate. "The Met is on fire."

"There's nothing you can do."

"Chris is there. I've got to warn him."

"He's been warned, Cate. He knows."

"How do you know?"

"The same way they knew at Hiroshima."

Within an hour after the lock-down, several platoons of National Guard troops had surrounded the CDC, prohibiting entry or exit. Sixty-five people were stranded above ground in the administration buildings, thirteen underground in the BSL labs. Within four days, Atlanta was racked by riots and looting. The governor declared martial law.

There had been massive troop desertions, so when the semi roared down Clifton Road toward the CDC early that Wednesday morning, there were only a few soldiers still guarding the compound. The truck smashed through the main gate, tossing the concrete barricades aside.

The rest was only heard distantly: the screech of tearing metal; the staccato burst of firearms discharge; the *whoosh* of plasma pods arcing through the air; then a deafening blast that shook the BSL labs, more than eighty feet underground at the rear of the compound.

In the cafeteria, where Cate lay sleeping, emergency lights flicked on. Acoustic ceiling tiles popped out of their frames, wafting to the floor.

"We've been nuked!" shouted someone.

"No way. No way," said another in a tone that nevertheless did not deny the possibility.

"Jesus!" shouted a third.

Cate sat on the floor by her cot, pulling her blanket around her. The thunder above continued.

Ron Ashby put his head in his hands. "Check. And mate."

After the explosions, the security cameras went blank and the internal phone system failed. As per safety procedures, the underground warren of BSL labs were lit with their own generators, supplied with their own water, and the air scrubbed clean with their own purifiers.

"EMP," whispered Ron. "Worse than a nuke."

"We still have electrical power," said Cate. "A pulse knocks all that out."

"We're underground."

"Not that deep," said Cate. "We're not insulated for EMPs or nukes. We're just biocontained."

"Same diff. Cut off. Limited supplies. It's just a matter of time."

Cate returned to her meal. After her initial panic about getting to Chris, Cate had accepted the reality of the situation. He was most likely dead, and had been since the early days of the outbreak. Her parents too. She shed many tears for them, for Chris, and for herself. She knew she would not likely get out of the BSL labs, and if she did, they had no idea where the virus would be hiding up there in the green, wet world. Anywhere. On anything. Waiting. Crystalized and hard-shelled. No heartbeat. No mind. Nothing but pure instinct whose prime directive was to invade, replicate, and destroy.

EIGHTEEN

INTO THE WORLD

"It's been long enough," said Dr. Cloudburst. "We're going to open the doors."

The thirteen of them sat in the cafeteria. The security cameras had been blown out three months before in the explosion, and the monitors were dark.

"Is it safe?" asked Cate.

"Well, there's no communication. Everyone above is either dead or they're treating this place like Roppongi. Either way, we're on our own."

"But is it *safe*?" repeated Cate.

"We have no idea."

"What is this *we* shit?" barked Ron. "*We're* the we, aren't we? Do *we* get to vote before you open the doors and infect us all?"

Cloudburst looked at each person in turn. Cate had grown to admire her. She'd kept them on track, slowly unraveling the RNA one combination at a time. She'd kept them busy and alive.

"I meant the *royal* we," said Cloudburst evenly. "We're low on supplies, but the biggest reason is we're not making progress. We've lost focus; we aren't working to our capacity."

"Who's going?" asked Cate.

"We haven't voted yet," said Ron angrily.

Cloudburst sighed. "Okay, let's vote. How many of you want to go upstairs and see what's going on?" Immediately, six workers raised their hands. "Opposed?" Ron, Terry, Deke, Brad, Cynthia, and Donna raised their hands. Everyone looked at Cate.

"It's tied, Cate," said Ron.

Cate got to her feet. "I wanna see the sun."

The elevator didn't work, but the stairway was free of debris, and it only took Deke a few minutes with a crowbar to pry the door open. They crossed the lobby and walked out under the porch. It was cold, everything was gray, and it was pouring rain. "That's luck," said Cloudburst. "The rain will wash everything clean."

"Unless Cobalt is in the water," said Deke glumly.

Cate said, "We have no evidence—"

"Shut up," said Deke. "We don't know shit about this monster, so quit acting like you do."

"That's enough, Deke," said Cloudburst, walking out into the rain. She stretched her arms out. The rain poured down on her and she didn't move for a long time, drinking in the moment. Cate and Deke exchanged a look, and Cate walked out into the rain as well. She took a deep breath; the air passing through the ULPA filter was humid but fresh. "I think it's safe," she said.

"How do you know?" asked Deke, still standing under the corrugated porch roof.

Cate smiled at Cloudburst through the downpour. "I just do."

When they returned, they were sprayed with disinfectant in the airlock and moved directly to the Slammer, where they waited for forty-eight tense hours before being released.

The next expedition involved Brad Palmer and Donna Major. Brad refused to wear a Racal suit. Instead, he wore gloves and a ULPA-NB respirator. They went out, looked around at the sunny, chilly day, then returned, spent a day in the Slammer, and were given a clean bill of health.

The third expedition involved Cate again, and they made the rounds of the compound. The blackened hulk of the semi truck sat in the main lobby of the administration building. They found a dozen bodies in the cafeteria. Using a greensman's wagon, they hauled them to the incinerator at the rear of the compound and burned them. As the smoke poured out of the chimney, unable to resist any longer, Cate took off her mask.

"Don't!" yelled Ron, trying to force the mask back on her face.

She pulled away. "I'm tired of wondering." She pulled off her gloves, knelt, and picked up a handful of fallen oak leaves, holding them to her nose and taking a deep whiff.

"Cate!" shouted Ron.

She turned toward the sun, which glimmered through the bare trees, and inhaled the cold, crisp air. "I don't care. It feels so good. So . . . *good.*"

A week after first emerging from the labs, it snowed—just a light dusting, but everyone went topside and Ron and Deke made a snowman. They plopped Ron's red Braves cap on top, gave him sunglasses for eyes, and put a ULPA mask on him. Deke turned toward Cloudburst and extended his hand. "See ya, Doc."

"You haven't been released."

He just smiled and walked away, across the lawn.

Cloudburst turned to the others. "We've got to continue our research. Cobalt is still out there."

Ron pointed southeast. "I live in Decatur. I need a decent coat. Anybody wanna come along?" He looked at Cate, who looked away.

"Cate? Will you stay?" asked Cloudburst.

"I'm going to Virginia, to see if my parents made it."

Ron walked over to Cate and whispered, "I'll go along, if you want company."

Cate knew what that would entail. His constant, clumsy advances, coupled with his general disagreeable personality, would make for a truly agonizing journey. "No. Thanks."

"I love you," he said abruptly.

"Oh, Ron, I don't know what—"

"You know your opera singer is probably dead," he said.

"Probably," she said, stunned at his insensitivity. "But it wouldn't matter anyway, Ron. You're not my type." She looked away, surprised at her own brusqueness.

Ron looked mortally wounded. "What type is that? A selfish jerk who was more interested in his career than he was in you? I'll bet he never even told you he loved you, like I just did."

"You're right, Ron. He never told me he loved me . . ." She walked three paces, then turned back. "Like *you* just did."

She turned and strode across the lawn, stretching her strides to match Deke's footprints in the snow. By the time she reached the sidewalk, she was running and crying.

NINETEEN

SINNERS AND SAINTS

Cate's first week on the road was uneventful. She found a hybrid mountain bike, a solar-assist rock-hopper that suited her well. She pedaled across the rolling hills of I-85, heading for the Appalachians. After months cooped up in BSL labs, she relished the workout. She scavenged food from grocery stores in small towns, most of which had already been picked over. There must have been a lot more people around than they first guessed, but she saw very few, and the ones she did see were armed and cautious. Her muscles eventually quit complaining, her sunburn peeled and settled into a tan, and she felt better than she had in years. At this rate, the trip might only take a few weeks.

One evening, just a few miles after crossing the Savannah river into South Carolina, she came upon a vehicle pileup that stretched across an overpass. As she coasted down the off-ramp to avoid it, she thought the crash looked a little too orderly, and she knew her mistake when she rode past the underpass and heard a car engine roar to life. She pumped up the on-ramp. A red Chevy truck roared out of the tunnel. She couldn't outrun it, so she steered onto the shoulder, bounded over the bunch grass, then dropped the bike and raced toward a chain-link boundary fence. The pickup stopped and someone yelled. She heard doors open and feet on gravel. She was almost over the fence when someone grabbed her foot. She kicked, connected, heard someone cry out, and dropped to the other side.

"Hold it there, missy," said a black man wearing an army fatigue jacket. He had a plasma rifle aimed at her. "Tired of chasin' you."

Cate glanced behind her. It was twenty feet to the safety of the tree line. The black kid on the ground in the mesh shirt, the one she'd kicked, sat up and spit blood. "Bitch kicked me!"

Cate backed away slowly.

"Why you running?" asked the man with the gun. "What's wrong with you?"

"It might be your gun," said Cate, taking another step toward the trees.

The man cocked the rifle. "Stop. I mean it."

"If you shoot me, you won't have any fun."

"Maybe we will," said the man. "Skate here likes it any old way."

Skate shrugged. "He's right. It don't matter to me."

Cate took another step and the gun went off, lifting up a chunk of sod by her feet. "Better listen to me," said the man. "Skate, jump over that fence and take hold of her."

Skate leapt up on the fence like a cat. In an instant he was on Cate's side. She relaxed a little. He was a full head shorter than she was. He came toward her. "Ain't gonna hurt you," he said, pulling out a switch blade. "Just wanna talk."

Cate stepped to one side, putting Skate between her and the man with the gun. Skate wore slip-on tennis shoes; she had on mountain boots. In a flash, she dropped and whirled around, her boot catching Skate at the ankle. The roundhouse toppled him, and he cried out, clutching his ankle. Cate picked up the switch blade and pulled him in front of her, the blade against his rib cage.

The man with the gun laughed. "Shit, Skate, she kung-fu'd you!"

"Rooster, she's got my blade. Shoot her!"

"Might hit you, Skate. You want that?"

"Then get over here! You got the gun; you can get the blade from her."

"Maybe I'll just shoot you both," said Rooster, raising the rifle.

"No!" shouted Skate. "We're friends!"

"Friends?" said Rooster. "Shit, man, I know you a couple a days and already I'm sick of your bullshit."

"Rooster!" wailed Skate. "Come on, man, help me!"

Rooster considered his options for a moment, then slung the rifle over his shoulder. "Shit," he said, and started scaling the fence. At that instant, Cate released Skate and bolted towards the woods. In an instant Rooster was on the ground, loping toward her. When he passed Skate, though, Skate reached out and snagged his jeans. Unbalanced, Rooster fell. He got up, cursed, whirled around and shot Skate dead, then turned toward the woods. Cate was gone.

Cate soon found another bike and got going again. She was in good shape by now, and sometimes rode up to twenty miles a night. When she needed supplies, she dabbed on makeup, covering her face and neck with black and blue bruises, simulating Cobalt. That always kept people at a distance, even the friendly ones. Sadly, you never knew if they were friendly or not until they were too close anyway.

One night in the Blue Ridge Mountains south of Roanoke, she was riding along, lost in the routine of pedaling, when someone stepped into the road in front of her with a lantern held high and a shotgun in the crook of her arm. Cate stopped, intending to turn back, but the woman stepped off the road to let her pass, lowering the gun. As Cate warily passed her, the woman asked, "Where you going, sick like that?"

Cate stopped. Since her attack on the Savannah River, she'd made it a priority to get a gun. The .22 pistol she'd found was tucked in her waistband, hidden by her windbreaker. For some reason, she didn't pull it out. Besides, the woman was so old, she probably couldn't see well enough to shoot her anyway, not in this poor light. "I'm okay, really," said Cate.

"Oh, honey," said the woman. "You won't make it where you're going—you got the Cobalt."

Cate remembered she still had on the makeup. "I'm not going far, just up the Shenandoah."

"I can help, if you want," said the woman. "Stop the hurt."

Cate felt her emotions unraveling. In a bizarre way this stranger was offering the greatest kindness she'd encountered since the outbreak. She looked at the old woman, standing there in an old floral housedress, holding the shotgun. "My name's Cate Seagram."

"I'm Alice Jansen," said the woman. "Live over there." She nodded toward a small white clapboard house set back from the road, a candle burning in a window. "They call me Mother Janice."

"Mother Janice?"

"My daughter couldn't say Jansen, only Janice. Name stuck. I'm a midwife. I used to bring people into the world. Now I help 'em go out. I can help you—see to it you get a decent burial. You accept the Lord Jesus as your savior?"

"Uh, no," said Cate. "I haven't."

"You will, when He takes your hand. Your worries fall away and He guides you straight on to paradise."

"Sounds nice," said Cate, not merely humoring her. "But I don't believe in God."

Mother Janice set the lamp down. "Don't matter. He believes in you, child."

Cate smiled. "You sound like a preacher. Mother Janice."

"I am. I preach love. Tough love: slap the babes on their way in. Motherly love: feed and care for the young. Tender love: holding a dying soul's hand on the way out. Even romantic love, once or twice in my life." She winked.

"Not much love left in this world," said Cate.

"If you need some, just say so."

Cate looked at Mother Janice's rifle. The offer was strangely appealing. Everyone she cared about was likely dead: Mom. Dad. Her sisters. Chris. It was only a matter of time for her too, and if she left Mother Janice's knobby but kind hands behind, what were the chances she'd get a proper burial?

"Don't need to be *this* way," Mother Janice said, patting the shiny rifle barrel. "But you can't wander off. I'm old and can't chase after you. There's a little place out back. I can put you up there, leave food for you until your day comes, which won't be too long now by the looks of you. Then I'll take care of the end. Fix it up so you're ready to meet your Lord. How does that sound?"

"Sounds good," said Cate. "And when the time comes, I'll come back. I promise."

"It's coming soon, child. You're sick."

"I'm going to see my folks in Winchester, up north. If they're gone, then I'll come back and say hello."

"I'll be waiting, Cate. I'll introduce you to the Lord. He loves you."

Cate almost believed it, coming from this old woman standing there holding a shotgun.

Two weeks later, Cate rolled into Winchester, Virginia, at the top of the Shenandoah, where the valley opens out into the rolling hills of Maryland and Pennsylvania. According to the letter left on the front door by a neighbor, now also dead, her parents had succumbed just two weeks after the New York outbreak.

Inside the house, on the kitchen table, her mom left Cate a note, along with letters for Abigail and Candice. As she looked down at the two other unopened envelopes, Cate knew it would be pointless to search for them now. If they hadn't made it here to say goodbye, they were already dead.

Cate took her letter out on the back porch and read it, then cried for almost an hour. Then she dried her eyes and walked over to the cemetery, taking a spray of lilacs with her. The neighbor's note gave her the location of the graves. There were no headstones, but the ground rose a little over the plots. Cate trimmed the bluegrass back, took a vase from a nearby grave, and set the lilacs in it. She set the picture she'd taken from the mantle on the graves and stood back, looking at Don and Louise smiling in happier times.

She returned to the house, put on the ULPA mask and surgical gloves, and cleaned it thoroughly, taking all the bedding and towels into the back yard and burning them. That night, she slept on a bare mattress in her old bedroom and could almost hear, in the house's routine squeaks and groans, her mother's light step in the hall or her father's gentle snoring in the next room.

She stayed three days, then suddenly found herself in the front yard one morning, hyperventilating, clutching herself, staring wide-eyed at the house. A terrible dream, full of grasping, dead hands clawing at her from mounds of overgrown grass.

She finally calmed down enough to go back inside, but within twenty minutes she had filled her backpack with family pictures and a Hummel figurine her mother treasured, and hit the road. By noon, she was out of the small town, headed south again.

TWENTY

BEHIND THE STARS

On her return trip, as promised, Cate stopped in at Mother Janice's, but a note on the door said she was gone "doing God's work." Cate smiled and got back on her bike. She rode another two days without seeing anyone. Then one night, as she passed a little white church outside a small town, she heard singing. She leaned her bike against the fence railing surrounding the dirt parking lot and went over to the church to listen.

Behind the closed wooden double doors, they were singing about gathering at a river, and then came a reedy voice. At first, the voice was meek, and it praised God for sparing them and asking that His grace be with those who had passed on. Cate wondered how many daring souls, drawn together by the superstition of faith, were inside.

The Voice (for that's how she heard it) soon rose in volume, becoming more strident. It began telling the listeners not just what had happened, but what it meant. Because of wickedness, God sent Cobalt to humble the world. "As in the days of Noah, He has destroyed the most wicked. Now He is watching *you*. Will you repent or will you continue in your prideful ways? Will you deny God's power? Will you deny His hand in all things?"

Cate straightened; she'd heard enough. She walked across the gravel parking lot. Suddenly, the door behind her flew open. "Come out of the darkness!" shouted the Voice.

Without looking back, Cate ran to the bike and swung a leg over the cross bar. The Voice stepped outside the church and pointed at Cate. "Do not fear the light!" He started down the steps toward her.

Cate still hadn't looked at him. She couldn't seem to push down on the pedals.

"You believe you are enlightened, but you worship the darkness of men!" shouted the Voice, striding across the parking lot toward her. "Your false gods will devour your soul!"

Cate squeezed her eyes shut, straining, trying to get the bike to move.

"You see the sun, yet you deny the Light!"

Cate finally opened her eyes. To her horror, the Voice stood before her. He was tall, pale as moonlight, and had a shock of white hair falling across his forehead. He looked solemnly at her, his thin lips pursed. "Open your heart, *Cate*."

She tumbled off the bike and scrabbled away. She reached for her pistol, but it had fallen out of her waistband. It lay on the dirt between them. The Voice bent and picked the gun up. He moved toward her, holding it in his palm. "You cannot hide from the truth."

"I'm not hiding!"

"Do not turn your back on your soul's deliverer."

"What deliverer?"

"He is the answer." The Voice held the gun out to her. "Force of arms is the path of death." She grabbed the gun and got to her feet, pointing it shakily at him. But the Voice had already turned and was walking slowly away. Inside the building, the singing began again, twenty voices lifted up in mournful praise. The Voice laboriously climbed the steps and went inside without looking back. The wooden doors creaked closed behind him.

Cate got on her bike and bore down on the pedals. Soon the church disappeared behind a curve in the road. Moonlight dappled the asphalt in silver light. She stared blindly into the darkness. *How did he know my name?*

∧∧∧

Since childhood, Cate had been taught that religion was at best a childish superstition and at worst a dangerous insanity. Immortality of the soul. Heaven. Hell. Life after life. Reincarnation. Past lives. Life between lives. Astrology. Crystals. Auras. Channeling. All of it was nonsense.

Yet the Voice knew her name. How could she explain that?

Cate had discussed something like this once with Dr. Cloudburst. "When you die," said Cloudburst, "your brain sends out electrical discharges. The white light people see is just the brain lighting off one last fireworks display before shutting down."

"And then what?"

"Then nothing. Freud was right. We invent a bright afterlife because we fear the darkness of death."

"Do *you* fear it?"

"No," said Cloudburst. "But, like Woody Allen said, 'I don't want to be around when it happens.'"

Cate laughed and changed the subject, but she secretly questioned the dogma that science would eventually answer all metaphysical questions. Quantum mechanics took the most recent stab at it. It maintained that we were living in many parallel universes at once, and sometimes we got a glimpse into another universe through dreams and so-called past life memories.

It sounded plausible, but it still didn't answer the key question: *Why are we living in* one *universe, let alone many?* Only believers in God had an answer to that: we're here because He/She/It put us here. That begged another "why," but it was one answer more than science, which said we were here because of an accident. No reason, no rationale, no purpose.

As Cate biked along the rolling hills of northern Georgia late one evening, she wondered what Chris would say about this. He'd once told her about being lost in the Sudanese desert, almost certain he was going to die. But when he looked up at the stars, his spirits lifted. Sure, they were just fusion furnaces, burning themselves cold in the emptiness of space, but they still made him feel better. He couldn't explain why.

Cate looked up at the distant, icy fires in the same sky. They made her feel better too. She couldn't explain that either, anymore than she could explain her feelings for Chris. Quantum mechanics couldn't explain love. It existed beyond science. Chris had loved her, and she had loved him. Theirs was an alliterative amour. He was Chris. She was Cate.

Just like the Voice said.

When Cate returned to Atlanta, she walked into Cloudburst's office down in the BSL labs and was surprised to see Donna Major sitting at the desk. Donna looked up, saw Cate, and tears filled her eyes. "She said you'd return, but I didn't believe her."

"Where's Cloudburst?"

"Somewhere in Nevada. About a month ago, she got a SatPhone call. Startled all of us; we thought the system was completely off-line. Anyway, two hours later, a helicopter came for her."

"We don't have a lab in Nevada," said Cate. "What is she doing out there?"

Donna shrugged. "Did you come back to work?"

"What's the point? I think Cobalt wiped the slate and then went to ground."

Donna shook her head. "Some people got together down in Peach Tree, in southern Atlanta, thinking Cobalt was over. They started working on getting the power back on, things like that. No one heard from them for awhile so a guy went out to check on them. Everybody was dead."

Cate shook her head. "So it's still out there."

"You're the only one who has returned," said Donna.

"Where else would I go?"

"Your boyfriend's?"

Cate felt tears building behind her eyes. Donna came around the desk, reaching for Cate, who recoiled. Donna put her arms around her. Soon they both were crying. After awhile, Cate pulled back. "I haven't been touched in six months," she said.

Donna sniffed, nodding. "Me neither."

They hugged and cried for a long time.

TWENTY-ONE

LIGHTNING TREE

The narrow path was muddy as K'tanu and his father climbed up the steep caldera wall. It had rained all morning, assisting them in their hunt, allowing them to get much closer to the antelopes than they normally could. K'tanu glanced back at M'uano, who carried the spiral-horned eland across his broad shoulders. It was hard to believe this was his father, for though he recognized M'uano's laugh, his body was another story. He seemed to be the same age as K'tanu.

As they reached the switchback turn, K'tanu stopped and looked past the large granite boulder. He felt a hand on his shoulder. "There are no tombs, Son," said M'uano.

"I know. But I cannot help looking."

"Then you must look in the huts in the village. They are all there. Alive."

"Are we truly alive?" asked K'tanu. "It is hard to believe this is Lightland."

"It was hard for me as well," said M'uano. "The Bleeding Sickness took me; I remember dying, hoping you would survive." He started up the trail. "Now that we are here, I wonder why we fear death, for we are all here, together." He stopped and looked back. "This *is* Lightland, K'tanu. I can imagine no brighter place than this, even when the day is cloudy."

He continued on. K'tanu matched his father's muddy footsteps, climbing toward the rim. His eyes turned toward the caldera. Suddenly, the clouds parted, and a ray of sun shot through, white as lightning, crowning an acacia tree out in the middle of the crater with golden light. For an instant, it seemed that the tree was on fire, then the clouds closed and the ray of light disappeared.

Lightland, thought K'tanu, trying to convince himself. *I am in Lightland.*

That night, as they lay in their hut, listening to the children's breathing as they wandered in the Other World, K'tanu whispered to Maya that old Antram had been wrong after all. Though it might be true that you would die if you perished in the Other World, when the Waking World came to an end and a soul entered Lightland, the Other World still continued. "Maybe this is not Lightland," he said. "Maybe *this* is the Other World. This afternoon, when we were returning from the hunt, I saw the lightning tree, exactly as I saw it a few nights ago, when I wandered in the Other World."

"This is not the Other World," said Maya. "There is no sickness and death, as there is there."

That is true, thought K'tanu. "But we are the last."

"They are here, my husband. They are with us. There is no reason to grieve."

K'tanu got up on one elbow and looked at Maya. "But no more are coming. Almost all of the people we knew in the Waking World are here. And our children, who died as children, will have no children of their own."

"You don't know that," said Maya, but there was a trace of doubt in her voice.

"Is anyone pregnant?" asked K'tanu.

"I don't think so, but we have not been here long."

"But many others have been here a long time. Have they had children?"

"What is troubling you, K'tanu?"

K'tanu lay back. "I am uneasy. The lightning tree fills me with dread. My heart hurts—like that day."

Maya threw her arm over K'tanu's chest. "I feared we might lose you."

"I was afraid too. But where would I go? There is only one other place."

Maya shuddered in his arms. "Do not speak of it."

K'tanu took a deep breath. "Perhaps I do not belong here, Maya."

"You are good, and all that is good is here. The evil ones, the ones that killed us, are not here. They are in the other place. They can never come here."

"We do not know that," said K'tanu. "The elders tell us to keep our spears sharp."

"Old habits," said Maya. "The old ones find it hard to change."

"They are not old, Maya," said K'tanu. "They are as young as you and I." He looked beyond her to their sleeping children. "Do you think they will grow up?"

"What? Of course."

"Then one day our village will be without the laughter of children. One day we will all be the same age, doing forever what we have done forever: hunt, eat, and sleep. Nothing more."

"What is it, K'tanu?"

"Something is coming," he said, sighing deeply. "I feel it. A change."

They were sitting by the fire pit, eating breakfast, when suddenly, there was Antram. K'tanu jumped to his feet and ran to him. Antram backed up, afraid. "Just today, I buried you!" shouted Antram, his eyes wide with terror. "You are dead!"

"Look," said K'tanu, holding Antram's own hand up before his face. "Your hand."

Antram looked at his hand, turning it over. "This is not my hand!" He backed away, but the people had gathered around him, and they kept him from running. Antram, his thin, silver hair now thick and black, turned around. Then someone shouted, "He is here! He is here!" and a stout woman burst through the throng, throwing her arms around him. "Antram, my husband! Antram!"

Antram fainted. His wife, the portly E'lahu, picked him up. He had always been a small, thin man. She looked heavenward, tears running down her cheeks. "Father Sun! Mother Moon! Thank you! He is here, my Antram! He is here!" She carried him to their hut.

Maya touched K'tanu's arm. "It was like that the day you arrived."

"I did not faint," said K'tanu.

"Everything but," said M'uano, who had leaned close. "You were shaking with fear."

"I was not," but those around him were smiling. "Well," said K'tanu, "it is to be expected. I was the last one he buried, I suppose, just before the Bleeding Sickness took him." At the mention of the illness, many people turned away. Talk of the trials and hurts of the Waking World were not encouraged here.

"You should speak to him when he awakes," said Maya. "He will have many questions E'lahu cannot answer. She died many years before he did, remember. She knows nothing of the Bleeding Sickness."

K'tanu did as Maya advised. He stood outside the hut for a long time before Antram finally appeared, assisted by E'lahu. "We are in Lightland?" asked the shaman, doubtful but smiling.

"Yes."

"And you made it after all, didn't you?"

"And you as well," said K'tanu. "It seems our fears about not reaching this place unless we were properly buried were wrong."

"No," said Antram. "Not wrong. I prepared myself as best I could, after I placed your body in your tomb with your family. I put your heart in the jar and rolled the stone back. Then I crawled into my own tomb and lay down next to E'lahu's bones. She has put on a little weight since then, no?" he whispered, nodding at his wife, who was being congratulated by her friends.

K'tanu laughed. "She will probably always be fat. And you will always be thin, Antram."

Antram touched K'tanu's arm. "You are cold," he said. "And dark!"

K'tanu shook his head. "We are all dark—"

"K'tanu!" shouted Maya, running toward him. It was as if a shaft of blackness had fallen upon K'tanu, leaving him in shadow while the rest of the world remained in light. Darkness filled his eyes, and he felt a pulling at his sternum. He put his hand on his chest. It was cold.

Suddenly, he was pulled backward, stumbling. His vision narrowed, and darkness closed in. Things grew hazy, people became mere white shapes in a black void. Maya ran toward him, arms outstretched. He could barely hear her cries. He reached for her, but could not even see his own hands. The pulling yanked him back another step. Cold knives pierced his heart. He doubled over, gasping in pain, hands clutching at his chest.

"K'tanu!" shouted Maya from far away.

He looked up. Tiny white dots in a pitch-black field floated before him. All sound had ceased. Tears spurted from his eyes; every nerve in his body was screaming. He wanted to cry out, but could not.

Then suddenly, he felt a great tearing as he was pulled from his body, which lay limp in Maya's arms. She sobbed and looked heavenward, calling upon Father Sun. Antram kneeled nearby, his head bowed. For an instant, K'tanu looked down at the strange tableau of his wife and Antram holding his still body.

And then, nothing.

RAISING LAZARUS

"Everybody back up a little," said Dr. Adamson. "Give me some room."

Sally Cloudburst obediently took a step back. The day they had so long anticipated was finally here. She could hardly believe it. Joanna screamed again and Cloudburst wondered for the tenth time why they hadn't given her any medication. Dr. Adamson said since they didn't know what deleterious effects it might have on the baby, they'd better not take any chances. "Now breathe, Joanna," he said. "And push. Gently."

"Gently?" bawled Joanna. "Oh, God! Oh!"

Cloudburst, never a mother herself, was as astonished as any man present at his first birth would be. The amount of blood was incredible. It was hard to watch, or hear.

"Oh, oh, oh!" cried Joanna. The nurse held her shoulders, whispering to her, pacing her breathing and, hopefully, her contractions. "Damn you all for making me do this!" screamed Joanna, sweat popping on her forehead.

"Almost there," said Adamson gently. "A couple more is all it will take. He's crowning."

And suddenly, with a gasp and a mighty push, the baby came out. He was long and slender, and his head was terribly misshapen.

Cloudburst took a step back in horror. Dr. Adamson saw her reaction. "Perfectly normal. Narrow canal, round head. Something has to give. He's okay."

The baby was coal black and covered with blood. A nurse suctioned mucus from his throat. Then Adamson did something Cloudburst thought they only did in movies. He held the baby upside down by the feet and whacked it on the fanny. It let out a wail that startled her, the little face an explosion of anger and surprise. A long moment passed as he inhaled, then he wailed again. Adamson smiled. "His lungs are fine," he said, handing the child to the nurses, who quickly cut the umbilical and wiped him clean.

In another moment, they had wrapped him in a blanket and handed him to Cloudburst. She cradled the infant in her arms, his face still scrunched up, wailing at his rude entrance into life.

Adamson looked up at her. "Well, you finally have it, Doctor: your miracle. Let's hope so, for all our sakes."

Cloudburst looked into the tiny, dark face, still crying loudly, obviously vibrant and healthy. If this moment was any indication, this boy would be strong. He would have to be. She smiled, tears in her eyes, holding the baby close. She rocked him gently and cooed, "Welcome back, Lazarus."

PART THREE

NORTH AMERICA

2035 A.D.

ONE

ADVENTUROUS SPIRIT

Chris looked at the calendar. It featured a pair of bears fighting over a salmon on a rock in the middle of a rushing river. He ran his finger along the boxes, not knowing what day it was. All he knew was that this was the sixth winter he'd spent on the Flathead River in Montana. So it must be 2035. From the looks of the snowy mountains to the east, spring was a ways off. January, probably. No later than February. He sat back down in the lounger facing the circular fireplace. The fire crackled. He tossed another book into the flames. "Good one, Mr. Defoe," he said. "Hell of a story."

Along one wall, hundreds of library books were stacked neatly. Every time he went to town, Chris "checked out" a few, feeding each one into the fire when he was finished, ignoring the part of him that recoiled from book burning. There were a million libraries in the United States and they all carried basically the same books. So what if the Kalispell library was missing one of its five copies of *Robinson Crusoe*?

He picked up the next book off the stack and turned it over. *King Solomon's Mines*. He'd been reading nineteenth-century adventure novels and had grown fond of the characters. Strong, brave, unconflicted British imperialists who could kill an attacker without spilling their tea. Like Chris Tempest.

He laughed ruefully; he was no adventurer. A week ago, a bear nosed around the house, and Chris huddled inside, the Winchester clutched in his shaking hands, too afraid to get up and lock the door, wondering if a grizzly knew how to turn a doorknob. His fear included his own species too. From the bulletins taped to the courthouse's glass doors, he knew there were probably fifty or sixty people still alive in the area, yet his contact with others was rarely more extensive than a distant wave.

He kept to himself, reading his adventure novels. *Ben-Hur* touted itself as the most popular novel of the nineteenth century. *Lord of the Rings* took the prize for the twentieth. He wondered what the winner in the twenty-first century would be, or if there would even be one. He considered writing his own entry. For days he thought about titles. *A Survivor's Story. The Cobalt Catastrophe. Me and the Virus.* Or should that be *The Virus and I?*

He didn't write it. Instead, he read and listened to ham radio. Though he had Charles Seidel's Winchester .388 rifle, he hadn't gone hunting, even though others were getting fresh venison, and they didn't have to go far for it either. One crisp, bright morning he looked up from his reading to see an elk bound past the picture window in the extensive, sloping back yard, followed by two men firing guns. The elk jumped into the icy river, swam across, and disappeared into the woods on the other side. The hunters stood awhile on the river bank, then turned and started back toward the house. Chris ducked below the window sill.

He heard the men stop near the house and watched through the blinds as one man pointed to Chris's footprints in the snow running between the stacks of cordwood and the house. The man called out, "Hello? Anybody home?" Chris shrunk back. He had a gun—what was he afraid of? After awhile, the two men slung their rifles over their shoulders and walked up the snow-packed driveway to the main road.

People were getting on with life—hanging out together. "Hey, Bob, let's go hunting tomorrow, what do you say?"

"Sure, Pete, sounds great. Let me ask the wife."

Then Bob and Pete, both Cobalt widowers, would shake their heads sadly and agree to meet the next morning and chase an elk across Chris's back yard while he cowered inside the house like a timid child. They must be crazy. Or he was.

One afternoon, halfway through *King Solomon's Mines*, Chris fell asleep. Leaden winter clouds hung low over the valley. The icicles on the eaves were two-feet long. The thermometer outside read nineteen degrees. Chris dozed by the fire, his feet toasty and his stomach full of tomato soup. He dreamed he was standing with the famous British explorer Allan Quatermain on a ridge overlooking an impassable desert, beyond which rose the misty peaks of majestic snow-capped mountains. Somewhere in those mountains were the mines of King Solomon, with enough diamonds to make them the richest men on earth. Quatermain wore a dusty pith helmet and explorer khaki. He looked out across the sun-blasted expanse, his handlebar moustache drooping from the heat. "No return from this journey, eh?"

"What is that?" asked Chris, pointing.

Out in the middle of the barren desert was a tree, spindly limbs jutting from a squat trunk underneath a flat canopy. "The thorn tree?" asked Quatermain. "Didn't see it before. Jove, that's strange."

Then suddenly, out of a clear blue sky, lightning arced, striking the tree, accompanied by an immense thunderclap that knocked both of them to the ground. When they got to their feet and sight came back to their eyes, Chris saw the tree, still intact, but the ground all around it was burned black.

"Hells bells," said Quatermain, dusting himself off. "That was something, wasn't it?"

"It's a warning to stay out of the desert," said Chris. "I will not enter it."

"You've no choice, lad. I hired you to go, and go you will if I say so."

Chris looked down at his hands. They were black, with long, thin fingers. His chest was bare, muscular, and hairless. He wore a / leopard-skin loincloth, and he had bands tattooed around his ankles.

In one hand he held an oval leather shield; in the other, a long spear topped with an iron blade. "Me?"

"Of course, K'tanu," said Quatermain. "It's what you signed on for."

TWO

ISOLATION

Cate had been back in Atlanta for more than three years, still crunching Cobalt RNA. She and her staff watched the single hour of news broadcast by the government each week. It was the only way to keep up on what was going on. The Internet was down; the dusty, unpowered servers were sitting in empty university labs nationwide. Cell-phone service was a pipe dream; land lines even scarcer. The power was on at the CDC, but the dinner most of the nation ate while watching the solar-powered broadcast was cooked over a campfire. The news reported continuing Cobalt outbreaks nationwide. The outbreaks, fortunately, were small and localized. People had learned to be careful around others, but when the virus got inside a close-knit group, it was still stunningly effective.

Because of their priority status, Cate and her staff had been quarantined from the outside world by the military. Once inside the compound, the workers were discouraged from leaving; if they did, they would not be allowed reentry. None of the twenty researchers Cate and Donna trained were allowed closer than fifty yards to the chain-link perimeter fence. Twice a month the military, which had encamped around the CDC, opened the gates and delivered food and supplies to the empty parking lot in front of the old admin building. Cate and her team had been instructed to wait until the forklift operator (outfitted in a Racal suit) was back outside the locked compound gates before leaving the building and approaching the shipment. Notwithstanding the precautions, some of the staff still feared the parcels might be contaminated, even though there was no verifiable data on Cobalt transmission via inorganic substances. They donned their own Racal suits and took the shipments apart carefully, exposing everything to ultraviolet light or pouring bleach over the containers.

Because of their isolation, Cate was startled one evening when the SatPhone rang. She stared at it blankly, wondering who it could be. The only calls she ever got were from HHS headquarters in Washington, someone asking for an update, which Cate dutifully gave, and which never pleased the caller. She lifted the handset from the charger and said, "CDC, Special Pathogens Branch."

"Cate?" came a distorted, hollow-sounding voice. "Cate? Is that you?"

"Dr. Cloudburst?" She hadn't heard from Sally Cloudburst in over a year, and then it was just a cryptic note telling her "things were progressing" and that she would keep Cate "in the loop," which she had failed to do. "Yes, it's me," said Cate. "How are you?"

"Doing great. I'm glad to know you're all right."

"Well, if not making any progress is doing all right, then I guess we are."

Cloudburst laughed. "Well, we're making enough progress here for the both of us."

"Sally, where is *here*? I know you're in Nevada, but where?"

"In an installation set up long ago, before the outbreak."

"A biological-research installation?

"Among other things, yes."

"How come I never heard about it?"

"You're hearing about it now. How would you like to visit us out here?"

"Out there?"

"We've made a marvelous leap forward, Cate. We've been working on Stage One for five years now, and it's nearly complete. Stage Two is about to begin, and I need your help."

"Stage Two?" asked Cate. "What is this, a NASA project? We going back to Mars?"

"Only slightly less ambitious," said Cloudburst. "This may be the biggest thing ever—it's certainly the most important, given what Cobalt has done. I want you out here."

"But who'll take my place here?"

"Donna can handle it. We've got everything you need out here. And more. You're coming."

"Are the roads open out west?"

"You're not going by road. Get packed. They're picking you up tomorrow morning."

"Seat belts secure, ma'am?" asked the pilot from the front seat.

Cate nodded, then remembering, said, "Roger."

"Name's Commander Dalton." He flipped an overhead switch. "Been up in a jet before?"

"Airliners," said Cate.

"Dinosaurs," laughed Dalton. "You have breakfast this A.M?"

"No," said Cate. "They told me not to."

"That's good," said Dalton, his finger on the ignition button. "'Cause anyone who pukes in my jet eats it twice." The two turbines roared to life. The instrument panel in front of her lit up. "Hartsfield unicom," said Dalton in his pilot monotone, "this is Raptor x-ray two-niner-niner, taxiing to runway three-one via charlie." In her headset, Cate could hear nothing but static. "Thanks, y'all," drawled Dalton. "Glad you guys are on top of it." He eased the throttles forward and the jet moved down the taxiway.

Cate tightened her seat belt again. "Does this have an ejection seat?"

"Yes, ma'am, but you won't need it. I've only crashed once, and that was early on in flight training."

"How long ago was that?" asked Cate, knowing she sounded about eighty years old.

"A couple of years ago. Out in Colorado. Electrical fire. Walked away, though. Those little Cessnas are easy to land. Engine quits, you just lift the nose, slow her to seventy knots, hunt for a flat place, and glide in. Unfortunately, these Raptors drop like stones if the power plant fails. But don't worry, I'll get you out if that happens, and the only thing you'll have is a sore tailbone."

"Tailbone?"

"The ejector seat hits the ground at about twenty-five miles an hour, which tends to compress the spine a little. But you'll walk away. Or limp, rather." He chuckled.

They taxied past the terminal. Over fifty big jets sat at the gates, their once shiny skins dirty from nonuse. Theirs was the only aircraft that was moving or was likely to. "Hartsfield traffic, Raptor x-ray two-niner-niner is holding at runway three-one," said Dalton.

Nothing on the headset. Cate was about to ask about that when Dalton said, "Nothing's on my scope, but you can bet that if I didn't check in, I'd get clobbered by some VFR fool on a short final." He pulled out into the runway and the engines cycled up. "Hartsfield traffic, Raptor x-ray two-niner-niner is rolling on three-one. Adios." The runway numbers passed below them. Dalton shoved the throttles forward and suddenly Cate's seat belts loosened as she was pressed deep into her seat. Within seconds, they were going straight up, and Cate could see only sky. Her stomach churned emptily. She tasted bile in her throat and tried not to panic.

"Be in Nevada in a couple of hours," said Dalton. "In the meantime, just enjoy the ride." With that, he smoothly rolled the aircraft once and headed west at twice the speed of sound.

THREE

YUCCA MOUNTAIN

Cate stood on the dirt runway. It was just after noon, and the sun beat mercilessly on the parched, cracked flats, bleaching all color from her sight, except the shiny silver of the F-45 Raptor, which was already taxiing away. Suddenly, out of the shimmering heat haze, an olive-green Hummer appeared. Dalton had told Cate to stand still, her empty hands at her side. She did as she was told, sweating through her white tee shirt.

The Hummer stopped a few paces away and two men got out, outfitted in bright blue Racal suits. They both had holstered sidearms. She could not see their faces behind their face plates. One dropped a Racal suit on the ground in front of Cate and stepped back.

"Where's Dr. Cloudburst?" asked Cate, sitting down and putting one leg into the suit.

The men did not answer. They simply watched her suit up. She poked her head into the helmet and zipped up, patting the Velcro over the zipper. She activated the internal fans with her chin and a blast of hot air circulated. One of the men gave her a thumbs up and she reciprocated. They opened the Hummer tailgate and she got in with her duffle. The door shut soundly behind her. The engine started and the Hummer lurched forward, kicking up white dust.

From the air, Cate had noted that the surrounding desert was made up of barren, shallow, alkaline valleys interrupted by low, gray, eroded hills. The Hummer approached a long rill running north and south, no more than five hundred feet at its highest point, the only indication of habitation being the antennas and satellite dishes clustered on its spine. As they got closer, she saw a half circle cut into the side of a hill, cleverly disguised to be virtually invisible from the air. From the ground, however, it was obviously an entry portal. A giant double door, a good twenty feet tall, was opening for them. Two angular matte-gray Comanche attack helicopters sat near the entrance. The Hummer passed between the two doors, which immediately began closing behind them. Fluorescent lights far overhead illuminated the darkness of a great staging area, but Cate's eyes took a while to adjust. There were a number of vehicles parked inside, and two freight elevators at the far end.

The Hummer pulled into a parking space. The rear hatch was opened. Cate grabbed her duffle and got out, heading for the elevators, which were labeled with nuclear and biological hazard stickers. Cate sighed. She was home.

"What is this place?" asked Cate, sitting in Cloudburst's tiny office, deep underground, drinking a Sprite and feeling wilted, even though the air conditioning made the room frigid.

"Feels familiar, I'll bet," said Dr. Cloudburst. She had dropped a lot of weight since Cate had seen her last, almost four years ago. Her high, wide cheekbones stood out sharply, making her normally round face triangular in shape. Her black hair was quite short and she wore fatigue pants and an olive tee shirt.

"You're in the Army now," said Cate, stating the obvious.

"This is a USAMRIID installation," said Cloudburst, pronouncing it "you-sam-rid." The United States Army Medical Research Institute of Infectious Diseases had its headquarters at Fort Detrick in Frederick, Maryland. It rose to prominence after helping to contain the Ebola-Reston viral outbreak in the late 1980s. Long before the Special Pathogens Branch of the CDC built its own warren of biosafety-level 4 labs in Atlanta, USAMRIID had similar facilities in Maryland, and following the first viral outbreaks, a turf war began between the two competing agencies. Cate thought the CDC had won.

"Obviously, they didn't give up stateside virus studies after all," said Cate. "You say they have over a dozen Level 4 labs? That's more than we had."

"Amazing how much funding you can get when your program is off budget," said Cloudburst. She leaned forward. "Everything here is state of the art. Three electron microscopes and a crack staff that was never affected by the outbreak."

"How did they manage that?" asked Cate. "They shoot everyone who came near?"

"You saw the place on approach," said Cloudburst. "Yucca Mountain has long been a restricted area because of the nuclear storage facilities. It's also the perfect place to study Cobalt."

"How long have the labs been here?"

"There was a Cobalt outbreak in the Congo in 2017. It was kept quiet because we didn't know what we were dealing with and we had our hands full with Ebola-Djakarta. But we knew it was something unprecedented when those three lab workers died in Fort Collins."

"I thought they died from Marburg-Ivory Coast. Failure to follow safety procedures."

"There was no breach of safety protocol. The bodies were incinerated, the labs sealed, and the samples moved out here, all quietly. Cobalt's first American victims died in 2018, not 2029." She looked squarely at Cate. "This lab has been working on Cobalt since then."

"Wait a minute," said Cate. "You mean we were replicating in Atlanta what you had already done out here?"

"Not exactly. When initial study revealed the stunning complexity of the Cobalt RNA, they divided up the workload. Our job in Atlanta was to take the conventional approach: go after Cobalt one protein at a time; search the entire human genome for the gene that might turn the virus off before it turned us off. That's what you've been doing."

"Unsuccessfully," said Cate. "Apparently, there is no such gene. And Cobalt's RNA contains a billion possible recombinants that mutate constantly, putting us back to square one each time." She settled back in the chair. "There is no conventional answer to Cobalt, Doctor, so I hope your *unconventional* approaches have been more successful."

"That's exactly what *did* succeed," said Cloudburst, standing. "Come with me. There's someone I want you to meet."

Cloudburst took Cate down the elevator another twelve floors and along a long, curving hallway. They stopped before a doorway and Cloudburst punched in a code. The door clicked open. They entered a large, low-ceilinged room with fabric-covered cubicles filling the center. It was warmer in here; a supercomputer was near, churning out answers and heat. Cloudburst led Cate past a number of cubicles. Inside each one was a tech working at a computer. No one paid any attention to their passing.

Cloudburst headed toward a double door at the far end of the room labeled RESTRICTED ENTRY. Another code, and suddenly Cate found herself in a luxurious living area, furnished with sofas, bookshelves, throw rugs, a couple of HPs, and all along one wall, big plastic boxes overflowing with toys. Children's artwork was posted all along the right-hand wall, ranging from finger paintings to stick figures and finally to houses, animals, and even one of Dr. Cloudburst.

"Day care?" asked Cate.

"You could say that."

The doors off the main room led to a kitchen, baths, and bedrooms. Cate counted three bedrooms, but only one was apparently occupied. They stopped before a closed door, a large rectangular window just past it. Cloudburst touched the glass and the reflective surface became transparent.

Inside, sitting on a couch, reading, was Ron Ashby. He looked up and squinted, and from that, Cate guessed the window remained a mirror on his side. He went back to reading. Sitting opposite him at a desk was a black boy about sixteen, tall and slender, with large eyes and closely cropped hair. He wore green surgical scrub pants and a tie-dyed tee shirt. He tapped a stylus on a ComPad.

"Our breakthrough," said Cloudburst. "His name is Russell."

"What kind of breakthrough?"

"He's immune to Cobalt."

Cate's mouth dropped open. "How?"

"That's why you're here."

"How long has he been here?"

"About five years," said Cloudburst. "Would you like to meet him?"

Cate was stunned. Immune to Cobalt? Impossible. "You're sure it's safe?" she asked. "I mean, if he's immune, he might be a natural reservoir and dangerous to us."

Cloudburst laughed. "Do you think I'd let Ron in there if he was?" Cate laughed, and so did Cloudburst. "No, really," she said. "I wouldn't expose even Ron to such a thing. It's safe. We don't know why Russell is immune; that's why you're here: to find out." She opened the door.

When Cate stepped into the doorway, she saw all color drain from Ron's face. He stared at her. "Hello, Ron," she said, remembering their last, uncomfortable encounter.

Ron got to his feet. He had put on weight and was now a good thirty pounds above what he should be. "Cate," he said, his face beet red. "I didn't know you were coming." He gave Cloudburst a quick, angry look.

"We weren't sure she *was* coming," said Cloudburst. She turned to the boy. "And this," she said, "is Russell. Russell, this is Dr. Seagram. She's going to work here now."

Russell looked up at Cate blankly, then went back to tapping on the ComPad.

"Nice to meet you," said Cate, holding out her hand.

Russell took her hand limply and then went back to his work. Cate looked to see what he was doing, expecting a composition or arithmetic. Instead, he had been copying a series of capital letters in a large, unsure hand.

"Very good, Russell," said Cloudburst. "Pretty soon, we'll start on cursive, right?"

The boy nodded, completing a shaky capital "D."

Cloudburst took Cate's arm and led her out. Ron attempted to follow them, but Cloudburst shook her head. Ron turned back, but not before saying to Cate, "I'm glad you're here." Cate nodded, not knowing what to say. The door shut and she and Cloudburst looked through the one-way window. Russell still focused on the ComPad.

"Is he . . . retarded?" asked Cate.

"No, he was just surprised. I think he missed you."

Cate laughed. "Not Ron, the boy! Is he slow or something?"

"You might say that. But we're doing the best we can to help him."

"What about his parents?"

"Dead."

"Cobalt?"

"I suppose so. We're all the family he has."

"Are there others?"

"No," said Cloudburst. "Russell is the only one we know of."

"Have you been studying his DNA? Any abnormalities? Mutations? What are you comparing it to? Who's your control group? You'd better, you know, get a serotype similar to his to compare—"

"All in good time," said Cloudburst, steering Cate away. "After a night's rest, you'll start. And maybe, with your help, we'll finish the job we began so long ago."

Cate nodded, her mind awhirl with possibilities, and let Cloudburst lead her away.

F O U R

RUSSELL

Russell frowned at the paper in front of him. When he tired of drawing things he'd seen on holos or in books, he liked to draw security-cam views, even though they were all the same. Flat, white ground with low, gray hills. Sometimes he put houses on the flat ground and trees on the hills. He didn't have brown in his watercolor set, but he could make it by combining red and blue and yellow. If he put black and white together, he got gray, so with brown and gray, he had most of the colors he needed. And blue, mixed with white, for the pale sky. He wondered if those were the real colors, or if the monitors changed them. Captain Lomax sighed and said the colors were as Russell had painted them, pretty much.

Russell had to take his word for it; he had never been above ground. He'd never felt the rain on his face or seen the sun rise, except on the security cameras. He liked to get up early and go as far up as they'd let him, just a few floors below ground, to the security pod, and watch the sun come up on the monitors. As the cameras cycled, one view nearly identical to another, he listened to the soldiers talk about the "good old days" before Cobalt, the disease that killed everyone who lived above ground. Everyone that is, except Russell. It made him feel special, not birthday-party special, but more like strange special or weird special. He tried to remember the good old days when he used to live up there, above ground. They said they'd found him in a big city, lost, but he couldn't remember that. His first memory was Dr. Cloudburst's brown face smiling down at him. She wasn't his mother, but she was like a mother. He couldn't remember his mother at all. Mama Cloudburst said she had died from Cobalt too. So had his father. He was alone, but he was *special*, and so he had to live down here underground until they found out why.

He looked up from the desk. All along the wall were his pictures. He knew they were his because he had signed them, though he didn't remember most of them. His memory was like a ball that rolled under the couch. You knew it was there, but you couldn't see it.

He scooped green into the mixing area on the plastic palette and added yellow and a little red, making a light brown. He painted a horizontal line and filled in the foreground, varying the color a little until it looked like a long way to the horizon. He wanted to make it as much like the dream as he could. He clenched his sore fingers, then dipped the brush into red and added yellow to make orange. He drew a half circle just above the horizon, the setting sun. Above it he put low-hanging gray clouds, tinted a little with yellow from the sun. Captain Lomax taught him to do that, to let the light touch things in a picture. Then he painted a tiny black tree far off in the distance, almost to the horizon, with long, thin branches and a flat top of green leaves.

Russell leaned back. Something was missing, but he didn't know what. He put the brush into the cleaning water and stood. The paper was curling from the wet paint. It was a good picture, but it wasn't done. He smiled. He'd just drawn something he'd never seen before, not even in a holo. It might exist somewhere on top of the ground, up in the world he might never see in person. He thought it was probably real because looking at it made him feel happy.

Cate studied the mucus cells scraped from Russell's throat, cells that in everyone else were susceptible to Cobalt. Twenty-four hours ago, she had introduced a Cobalt virus into the cells, which had ingested it, but the Cobalt Trojan Horse just sat there while Russell's lysosomes steadily ate away at its protein shell, finally exposing the RNA and consuming it too. In the end, the virus was reduced to nothing but tiny, harmless bits floating in the watery cell cytoplasm.

She knew there were a dozen steps along the way where the key to killing Cobalt might lie, but each step contained almost countless protein and enzyme combinations that might or might not be responsible. Why didn't Cobalt, once inside Russell's cell, commandeer its DNA and start making replicas of itself? Why did it just sit there while the cell gathered its resources and destroyed it?

There was something else, too. Cate had studied thousands of cells. She had learned to distinguish between simian and human cells, even between humans and lemurs, mankind's closest cousin. She could look at chromosomes of any organism and know roughly what genus it was, and sometimes even the species.

She opened an electron-scope view of Russell's chromosomes, the forty-six tightly wound packets of DNA contained in the nucleus of every cell. She examined the threadlike DNA strand from Chromosome 21, one of the shortest chromosomes, containing just fifty million nucleotide bases that coded just a few hundred genes. But though they knew the total number of genes in Chromosome 21, they didn't know what ninety-five percent of them actually *did*.

She zeroed in on the tip of Chromosome 21, a repeating string of DNA molecules called *telomeres* that acted like the yellow ceramic bumps on a freeway warning drivers of an imminent stop ahead. In young cells, telomeres were quite long. Each time a cell split, the telomeres shortened a bit, as if someone had pried loose a few of those ceramic bumps. When a cell was old and nearing the end of its life cycle, the telomeres became very short.

Cate frowned. The telomeres at the tip of Chromosome 21 were very short. And that meant Russell was *very* old.

Via Satellite

Chris stepped out of the library with a pillowcase full of books slung over his shoulder, a kind of perverse Santa Claus, taking instead of giving. It was high summer and the brown grass in front of the Post Office across the square was a foot high. Someone had attached a corkboard to an exterior brick wall. Several people waited in the square to look at it. When it was his turn, Chris approached the bulletin board, reading the notices. Bill Grady shot a buck and was curing the meat. He would leave it on the tables in front of the Smith's supermarket on Friday for anyone who needed any. Dorothy Harrison was sick, but only with a cold. Lynn Dimick needed someone to clean her chimney, which was plugged with creosote.

But dominating the board was a large, neon green sheet with OFFICIAL GOVERNMENT NOTICE: SPECIAL SATELLITE BROADCAST printed at the top. Underneath the caption, it read THURSDAY, JUNE 7, 9:00 P.M. EASTERN TIME.

The government updates were usually broadcast the first Monday of the month. President Burrows, her hair gone from auburn to mousy gray, generally talked about the progress they were making in getting the country back on its feet. Power plant restarts, road-clearing efforts, food distribution. But no convoy had ever delivered food to Kalispell. Chris didn't expect one—in the last election, Montana's electoral votes went to Burrows' rival. He turned and shouted to the man well behind him. "What day is it?"

"Thursday the seventh," yelled the man.

Chris looked at the green flyer again. The broadcast was tonight.

That evening, Chris pedaled his bike down to the Seidel cabin, which had a solar-powered satellite receiver. He poured himself a drink of Seidel's eighteen-year-old single malt scotch and made himself comfortable on the leather sofa. He keyed the remote. An image of the world popped up above the holo projector. He lit one of Seidel's cigars and leaned back. Smoking was a retro habit he'd taken up, in addition to hunting with Seidel's Winchester rifle. He'd even killed a deer last winter, and when he ate the barbecued venison, it was so good tears filled his eyes. Perhaps he might survive after all.

When Chris first entered the empty Seidel place back in '29, after being scared shitless by the towering stuffed grizzly, he checked out the house. Most people died in their own beds. Where was Seidel and his family?

Then one afternoon almost two years later, while walking back toward the house after being down by the river looking for a good place to set a trout snare, he finally met Charles Seidel. Charles was sitting with his back against the garage wall, a skeleton in a flannel shirt and jeans. Grass grew up through his rib cage. On the ground a few feet away was a snub-nosed .357 S&W revolver. There were five bullets remaining in the cylinder and a hole in Charles' skull. *Why did you do it?* thought Chris. *You survived the outbreak, and yet you still cashed it in. Why?*

Looking around, he found the answer. A few yards away, on the overgrown riverbank, were four grassy mounds. Chris looked back at Seidel's skeleton. Though Seidel's "my four-by-four is bigger than yours" lifestyle initially repulsed him, he now saw that Charles Seidel wasn't such an ogre after all. He was merely a throw-back, and when Cobalt broke, he was probably as prepared as anybody could be. When his family died, he buried them, cleaned and straightened the house, sat down behind the garage, smoked his last cigar (Chris found the butt on the ground by Seidel's left hand), and raised his gun. Seidel was a realist, and his was the only realistic solution.

Waiting for the satellite broadcast to begin, Chris puffed the cigar. *I misjudged you, Chuck,* he thought, looking at the hunting trophies crowding the paneled walls. *You didn't kill for pleasure; you killed because, unlike the rest of us, you knew how things actually* were. *You were prepared to do whatever it took to care for your family. And when you were done caring for them, you sat down, had a good smoke, and joined them.* Chris lifted his tumbler of amber liquid. "Way to go, Chuck. You did all right."

The music fanfare ended and the hologram changed. The Presidential Seal appeared, then dissolved to a podium in front of the White House Seal, though Chris doubted President Burrows was still in Washington. She was probably ensconced in some hardened bunker, giving orders and eating little better than everybody else. Finally, the politicians knew how ordinary people lived. If there ever was another government—a *real* government, not just a monthly chest-thumping news conference—the leaders might actually be attuned to the people. But then, Chris was an optimist.

President Burrows appeared, dressed in a gray suit, which nicely complimented her steel-gray eyes. The old gal's calm demeanor, ever matronly and capable, still shone through. Though the times had put more than a few years on her face, she still looked like someone who could wrestle any senator to her point of view. "My fellow Americans," she said.

Chris raised his glass. "At your service." A good buzz was coming on.

"After years of tragedy, it is my profound pleasure to share with you the best news we've heard in a decade. Though our country has been decimated, the government has continued working to defeat Cobalt. Now, finally, after more than ten years of study, scientists at the Centers for Disease Control have achieved a remarkable breakthrough. I will now turn the time over to the director of the Special Pathogens Branch, Dr. Sally Cloudburst, who comes to us from her research labs."

Chris nearly spilled his scotch. Wasn't that the name of Cate's supervisor in Atlanta?

The scene changed and after a moment of ghost imaging, Cloudburst appeared in a white lab coat, standing in front of the CDC logo. "Thank you, Madame President. As you know, Cobalt is a virus that invades a cell, hijacks its DNA, and uses the cell to make copies of itself—so many copies that eventually the cell explodes and dies, releasing thousands of new Cobalt viruses, which then seek other cells to invade and destroy. This is true of all viruses, but Cobalt has a unique characteristic: it constantly changes its genetic structure, making study of it nearly impossible. Because human DNA is non-resistant to Cobalt, studying the virus itself was the only way to solve the problem, and we have had, sadly, very little success. Until now. We have found someone who is immune to Cobalt."

Chris almost came out of his seat. The scene changed and there was a black teenager sitting on a couch, looking into the camera. Cloudburst's voice continued: "His name is Russell, and he has been the subject of rigorous study for the last five years. The Cobalt viruses that invade Russell's cells do not destroy them. In fact, Russell's cells destroy the Cobalt virus as easily as your and my cells overcome a flu virus. Hello, Russell," said Cloudburst's voice. "How are you today?"

Russell smiled at the camera, the kind of fake smile kids put on. "I like to draw."

"You certainly do," said Cloudburst. "How do you feel today?"

"Okay, I guess. Bored. I like the desert. It's really big—"

"Yes, it is," interrupted Cloudburst. "You know you're the only person we've found that is immune to Cobalt, don't you?"

Russell nodded.

Chris frowned. Why was she talking down to the kid?

"Why do you think that is?" asked Cloudburst.

"Just lucky, I guess. I wish I could see a tree. On the monitors, there aren't any—"

The camera cut back to Cloudburst, who began detailing Russell's daily routine. A film clip popped up in a corner of the holo, showing a living area with toys and crude drawings hung on a wall.

Russell entered the frame and the camera followed as he went into a room and sat down with a ComPad and started writing. Several cuts showed him exercising on a weight machine, running on a treadmill, eating cereal at a table, and watching the HP.

The clip ended and Cloudburst said, "Russell is an amazing boy, and in his cells is the secret to defeating Cobalt. Our team of scientists"—and here the scene shifted to a large room of cubicles, the camera dollying past several of white-coated people studying printouts and holograms—"are doing everything in their power to unlock its mysteries."

Chris dropped his drink. Cate was on-screen, sitting in a cubicle, looking at a hologram that filled the air between her and the camera, her eyes intently searching a slowly rotating DNA molecule. "Cate!" he barked. The scene changed and a group of scientists was sitting around a mahogany conference table. And there Cate was again, using her hands as she talked, the way she always did. "You're alive!"

Cloudburst's voice-over continued. ". . . and we are making progress. It is much easier to study the one, static cell type that defeats Cobalt than the ever-changing virus itself. Our researchers, the best the country has to offer, have been gathered here—"

"Where?" shouted Chris. "Where the hell are you?"

". . . the President has given us access to all the resources of the federal government—"

In one of the shots, the camera moved past an olive-uniformed soldier at parade rest, his hands behind his back, standing in front of a doorway. The patch on his shoulder had an "M" with three interlocking ovals below it. Then it was gone.

As Cloudburst droned on, Chris shouted, "Cate, where are you?"

At last the scene shifted back to Cloudburst. "With Russell's invaluable help, we are certain that a cure for Cobalt is near. It is only a matter of time. Madame President?"

The transmission cut back to the President. "Thank you, Dr. Cloudburst. My fellow Americans, it has been a grim five years. Most of our countrymen are dead, and the rest of you are struggling to stay alive. Help is on the way. We believe it is, to echo Dr. Cloudburst, 'only a matter of time.' In the meantime, please cooperate with the authorities, and above all, have hope, which has always been our greatest strength. And may God bless America." The Presidential Seal appeared on the holo. Chris sat back, stunned. *Haven't heard that in a long time,* he thought. *God bless America.*

If Cate were still alive, maybe there was a God, and maybe He actually did.

He fell asleep in the lounge chair that night, his feet warmed by the fire of *The Time Machine*, a book with particular resonance to Chris. He, too, was in a time machine, only instead of a fearful future, he had been hurled into a dark past, where you had to burn books for light to read them by.

Suddenly his eyes popped open. *He mentioned a desert with no trees. Why, then, did the guard's arm patch have a tree on it?* He reached and tossed a couple of unread novels into the fireplace and opened an old road atlas. Soon the room was full of light. No deserts back east—it had to be out west. Somewhere far from people, but not too far. You needed construction crews to build installations as big as the CDC needed. He flipped pages. It had to be somewhere in the Great Basin. To the south. Only five possible locations: Utah, Nevada, California, Arizona, or New Mexico. He turned to the map of California. Big enough, and there were remote areas, but California had had a federal building moratorium since 2015, due to environmentalist lobbying.

What about Arizona? Also the site of a burgeoning environmentalist culture. Whenever a trial balloon was lofted about a government project, they came out in force, blockading roads and sabotaging earth movers. Besides, for the last fifteen years, the governor of Arizona had been a Green Party leader. No, not Arizona.

New Mexico? Too unstable politically, shifting constantly from liberal to conservative.

Utah? Too weird for nonmilitary installations, but ideal for military bases. Several had been constructed there since the turn of the century. It might be Utah. Or Nevada, with the largest tracts of desert in the whole country. Utah or Nevada. His road was clear for the first two hundred miles, anyway: south.

S I X

SCRATCHING THE SURFACE

Chris stood on the highway just south of Jackson Hole, Wyoming, looking down at the flat tire on his bike. The sun had slipped behind the mountains and the sky was a deep, perfect blue. Before he left Kalispell, he buried Charles Seidel next to his wife and children, cleaned up the house and locked the doors, placing the key under the mat. He did the same at the Allen place. A stack of books remained, unread and unburned, next to the lounge chair, in case he ever returned.

He filled his knapsack with protein bars and bottled water, and headed south. The first fifty miles were an easy ride. Then the road climbed into the mountains, heading for Missoula. Wet weather trapped him for two days in a musty motel room in Evaro. He ate canned fruit and watched sheets of water cascading off the eaves, turning the parking lot into a shallow lake.

He fished in streams along the way. The rod and reel was one of only two things he'd taken from the Seidel's. The other was the .357 pistol, Charles' five remaining bullets still in the cylinder.

Standing now at the side of the road, Chris looked back at Jackson, wondering where he should bed down for the night. Just then a big blue GMC pickup rumbled around the curve in the two-lane road. Surprised, he nevertheless stepped aside to let it pass. It stopped a few yards beyond him and the driver waved him forward. Chris walked to the passenger side, the .357 held loosely in his quilted vest pocket. The window rolled down. Inside, a hatchet-faced man with piercing blue eyes, long gray hair, and a Seattle Seahawks baseball cap eyed him.

"Hi," said Chris. "My tire's flat."

"Hey," said the man. He had a Slim Jim jerky stick poking out of his mouth like a cigar.

"I need a lift," said Chris. "How far you going?"

"All the way," said the man. "You can come along, but you gotta chip in."

"I don't have any money."

"I mean provisions. You scout, find us food and such. You okay with that?"

"Sure," said Chris. "I got a mask and gloves. I'll find what we need."

"Shit, Cobalt eats right through that stuff," said the man. Chris reached for the handle. "In the back," said the man. "And put on your mask."

"I thought you said they didn't work."

The man laughed. "How'd you live this long? For all you know, *I* might be the one with Cobalt."

The guy's name was Elvin Udall, and he was from Twin Falls, Idaho, but had come to Yellowstone to hunt gray wolves. He showed Chris a big furry coat he'd made from their skins. "Keepin' the balance, now that the rangers are gone," he laughed.

Chris liked Elvin immediately. Spending time with the ghost of Charles Seidel had prepared him for Elvin's type. If there was trouble, Elvin could probably handle it, but his one shortcoming, besides never taking the jerky out of his mouth, was his gift of gab. Inside of an hour, he'd worn Chris out, talking out the window as they slowly tooled up the winding canyon road, forcing Chris to yell back. Chris was soon hoarse, so he slumped down behind the two fifty-gallon gas barrels that sloshed next to him. He wondered where Elvin had gotten so much fuel.

At a rest stop, Elvin said that diesel was basically Jet-A fuel, so he siphoned gas from airplanes. "I got four-wheel drive, too," he said proudly. "And you need it, because there's pile-ups on the road, usually thrown up by outlaws. That's why I got these." He walked over to the truck bed and threw an oily canvas tarp aside. Inside a wooden box were two-dozen hand grenades, resting like eggs in fibreboard cups. "I just toss one of these in their direction, hit the gas, and breeze through. Now that you're in the back, you can chuck 'em if we need to."

Chris blanched. He'd been bouncing along next to the grenades all afternoon.

They were at a rest stop in the mountains overlooking Star Valley, Wyoming, the Palisades Reservoir glistening below them. Chris had been admiring the view through his binoculars. He laughed. "Hey, some guy's water-skiing."

"Why not?" said Elvin. "He loves to ski, I love the road, and you love . . . what, Chris?"

"A girl, I guess."

Elvin hooted. "Why that's the best hobby of all! She still around?"

"She's still alive, I know that. But I don't know exactly where she is. I saw her on that satellite broadcast about a week ago, you know, where they showed that kid who's immune to Cobalt."

"Oh, that," said Elvin, snorting. "That's just a bunch of happy horseshit they feed us so we don't go starting another country without 'em. There's no breakthrough."

"Cate was on that holo, working at the place where they're studying Cobalt. I haven't seen her since before the outbreak. Now that I know she's alive, I want to find her and tell her something I've been meaning to say for five years."

Elvin chewed his jerky, considering. "So it's a quest, huh? True love and all that?"

Chris nodded, a little embarrassed.

Elvin opened the passenger door, gesturing for Chris to get in. Then he got in the driver's side. "Now that's a good reason for a journey."

They stopped on the eastern shore of the Great Salt Lake. The sun was setting and the perfectly still lake was a mirror of blue sky and pink, wispy clouds. "You know," said Elvin out of the blue, "your trip is kind of like a knight's errand—rescuing a princess."

Elvin was an interesting guy. He'd read a lot, traveled extensively, and served eight years in the military. When he heard that, Chris described the guard's arm patch he'd seen on the holo, hoping Elvin might know something about it.

"Draw it," said Elvin, indicating the ground.

Chris kneeled on the road shoulder. "Something like this," he said, scratching in the dirt with his finger:

Elvin laughed. "How'd you live this long?"

"You know what it is?"

"I'm surprised you don't, being a college boy and all." Elvin took a stick and traced the drawing. "Of course, that's the atomic symbol at the bottom. Above it is an 'M.' But you missed the other letter."

"What other letter?"

"The 'Y,'" said Elvin, "Inside the 'M.' Get it now?"

Chris frowned at the drawing. "M-Y. Y-M. Atoms." Then he saw it. "Ah! The nuclear waste repository at Yucca Mountain."

Elvin nodded. "Yup. Nevada."

OLDER THAN HIS YEARS

"No, it's spelled with a 'C,' not a 'K,'" said Cate, leaning over Russell's shoulder, watching him write her name. His cursive was coming along well, considering he only learned to block-letter a couple of weeks ago. He looked up at her, confused. "But that's wrong, isn't it? Shouldn't it be a 'K'?"

"Names don't follow the usual rules."

"Mine does," said Russell. "Two 'S's and two 'L's. That makes it easy."

"Yes," said Cate. "Your parents were wise. Mine were trying to be creative. My name is actually Catherine, and Cate is just a shortened version of that."

"Shouldn't it be Cathy, then?" asked Russell.

Cate smiled. Russell had turned out to be much smarter than she originally thought. He wasn't slow or retarded, he was just unschooled. Dr. Cloudburst said when he came to Yucca, he didn't know how to read or write, and his memory was jumbled. When Cate asked him about his parents, she got a blank expression, even as Russell showed her a picture of his mother. "Her name was Joanna," said Russell. "Do you think I look like her?"

"A little, but her nose is different than yours. Maybe you take after your father. Do you have a picture of him?"

Russell shook his head.

"Do you remember him?"

Russell shook his head again.

"But you remember your mother."

Russell looked up. "No. Just from the picture." His hands trembled, the knuckles knobby and red. She often saw him rubbing them, as if they pained him.

"Russell, when did you come here? Do you remember?"

"I don't remember anything."

"Nothing before the outbreak, like where you lived?"

He shook his head.

"They found you in Seattle after the outbreak. Do you remember Seattle?

"No."

"Very green. Rains a lot."

He shook his head, staring past her.

She could tell he was getting upset. "A nearby volcano with snow on the top?"

"A what?" asked Russell. "I know what snow is—I've seen it on holos. But what's a volcano?"

Cate looked at Russell. Who doesn't know what a volcano is? "It's a mountain that's made from molten rock—looks like a pyramid, sort of."

His expression indicated he didn't know that word, either.

"My head hurts," said Russell.

She patted him on the shoulder. "Okay. Why don't you take a nap?"

"Okay," he said, getting to his feet and shuffling off, his back bent like an old man.

Cate turned into the conference room. Dr. Cloudburst was supervising the placement of the HoloCams. The CDC banner hung on the wall behind a Plexiglas podium. Cloudburst looked up. "I have an idea, Cate. Let's put you on camera this time. This scares me to death."

"I wouldn't know what to say," said Cate. "You're planning another broadcast?"

"The President wants regular updates. She's going to dish out the good news a little at a time, to keep the public encouraged."

"When you said, 'It's only a matter of time,' you certainly raised expectations."

"Yes, but Ron says we've eliminated over half of Russell's chromosomes, the ones that don't code resistant to Cobalt."

"It's really closer to one-third. That still leaves more than thirty we haven't looked at—and those include Chromosomes 1 through 5, the biggest ones. Ron's being optimistic."

"And you? What are you being? Pessimistic?"

"I need to talk to you."

"I'm really busy here, Cate. Can it wait?"

"No, it can't."

Cloudburst saw there was no arguing. "My office, then. Fifteen minutes."

"You're not telling me everything," said Cate, sitting on the sofa.

Cloudburst sat behind her desk. "What do you want to know?"

"How old is Russell?"

"We don't know exactly. Maybe seventeen. Why?"

"He looks twenty," said Cate.

"Okay," nodded Cloudburst. "He looks twenty. Mature for his age. And?"

"I've been here, what, almost six months, right? When I got here, he looked twelve."

Cloudburst shrugged. "Adolescence. He's grown a couple of inches in the last year."

"His telomeres are truncated."

"His what?"

"His telomeres!" said Cate. "You remember telomeres, the stop-coded DNA that terminates a chromosome?"

Cloudburst got to her feet, crossed the office, and closed the door. She turned to Cate. "I know what telomeres are. What's your point?"

"They're *shortened!* That means they're old. Russell's chromosomes are very old."

Cloudburst went back to her desk and sat down, looking intently at Cate. "Really. Then maybe we should focus on that. The telomeres might hold the key."

"Doctor!" said Cate, leaning forward. "Cut the shit. You're not dealing with some low-level cell-slicer here. I'm a better genetic engineer than you are. Something is wrong with Russell. He's aging prematurely. He has arthritis and low bone-calcium density."

"You don't have to be old to have that."

"Goddammit!" yelled Cate, getting to her feet. "Russell is not a seventeen-year-old boy! He's older than I am, older than you! Hell, he's older than anyone in this lab! I figure he's so old, he ought to be dead!" She paused, seething, glaring at Cloudburst. "Well?" she shouted.

"Sit down," said Cloudburst flatly. The authority in her voice pushed Cate back down onto the couch. "You're right," she continued. "Mostly. Russell is not that old. But his DNA is."

Cate shook her head to clear it. "That means he's . . . "

Cloudburst nodded. "Yes. He's a clone."

"A clone?" asked Cate. "A clone from whom?"

"We're not sure," said Cloudburst. "They found him—or rather, his prior self—wandering the streets of Seattle, after the outbreak. He was dazed and dehydrated, but he was not infected."

"How old was he?"

"In his late fifties."

"You said his prior self. He died?" Cloudburst nodded. "How?"

"Heart failure, not Cobalt-related. A cloning procedure was immediately initiated. I first heard about it when they finally obtained a viable embryo. Russell was born shortly after I arrived here, almost five years ago."

"Five years?"

"Yes," said Cloudburst. "They took one of his former self's mature cells and starved it of nutrients to reset its internal clock. Then they removed the nucleus from an unfertilized egg and electrically fused the egg and the adult cell. It took a few tries, but eventually they had a viable embryo."

"Who was the surrogate mother?"

"A service person working here. Her name was Joanna."

"At least you didn't lie about that," spat Cate. "Where is she now?"

"To avoid complications, we transferred her. Russell stayed behind."

"But she's his mother!"

"Not really. He has none of her DNA."

"What about mitochondrial DNA? The DNA in the cell cytoplasm?"

Cloudburst shrugged. "Negligible."

"Cloning is illegal," said Cate.

"In what *nation*, Cate?" said Cloudburst testily. "What Supreme Court exists to ban it now?" She shook her head. "Those laws were ridiculous anyway, passed by an uninformed legislature."

"But they *were* passed," argued Cate. "Overwhelmingly, after it was discovered that Mark Tollman, the crazy billionaire, was cloning himself for kidneys, livers, and even hearts. Dozens of clones trussed up in cages like lab rats, all to serve his insane desire to live forever."

"He was a madman. A Dr. Moreau."

"Funny you should mention him," said Cate. "Moreau was a doctor, like you. And you're exhibiting the same sort of megalomania he did."

"That's a novel, Cate. It's true, Tollman was borderline insane, and it was right to outlaw that kind of 'spare parts' cloning. But the kind we're doing here is completely different."

"So you say," said Cate, but she knew Cloudburst had a point. She was mostly angry at not being told about this before now. "But what's wrong with Russell? You say he's only five years old? Then why does he appear four times that old?"

"When the adult blastomere is starved to set its clock back, some genetic damage inevitably occurs. In addition, through *in vitro* gene therapy, we increased the somatotropin secretions in the pituitary gland."

"Why?"

"Because we had to see, as soon as possible, if his Cobalt immunity would last. Throughout his entire life, or only through adolescence? You know different genes turn on at different times—some in infancy, others in childhood, still others in adolescence, adulthood, and old age."

"So you're killing him."

"We're not killing him," growled Cloudburst. "And what would *you* do? Risk losing another generation of Americans before you knew why Russell was immune to Cobalt?"

Cate looked down. Of course she wouldn't. "And if he dies, there's always another, right?"

Cloudburst looked at her, eyes slitted, saying nothing.

"You've got scores of fertilized embryos in the freezer right now, don't you? Just in case this one doesn't pan out."

"You claim to be a geneticist, why don't you act like one?" spat Cloudburst. "Your moralizing is mere posturing. You're just angry we didn't tell you everything. Well, I just did. We have a subject who is immune to Cobalt. We intend to prevent the complete eradication of human life on this planet. And if that's not a lofty-enough goal for you, you're free to get the hell out of here."

Cate looked away. After the stem-cell debates of the century's first decade were settled and cloning of humans became possible, it was provisionally approved in rare instances only, like helping childless couples bear children. But when the Tollman atrocities were discovered in 2019, the public recoiled and all human cloning was banned outright. The cloning that Cloudburst was engaged in was a step back toward the horrifying Mark Tollmans of the world: rich people creating copies of themselves for use as spare parts.

But they were not doing that here. They were trying to solve the world's worst catastrophe, and whatever solution they could find would be used. But then Cate thought of Russell's dark, liquid eyes, so full of innocence and confusion, looking up at her for answers. The answer she'd just been given was, of course, one she could not share with him. "I just wish it weren't Russell."

"I held him in my arms when he was born," said Cloudburst softly. "I wouldn't do anything to hurt him. I love him."

"Do you really?"

Cloudburst nodded.

"Then why don't you tell him?" asked Cate.

"I will," said Cloudburst. "When the right time comes, I will."

Cate lay in bed a long time before falling asleep. After her talk with Cloudburst, she visited Russell again. She knew the security cams were monitoring her and if she said something wrong, she'd be whisked away. Russell would be given a prostatin injection, which would erase his short-term memory of the incident, and she would never be allowed to speak to him again.

So she just chatted with him, trying to gauge his general health. His skin was dull, not lustrous as it should be in a young black male. His hairline was already receding, though he had a high forehead to begin with. His hands trembled a little, which she now recognized as a side effect of the somatotropin on his pituitary gland. He tired easily. He was irritable and prone to emotional responses.

And he was very, very lonely. He'd taken to holding on to Cate's sleeve when they talked, and she knew he slept with a little stuffed toy that looked like a unicorn—another fictional creature, like him.

In her dream, Cate stood facing an earthen wall. It was cold and the wind whipped her hair about her face. Before her was a large round stone. When she reached out toward it, it rolled slowly to one side, exposing a small, rough-hewn cave opening. She bent down and peered inside. The air was musty and stale. She crawled in and followed the tunnel as it bent to the right. The floor was firm, flat, and dry. This was an excavated cave, not a natural one, and it was pitch black inside.

There was a burst of lightning outside, followed by a crack of thunder. After crawling a few feet, she touched an animal skin.

Something bulged under it. She tugged the skin aside. Lightning flashed again and imprinted the scene on Cate's retinas. She recoiled in horror. Several bodies lay in front of her, wrapped in black, glossy bandages. By each mummy's head was a white stone jar.

She had crawled into a tomb. Horrified, she backed out quickly, bumping her head on the low ceiling, drawing blood. Outside, she got to her feet and turned. She was standing on a narrow path cut into a steep, rocky cliff. The land fell off sharply to a rolling, grassy plain hundreds of feet below. Silver moonlight shone through tears in the low clouds hugging the walls surrounding the plain, illuminating the enclosed valley. A lone, spindly tree stood far out in the middle of the plain. She could make out a man standing by the tree, holding something large in his arms. A body?

Then another bolt of lightning stabbed earthward, striking the tree, sending up a shower of sparks, momentarily lighting the entire area around the tree. Darkness fell again, and the man with the burden was enveloped in black. But his face somehow remained, etched into Cate's brain.

Russell's face.

EIGHT

REUNION

"Get down!" hissed Elvin, tugging on Chris's pant leg. "They'll see you."

"So what?" said Chris, still standing, arms folded.

Elvin, much stronger than his wiry frame would admit, pulled Chris down flat on his stomach. "Listen, kid, I've been in the military, you haven't, so don't argue. Here." He gave the binoculars to Chris. "Check it out."

Chris put the glasses to his eyes. "What am I looking at?"

"See the entrance? That big half circle in the hillside?"

"Yeah. So?"

"See the choppers next to it? Those are thirty-millimeter chain guns slung along the side. And those big pods under the bellies? Hellfire rocket launchers."

"So?"

"So I'm just saying it ain't a sightseeing chopper. See those blinking red lights on those poles around the entrance? Motion detectors or cameras. I'm surprised they're not already shooting at us."

Chris gave the glasses back to Elvin. "Cate's in there, I know it." The sun had slipped below the horizon behind them. The entire desert glowed orange, the cloudless sky a brilliant red. It was insanely hot, and no breeze blew. "Why did they put this stuff way out here?"

"Ellis Air Force base is in Vegas, only a hundred miles away. This used to be a firing range, before they built the nuke-waste deposit," said Elvin, unfolding the sectional map in front of them. "See? All these restricted areas? And we're smack-dab in the middle of one."

"Maybe I should just go down and knock."

"How'd you live this long? They probably got remote gun placements. None of this 'Halt or be fired upon!' shit. You'll feel the air move and then a second later, you'll be lying there with a fifty-caliber slug through the chest."

"Thanks for that image," said Chris. "You don't need to stay, you know."

"You're gonna get killed."

"A knight's errand," said Chris. "Like you said."

"I say a lot of things. That don't mean you have to listen to them." He handed Chris the glasses and the map. "I'm going back to that little deserted town we passed. I'll wait a couple of days. If you make it out of there with your lady friend, stop in." He held out his hand. "You're a damn fool, Tempest."

Chris smiled, taking Elvin's hand. "Takes one to know one."

When the dust plume from Elvin's truck dissipated, Chris turned back. A sliver of moon hung behind him on the western horizon. His watch said 9:17. Calling Yucca Mountain a "mountain" was being generous. It rose no more than a thousand feet above the plain, looking just like any other gray, eroded, barren hill in the southern Nevada desert. He could not see one distinguishing feature to explain why they chose this place to store depleted uranium for the next hundred thousand years.

The facility entrance was camouflaged to match its surroundings. The dirt roads were devoid of tracks. All transport must have been by helicopter. Elvin was probably right. If he just walked down there, he'd probably get shot. He couldn't call them on the phone. There wasn't even any sage brush he could light as a signal fire. It was at least a three-mile hike to the entrance. There was another door in the mountain a half mile north, but a sand dune had blown up against it. He dug his toe into the sand, thinking.

"Hey, Captain, take a look at this."

Captain Lomax peered into the screen. "Huh. I'll be." He ran his hand through his crew cut, frowning.

"What is it?" asked Russell, still in his pajamas. Fascinated by sunrises, he liked to get up early and watch the monitors as the sun came up.

"Looks like we've got an intruder," said the corporal. "Shall I call the alarm?"

"What is that on the ground?" asked Lomax. "Switch to infrared."

Corporal Jennings flipped a switch. The visual instantly shifted to a bright whitish-green. They squinted into the monitors, their eyes adjusting to the light.

"Hey!" said Russell. "It says 'Cate.'"

"What?" asked Lomax. "Where?"

"There!" said Russell, tracing the arc on the monitor. "There's a 'C' and then an 'A' and a 'T-E.' 'Cate.' Like Dr. Seagram."

"Is that her first name?" asked Lomax.

"I still don't see it," said Jennings, adjusting the monitor's intensity.

"That's her name," said Russell proudly. "Cate. That's her."

Lomax nodded. "Russell, go wake Dr. Seagram. Tell her she's got a visitor."

The sun was just coming up over the Sheep Range to the east, sending long shafts of light across the dusty flats. Chris sat on the ground a mile west of the main entrance, feeling the sun on his face. Behind him, on the western horizon, Orion was setting.

During the night, he etched Cate's name into the cracked, soft earth in fifteen-foot letters. Afterward, he had an experience eerily similar to the one he had in the Sudanese desert back in '25. The black night sky was vivid, the steamy band of the Milky Way rising from the Sagittarius teapot. The air was utterly still, as if everything were holding its breath, and Chris did too. As he lay back on the warm ground, he marveled at the immensity of space and his tiny place in it, and felt, just below him, hundreds of feet underground, Cate breathing quietly, asleep.

He drifted down through the soft dirt, passing through concrete, his feet touching down on the floor of a dark hallway. He was covered head to toe with gray dust. He crept down the corridor, navigating by the homing beacon of Cate's steady heartbeat. Turning into a room, he saw her, sleeping, her short blonde hair framing her delicate features. He reached out to touch her cheek, and the alarm went off.

The air was suddenly full of a pulsing *whoop whoop whoop.* Chris came back to the present and scrambled to his feet, looking eastward, shielding his eyes from the sun. A Comanche helicopter was heading toward him, the underbelly rocket pods rotating into firing position. He raised his arms overhead and didn't move. The chopper set down twenty yards away. The turbine scream was deafening. A side door opened and someone jumped out in a blue Racal suit. The rotors raised a storm of dust, but he knew it was Cate. She undid the helmet latches as she ran toward him. He dropped his hands and ran toward her. Cate pulled her helmet off, tossing it aside. Her long hair flew out behind her. "Chris!"

They met like lovers in an old movie, embracing. She smelled like Dove soap and shampoo. He lifted her up and spun her around. She kissed his cheeks. "Chris, Chris, Chris."

Inside the chopper, the rotors slowed. They had lost Cate in the churning dust, but now they saw her again, hugging and kissing Chris. Captain Lomax pushed Jenning's rifle barrel down.

"She's insane!" said Jennings. "He might be seropositive."

"But he isn't," said Lomax. "We're not licked yet."

"What do you mean, sir?"

Lomax turned back. Cate was kissing Chris passionately. "Us. People. There's still hope."

ⅤⅤⅤ

"You violated security procedures."

Captain Lomax looked up. "Dr. Cloudburst. You're up early."

Cloudburst stood in Lomax's office doorway. She flipped on the lights, illuminating the room.

"I can't see the monitors," said Lomax.

"What difference does that make?" spat Cloudburst. "You let everyone in anyway! And why wasn't I informed about this?"

Lomax, a large, graying, jowly man, folded his arms. "Didn't see any reason. It wasn't your name scratched out there on the hardpan."

"So you're saying that if someone had written *my* name in the dirt, you'd have let *them* in?"

"Now, who'd write *your* name in the dirt?" smiled Lomax. He'd never liked Cloudburst. He'd known a lot of Indians growing up in Arizona, but never one as obnoxious as she was—like she had something to prove every time they spoke. A thoroughly boring and pedantic shrew.

"And you violated security protocols when you let her leave!"

"She was coming right back. The guy's her boyfriend. Besides, she was wearing a suit. "

"She removed her helmet and risked exposure!"

Lomax shrugged. "Talk to her."

"You should have checked with me first!" She was seething, hands on her broad hips.

Lomax shrugged. "What did you want me to do, shoot her?"

"Not her, asshole! Him! You should have shot *him*!"

"It was such a shock, seeing you on that holo broadcast in June," said Chris. "Your hair's longer."

"You like it?"

Chris nodded. "Yes. You look . . . *wild*." Cate laughed and hugged him again. They were sitting on the bed in her room. She kissed him. When they parted, Chris said, "I'm not infected, you know."

"I don't care," said Cate, kissing him again. "I can't believe you're really here. All those years in Montana. You must have been so lonely."

"Somehow it was easier, thinking you were dead. But if I lost you now, I don't know what I'd do."

"You're not going to lose me. For the last six years, there hasn't been a day go by that I didn't think about you. I'd look up into the night sky and imagine you still alive, one of the survivors."

"Speaking of survivors," said Chris. "What's going on here?"

"You saw the holo. We're getting close to a cure."

"I didn't really believe it. I just knew I had to see you." He kissed her deeply, tasting her, inhaling her fragrance. He pulled her close and cupped her breast with his hand. She sighed.

"Cate?" Dr. Cloudburst stood in the doorway.

Embarrassed, Chris stood, extending his hand. "I'm Chris—"

Cloudburst took a step back, raising her hands before her. "Cate may be certain you're not infected, but I'm not."

"Of course." He started unbuttoning his flannel shirt. "Look, no bruises or anything—"

"That will do," said Cloudburst. "Since Cate has already exposed herself, I'll leave it up to her to run the tests. If you check out, you may stay a few days, but then you'll have to leave. If you don't check out, you'll leave immediately."

"Dr. Cloudburst," said Cate. "This is Chris Tempest. You know, the opera singer?"

Chris looked at Cate, then at Cloudburst. "I don't sing—"

"Three days," said Cloudburst flatly. "If he's uninfected."

"Sally," said Cate. "Please."

"The blood work, Cate. Now." She turned and left, shutting the door firmly behind her.

Chris frowned and sat back down next to Cate. "What's up with her?"

"Anybody who comes within twenty miles of this place is supposed to be shot. How you got as close as you did is a mystery to me. You're lucky Captain Lomax is a sucker for romance."

"Speaking of romance, that's why I'm here. I'm on a knight's errand."

Cate folded her hands under her chin. "Pray, tell, Sir Knight."

"Rescuing the fair maiden being held in the icy clutches of a wicked witch! Now that I've met her, I see the situation is dire. Come, m'lady, let us fly from this dungeon, to once again breathe the fresh air of liberty!"

Cate laughed. "Not so fast," she said. "First I must know if you are worthy. What ordeals have you overcome on your quest?"

Chris struck a melodramatic pose. "Wind and hail and dark of night."

"You sound more like a mailman than a knight," said Cate. "Besides, I don't need rescuing. In fact, it is I who shall rescue *you*."

"And how will you do that, seeing that you are just a mere wisp of a girl, with no muscles and a tiny, empty brain?"

"How he mocks me!" cried Cate melodramatically. "Do not judge me, Sir Knight, for I have the sword that will slay the fire-breathing dragon." She pulled him to his feet. "I want you to meet someone."

"Who?"

"The one who gave me the sword."

NINE

THE STARS ALIGN

They entered the living quarters, a large room with doorways connecting to bedrooms, baths, classrooms, recreation, and a kitchen. There were toy boxes all along one wall, drawings pinned to corkboard along the other. They went into the rec room. The young man Chris had seen on the June holo broadcast was sitting with his back against the wall, listlessly rolling a basketball to the far wall and corralling it when it rolled back between his splayed legs.

"Russell," said Cate, "this is Chris. Chris, Russell."

Russell slowly got to his feet. Chris held out his hand. "You saved my life up there. Thanks for not letting them shoot me."

Russell nodded. "I can read," he said. "I read her name."

"Were you playing basketball?" asked Cate.

"No, just thinking."

Chris studied the young man, who seemed much older than the sixteen years Cate said he was. He was graying at the temples and his knuckles were as knobby as an old man's. He was tall, over six feet, but he stooped a bit. Chris looked down, expecting to see ornate tattoo rings on his ankles. He saw gym socks instead. He wondered why he thought Russell would have tattoos.

"Chris?" repeated Cate. "Russell asked you how the sunrise was."

"Sunrise? Good, I guess. Why?"

"I've only seen them on the monitors. Was it warm? It looked warm."

"Yes. It was warm. The night was chilly."

"I would like to feel that," said Russell.

"Russell has been in here most of his life," said Cate. "We try to protect him."

"I don't need protection from a sunrise." Russell looked like any disappointed teenager.

"I agree," said Chris. "Russell is old enough to decide for himself what to do."

Russell smiled. "Can you stay?" he asked. "We could play ball."

Chris nodded. "Yeah, Russell. I want to play ball with you."

Ron Ashby entered Cloudburst's office. He never liked being summoned here; it was always for a reprimand. He took a chair in front of her desk. She was reading something and didn't look up. "Close the door, " she said. Ron got up, closed the door, and sat down again, lacing his fingers across his stomach. Cloudburst looked up. She was angry. Ron straightened. What had he done?

"Cate's boyfriend is here."

Ron blinked. "Who?"

"The opera singer."

Ron's heart stopped and the blood drained from his face. He'd been making steady, if slow, progress with Cate in the past few months. They often lunched together with Russell, and he liked to think of himself and Cate as parental surrogates for the boy—they were kind of like a family. Now the boyfriend shows up. "How did he find her?"

"He saw her on the holocast. How he put that together with Yucca Mountain is a mystery to me."

"You're not letting him stay, are you? He might be infected, you know."

Cloudburst snorted. "He's got three days and then he's gone."

"That's good, because if he finds out—"

"Well, we won't let him, then, will we?"

"You want me to keep tabs on him?"

"That's a great idea, Ron. Why don't you? Find out why he's *really* here—I can't believe it's just for *her*." She shook her head at such foolishness.

Show's what you know, thought Ron. Why, he himself would swim the Pacific for Cate Seagram. Or do whatever it took to stop an old boyfriend from bothering her. "He's a security risk," affirmed Ron. "He could disrupt everything."

"And we can't have that, can we?"

Ron shook his head. No way.

Cate and Chris sat in the dining area, eating lunch. Chris was just moving the food around his plate, lost in thought. Cate watched him, overjoyed he was here, but there was something bothering him. "Chris?" she asked. "Are you okay?"

"This food is pretty bad."

"At least it's hot. On my trip, I ate out of cans. Cold."

"Where else have you been, besides Virginia? You make it up to New York?"

"No. Not after the outbreak. Why?"

Chris put down his fork and glared at her. "Quit lying to me."

"I'm not lying—"

"Knock it off! You know as well as I do—"

"Hello, Cate," came a voice. They both turned. Ron Ashby stood there in his pale-green hospital scrubs. Neither Cate nor Chris said anything. Ron held his hand out to Chris. "You must be Chris. From New York."

Chris took it absently. "Yeah. That's me."

"I've wanted to meet you for a long time," said Ron, seating himself in an empty chair opposite them. "Cate has told me almost nothing about you." He smiled knowingly at her.

Cate flushed. "That's not quite true—"

"Of course I'm joking," said Ron. "For years, you've been all she's talked about. And now, here you are, back from the dead."

"Yeah," said Chris. "Back from the dead. Guess I came to the right place. You're miracle workers here, right?"

Ron nodded proudly. "No miracles yet, but we're working on it." He winked slyly at Cate.

Cate wanted to jump up and bolt from the room.

"Oh, you're too modest," said Chris, looking evenly at Cate. "You've already performed a major miracle, haven't you?"

"So what brings you to the desert?" asked Ron. "Besides Cate."

"Nothing. I just wondered what she was up to."

"Just Cobalt," said Cate, disoriented.

"Just Cobalt," repeated Chris, getting to his feet. "Nice to meet you, Ron." He turned and strode from the room.

Cate started to get up, but Ron grabbed her arm, pulling her back down. "Lover's quarrel?"

She pulled her arm free. "What was *that* about, Ron?"

"He seems upset about something."

"What do you want?"

"Just curious. I always wanted to meet an opera singer."

Cate had turned to see the cafeteria door shut behind Chris. She turned back to Ron, steel in her eyes. "Well, *I* know why you're here: to get between Chris and me. Well, it won't happen. I love him and he loves me. And your little game, trying to goad him, won't work."

"What upset him had nothing to do with me," said Ron, reaching out for Cate. She recoiled, disgust on her face. A sudden clarity came into Ron's mind, showing him how things truly were, turning his heart to ice. "Fine. I'm only trying to help. But if you'd rather be with an unstable, immature . . . child, you'd better run after him." He nodded toward the door.

"Ron," said Cate quietly, "go to hell." She stood and strode from the room.

After almost twenty minutes of searching, she finally found Chris in a stairwell, sitting on the concrete landing. She shut the door behind her. "What is it?" She went to sit next to him, but instead, he stood and faced her.

"Who the hell was that?" Chris barked, his voice echoing.

"Ron? He's just a guy."

Chris grunted. "He's *your* guy, isn't he?"

"Chris, you are *not* jealous. You were mad about something before Ron showed up. If you want, we can talk all about him later, but right now I want to know what's bothering you. You've been angry ever since we left Russell."

Chris put his hands on his hips. "Exactly."

"What is it?"

"Who is he, Cate?"

"He's just a kid who's immune to Cobalt."

Chris pounded the railing. "He is *not*!"

"I beg your pardon? He *is* immune—"

Chris grabbed her wrist. "No! He's not just some *kid*."

Cate wrenched her wrist away, but she wasn't innocent. She hadn't told him the whole truth. Suddenly all the strength went out of her and she sat down, her back to the door, and took a deep breath. "Okay. Russell isn't just some kid we found."

"He's a clone," said Chris flatly, sitting down opposite her on the floor.

"How did you know?"

"How would *I* know? Cate, quit lying!"

"We found him, or the previous him, wandering in Seattle, shortly after the outbreak there."

"Really," said Chris.

"It's the truth!" countered Cate, looking around, suddenly aware of their echoing voices. She looked up, scanning the ceiling. There were no security cameras in the stairwell—at least on this level. She lowered her voice. "He had been in a hot zone for weeks and showed no trace of Cobalt. They brought him here, but he died shortly thereafter. They used his cells to clone Russell."

Chris snorted derisively. "Do I look that stupid?"

"It's the truth!"

"Okay. Have you *seen* the body they cloned Russell from?"

Cate was stunned. "No."

"Then how do you know it was him?"

"Who else would he be? And how did you know he was a clone?"

"Quit lying!" shouted Chris. "I know who he really is!"

"Okay, Chris, who is he *really*?"

"Look," he whispered, "level with me. You stole it, didn't you?"

"Stole what?"

"The mummy. The heart. You guys took them."

"What are you talking about?"

"The day Cobalt broke in New York, I went to the Met to see what I could salvage. It was on fire. There were riots, police and soldiers everywhere. You saw it on the holos."

Cate nodded. It had been terrible. She'd gotten a headache from scanning every face in the broadcast in hopes of seeing Chris. Or dreading seeing him hurt or dead.

"I went down to the basement where we were keeping the artifacts I brought back from Tanzania. The mummy. The canopic jar containing the heart. They were gone. Stolen."

"And you think *we* took them?"

"Who else?"

"Why?"

Chris glowered at her. "Because the tissue was immune to Cobalt, that's why. Remember?"

Cate's mouth dropped open in surprise. It was the first time she'd thought about that since that hurried conversation almost six years ago. She shook her head. "Chris, I swear, we didn't take the mummy." A long moment passed, and then, "At least *I* didn't." She crawled over by him, taking his hand. "I didn't know anything about it."

"Well," said Chris, feeling his hand stiffen in hers. "Someone knew."

Cate looked up at him. His hair had gone salt and pepper since she saw him last. He was thin, haggard, and sunburned. And angry. Softly, she said, "Why do you think we stole the body?"

"Because I just saw it again. On the basketball court."

Cate's blood went cold. "You're saying the mummy is . . . *Russell*?"

"At the Met, we used a computer simulation to see what the mummy looked like when he was alive. Russell is *him*. A six-thousand-year-old man who was immune to Cobalt. You guys took his heart and cloned him from it."

Cate rested her head against the light-green concrete wall. "Chris, you've got to believe me. I didn't know."

"Well, you know now. So what are you going to do about it?"

LAZARUS

It was just after 1 A.M. when Chris felt a hand on his shoulder, waking him. On Cloudburst's orders, he'd been relegated to the Slammer, even though he'd had contact with a half-dozen people in the complex, including their prize pupil, Russell. But Chris and Cate both knew the order was more symbolic than real; that Cloudburst was just reminding them who was in charge.

Cate led him out of the room, down a wide hall and up a flight of stairs. Two levels up, she stopped in front of Dr. Cloudburst's office. She turned the knob gently, let out a sigh of relief, and turned to Chris, whispering, "We just learned something very important—something that gives us an advantage." She led him inside the dark office and shut the door quietly.

"What?" whispered Chris.

"We know they don't know about our conversation in the stairwell," said Cate, crossing to Cloudburst's desk, "or she'd have locked her office." She settled into Cloudburst's chair and waved her hand across the flat desk panel, which glowed, then configured into a keyboard, rising slowly from the flat desk surface, forming three-dimensional keys.

Chris pulled a chair over and sat next to Cate. "How are you going to get past her firewall?"

Cate started typing. "I've stood behind her a hundred times as she entered security doors. I think I can figure out her password."

And within a minute and just a half-dozen tries, she'd accessed Cloudburst's computer, initiating a Boolean search using "Russell" "origin" "cloning" and, just for fun, "Christopher Tempest." The search returned nothing except a list of files on cloning procedures and support documents. Chris asked for a hard copy of one such article as Cate continued searching. "I thought cloning was illegal," he said, turning the pages.

"But you're not surprised to know that we're doing it anyway."

"After seeing Russell, nothing surprises me."

Cate's hands stopped. "Well, well. This surprises *me*."

Chris looked up. A long list of phone records hung in the air before them. Cate raised her hand and touched one, highlighting it, attempting to open it. Nothing happened.

"That's my office number," said Chris. "Serves us right, calling each other from work."

"Check out the dates," said Cate. "August 11, 14, and 22, 2029. Just before the outbreak. They were eavesdropping." She shook her head. "I think we've found our smoking gun."

Chris shook his head. "Not yet. But I'll bet it's around here somewhere."

Before they left, Cate did a security-system scan. She knew that, as director of the installation, Cloudburst had access to everything the guards saw, and maybe even a couple of cameras they didn't know about, like the one pointed at the guards from out of their own security panels. On one such camera, Cate watched the night-duty guard dozing, his feet up on the panel, snoring softly.

They moved quietly through darkened corridors. Yucca had a staff of about sixty, with fifteen military. But at night, in a secured, locked-down, hardened-concrete encasement a thousand feet below ground with just two working elevators, they didn't need a division of Army Rangers to guard the place; just a sentinel up top in the security pod, who happened to be asleep at the moment.

They took a stairwell down many floors, painfully aware of the echoing sound of each footfall. As they descended, Chris began to appreciate the size of the place. There had to be at least ten working levels above them. The BSL4 labs, according to Cate, were located near the bottom, for safety reasons. But then there were an additional twelve levels below the Level 4 labs, and when they stepped out onto the lowest landing, Cate cast her flashlight around and Chris drew his breath in sharply.

The place was a giant hub with a high, vaulted ceiling disappearing into the darkness above. In the center of the hall was an immense pillar with four huge freight elevator doors at ninety degree intervals around its circumference. Radiating from the doors were rail tracks set flush in the concrete floor. As the tracks flowed away from the elevators, they forked again and again. Chris scanned the hall perimeter, estimating that there were probably dozens of dark tunnels into which the tracks disappeared.

"The fuel rods came in these big lozenge-shaped containers," said Cate. "They were placed on specialized rail cars and transported to the storage tunnels. There are literally a hundred miles of tunnels down here, in extremely stable, dry rock."

"That's why they chose this location," said Chris. "No water or earthquakes."

"Yes. Our offices were originally designed as the command center, but were refitted when the government figured a Cobalt outbreak was inevitable. They're secure and totally self-contained."

"What's this?" asked Chris, pointing to a wall with strange, hieroglyphic-style writing on it.

"As an archeologist, you'll appreciate this," said Cate. "Since they were storing nuclear waste with a half-life of anywhere from sixty to sixty thousand years, they had to come up with a language that future generations of scientists would understand. It was wishful thinking to hope English would still be spoken a hundred thousand years from now."

"How much is down here? Nuclear waste, I mean?"

"All of it," said Cate. "But it's as safe as they could make it. They thought of everything."

"No one thinks of everything," said Chris. "But it's still pretty impressive."

"How will we find it? I'm sure it's down here."

Chris took her flashlight and walked across the floor, playing the light across the glinting tracks.

"What are you looking for?" asked Cate.

"Found it." He ran the light down the rail to where it disappeared into a black tunnel.

Cate came and stood beside him. "How do you know?" Chris went to the next track over and ran his finger across the rail. It came up dirty. He touched the rail they were standing next to. He showed his finger to Cate. It was clean. She smiled. "What color is the ceiling, Chris?"

Chris shrugged. "Dunno. That's why I'm an archeologist and not an astronomer."

They thought of turning on lights, but the power grid might spike, raising an alarm in a place where the slightest environmental change would be noticed. The track ran straight into the tunnel, but soon began branching right and left at regular intervals. "It's like a giant tree," said Chris, stopping at the first junction. He kneeled, saw the branching tracks were dusty, and continued ahead down the main line.

At the fourth junction, the left branching track was clean, and they entered the tunnel, which was about eight feet in diameter and curved slightly, following the general direction of the main spoke, like branches on a young tree. Shining his light ahead, far down at the end they saw a rail car with a large silver object in it, nearly filling the round tunnel. As they approached, Chris said, "That isn't a fuel-rod container, is it?"

"It's a nitrogen tank," said Cate, pointing to a green diamond-shaped label with a large "N_2" stenciled on it. Chris squeezed past the car, Cate following. Flexible hoses connected the silver canister to an eight-foot-long lozenge in the next car. It was different from the other storage containers they'd seen. The top portion was hinged and it sported a red LED readout. Chris touched the spun graphite surface. "It's cold," he said. "Radioactivity is anything but."

"Look. It says LAZARUS on it," said Cate. "Why?"

"Wordplay," said Chris. "Laz-A-Russ. Russell. Your New Man. My ancient Egyptian." He handed her the flashlight and began undoing the latches. As he raised the curved lid, white tendrils of nitrogen gas spilled over the lozenge edge. The inside of the lid was coated with frost, which glittered in the light. Chris waved the steam away. "Meet Lazarus," he said gravely, "before he became Russell."

Inside, wrapped in clear plastic, was the mummy, lying on its side facing them. Chris touched the head. "Missed you," he said quietly. Lying with the mummy was the blackened stone jar. Chris picked it up gently, removing the stopper. He frowned, showing the empty jar to Cate. "This contained the heart. It's probably in a freezer upstairs somewhere." He handed the heavy jar to Cate, who looked carefully at it. It was made of white alabaster, about ten inches tall, darkening toward the top, with three wavy lines around the waist and an orb stopper atop the lid. "This was unique?" she asked, handing it back.

"Completely. I believe our friend here was the first Egyptian." He laughed.

"What?"

"I was just thinking about Al McFadden, the archeologist who discovered Lazarus here—the credits on the paper I was going to write. 'M' before 'T.' McFadden, then Tempest." He placed the jar back inside the container next to the mummy. "Once upon a time, that kind of thing was important." He gazed down at the mummy with a look on his face that wouldn't be out of place at a funeral viewing. "At least they didn't cut *you* up," he whispered, placing his hand on the mummy's head. "At least they didn't do that."

On their way back upstairs, they agreed that Chris would stay with Cate instead of returning to the Slammer. After all, as soon as Cloudburst discovered they'd been on her computer, the secret would be out. "If she kicks you out, I'll go with you," said Cate, opening the door to her room.

"I didn't come here to stop your research—I came because I missed you."

"I know. But finding the mummy changes things."

"No, it doesn't," said Chris. "I'm angry about the theft of the mummy, but I told *you* about its immunity. Subconsciously, I must have known that only the CDC could use that knowledge." His shoulders slumped. "I'm sorry I got on you about it."

They settled down onto Cate's bed, pulling the blanket over them. Chris spooned behind Cate and whispered, "When we're *really* alone, we'll make up for lost time."

Cate smiled, feeling his arms around her. "It will be worth the wait."

Soon after, she heard his soft breathing and felt his arms loosen. Poor guy. He'd had a long day: guns pointed at him at dawn, an emotional reunion, a stunning surprise in Russell, and finally, the late-night discovery of the mummy in the repository catacombs. As he snored softly, she was once again amazed at his courage. He boarded a plane and went to Ground Zero in Tanzania, returning with the one thing that just might save the entire world. And he did it without a single thought about his own safety. She knew Chris would say he did it for selfish reasons, but when everything you do turns out in the end to be for the good of others, it's hard to make a case that you're acting solely in your own self-interest.

Again, her nagging doubts about humanity's insularity filled her, and she wondered if there were something bigger out there shaping the destiny of individuals and nations. What were the chances that she was a Cobalt researcher and he had discovered the only person on the planet who was immune to it? So, though she didn't really believe it, she *wished* it weren't a coincidence—that someone was in charge—because then, their feelings for each other might be more than just endorphins and hormones and firing synapses. They might just be something that survived death. Holding Chris's rough hands in hers and listening to his breathing, she truly hoped so.

Chris stopped and pointed. "Look!"

Quatermain squinted into the heat haze. There, in the shimmering distance, was the spindly acacia tree, as always, no closer now than five hours ago. But now there was a man standing by it, holding something in his arms. "Do you see him?" asked Chris, noting with only a trace of surprise that his own outstretched arm was black and tattooed around the bicep with three wavy lines.

"Who do you suppose it is?" asked Quatermain.

"It is Lazarus," said Chris.

"That would be a neat trick," chuckled Quatermain. "Finding Jesus out here in the African desert, carrying his old friend Lazarus in his arms."

"Lazarus is the one standing," said Chris. "I do not know whom he carries."

"It just occurred to me that you've no business even knowing who Lazarus is," said Quatermain, turning to Chris and surveying him closely. "You're no Jew."

"Yet I know his name." Chris looked down, noting his black skin, the tattoos around his ankles matching the ones on his biceps. He wore a leopard-skin loincloth. But now there was something new: hanging from his neck was a silver amulet. He examined it.

"The ankh," said Quatermain. "Symbol of eternal life."

"And of Cobalt," said Chris, surprising himself.

"Afraid I don't understand," said Quatermain. "What is Cobalt?"

Chris turned his attention to the umbrella-shaped thorn tree and man standing beside it. "He knows."

Quatermain nodded. "Well, then. Lay on, McFadden. Let's get the answer to this riddle."

Cate turned. The sky was black with clouds, and big raindrops began to pelt her. She covered up, ducking back inside the cave entrance, her eyes never leaving the dark panorama before her: an immense, collapsed volcano crater, the far wall vague in the mist. Overhead, the clouds parted and moonlight slanted down, illuminating the crater floor with silver light. Out in the middle was a lone acacia tree. And if her eyes didn't betray her, a man standing near it—

Suddenly, someone grabbed her from behind and she whirled, striking her head on the cave ceiling. She fell backward out onto the ledge. A flash of lightning, and she saw it: a mummy, kneeling in the entrance, a woman carrying a child's corpse, reaching out to Cate. "Where is he?" it cried in a croaking, dead voice.

Cate scrabbled away, stopping at the edge of the sheer drop-off behind her. The mummy crawled slowly toward her. The dead woman's eyes were empty black sockets, but tears flowed down her linen-wrapped face. "He is gone," she moaned. "Where have you taken him?"

Cate shook her head, unable to speak, shuddering with revulsion.

"He is gone," repeated the mummy, holding our her tiny, wrapped child. "Please, tell me where he is."

Cate looked over her shoulder. A shaft of moonlight lit the acacia, and suddenly, Cate knew the answer. "He is there," she said, pointing to the tree. "He is coming."

Tears spilled out of the mummy's empty eye sockets. "But he is blind and cannot find his way."

"I don't know the way," said Cate.

"You do," said the mummy, cradling her dead child. "You must bring him to me."

Russell lay in bed. His back ached. He often played hoops with Captain Lomax and the other soldiers without getting sore. But he didn't play basketball today. So why did his back ache so much?

You're old, came the voice in his head. All his life, he'd heard a man's voice in his head, speaking a strange language. But this was the first time he'd ever been able to understand it. *You're old,* it repeated. *Your body knows, but your mind will not believe.*

"I'm sixteen," answered Russell.

No.

"Yes. I'm sixteen, almost seventeen."

But you remember the painting. You know the one. You painted it just last year.

"I was watching the security cameras when I got the idea. It was the day Lieutenant Morris gave me the toy truck for my birthday."

How old were you?

"I was six," said Russell, surprised at how clearly he remembered. "The truck was red, with six wheels. Two in front and four behind. That makes six. That's how I know."

That was a year ago, when you painted the tree. You were six. Now you're sixteen.

Russell got up and shuffled across the dark room and opened the door. The common-area lights came on. His artwork hung on a cork strip on the wall to his left. He walked past his earliest finger paintings and then stopped at the one he was thinking of. It was a flat grassland with a single tree in the middle and an orange sun on the horizon behind it. He turned and went to the chests, sorting through toys. At the bottom was the red dump truck, the one Morris gave him. It wasn't as large as he'd remembered it. He looked back to the tree painting. Both on the same day?

One year ago. You were six.

Russell walked to the couch and sat with the red truck on his lap, still looking at the picture.

You know that place.

"I made it up."

No, it made you up.

Russell went to the painting and sat down before it. Suddenly, he found himself standing inside it. Dark clouds roiled overhead; rain was coming. To his left was the tree, just as he'd painted it, with crude, wiry black limbs and oversized green blotches for leaves. Then, as he watched, the clumsy trunk became many twisting, variegated branches and the canopy morphed into a kaleidoscope of slender waxy gray-green leaves. He looked down. A man's wrapped body lay at his feet. The face was horrible, with black holes where the eyes should have been and a gaping mouth. Russell opened his mouth to scream, but no sound came out. The mummy reached up for him.

Help.

Russell whirled around. It was the voice from his head. But where was he? The mummy's hand was still outstretched, its horrible jaw distended, white teeth whirling around inside like popcorn in an air popper.

Please. Help me.

Russell felt the first drops of rain. He looked up. He'd never felt rain on his face before. Tears came to his eyes. Then he felt something scrabbling at his leg. The mummy had his pajama leg clutched in its bony fingers. Russell jumped back.

Do not leave me.

"Why not?" The rain drops bounced off the hard, parched ground.

Because we are one. The dead man looked up at him with empty eyes and that terrible, swirling mouth. He held something green in his bony black hand. Russell reached for it and woke up shivering in the darkness.

ELEVEN

K'TANU, AWAKE

When Cate came back to her room, holding the printout, Chris knew he'd been given a clean bill of health. "I told you I didn't have Cobalt."

"And now we've got proof," she said. "She has to let you stay now. We can find something for you to do here, and we can be together."

Chris looked doubtful. "I thought you wanted to leave."

"If she won't let you stay, I'll go." She looked at Chris. "What?"

"I'm just not sure I want to spend the rest of my life down here." He pulled her down on the bed next to him. "I was hoping you'd come with me."

"Where?"

"Back to Montana. There's game in the mountains and we can grow our own vegetables. There's hardly anybody around and we'll be safe."

"But Cobalt is still out there."

"But it's far away. In here, you're working with it every day. Much riskier."

"But what about Lazarus—Russell, I mean? He's immune, Chris. He holds the key."

"You don't know that. All you know is he isn't dying of Cobalt."

"He isn't dying of anything."

"Yes he is. You guys screwed with his genes."

"They sped up his pituitary, yes. He gets growth hormones, yes. But he's not dying."

Chris picked up a sheaf of papers off Cate's desk. "While you were in the lab, I've been reading. The first mammal successfully cloned from an adult cell was the sheep they called Dolly, way back in the last century."

"Named after the buxom country singer," said Cate.

"Right," said Chris. "But Dolly aged prematurely, and soon she was suffering from arthritis, obesity, and a host of other age-related disorders—Alzheimer's, for all they knew. They had to euthanize her after only six years, and that's pretty young for a sheep."

"Her telomeres were shortened," said Cate, "the stop-codes at the end of chromosomal DNA strands that tell a cell how old it is. But not too many years after that, scientists discovered how to turn on a gene that codes for a hormone that prevents telomere shortening."

"Then why is Russell getting old so fast?"

"Because they couldn't use the hormone on him. Sometimes it causes cancer."

"So he dies from heart disease or cancer," said Chris. "Some choice."

"They had to speed up his metabolism because adult DNA is optimum for study." She noticed him looking critically at her. "Hey, it wasn't my idea."

"But you went along with it."

"What would you have done? You have the opportunity to cure the worst plague in history, but you won't use it?"

"You don't *use* people, Cate. That's all I'm saying."

Cate grabbed the papers from Chris and shook them in his face. "Science is nothing *but* hard decisions. Did you ever stop to think that those Maasai tribesmen who were attacking you might have had a point? Al McFadden was a grave robber—that makes you one too!"

"The mummy was already dead. You brought him back to life, just to kill him again."

"We didn't bring *him* back to life. We used his DNA. Russell is not Laz—"

Someone knocked on the door.

"Cate?" The door opened. Russell stood there, looking very agitated.

"What is it, Russell?" said Cate, turning the sheaf of papers face down on her lap.

"Can I talk to you?" asked Russell, closing the door behind him.

"Sure," said Cate.

Chris stood. "I'll leave you two alone."

"No, Dr. Tempest. I want you to stay."

Chris sat back down next to Cate. Russell stood by the door.

"Sit down, Russell," said Cate. Already, his name seemed foreign to her. He pulled a chair over and sat down. Chris saw the mummy's features in the young man, and felt a strange compulsion to tell the truth. "What's on your mind?" asked Cate. "You don't look so hot."

"I had a bad dream last night," said Russell. "But that's not why I'm here." He turned to Chris and said, "Yesterday, you looked at me funny, like you're looking at me now. Why?"

"Maybe he hasn't seen too many black people," said Cate lightly. Something ominous was about to happen, and she was suddenly afraid.

Chris snorted. "I've seen plenty of black people, Russell."

"Then why do you look at me that way?"

"You remind me of someone, that's all."

Cate resisted the urge to elbow Chris in the ribs. "See? Black people all look alike to him."

Chris gave *her* an elbow in the ribs, then said, "Russell, what's on your mind?"

"Who am I?"

Cate interjected, "You're a boy we found—"

"He was talking to me, thank you," said Chris. He turned to Russell. "Why do you ask?"

"Well," said Russell, "I don't think they told me the truth about how I came here."

"Why do you think that?" asked Cate warily.

"I painted a picture a year ago, the same day as my birthday, when I got a toy truck."

"Yes?"

"I was six years old. I remember. But Mama Cloudburst says I'm sixteen now." He touched his temple. "But I think I'm even older than that. My hair is going gray, like Captain Lomax's. And my hands and knees hurt. My back, too, like his does."

"We should check your diet, Russell," said Cate. "Maybe you need vitamins."

"You don't understand," said Russell. "Last year I was six. Now I'm sixteen."

"We *do* understand," said Chris. "And you're right. That *was* last year." He turned to Cate, silently daring her to withhold the truth from the boy now.

Cate sighed, defeated. "That's strange arithmetic, isn't it?"

The boy nodded. He looked so sad, sitting there, looking at his feet and rubbing his hands together slowly.

"That's because you're really only six," she said.

Russell looked up. "How can that be? What happened to those ten years?"

"You never had them. You're a clone," said Chris. "You know what a clone is?"

"No."

"They take a cell from someone's body and put it into an egg. You know, like a sperm?"

Russell, as dark as he was, went still darker with embarrassment. "I know about that." He looked at Chris, avoiding Cate's eyes. "When the man puts his . . . his . . . "

"Exactly," said Chris. "And when the sperm and the egg join, a baby is made, and it grows in the mother's stomach until it's born."

"That's how I was made?"

"Yes," said Cate, knowing they could not turn back now. She kneeled before him, taking his hands in hers. "They took your DNA, the blueprint that tells a cell what to do, and put it into an egg. But before they did that, they removed the mother's DNA from the egg. So instead of being part mother and father, the baby is just the father."

"You are your own father, Russell," said Chris. "You've had two lives."

Russell's eyes opened wide. "Two lives?"

"No," said Cate. "Just one. But before you were born, there was another man. He wasn't you, but he *looked* like you."

Russell's eyes teared up. Cate put her arms around him. "Then he was right," mumbled Russell.

"Who was?"

"The voice. The mummy's voice."

Chris leaned forward, startled. "What?"

"The mummy by the tree."

Cate's blood went cold. "What tree?"

"I dreamed it," said Russell. "I made a painting of it. The tree with the lightning. And the rain." He looked up, tears rolling down his cheeks.

Cate pulled back, horrified. For just an instant, his face looked like the mummy's face in the cave in *her* dream, streaming tears from empty eye sockets.

Russell looked at her, alarmed at her reaction. "I'm sorry!"

"Describe the tree, Russell," said Chris, thinking of Quatermain, the desert, and the distant snow capped mountains beyond from *his* dream.

Russell fished in his back pocket. "Here it is." He handed a folded piece of construction paper to Chris, who opened it. It was a crude painting of a strange tree that looked a bit like an acacia.

Chris showed it to Cate. "I dreamed this."

Cate's eyes were wide with surprise. "I dreamed it too."

They all looked at each other for a long, numbing moment, then Russell's eyelids fluttered and he fell forward against Cate. They picked him up and put him on the bed. "He's fainted," said Cate, feeling his pulse.

"What do you mean, you dreamed it too?" asked Chris.

"I was at a cave entrance, high up on a mountainside. It was a tomb. There were mummies inside. A woman's mummy spoke to me, asking me to help her find someone. I turned and saw that tree out on the flats." She pointed at the painting lying on the floor. "There was someone standing next to it."

"I saw him too," said Chris. "In *my* dream. Who was he?"

"I couldn't tell; I was too far away."

"He was carrying another man in his arms."

"It was me," said Russell, opening his eyes.

They both turned. "What?" asked Cate.

"I was by the tree," said Russell. "There was a dead man on the ground. He was crying and he said he was me." His face scrunched up. Chris pulled him close and Russell sobbed into his shirt.

Chris looked at Cate. "In my dream, I was black. I just realized who I was supposed to be."

"Who?"

Chris nodded at the boy in his arms. "Russell."

Though he was tall and appeared in his late teens, in most ways Russell was still a young boy, and his tears and fright wore him out like a child. He soon fell asleep on Cate's bed. Cate and Chris conferred nearby, whispering. "Simple telekinesis," said Cate.

"So what does it mean?"

"Just that we've all had the same dream. Nothing more."

"You blanched when he mentioned a voice," said Chris. "Why?"

"Shortly after the outbreak, on my way back from Virginia, I met a preacher at a little church. I've come to think of him as The Voice. He said some strange things to me."

"Like what?"

"That I was hiding. That there was a deliverer coming and that I'd meet him soon."

"Sounds like your typical second-coming scenario."

"He knew my name," said Cate, shuddering.

"Hmm," said Chris. "That's not easy to dismiss, is it?"

"What are you saying?"

"Maybe Cobalt effects some people in ways besides killing them."

"Like?"

Chris nodded at Russell, sleeping beside them, his chest slowly rising and falling. "Who knows? Voices that seem familiar. People on the road who know our names. Common dreams. This." He dug into his pocket and brought out a green object. It was carved out of serpentine stone, lying on a bed of beaten gold.

"What's that?"

"A scarab amulet. It was tucked under the mummy's hands. I've always kept it with me. I don't know why."

"What's that?" asked Russell, who had awakened.

Chris quickly hid the scarab. "Nothing."

"Can I see it?"

Chris looked at Cate. They were going to have to tell Russell about Lazarus. Best to ease into it. Chris held the scarab up. "It's a beetle. The Egyptians believed it represented eternal life."

Russell got up on his elbows to see it better. "Why?"

"They saw the beetle rolling little balls of dung—"

"He means poop," said Cate.

Russell laughed. "Really?"

"You want to hear this?" said Chris, fixing a frown on both of them. The others nodded, suppressing smiles. Chris continued. "They saw the beetle rolling balls of *poop* along, then later, they noticed that little beetles crawled out of the balls."

"Ick," said Russell.

Cate laughed in spite of herself.

"They thought the baby beetles were the big beetle being reborn. That's why they believed in a resurrection."

Seeing the blank look on Russell's face, Cate said, "They believed that your soul or spirit—whatever it's called—lives on after you die, that it's born again."

"Like me?" asked Russell.

"No," said Cate firmly. "Not like you. You are a completely different person than the one whose DNA they made you from. You look like him, that's all. There is no such thing as a soul."

The explanation seemed lost on Russell, who still eyed the amulet. "Can I hold it?"

"Sure," said Chris, handing it over. Russell held it carefully in both palms, looking at it. Then suddenly, he began to shake, and his eyes rolled up into his head.

He was standing inside a thorn-bush fence, facing a village of thatch-roofed mud huts.

"K'tanu!" shouted a woman.

Russell looked up. In the center of the village, people were getting to their feet, including a tall, slender black woman. She, along with everyone else, ran toward him, yelling the same word over and over. "K'tanu! K'tanu!"

Russell turned to see if there was someone behind him. There wasn't. He turned back just as the woman fell into his arms. "E gali nom kumbu!" she cried, hugging him fiercely. "K'tanu!" Russell felt wetness on his chest. She was crying. She looked up at him, tears rolling down her cheeks. "Na'om be luza, K'tanu! Na'om! Na'om!"

Russell, sensing her distress, patted her on the back. Who was she? Where he? He looked around at the people who encircled him. They were black, and like him, most were tall. They wore little clothing. He saw the women's bare breasts and looked away, embarrassed. The men held spears and decorated leather shields, like those he'd seen on holos about Africa. The woman was still crying, "K'tanu, K'tanu, Na'om!"

Then there was a commotion and a little naked boy burst through the throng, shouting "Baba! Baba!" and throwing his arms around Russell's legs. A crying woman held an infant out to him. He took the baby. And still the slender woman clutched him as if he would run away if she let him go. She put her hand on the baby's downy cheek. "K'tanu, en belungaza o Anja!"

Russell looked down at the woman, utterly confused.

She became aware that something was wrong. "K'tanu! Dara um kagara?"

He shook his head. What was she saying?

She looked up at him, tears standing in her eyes. "K'tanu?"

He realized that she thought his name was Ka-TAW-new. He shook his head, handing the baby to her. He pointed to himself and said, "Russell. I'm Russell."

"K'tanu!" answered the woman, hugging him again, apparently relieved he wasn't mute.

"No. Russell," he said, pulling away from her. The woman, who was looking at him strangely, was, like all the other women, bare from the waist up, and he averted his eyes.

She placed her hand against his chest. "Um e K'tanu," she said slowly. Then, she placed her hand on her breast. "Na e Maya. Maya."

"Maya," repeated Russell. "But I'm Russell—"

The crowd shook their heads. Maya held up the baby. "Ga e um chakula, Anja."

"Anja," repeated Russell, and Maya smiled gratefully.

The little boy at his side tugged on Russell's loincloth. "Na e N'kala," he said, pointing to himself.

"N'kala," said Russell. He looked somehow familiar.

Maya handed the baby to another woman and threw her arms around Russell. He felt her breasts against his chest and suddenly there was an embarrassing stiffening in his loins. He gently pushed her away, but as he did, a woman in the crowd laughed and pointed at the bulge in his loincloth. Mortified, he turned away. The crowd was laughing, not unkindly, and several women were nodding knowingly. Maya stepped forward and whispered, "K'tanu, hala um tisara n'gom. E na mume. Na mume."

Suddenly, someone grabbed Russell's shoulder and whirled him around. Before him stood a small, very thin man. "K'tanu!" he chortled.

"K'tanu ba e n'guka fala," said Maya to the man.

"Rasadi?" asked the man. "K'tanu? Na e hala na, Antram?" He pointed to himself.

Russell shook his head.

The man came closer. "E na umbadi? Umbadi?"

Russell shook his head again. Where was he? Who were these people?

The little man reached and snatched something from Russell's waist. Russell looked down and noticed that he had a small leather pouch secured around his waist by a leather cord. The pouch flap was open. He looked up. The man held half a human jaw bone in his hand. "K'tanu! Na gala e bengula? Eh?"

Russell took the jawbone from the man, who pantomimed holding it up to his ear. Russell obeyed. At first, there was nothing, then a tiny voice began speaking in a language Russell did not understand. He shook his head. The old man shook his fist near his own ear, instructing Russell to try again. Russell held the bone next to his ear again and listened. The voice, now joined by others, rose and fell, babbling. He was about to hand the bone back, when he heard, distinctly but faintly, "Fear not." He froze, his eyes wide with fear nevertheless. But the skinny man was nodding and smiling.

"Yes?" said Russell, holding the bone closer.

But the voice said no more. Instead, a melody began building, like water bouncing down a steep, rocky stream. It carried within it a sweetness, tinged with ancient anguish. The man gently pulled Russell's hand down, meeting his eyes. Russell watched as he took Maya's hand, turning her to face Russell. He took the baby from the other woman and gave her back to Maya. The boy N'kala was placed at Maya's side. "K'tanu!" whispered the little man. "Um fala e jamaa! Um jamaa!" He pointed at Maya, then Russell, rubbing his palms together, then pointed at the children.

Russell's mouth dropped open. This was his family? He looked at Maya. She was his *wife*?

The man then pointed to himself. "Antram, e fala e rafiki. Rafiki."

"Rafiki," said Russell. *He's my friend. Rafiki means "friend."*

Sudden awareness filled him. The people around him had jagged tattoos around their ankles and biceps. He looked at his arms, noting his own tattoos. The sun shone brightly in a deep blue sky. He closed his eyes, feeling its magnificent warmth on his face. A chill coursed up his spine and for the first time he fully grasped the meaning of a word he'd heard all of his life.

Home.

He knelt and held N'kala, feeling the boy's little arms around his neck. Then he stood and took the baby from Maya, cradling the child gently in his arms. "Ja binti?" he said. *My daughter?*

Maya burst into tears and threw her arms around him, squeezing him tightly. Russell suddenly felt an astonishing, overwhelming love for this woman. This beautiful, tender woman, who was his *wife*.

"K'tanu," she whispered, "you have returned to us."

"Maya," said K'tanu, holding her tightly. "My love. My love."

He felt a hand on his shoulder and turned. Antram nodded at him. "You are home, my friend." He touched the silver amulet hanging around K'tanu's neck. K'tanu touched the amulet. He knew now what it represented. Life. Eternal life.

Then suddenly K'tanu heard a thunderclap and felt a cold wind shake him. The air was rent by a horrible tearing sound. He reached for Maya, but she was suddenly on the other side of an immense, dark gulf. He was pulled backward into darkness. Her cries echoed across the empty, black chasm.

"K'tanu! K'tanu!"

TWELVE

PALIMPSEST

"Get it away from him!" cried Cate.

It took every ounce of his strength, but Chris finally wrenched the scarab free. Russell's grip was incredibly strong. He grasped at empty air, crying out, "Maya! E gara no kala!" Cate and Chris stared at each other. "Maya!" cried Russell one last time, then collapsed back on the bed, eyes still staring at the ceiling.

Cate put a hand on his forehead. It was feverish. "Russell," she asked, "are you okay?"

Russell's vision cleared and tears filled his eyes. "N'gua e malaa kawa. K'tanu. My name is K'tanu." He shook his head. "What happened?"

"You might have had a seizure," said Chris. "An electrical storm in your brain."

Russell looked at Cate. "I don't belong here," he said weakly. "I belong *there*."

"Where is *there*?" asked Cate.

"With my family. My friends."

"You're with your friends now," said Cate. "You're home."

"I have to go back!" Russell looked around wildly. Chris held the scarab amulet behind his back. Russell met his eyes and for an awful instant Chris was sure the young man knew what he was hiding.

Then Russell's hands went to his own waist, searching for something. "It's gone!"

"What's gone?"

"The mandible."

The color drained from Chris's face. He tucked the scarab in his back pocket and stood. "Russell," he said, helping the young man to his feet. "Come with me."

"Chris!" said Cate. "No!"

"It's time," said Chris, leading Russell to the door. "Time for answers."

Twelve stories below, they stood around the mummy's container in the narrow, tube-like tunnel. The ceiling was too low for Russell to stand up straight. Chris raised the container lid. White mist drifted over the lip. Chris put his hand on Russell's shoulder. "Remember we said you were a clone?"

"Yes," said Russell distantly. "Someone died. I'm him. I remember."

Cate was about to correct him, but Chris said, "Right. And here he is." He peeled back the plastic. When he realized he was looking at a body, Russell pulled back in horror. "Please," said Chris. "We have to know for sure."

"Have to know *what*?" asked Cate.

Russell looked into the container again. The body was wrapped in narrow cloth strips, blackened with age and covered with a brittle, yellowed resin. The face was a mere outline with just the barest hints of nose and jaw. "K'tanu," whispered Russell.

"Is that his name?" asked Cate.

"Yes. It is my name."

"This is the man they made you from, Russell," said Chris.

Russell touched the mummy's head. "Yes, it is my body." A tear spilled onto his cheek.

"I have to be sure about something," said Chris.

"Chris!" cried Cate. "He knows he's a clone! Why show him this . . . this . . . *horror*?"

"It is not a horror," said Russell. "It was beautiful and strong and held my soul the way a cup holds water."

"No," said Cate. "You share his DNA, that's all. *You* are you, Russell. He is *not* you."

Russell smiled at her. "You're right," he said, touching his chest. "*This* . . . is me."

"Yes," said Cate, relieved.

"My soul fills *this* cup now," said Russell.

Cate frowned. "But—"

"I think I know what he's saying," said Chris, pulling out a pocket knife. "But I have to be sure." He found a spot on the mummy's chest, just under the crossed hands. Using the blade, he peeled back several layers of cloth, revealing something white. He was about to pry it free when Russell reached and removed the object himself. "The weeping mandible," he said reverently, gently separating the bone from its ancient wrappings. He held it up to his ear and listened, eyes closed.

"What?" asked Cate.

"Shh," said Chris.

After a long while, Russell lowered the bone, considering it. "It does not speak."

"Why not?" asked Chris.

"I don't know. I am far from home. Perhaps it only speaks to me there."

"Where is that?"

"Near Mother Moon's birthplace."

"You were looking for the jawbone upstairs, weren't you?" asked Chris.

Russell nodded, cupping the bone in his hands.

"Russell?" asked Chris.

Russell did not answer.

"K'tanu?"

Hearing Chris use that strange name surprised Cate.

Russell looked up at Chris.

"What did you wear around your neck?" asked Chris.

Cate looked at the mummy. If it did have something around its neck, it was buried under layers and layers of resin-soaked cloth.

Russell touched his neck. "It was silver."

"Do you remember it well enough to draw it?" asked Chris.

"Yes," said Russell, pressing his finger against the frost-covered inside of the container lid and tracing a figure.

"Yes!" said Chris. "The ankh symbol!"

"God," whispered Cate, stunned.

Russell turned to her. "Yes, it also represents God, the creator of all life."

"No," said Cate. "I meant, 'God, it looks like . . .'"

"What?" asked Russell.

Cate drew in a deep breath. "It . . . looks like the virus. It looks like Cobalt."

"I'll bet he sleeps for two days," said Cate, closing the door quietly.

"I would, except I haven't got two days," said Chris. "Tomorrow I have to leave."

Cate put a finger to her lips and led him to her room. It was well after midnight. A few minutes earlier, when they appeared in the common living area, Ron Ashby poked his head out of his doorway, a few rooms down. His thinning hair was mussed and he was disoriented. "What time is it?" he asked, peering at the wall clock. Eleven forty-five. "Where have you been?" he growled. "You missed dinner!"

"I'm tired," said Russell as Chris led him into his room and shut the door behind them.

"We gave Chris a tour," said Cate. "I didn't know it would wear Russell out so much." She looked flatly at Ron until he rolled his eyes and went back inside his own room, shutting the door.

Back in her room, Cate sat on the bed and looked up at Chris. There was a strange look in his eye—an eagerness, an almost feral light.

"Don't tell me you believe it!" she said.

Chris ran his hands through his hair. "I'll admit it's unbelievable."

"Yes," said Cate flatly.

"But not impossible," amended Chris.

"Chris, please."

"I know. But what an impossibility! He had a . . . *vision*. I don't know what else to call it."

"Call it a delusion," said Cate. "Or a nightmare."

"No, I'm gonna call it a vision," replied Chris. "He spoke some strange language."

"How do you know?" asked Cate. "He might have just been babbling."

"I'll grant you that," said Chris. "But he knew about the jawbone."

"Not until you showed it to him."

"No," said Chris, sitting next to her. "Remember? He mentioned it right here in this room. He said he was looking for the *mandible*." He laughed. "How does a kid who's just six years old know a word like *mandible*, Cate?"

"He's very smart. He's fascinated with the human body."

"Come on," said Chris. "His vocabulary is small. He laughs at the word *poop!* Give me this one. He knew about the mandible."

"Okay, but that's all you're going to get."

"Two: he drew the ankh symbol."

"I've watched holos about Egypt with him myself," said Cate.

"But how did he know the mummy had one around its neck?"

"I'm not sure he did," said Cate, feeling like she was on the witness stand being cross-examined. "I never saw it. Besides, didn't most mummies have an ankh on them somewhere?"

"Yes!" exclaimed Chris. "In their hands! And yet our mummy, K'tanu, has one around his neck. I saw it on the CAT scan in New York." He smiled at her. "That's two you gotta give me."

She was about to give him hell. "Conjecture and supposition! He has a seizure, the lights go off, and he comes to babbling. So what? Chris, you try standing there, looking down at your own corpse, and then tell me you wouldn't freak out! We're lucky he didn't have a psychotic break!" She glared at him. "You were horrible, showing him that body. It was cruel."

"He took it pretty well," said Chris. "I was hoping you would, too."

"Why?"

"Because our young friend in there is the best evidence I've ever seen for life after death."

Cate rolled her eyes. "Please, *Doctor* Tempest, contain yourself."

"I mean it," said Chris, taking her hand. "Think about it! He lived six thousand years ago in a Stone Age culture in sub-Saharan Africa. He was killed. They bur—"

"He was killed?" asked Cate. "How?"

"He was run through with a spear. They buried him according to a custom that mutates a thousand years later into Egyptian cosmology, mummies and all. Which reminds me. We all had parts of the same dream. Yours was of the tomb, which, by the way, I have never described and you've never seen." He raised his chin triumphantly.

"If memory serves, you never saw it either," said Cate, frustrated. "What's your point?"

"He dies, Cate, and his soul or his spirit or whatever your want to call it . . . goes *somewhere*. It continues on as *him*, a unique individual with a family and friends, living in a world apparently a lot like the world he lived in here—"

"And that's heaven?" smirked Cate. "Where are the pearly gates and the angels?" She shook her head. "Hell, where's God, for that matter?"

"That's *your* idea of heaven. I didn't call it heaven. Russell didn't either. Maybe it was just another world, like quantum mechanics postulates."

"Quantum mechanics theorizes *parallel* universes, not immortality!"

"Now that's a quantum leap!" laughed Chris. "All it took was scientific terminology and suddenly you're defending a remarkably similar idea. But they may simply be different terms for the same thing! Russell was in this other universe, and when you guys cloned him, he was yanked out of that world and plunged back into this one, the one he'd left thousands of years ago."

"Do you miss your mind, Dr. Tempest?" mocked Cate. "Because it is *gone.*"

"Why? Because the idea's challenging? How come every theory that passes peer review in some bone-dry journal is treated like unassailable fact, but a theory from another source—say myth or even personal experience—is dismissed as mental illness? Isn't that just intellectual snobbery? Isn't it really just using different words to describe the same thing?"

"So you found Jesus down there in the basement?" laughed Cate. He was beginning to scare her and laughter was the only way she knew to hold back her rising fear.

"Jesus is one explanation. Buddha was another. Osiris a third."

"Quantum mechanics trumps them all," said Cate.

"It's still just a theory. What are you afraid of? Don't you know Western civilization has been brainwashed into not believing in God, just like other civilizations are brainwashed into *believing* in Him? Isn't it time for us to examine the evidence and decide for ourselves?"

"Because God is unprovable, Chris. Wishful thinking. Belief without empirical evidence."

"Yet you believe in telekinesis. How do you explain that?"

"I don't. Quantum mechanics does. Alternative universes, some very similar to ours, that leak over into our universe. Inevitable parallelism and redundancy."

Chris sat back and looked at Cate.

"It's not the same," she snapped. "*Soul* is just a section in the music store, Chris."

A smile began forming on Chris's face.

Cate got to her feet, agitated. "Similar universes, different dimensions, all existing at the same moment, not as islands in a stream of time!"

Chris looked up at her. "You want to know too, don't you?"

Cate plopped back down on the bed. "I'm too tired to argue about this now."

He pulled her back down on the bed and kissed her cheek. "I love you," he whispered. Cate's eyes inexplicably filled with tears. She really *was* tired, emotionally vulnerable. It wasn't fair of him to manipulate her this way. He whispered again, "How do you explain love, Cate?"

"Firing synapses," she managed weakly. "Hormones."

"Oh yeah?" said Chris. He kissed her deeply, then pulled back and smiled in his winning way. "Are you telling me that's just chemistry, Cate?"

She looked at him, her eyes brimming with tears. "I hope not," she said.

Cate stood outside Russell's door. The clock on the wall read 2:37 A.M. She'd laid in her own bed for two hours, listening to Chris's breathing, unable to sleep herself. Chris's face, lit by the red LED of the clock, was unlined and restful. He'd discovered something tonight, something that filled him with peace. She'd listened to him theorize wild ideas for years and not once had he ever evinced the same amount of certainty amid his passion.

You want to know too, don't you?

So here she was, her hand on Russell's doorknob. She didn't want to wake him, only to watch him sleep, wanting things to start making sense. All this talk of God and transmigration of souls. Only a fool believed in such nonsense. Like the rubes who blindly followed The Voice in that white clapboard church in South Carolina. But also people like Mother Janice, who had kindly offered to put Cate's hand into Jesus' hand by pointing a gun at her and squeezing a trigger. This was just the latest example of the futility of belief—it made you crazy.

You want to know too, don't you?

It was unmistakable. It was him. The Voice. The same gaunt man in the old-fashioned suit, holding the bike handlebars. And her, scrabbling backwards, terrified, simply because he knew her name. Was she still that fearful child, seeing monsters in the shadows thrown by the tree outside her window, crying for her mommy? Wasn't religion really just Mommy to a frightened child?

There were no answers, only harder and harder questions.

She turned the knob, being careful to make no noise. In the darkness, she saw Russell's bed, but he was not in it. Like her, he was awake, seeking answers to battle the terrifying shadows. *You want to know too, don't you?* she thought as she shut the door.

She found him in the tunnel, kneeling by the mummy, which lay on the cement floor on a blanket. Russell's eyes were closed, his head bowed, his hands stretched out over the body. As Cate approached, she heard him murmuring, "Maya, um taga n'halu nom jamaa. Maya."

It was a bizarre image. She'd said it herself: it must be a terrible shock to see yourself from the outside. *But it's not him*, she reminded herself. *He just shares the same DNA. No different than when you plop an avocado pit into a glass of water and it grows roots, then transplant it in the yard. After a while, you've got fresh avocados in your salad, clones of the pit in the drinking glass.*

Yet as she watched Russell kneeling, murmuring in a strange language, his outstretched hands trembling slightly, she knew it wasn't the same.

You want to know too, don't you?

The desire was too great. She stepped forward.

Russell opened his eyes and looked up. "Why did you do it?"

"Do what?"

"Bring me back?" He looked down at the mummy. "I was happy there. The pain was gone. There were no enemies, no sickness, no death." He looked up at Cate. "Why?"

Cate kneeled down opposite him. "You were the only person who was immune to Cobalt."

"We called it the Bleeding Sickness," said Russell. "It took all my people. My son N'kala. My daughter Anja. And my wife Maya. Took them all."

"But it didn't take you," said Cate, nodding at the mummy.

"It even took our enemies. Just as it is taking everyone in your world."

"That is why we must fight it."

"No. The death you fear is only a door. There is a reason for the virus. A reason for everything."

"Then why are *you* here, Russell?"

Russell looked down at the mummy. "I'm being punished." He looked up suddenly. "Where is my heart?" Before she could answer, he went on, "If it isn't in the jar, Father Sun will not be able to weigh it on the scales of justice!" He scrabbled at the corpse, pulling at the wrappings.

Cate gently took his hands in hers. "We have your heart. We cloned you from its cells."

"You must keep it with the mummy," said Russell. "It must be kept close!"

"It isn't far," said Cate gently. "It's here in the complex."

"What have I done to deserve this punishment?" cried Russell, looking up, his voice echoing in the dark tunnel. "To be separated from the ones I love?"

Cate thought of the years she'd been separated from Chris. The only way she survived was because he was dead and could no longer miss her. But what if there really were no death? How could she have gone on, knowing he was alive, but unable to find him?

"I cannot live without my family," said Russell, finishing her thought. "I do not want to." He slumped down, his back against the curving cement wall, shaking his head ruefully. "Lightland is like a large, bright room. Everyone and everything I've ever loved is inside that room. It makes this world seem like a tiny, dark closet. I would kill myself if I wasn't afraid I would not be allowed to return to them."

Cate looked up. "Oh, Russell!"

"But what would be the point? You would just clone me again and I would have to return. I cannot leave until I know why I have been sent here. Neither can you."

"What?"

"There is also a reason *you* are here, Dr. Seagram. You didn't know about the mummy. But Chris knew. He saw you on the holo broadcast. You came here so he would also come here and show me who I really was. You are both here for reasons you do not yet understand."

"What reasons?" she asked weakly. She'd wondered this very thing just yesterday.

Russell looked her frankly. He was no longer a little boy. "To help me return home."

Cate became aware of something in her pocket. She didn't know why she had taken it from Chris's quilted vest. She just wanted just to touch it, but once it was in her hand, it was the most natural thing in the world to put it in her pocket. She removed it and held it out to Russell.

"What is that?"

"You don't remember it?"

"Should I?" he asked, peering closer.

You want to know too, don't you?

Cate said, "You mentioned a doorway to a big room?"

Russell nodded.

"I think this is the key."

He reached out for it, but Cate pulled it away. "Last time you touched it, you had a seizure. When it passed, you began talking about the place you went to."

Russell's eyes opened wide. "Lightland."

Cate nodded, then opened her hand.

You want to know too, don't you?

"Russell," she said quietly.

Russell smiled. "You want to know too, don't you?"

She was not even surprised he said it. "Yes, I do, Russell. Take me there."

Russell placed his hand on top of hers, covering the scarab. "I will take you. To Lightland."

They shut their eyes.

THIRTEEN

EPIPHANY

It wasn't like in the movies, when the spaceship gets sucked into the wormhole and spirals down a roller-coaster vortex of swirling color and sound. Instead, it was perfectly silent and dark, except for a single, radiant flash of light, and then Cate stood on the narrow rock ledge looking out across the immense caldera. The sky was perfectly blue. The rising sun cast her shadow into the dark bowl of the collapsed crater. And also, she knew, behind her was the large, circular stone hiding the cave containing the mummies. She turned, but found nothing of the sort. No stone, no cave, no mummies. Of course. She was in Lightland. There was no death here.

Turning back, she looked out across the caldera. Waterfalls coursed down the distant crater walls. A lake stood in the middle of the rolling distance and a pink dot undulated on its surface. She had no idea what it was, but it seemed alive. She scanned the grassy floor for the acacia tree, but could not see it. Below her was an immense herd of square-headed wildebeests. A hyena howled and she jumped, startled, looking up.

Above her on the rim stood a small, thin black man wearing only a loincloth. He held a gnarled staff and had jagged purple tattoos on his ankles and arms. "E n'guaa na kelia," he frowned, pointing his staff at her.

Cate looked around for Russell. He was nowhere to be seen. She gave the man the universal sign of ignorance, shrugging. He gestured in an equally universal way: *Come up here.* Cate headed up the trail. When it crested the rim, she found herself in front of the little man, no taller than she was. "Um bata ya valara," he said.

"I can't understand you," she said. "Sorry."

He stabbed his staff into the ground and shouted. "Um bata ya valara K'tanu!"

Cate understood one word, at least. "K'tanu?"

The man nodded fiercely.

So you're the greeting party, she thought. "He was supposed to come with me." She felt foolish. Come where? She was having a dream. It struck her as funny and slightly pathetic. Wishful thinking. "Hey," she said, "where's St. Peter? I'm expected, you know."

The little man whipped his staff around and struck her in the stomach. She fell to the ground, gasping, the wind knocked out of her. He stood over her, shouting, "Um bata ya valara K'tanu!" pointing his staff at her. It had a sharp stone tip, and Cate realized her mistake. Stone Age cultures were all about respecting physical power.

She bowed her head. "I'm sorry. I don't know where K'tanu is." She didn't look up.

Then the man stretched his hand out to her. She took it. His skin was cool. He lifted her to her feet and looked into her eyes, touching his chest. "Um fala Antram. Rafiki ka K'tanu. Rafiki."

Cate nodded, hearing the familiar name again. Taking a chance, she pointed to herself and said, sounding it out, "Um fala Cate. Rafiki ka K'tanu."

The man smiled, then faced the caldera, saying nothing for a long time.

Cate waited.

"I was not expecting you," he said finally as he turned back to her. "I am Antram."

"You speak my language?"

Antram shook his head. "I do not think so. We speak heart to heart. As friends of K'tanu's, our hearts understand one another."

"I don't know where K'tanu is. He may still be in my world."

"He has been pulled back twice to the Waking World. It has a strong hold on him."

"What is this place?" asked Cate. "Is this . . . heaven?" She almost laughed at the notion, but remembered Antram's quick moves with the staff. Her stomach still ached.

"This is Lightland."

"I am dreaming," said Cate. On his puzzled look, she said, "Where you go when you sleep."

"No," said Antram. "This place, where we are now, is where my people go when our time in the Waking World ends. Your people must be in another place. You are here by mistake."

"I intended to come with K'tanu. He had an amulet of green stone. It looked like a beetle."

"The Khepr," said Antram. "Yes. I placed it with him when I prepared his body for burial."

"You buried him?" asked Cate. "How did he die?"

"In battle."

Everything thus far she herself could have invented from the details Russell and Chris had shared with her. This was without doubt the most vivid dream she'd ever had, but it was still just a dream.

"You do not believe this is real," said Antram, eyeing her.

Cate smiled. Of course. Antram was her creation and would know what she was thinking.

"I am *not* your creation," said Antram, perturbed.

"I'm sorry," said Cate. "I'm a scientist and I need proof."

"What is a scientist?"

"One who studies the world and learns why things are the way they are."

"Then I am a scientist too," said Antram, gesturing around with his staff. "I know why things are the way they are. If you are a scientist, why do you not know these things?"

"Because it is a dream—it doesn't feel real."

Antram looked at her critically. "How do you know what is real? You wear too many clothes; you are cut off from the world.

Your heart is full of pride; you are cut off from wisdom. Your soul is shriveled; you are cut off from truth."

"But I need *proof*," said Cate. "Otherwise, I'll wake up and know this was just a dream."

"What proof would you believe? You listen to your mind, which can lie to you, yet you ignore your heart, which never lies." He removed a leather thong from around his neck. A beaten silver ankh symbol hung from it. He put it around Cate's neck. "You are in conflict. Your heart must prevail."

Cate touched the amulet. Antram took her by the shoulders and turned her to face the caldera. "Listen," he whispered. "Listen with your heart, not your ears. See with your heart, not your eyes. Feel with your heart, not your fingertips. Know with your heart, not with your mind."

Cate looked out across the vast bowl, now rapidly filling with sunlight. High overhead, an eagle soared. She got on her tiptoes, aching to fly with the eagle. Her feet left the ground. In an instant, she was soaring, not in her own body, but in the eagle's, seeing the world through its eyes, high above the caldera. She saw herself and Antram far below on the crater rim, looking up at her. Then she was diving steeply toward the ground. And there it was, the acacia tree, standing alone in a sea of waving dry grass, out in the middle of the caldera. She swooped low, soaring under the tree's canopy and suddenly found herself sitting on a granite outcropping, licking a large, fuzzy paw. She shook her head and a large mane entered her field of vision. She rolled over, arching her back.

Then she felt a cold wetness and slipped between rocks in a stream, her vision two separate, distorted views. She glided through the water. No thought except *food*.

Suddenly, she was pulled out of the water and was flying through the air, caught in strong claws. Now she was the hawk, wings beating fiercely at the air, with scarcely more thought than the fish, a mind focused solely on feeding.

In a nest high up in a tree on the caldera rim, she delivered the fish to three mottled gray hatchlings, who gobbled up the feast hungrily. A feeling of satisfaction entered her.

Then a stone struck her in the head and she fell to the ground. A large, warm hand scooped her up and now she was running toward the village, her slender dark legs churning. Entering the village, she handed the bird to a woman with a delicate, triangular face. "Thank you, N'kala," said the woman, smiling.

And then she was the woman, looking proudly down at her young son. She handed the bird to another woman. "Look what N'kala caught," she said. "He is a wonderful hunter."

Cate looked down at herself. She wore a simple cloth wrap around her hips. Her breasts were bare and at her neck was a silver pendant, the ankh symbol. She shooed N'kala away, sat, and once again took up her weaving. Her hands moved swiftly, crafting a reed basket, and Cate felt the woman's thoughts crowd out her own.

Where is he? she mused. *One moment he is with us and then suddenly he is gone.* She touched the pendant, cool at her neck, and Cate felt a burning within her that pushed away all other thoughts. K'tanu. This woman, whose soul Cate was sharing, was Maya, his wife. Her children were N'kala and Anja. She had watched her husband die, run through with a spear, even as she lay dying herself, holding their tiny, unnamed child. *Oh, K'tanu!* cried Maya's heart. *My love, where are you? Why can you not be with us? We need you. I need you.* Cate felt the woman's heartache as her own. A terrible doubt lingered in her mind. Was he coming back? Would she be alone, without him, for eternity?

No, thought Cate. *He will return.* She thought of all the years she'd spent without Chris, a loss so great at times that all she could do was cry. *He will return,* she repeated, reaching out to Maya. *You must have faith.*

I must have faith, thought Maya. *I must believe.*

"Do you believe?" asked Antram.

Cate had crumpled to the ground, her hand still clutching the silver amulet. She looked up at Antram, but could not speak. He helped her to her feet and Cate saw a different world than before. Infinite varieties of life, each with its own consciousness, seeking to live life to its fullest. Even the very stones beneath her feet were alive, each aching to fulfill its own, unique purpose. Tears rolled down her cheeks, as alive as she was, each aware of its part in the greater whole. The entire world in a single teardrop—a fractal universe. The eagle, the lion, the fish, the water, the hawk, the child, the woman. K'tanu. Chris. Cate. Even Cobalt. Each had a purpose. Each ached to understand and fulfill that purpose.

And something with infinite wisdom had organized it all.

She stood on the crater rim, her heart bursting. She turned to Antram, barely visible through her tears.

"Now you know what is real," he said. "All is order. All is as planned. All is love."

Unable to speak, she nodded. It was true. No further empirical investigation was necessary. All the facts were in. All the double-blind studies were complete, the results catalogued, collated, and recorded. All the peer reviews had been submitted. All the skeptics were silenced. All was love.

"I never knew," she managed. "How much I . . . " She broke down in tears.

Antram put his arm around her. ". . . how much you were loved."

"Yes!" she cried. "I feel like I'll melt! Who is it? Who could possibly love me this much?"

Antram gestured around. "Everything."

Cate fell to her knees as tears coursed down her cheeks. *Now I know why people pray*, she thought as the last remnants of consciousness fell away into white emptiness.

It's to give thanks.

"Cate. Cate." Russell held her head in his lap. "Wake up."

She opened her eyes and threw her arms around him. "Oh, K'tanu! It's so beautiful!" She pulled back and saw the surprised look on his face. "She is there! Maya! She wants you to come home! She loves you so much! So much!" She hugged him again. "So much!"

"What happened?" asked Russell. They were still in the cool, dark tunnel, next to the icy storage container. He still held the amulet in his hand. "Why couldn't I go with you?"

"She is there, K'tanu. She is there!"

Russell looked down at the amulet. "Then why can't I go to her?"

Cate got to her knees. The mummy lay near them. "I don't know, K'tanu. I don't know. I saw Antram there. He showed me everything." Tears started in her eyes. "I never knew! I never knew!"

"I wish I could have seen it."

Cate took the amulet. "Maybe it's because we were both touching it. Here. You try it alone."

Russell straightened and closed his eyes. Cate placed the amulet in his open hands. After a moment he opened his eyes. "Still here," he said. "Perhaps the key no longer works."

"Let me try," said Cate. She took the amulet, closed her eyes, and waited. Nothing. When she opened her eyes, she saw tears forming in Russell's eyes. "K'tanu?"

"The door is closed." He sat back, shaking his head. "I can no longer return."

"Yes, you can!" said Cate, taking his hands in hers. "You must return! It's the only thing that matters. I see that now. Everything depends upon you going *home*!"

"Perhaps I am supposed to stay here. To help you cure Cobalt."

"No!" cried Cate. "You said all things have a reason. I know what my reason is now. I'm supposed to help you go back to Lightland. Nothing else matters! I know it!"

"How do you know it?" asked Russell. "Maybe what you saw wasn't real."

"I know what is real," said Cate firmly. "It's so real, my heart is about to burst!" She got to her feet. "We've got to tell Chris about this, K'tanu."

Russell shook his head. "Why do you keep calling me that?"

Cate looked down at him, steel in her eyes. "Because that is your name."

ALLY

Chris opened his eyes. Cate could tell he was completely disoriented. "It's Cate," she whispered.

"I know that," he frowned. "I just don't know who *I* am."

"You're going," said Cate, pulling him to his feet. Russell stood in the doorway, dressed in military fatigue pants and a green scrub pullover, a backpack slung over his shoulder.

"What time is it?" asked Chris.

"A little before four," said Cate. "I need you to take K'tanu upstairs as quickly and quietly as possible."

Chris pulled a sweatshirt over his head. "K'tanu?"

"His real name."

Chris frowned. "Where are *you* going?"

"To make sure he really *is* one of a kind." She winked.

"So I guess you're going with me after all," said Chris.

"Going where?"

"Crazy."

"This way," whispered K'tanu, leading Chris to the stairwell. He wore a hooded gray sweatshirt over his scrubs. It was so quiet Chris could hear the sighing of the air in the A/C vents. They entered the stairwell and started up. "It's seven floors to the upper level," said K'tanu excitedly.

"What's going on?"

"It will be easier if Cate tells you."

"You've never been outside, have you?"

Ahead of him, K'tanu shook his head. "Not in this life."

They reached the top level and exited the stairwell, finding themselves in a lobby with two elevators on their right and the glass-walled security pod on their left. At the end of the vestibule was something covered with blankets on a stainless-steel gurney. Chris pulled the blankets back, revealing the mummy. "We're bringing this along too?"

"We are," said a deep, resonant voice.

Chris turned. Captain Lomax stood with his hands on his hips, the heel of one hand on the butt of his holstered gun.

"Captain Lomax is going to help us," said K'tanu.

"Help us do what?"

"Escape," said Lomax, picking up an olive-green bundle and tossing it to Chris, who found himself holding a zippered vinyl body bag. "Help me stow this boy's better half."

Chris unzipped the bag and they gently placed the mummy in it.

"I thought he'd weigh more," said Lomax.

"We're seventy-five percent water," said Chris. "All of that is removed in mummification."

"By the natron salts," said Lomax, carefully tucking the head inside the bag.

"How did you know about that?" asked Chris.

Lomax reached inside his shirt and pulled out his dog tags. A tiny silver ankh symbol hung next to them on the chain.

"Disciples of Osiris," said Chris, amazed. He turned to K'tanu. "Did you know?"

"I'd seen the amulet," said K'tanu, "but until an hour ago, I didn't know what it meant."

"I guess he saw it when we played basketball," said Lomax.

"Why are you helping us?" asked Chris.

"Grave robbing is against my religion," said Lomax flatly, fixing Chris with a disapproving look. "Russell told me what happened with the scarab amulet, and Cate's experience as well."

"Captain Lomax," said K'tanu. "Remember?"

Lomax nodded. "Right. K'tanu. Sorry, son."

"What happened to Cate?" asked Chris.

"She should be the one to tell you," said K'tanu. "She'll be here soon."

"What's taking her?" asked Chris.

"A few last-minute chores," said Lomax.

"But why are we bringing the mummy? The heart is what they used to clone him with."

"Without it, K'tanu cannot return to Lightland," said Lomax.

"You believe in Lightland?"

"Of course. All intelligent people believe in God, Chris."

"And why is that?" asked Chris, perturbed at the subtle dig.

"Because the universe is endless, right?"

"That's what they say."

"So something that goes on forever has room for everything— even God." He clapped Chris on the back. "You'll get used to the idea. K'tanu here," he said, nodding toward the young man standing by the gurney, looking solemnly down at his own body, "is pretty convincing evidence."

"Convincing enough to risk your life?"

"I've risked my life for a hell of a lot less."

"So where are we going?"

"We're going to place his mummy in the tomb with his wife and children."

Chris blinked, surprised. "You know where that is, don't you?"

Lomax nodded. "Yes, I do. Africa."

Cate shut the Level 4 door and plugged in her air supply. She waited a minute as the forced air cleared the faceplate fog. Then she picked up the bolt cutters and approached the bank of freezers. The one on the far left was padlocked. She had always wondered why that particular freezer was bolted; now she knew why. The bolt cutters made quick work of the lock, and she opened the freezer door. She turned and opened the backpack, withdrawing the white stone jar, removing the orb-topped stopper. Then she reached into the freezer and removed a plastic container with a snap lid. Opening it, she removed a zip-lock bag, holding it up, peering at it.

"Well, K'tanu, no one can say you don't have a heart," she whispered. "Or two." She placed the bag into the canopic jar and replaced the lid, putting it in the backpack. She turned back to the freezer, where twenty glass vials hung in plastic clips in four neat rows. Then she picked up the bolt cutters again, feeling their satisfying weight in her hands.

Lomax pointed at the bank of security monitors. On the top row were several angles of the main entrance. Two choppers sat in the predawn darkness. "I don't think they'll shoot at us as long as have him." He nodded toward K'tanu, still standing beyond the glass wall, looking at the mummy on the gurney.

"They'll force us to land and then they'll shoot *us*," said Chris. "You know that."

"We'll try to avoid that."

"That's your plan?"

"The best I could do at a moment's notice. Anyway, when we get topside, while I prep one of the Comanches, I want you to disable the other one."

"How?"

"Were you ever a teenager? Ever pee in somebody's gas tank?"

"No!"

"Well, I won't ask you to do it now. Use sand instead." He sat down at the console and started typing. "I'm initiating a security system self-test. Takes about two hours, during which time the system goes offline. We usually do it during the day, when we can post guards. Today, we're starting it . . ." He pressed a button with a flourish. "Now." The monitors went blank.

∧∧∧

A single beep awakened her. Cloudburst rolled out of bed and pushed a button on the HP module on the night stand. A holo appeared. SECURITY SYSTEM SELF-TEST IN PROGRESS, it said in quavering red letters. She rubbed the sleep from her eyes. At this hour? She lay back and closed her eyes. They had one of these last week, didn't they? And weren't they usually during the day? She opened her eyes, sat up, and picked up the phone, punching Lomax's extension.

The phone rang and rang. All right, he was running the test, but why now? She stood, pulled on her robe, and crossed to her computer module, waving her hand across the featureless desktop. The keys emerged from the flat surface and a blank holo appeared above, a sparkling, misty cloud. "Security pod visual," she said, and the color coalesced, forming an image of the pod from a high angle at the rear of the room. Lomax was in a chair, his head hidden by the high back. The monitors showed their usual views of the complex, over forty in all, cycling between sector cameras.

Wait a minute, she thought. *Those monitors go blank during the test.*

She was about to key the intercom when Lomax swivelled his chair and reached out to adjust a monitor. Only it wasn't Lomax; it was Lt. Jennings, his second in command. She was about to press the button and speak to him when she stopped. *Where's Lomax?* She glanced at the clock on the wall. Five thirty-seven. Where would he be at this hour, if not in security overseeing the test? She picked up the phone and dialed the security pod extension. It rang several times. She looked at the holo, expecting to see Jennings reach for the phone. He didn't. Then she noticed that the light on the phone module was not flashing. She hung up and dialed again. It rang on her end, but the light on the phone in the pod did not illuminate.

Cloudburst cursed and stood up so fast she knocked her chair to the ground running from her room.

〰〰〰

"Who was that?" whispered Chris, still looking at the phone, which had just stopped ringing. They were standing in the security pod.

"One guess," said Lomax, turning to a large metal cabinet. He dialed the combination and opened it. There was a large selection of firearms inside. "Take your pick."

"Do you have a pistol in there, like the one you carry?" asked Chris.

"Standard issue nine-mill Glock," said Lomax, tossing one to Chris, along with two clips. Chris stuffed the gun into his waistband and the clips in his vest pockets.

"Never point that thing at your future," said Lomax, slapping him on the shoulder.

Chris removed the gun and put it in the pocket of his quilted vest. *You're assuming I have one*, he thought.

"Where's Captain Lomax?" asked Jennings, pulling on his pants and shirt.

Cloudburst stood in the doorway, glaring at him like *he* had gone AWOL. "Something's up," she said, turning from the door.

Jennings pulled on his boots and grabbed his pistol off the night stand. She was waiting for him outside. The doors to the other soldiers' rooms were shut. "Did you check his room?" asked Jennings, tucking his shirt in.

"He's not there. He's not in security—you are."

"Me?"

Cloudburst turned and headed down the corridor. "Morons," she said to herself.

Cate burst through the stairwell door. Chris jumped to his feet. "Where have you been?"

She ignored him and went straight to K'tanu, who still stood by his mummy, as if guarding it. "Here it is," she said, handing him the backpack. He carefully unzipped it, looking inside.

"Okay, we're ready," said Lomax, indicating the elevator call button. "Once I touch this, the alarm will sound."

"Can't you disable it?" asked Chris. "What were you typing in there?"

"I disabled the cameras, that's all," said Lomax. "Part of the self-test is a lock-down of all exterior entrances. I bypassed it for this one elevator. We'll take it topside, disable it, and be on our way. It'll take 'em a few minutes to override, but by then we'll be long gone." He punched the button, and immediately a klaxon blared. The steel double doors opened. Lomax wheeled the gurney inside, followed by the others. The door closed and the elevator began its slow ascent.

Lomax turned to Chris, smiling. "Gotta pee yet?"

FIFTEEN

WRITTEN IN STONE

The elevator door opened into complete darkness. Lomax edged past the gurney. "I'll get the lights. Chris, prop the door open. Cate and K'tanu, bring the gurney!" He trotted away. K'tanu and Cate pulled the gurney out of the elevator. Chris watched them move across the concrete floor, disappearing into the darkness. The light thrown by the interior elevator light began to thin and he whirled around. The doors were closing. He thrust his arm out, stopping them. "I need something to prop these open with!" he shouted. The other elevator bell chimed, the down light illuminated. "The other one is going down! I thought you said you disabled them!"

Suddenly the overhead lights went on. Far across the staging area, by the two immense exterior doors, Lomax was working on a panel. Cate and K'tanu had almost reached him with the gurney. Chris was trapped, unable to move. The doors constantly tried to close. He couldn't take his eyes off the down arrow above the next elevator. Someone was going to step out of that car in a couple of minutes and shoot him dead. "A little help!" he yelled, trying not to sound frantic.

"Be right there!" called Cate, running back toward him, snagging a wheeled utility cart on her way.

The elevator next to Chris chimed again. He waited for the up light to illuminate, his heart in his throat. Cate arrived with the cart and shoved it between the doors. The doors hit the cart, retracted, and hit it again, each time nudging it a little. "This won't work," said Chris.

Cate upended the cart and pushed it between the doors, its wheels spinning in the air. As she hauled him away, he looked over his shoulder. The up arrow on the other elevator still had not lit.

Lomax was just shutting the panel. "Okay, the pneumatics are bypassed. We'll have to push. Ready? One, two . . . " He placed his shoulder against the heavy door and grunted. "Three!" The immense doors slowly opened. Though still fully dark, the jagged outline of the low hills to the west was visible by starlight. They wheeled the gurney outside and it was immediately mired in drifted sand. "Afraid of that," said Lomax. "Gotta carry him. Cate and K'tanu, see to it." He turned to Chris and pointed at the first Comanche, then trotted toward the second chopper.

Cate and K'tanu took the body bag and shuffled toward the chopper, a good thirty yards away. As they walked, their backs bent with effort, K'tanu sniffed. "What's that smell?"

"What smell?" asked Cate. "I don't smell anything."

"It's sweet."

"It's sage," called out Chris. He found the Comanche's fuel port. He scuffled his feet—the cement under the choppers had been scoured clean by rotor blast. He ran back to the main doors, where sand had drifted against them. Far across the cavernous interior staging area, the elevator dome light still shone, the upended cart still in place, but he could not tell which of the two arrow lights were lit above the second elevator. He pulled off his boot and scooped sand into it, then trotted back to the chopper. Just then, the second Comanche's rotors began to turn. A shrill, rising whine filled the air. The cargo door slid back and Cate and K'tanu trundled the body bag inside. Lomax was in the pilot's seat, feverishly flipping switches, glancing repeatedly toward the entrance doors.

Chris upended the boot, dumping sand into the fuel spout. It clogged and he had to poke it down with his fingers. It was too dark to tell how much had gone in and how much he'd spilled on the ground. He ran back to the drift to get more. He filled the boot again and ran back to the chopper. His hands shook as he poured sand into the fuel spout, unable to see much because his body threw a shadow across the spout. He heard yelling, shouting for him to hurry. He looked back at the entrance. The interior elevator light had gone out—the doors had somehow closed. "They're coming!" he yelled, forcing sand down the fuel spout. He needed something to wash it down with.

Inside the other chopper, Lomax keyed his loud-hailer mike. "Chris, let's go!"

Chris ran around the nose of the other Comanche, zipping his pants. At that same moment, deep inside the staging area, the elevator dinged, the doors opened, and several people emerged at a run. Chris sprinted toward the chopper, which was throwing up so much dust it blinded him. He bumped his head on the fuselage, whirled around, felt someone grab his vest, and was hauled inside. The chopper lifted off while he still had a stockinged foot on the ground, his boot clutched in the crook of his free arm.

"Got you!" yelled Cate, pulling him inside and slamming the sliding door shut.

Below, just outside the steel doors, Lt. Jennings lifted his sidearm, aiming at the chopper.

Cloudburst pushed the muzzle down. "Not that way. Not yet."

"What, then?"

Cloudburst scowled, watching the Comanche disappear into the darkness. "Go wake Zuñiga."

"Get up here!" shouted Lomax. Chris crawled over the center console and into the copilot's seat. Lomax handed him a headset, and he put it on. "What took you back there?" shouted Lomax.

"The sand wouldn't go down the spout," said Chris. "There was a screen or something."

"I saw you zipping up. I was kidding about pissing in the tank, you know."

"Couldn't think of anything else."

"If you can make water in a tight fix like that," said Lomax, "you might make a soldier after all."

Chris looked out the window. They were barely fifty feet above the ground, which was just a shade darker than the starry black sky. "Where we headed?"

"West and north to go east," said Lomax. "Empty country." He yanked the stick sharply to the right and the horizon out his window disappeared, replaced by empty, black sky.

"Will they follow us?" asked Chris, hanging on for dear life.

"Not if your aim was any good."

"I can't find Russell," said Ron. "He isn't anywhere."

"He can't not be *anywhere*!" said Cloudburst. They were in the security-pod. Ron was still in his pajamas, his hair wild, his face red from running up the stairs. Jennings was bent over the console, trying to undo the changes Lomax made to the security protocols.

"Well, he's not below," said Ron. "Did he go with them?"

"He's got this thing screwed up pretty good," said Jennings, punching keys.

"Shit," growled Cloudburst.

"There's more," said Ron.

"What more?" *Didn't either of these morons have answers, instead of insipid, stupid ques—*

"She took the mummy's heart."

"What in the hell for?"

"It *was* the DNA source; we could have used it to clone him again. And she destroyed the embryos."

"Dammit!" howled Cloudburst. "Why is she *doing* this?"

Ron shrugged again.

If he shrugged once more, Cloudburst was going to let Jennings shoot somebody after all.

"The body's gone, too," added Ron.

Cloudburst was so surprised she laughed. "What in the world for?"

"It *was* Tempest's mummy," said Ron. "I guess he wanted it back."

Cloudburst glared at the two men, both of whom looked away sheepishly. "Gentlemen, you know who is *really* gonna benefit from cloning?"

Ron didn't say anything. Jennings looked confused.

She scowled. "Women—we won't need men anymore."

"Keep your eyes open," said Lomax. They swung in a tight arc around a low, barren hill. Chris looked out the window, his stomach in knots. The ground looked about ten feet away. When they leveled off, he noted that the eastern horizon was brightening.

"They'll come from the south, out of Nellis AFB."

"Helicopters?"

"Probably. If we can make it to the Grand Canyon, I might be able to lose them in there."

"Then let's go!"

"Negative. We'd have to fly right past Nellis to get there." He flipped a switch and a 3-D map appeared on the glass panel in front of them. He pointed at a small red blip. "That's us. This is Vegas. Grand Canyon. Nothing much else, except . . . " He pressed an arrow key and the display panned to the east. The colors changed from yellow to deep browns and greens, indicating steep topographical changes.

"What's that?" asked Chris.

"Virgin River Canyon," said Lomax, tapping the screen. "We might have a chance in there."

Back in the cargo area, Cate and K'tanu held on for dear life as Lomax hugged the terrain, swooping and diving, nearly flying upside down at times, it seemed. The mummy was strapped on a litter between them. Cate watched as the eastern horizon grew brighter. Cloudburst would have jets in the air in minutes, though she doubted they would fire on them. No, they'd probably just force the chopper down, grab K'tanu, shoot everyone else, and leave their bodies to rot in the sun.

What did she expect? She'd just put the fate of the world in jeopardy because she believed she'd been a hawk in a bizarre African afterlife hallucination. She put her head in her hands. Is this what faith really was? Self-destructive insanity?

Cloudburst dialed Samuel Fox, Director of Central Intelligence. He was a hard-nosed military vet who, some whispered, had masterminded the mainland Chinese coup a dozen years ago that had fractured the country in two, turning its hegemonic tendencies inward, much to the relief of the West. Fox was arguably the power behind the throne, a close personal friend of the President.

Fox consulted this watch and frowned. "Where are they headed?"

"No idea," said Cloudburst.

"There's little air traffic these days, so that gives us an advantage. But if they dump the chopper and go to ground, we might lose them."

"What can we do?"

"I'll scramble Nellis." He flipped through a notebook on his desk and then looked up. "You have another chopper there, don't you? Why aren't you after them?"

"It's been sabotaged."

"Hmm," said Fox. "Range on the Comanche is just over four hundred miles."

"Can we see them on satellite?"

"Checking on that now," said Fox. "The closest one doesn't enter that airspace for another twenty minutes. Plus, I hesitate to re-task a satellite unless it's absolutely necessary." He looked squarely into the VidPhone and waited.

Cloudburst looked back, not knowing what to say.

"You're supposed to tell me why it's absolutely necessary," said Fox.

"They've got Lazarus! They've destroyed the embryos and taken the source material. Without him, we're dead in the water!"

"Fair enough," said Fox. "Choppers will be in the air in five and over you in ten. Do what you can on your end." The visual blinked off.

Cloudburst leaned back in her chair, relieved. Lomax obviously had no idea with whom he was tangling. After they found the Comanche and forced it to land, she hoped Lomax did something *really* stupid. She'd like to see the look on his face when real soldiers took control of the situation.

The Shoshones were the largest range of mountains anywhere near Yucca Mountain, but they still only rose three thousand feet above the flat alkaline plains. So it wasn't until he swung the chopper around the southern end of the formation, putting the hills between them and Yucca Mountain, that Lomax relaxed. Nevertheless, he still kept the chopper impossibly low, and their steep climbs and dives made the scariest roller coaster seem tame by comparison.

Suddenly, Chris yelped with surprise. "Turn back! Turn back!"

"I don't think so," said Lomax

"I just saw my name written down there! Turn right!"

Lomax muttered something but swung around anyway, and Chris saw the letters again, formed out of rocks. Near them was a dirty blue pickup and a man standing by it, waving his arms.

"It's Elvin!" cried Chris. "We've got to land!"

"They've probably got jets scrambling at Nellis as we speak," said Lomax irritably. "Who is this guy?"

"He's a friend. Land, please!"

Lomax shook his head, dipped the nose, and lost about a hundred feet in two seconds, putting Chris's stomach in his throat. The skids touched the ground twenty feet from Elvin's truck.

"Why are we landing?" yelled Cate from the back.

"It's Elvin," said Chris, jumping out.

"You got one minute!" yelled Lomax.

Chris ran to Elvin. "What are you doing here?" he yelled over the rotor blast.

"I wasn't gonna leave you, no matter what I said," yelled Elvin. "So I parked here and hiked up there to see what happened." He pointed at the hilltop separating them from Yucca Mountain. "When they came out the next morning, guns deployed, I worried some, but when I saw your gal, I knew you'd be all right."

"We're escaping," said Chris.

"I figured you'd wear out your welcome before long."

"Chris!" yelled Cate from the open cargo door. "Time's up!"

Chris turned to Elvin. "Come on!" He reached for Elvin, who backed up a step.

"Not so fast. Why are they after you?"

"They'll think you were in on this," said Chris. "Those chain guns are for real."

Elvin considered this a moment, then opened the truck door, grabbed a handful of Slim Jims, and trotted after Chris toward the chopper.

SIXTEEN

EYE OF THE NEEDLE

K'tanu was bent over, his face drained of color. The smell of vomit filled the cabin. "Havin' fun?" asked Elvin, buckling his harness. He bit off a piece of jerky and leaned back in his webbed seat, smiling.

The chopper flew north, no more than fifty feet off the ground. When the Shoshones gave out after about fifteen miles, Lomax turned into sun, just now peeking over the horizon, blinding them. Lomax lowered his visor and piloted by instrument, his eyes glued to the panel. "Gonna have company soon!" he said. "Chris, you're the gunner. You will arm your weapons *only* when I tell you, and then engage *only* when I command. Got it?"

Chris nodded.

"I need verbal responses," said Lomax, still focusing on the terrain ahead.

"Aye aye," said Chris.

"In the Army, we say, 'Affirmative,' or 'copy.'"

"Affirmative," said Chris.

"The trigger on the stick between your knees fires the chain guns. The red button fires the missiles," said Lomax. "I'll disengage your stick from flight control. You'll be free to aim and fire. Use your HUD. Got it?"

"Affirmative," said Chris.

"They'll come low and fast if they're choppers, high and shit-in-your-pants fast if they're jets."

The sky was pink, the sun in their eyes. Chris began to realize just how exposed they were out there in the flat, even this close to the ground. "How far to the Virgin River Canyon?"

"Three hundred kilometers," said Lomax. "About twenty minutes."

"How long before they find us?"

"Sometime between now and then," said Lomax. "You got a problem firing back?"

Chris gulped. "No."

The sun was so bright through the windscreen, Chris couldn't see a thing. "Didn't the Red Baron always come out of the sun?" he asked.

"You want to drive?" asked Lomax.

"No, sir," said Chris, his stomach falling away as Lomax pushed the stick forward.

Jennings turned to Cloudburst. "Satellite has them headed east, about sixty nautical miles north of us, just past Groom Lake." He listened for another moment. "Choppers are scrambled. ETA Mesquite in thirty minutes."

Lieutenant Zuñiga appeared in the security pod doorway, wiping his hands on a red rag. "Good news, Director. The sand didn't get into the engine. We're flushing the fuel tanks—we'll have her airworthy in twenty minutes."

Cloudburst jammed a clip into her gun. "And I want to be in the air a minute after that."

Elvin pointed at the blanket-wrapped shape strapped to the litter behind them. "Somebody hurt?"

"It's my body," said K'tanu, who now felt a little better after emptying his stomach. Once the hills gave way to empty, flat desert, Lomax had no choice but to fly straight and level.

"*Your* body?"

"K'tanu is a clone. That is his body."

Elvin nodded and Cate wondered if he was just humoring her. "We had to stop them," she said, "so we took him and his heart. We're taking them both back to Africa."

That got Elvin's full attention. "Isn't that where Cobalt came from?" K'tanu nodded and Elvin looked at Cate. "I can see why he's okay with it, but you're not immune, are you?"

Cate shook her head.

"Now I know why you and Chris are a pair. You're as crazy as he is."

"Helicopters!" shouted Chris, pointing out his side window, to the south.

"Where?" asked Lomax, still focused ahead.

"Behind us!" yelled Chris. "Four o'clock!"

"High or low?"

"Even!" shouted Chris.

"Shit!" yelled Lomax.

From over a rise behind them, two sleek black Comanches appeared, falling into the chopper's wake. Lomax reached over and flipped on Chris's HUD. Suddenly, Chris was looking at the rear view camera, the two choppers plainly visible behind them.

"Half mile behind us," said Lomax. "Weapons systems!"

There were dark bands at the top and bottom of Chris's HUD display, filled with red icons with three-letter acronyms like DSI, HGT, and CGO. "What's CGO?" he asked.

"Chain gun outboard," said Lomax, making wide, sweeping turns, forcing the pursuing choppers to weave to stay with him. "Canyon in fifteen clicks. Keep 'em off us."

"How?"

"Fire a few rounds. Back 'em off."

"Okay," said Chris, flipping up the safety catch and moving the stick. The HUD moved as well. He centered the red box on the lead chopper. It turned green. He squeezed the trigger. The tracer rounds, the first couple of bullets of every burst, hit the chopper, but by the time the live rounds arrived, both helicopters had broken high and away. "They're backing off," shouted Chris.

"They'll be back," said Lomax. "Ten clicks! Heads down back there!"

Within moments, the two choppers were behind them again, this time in tandem formation. *Smaller target*, thought Chris. He watched in horror as their missile outboards swivelled into position. "I think they're going to fire," he said. Just then, a puff of smoke erupted from the lead chopper. "They fired! Incoming!"

Lomax banked left. The missile impacted on a low hill in their wake. The chase choppers burst through the smoke, closing the distance.

"That was close!" said Chris.

"It wasn't locked on," growled Lomax. "If they'd wanted to hit us, they would have."

"Here comes another one!" yelled Chris. A missile flared from the lead chopper, this time racing above them, impacting on a hillside as Lomax banked steeply left. "I think they want to hit us!" yelled Chris.

"Shut up and fire!" yelled Lomax.

Chris squeezed off another three short bursts, but the pursuing choppers anticipated it and pulled up. The rounds went harmlessly into empty air.

"Five clicks!" shouted Lomax.

Before them, the red and yellow cliffs of the Shivwits Plateau rose abruptly four thousand feet from the desert floor. Lomax thrust the throttle all the way forward and nosed the chopper down, reaching two hundred fifty knots. It looked to Chris like Lomax intended to ram them right into the cliffs. "Where are you going?"

"Keep firing!"

Chris fired twice more, but he couldn't take his eyes off the mountains. If they didn't start climbing *now* they'd never make it over. "Isn't there supposed to be a *canyon*?"

"You do your job, I'll do mine!"

Chris looked in his rear view. A single chopper pursued them. "One of the choppers is gone!"

"He read my mind!" shouted Lomax, veering left so suddenly that Chris inadvertently squeezed the trigger, sending more than fifty rounds harmlessly into the air behind them.

"Our seven!" shouted Lomax. One of the choppers had arced to the left and was headed at breakneck speed toward the cliffs. "He's going to cut us off," yelled Lomax.

Then Chris finally saw it, a small cleft in the sheer cliffs that grew ever more distinct. It was not more than a hundred yards wide at the bottom of the cliffs. Out of it ran a glistening, green ribbon, the Virgin River. "We're going into that?"

"Lose 'em in there," said Lomax, dropping the nose even further to achieve maximum speed. Directly out of Lomax's window, at nine o'clock, the other Comanche also raced toward the defile. "Since we brought the family," said Lomax, nodding toward Cate and the others, "he's faster than we are."

The chopper behind them began to slow and rise. "The one behind us is letting us go," said Chris.

"This one isn't," said Lomax, gesturing at the chopper racing neck and neck with them toward the canyon opening. And then, for just an instant, the chopper hesitated and Lomax smiled. "Got him," he said, plunging into the cliff shadow and then into the narrow canyon, turning them nearly sideways as he did. Chris saw the winding river below them. He looked at his rear camera. The chopper was following them inside the canyon, but it had fallen back, pacing them. Lomax hooked left, rounding a hairpin turn.

Chris fired, but the canyon walls were so close that his rounds hit before the other chopper even appeared. "Narrow section coming up," shouted Lomax. "Engage Hellfires."

Chris flipped the safety back and put his thumb on the red button. Using his HUD, he blinked twice at the flashing red missile icon. It would not turn green. "I can't lock on!"

"Don't worry, just fire when I tell you to!"

They followed the freeway up the canyon, which mimicked the river's winding path. Above them, the sandstone cliffs glowed gold in the morning light. "Okay!" yelled Lomax. "Three, two, one, *fire!*" He turned sharply right, around a fin of red rock protruding from the canyon wall. The pursuit chopper slowed to make the turn, and when Chris pushed the button, it wasn't even visible. The missile impacted on the rock fin. It dissolved in a burst of white light, and rocks tumbled off the summit just as the other chopper appeared. The pilot swerved wide to avoid the rock fall and grazed the opposite canyon wall. The chopper's tail impacted the cliff, destroying the stabilizer fan. Without a rudder, the chopper wobbled out of control. It struck the canyon wall, exploding. An instant later, Lomax turned sharply left, and the chopper disappeared behind another turn.

"Got him!" shouted Chris. He looked back and met Cate's eyes. She glared at him, no doubt responding to his juvenile video-arcade bravado. He looked back at Lomax, chastened.

Lomax saw his look and said, "They were shooting at you." He nodded out the window. "Where's the other one?"

Chris blinked at the rearview icon in his HUD. "Not down here," he said.

Lomax began to climb. "He's up top." The river fell away and Chris's stomach plunged as he watched the cliff walls move quickly downward. When they popped up to plateau level, Lomax turned the chopper around, facing west. Several canyon turns back, a plume of oily black smoke rose. "Where is he?" asked Lomax.

"There," said Chris, pointing. Rising up out of the canyon near where the other chopper went down was the second Comanche.

"He's on us," said Lomax, turning and dipping the nose, heading down into the canyon again. All Chris could see was ground rushing up at him. They leveled off twenty feet above the river. Behind them, the other chopper appeared. "We're running out of canyon," said Lomax. The pursuing chopper was well back, pacing them, unwilling to suffer the same fate as the other pilot.

"He's not going for it," said Lomax, making a U-turn and heading straight back for the other chopper. It pulled up just in time and they roared beneath it, headed back into the narrowest part of the canyon. "Come on, buddy," whispered Lomax, looking at the rear display as the chopper hesitated. "Where's your killer instinct?"

The chopper's nose fell and it started after them. "Attaboy," smiled Lomax. "Chris, arm a Hellfire."

"It's armed," said Chris.

Lomax swerved through several hairpin turns, slowing as he did.

"He's gaining!" yelled Chris.

"Good," said Lomax, slowing even more.

"He's right on top of us!"

Just then they rounded a bend and saw nothing but smoke in front of them. Lomax pulled back on the stick so sharply that all Chris saw was sky. Below them, the other chopper raced around the bend and disappeared into the smoke. Lomax pointed the nose down. "Fire into that."

Chris pressed the red button. A missile shot out from under the Comanche and disappeared into the smoke. A great explosion was heard and flames erupted from the smoke, consuming it in an immense fireball. Lomax lifted them straight up.

Chris couldn't see a thing. "What the hell was that?"

"I keyed on the wreck's heat signature. The explosion got the other one."

They finally cleared the rising smoke, finding themselves above the canyon. Lomax turned the chopper east, into the sun, and dipped the nose.

SACRED ARCH

Dr. Cloudburst stood next to the rail car, pointing a flashlight into the empty container. "At least now we know why Tempest was here," she said. "He found out we had the mummy." She turned to Ron. "You studied it, didn't you?"

"What do you mean?"

"Was there anything about it that was . . . unusual?"

Ron shrugged. "What do I know about mummies? Anyway, the viable tissue is in the heart."

Cloudburst frowned. Taking the heart she could understand, but the mummy? She ran her hand along the frosted container edge. "So, what is so important about the mummy?"

"Well, it's too late now," said Ron, turning away.

Cloudburst watched him go. *That's right, Ron, walk away. That's why I'm in charge, not you. You give up too easily.* She turned back. *Something is going on and I'm going to find out what it is.*

"See that?" said Lomax, pointing.

Chris squinted into the sun. "That round-topped mountain?"

"Navajo Mountain," said Lomax. "Biggest in the area. At the foot, on Lake Powell—or what used to be Lake Powell—is Rainbow

Bridge. Lots of overhanging cliffs. We'll land and wait these guys out."
He swung low over Glen Canyon Dam. In its heyday, Lake Powell
provided water and electricity for most of Arizona and southern
Utah. But twenty years before, environmentalists successfully
lobbied for the draining of the lake, asserting that ancient Navajo
ruins had illegally been drowned fifty years before. Now the water
was down hundreds of feet below its former levels, and the sheer
red canyon walls were stained with black mineral rings like a giant
bathtub. "There was no one left to enjoy it anyway," said Lomax as
they cruised up the canyon just above the slowly flowing Colorado
River. "Still, it was a great place to water-ski."

Chris had never seen anything like it. It was like the Grand
Canyon on a smaller scale. While the Grand, fifty miles downstream,
was incredible, it was too just big to comprehend. On the other hand,
Glen Canyon was just big enough to stun you into silence: an alien
planet with no vegetation, just sheer cliffs of red and ocher stone,
streaked black above the muddy, meandering Colorado River.

They were flying so low that Navajo Mountain could not be
seen above the stark cliffs on either side of them. Lomax pointed to
an ancient buoy lying on a sandbar, then turned south into a narrow
canyon, tighter even than the Virgin River canyon. Lomax slowed.
As they eased up the canyon, there were times Chris thought both
rotor tips would scrape the opposing rock faces.

Then they came around a bend and there, high above them, was
Rainbow Bridge. When Lake Powell was at its height, you could boat
right up to it. Now a small stream flowed under the arch, falling over
a cliff, cascading to a pool a hundred feet below.

Lomax guided the chopper to a strip of land just below the bridge
and landed. The turbines whined down and the blades retracted. He
hit a button on the panel and the chopper's skin began to transluce.
As Chris helped Cate and K'tanu out, the surface of the Comanche
changed color, picking up on the surroundings. After five minutes, it
was the same reddish brown color as the rock around it.

"Neat trick," said Elvin, chomping his jerky. "Didn't know they
could do that."

"Microphoto receptors," said Lomax. "Developed during the Indonesian terror war."

K'tanu was not looking at the chopper's remarkable color-shifting abilities. He walked slowly toward the bridge, a massive arch almost two hundred feet high at its tallest point, carved by wind and rain and water.

Cate joined him. "Cloudburst won't think to follow us here," she said.

"Why not?" asked K'tanu.

"For a couple of reasons: she'd never think we'd stop at a place with no food, shelter, or drinkable water. Also, the arch is sacred to her people. They rarely come here." She pointed east. "Navajo Mountain—up beyond that cliff—is where they believe the world began. They say spirits dwell there."

K'tanu nodded. "We're trespassing?"

"In a way."

"Then maybe we shouldn't be here."

"We have no choice, K'tanu," said Cate. "They'll find us and take you back."

"We shouldn't have killed those pilots," said K'tanu. "My life is not worth another's life." He sat down and bowed his head. Cate sat by him, not knowing what to say.

"We have reports of smoke in Virgin River Canyon," said Jennings. "Looks like a crash."

"What do the pilots say?" asked Cloudburst.

"No contact."

Cloudburst keyed the intercom. "Zuñiga, how long before we're airborne?"

"Five minutes."

Cloudburst looked at Jennings. "I want you and two others. Armed." She strode from the room.

∧∧∧

"So he's the Messiah," said Elvin, indicating K'tanu, who was sitting high up on a shadowed ledge near where the bridge began its graceful arch over the narrow canyon.

"Who calls him that?" asked Cate. She had been sitting by Chris, just looking down the narrow canyon, saying little, thinking.

"Everyone out there. They call him the Miracle Man, too."

Cate looked up at K'tanu. "He's a miracle, all right." Yet the heat and clarity of the day were making her question plans that seemed irrefutable in last night's dark excursions.

"Then why are you taking him away? He's the key to Cobalt, right?"

"He's more than that," said Cate. "He's someone who lived six thousand years ago. What we didn't know, what we never imagined, was that when we cloned him, we interfered with his *soul*. He was in the afterlife, living with his family." She stopped, aware that what she'd just said was absurd, and she looked up at Elvin for a reaction.

Elvin shrugged. "So?"

"So," continued Cate, "he was pulled back to earth. Turns out the body and the soul are connected."

Elvin switched his jerky cheroot from one side of his mouth to the other. "Okay. So?"

"So . . . we interfered! We had no right to do that!"

Elvin nodded. "Ah! And he wants to go home?"

Cate nodded.

"But don't we need him?" asked Elvin. "People, I mean."

Cate nodded again.

"Have you asked him to stay?"

"No," said Cate, finally looking directly at Elvin. How had she not thought of this? She'd been so caught up in her astonishing discovery of life after death that she'd naturally assumed that the upshot of it all was that they were supposed to help K'tanu get back to Lightland. Like he said, why else had they all come together?

Elvin looked back at her, chewing his jerky thoughtfully. "You ought to ask him before you get him killed," he said. "This life is his too."

They looked up. K'tanu was not on the ledge. Cate started, then felt a hand on her shoulder. She turned. It was K'tanu, the backpack slung over his shoulder. The look on his face told her he'd heard their discussion. "If you want me to, I'll go back," he said.

"We'll do whatever you want," said Cate, taking Chris's hand, squeezing it. Chris nodded.

There was a long pause. Elvin looked at K'tanu. "What's in the jar?"

"My heart," said K'tanu.

"The heart tissue was alive," said Cate. "DNA disintegrates at death. But the DNA in K'tanu's heart cells was intact."

"After six thousand years?" asked Elvin.

Cate nodded.

"What are the chances of that?"

"None," she said. "It's impossible."

Elvin looked up at K'tanu. "And you were in heaven?"

"We call it Lightland. Yes, I was there, with my family."

"I've seen it, too," said Cate.

Elvin looked at her. "And what are the chances of *that*?"

Cate shrugged.

"I think I know what Elvin's getting at," said Chris. "Everything we've seen is impossible, yet it happened. The big question is *why* did it happen? Was K'tanu sent here as a punishment, as he fears? Is going back to Lightland the right thing for him to do? Or should he stay here and help us eradicate Cobalt?"

No one said anything. There was no easy answer.

K'tanu turned away and climbed back up on the ledge. He looked at the bridge. A strange desire to cross it filled him. It was wide enough, but the surface was loose, slippery shale. Still, he wanted to cross the bridge. Why, he could not say.

"Can I join you?" asked Cate from below.

"Sure," said K'tanu, helping her up on the ledge.

"I've never seen the sun before," said K'tanu. "Even though I've lived all my life in the desert." He scooted to the edge of the ledge, his long legs dangling over the chasm, raising his chin and closing his eyes, feeling the morning sun's warmth on his face. "But I *have* felt it before," he said. "It's like there are two of me. I thought I was Russell, but Russell never saw the sun, never felt it on his skin. But now I remember how that feels because I'm K'tanu, too. Whenever Russell sees something for the first time, I see it new through his eyes, but then I know K'tanu has already seen it and then Russell's impressions kind of fade. Soon Russell will be just a dream, what my people call 'walking in the Other World.'"

"I feel like I've been dreaming all my life," said Cate. "And there's only one of me."

"Why?"

She sighed. "We're so damn *sure* of ourselves. We assumed that our advances in technology really *were* advances. Then Mother Nature threw us the Cobalt curve ball and we struck out. Everything fell apart, and all we have left is a world like the one you lived in six thousand years ago. The Stone Age. Tribes. The elements. Fear. Hatred. War."

"It wasn't just those things," said K'tanu. "We also had family and friends. We had love. Maybe it's because I've never really been loved in this world that what I felt in Lightland meant so much to me. The amount of love there is incredible. It flows around you, like a river. You could drown in it, but you wouldn't die."

Cate nodded. "No, you don't drown. You breathe it like air." She looked at K'tanu. "So now we're back in your world, K'tanu. What do we do now? How do we survive?"

"I don't know."

"You want to return to Lightland?" He nodded. "What about staying?"

K'tanu pulled out the green scarab amulet. "Something inside says I should go, even though the Russell part of me knows that millions have died and I might be able to save those who are left. But I know that maybe a hundred billion people have lived on this earth. And ninety-nine percent of them would be dead anyway, even without Cobalt. We're *all* going to die, eventually, no matter what your or I do. That's not the point."

"What is?"

"When you know there's something *after* death, you also know you *can't* really die."

"But aren't we supposed to try to live as long as we can?" asked Cate.

"I don't know. There might be more important things. How we face life—and death—maybe *that's* what really matters. I died trying to protect my family. I failed, but in trying to save them, I showed my love for them. Without fear of death, no one would ever know if they were a hero or not."

"Listen to you," said Cate. "Just a few days ago, you were struggling with cursive writing. Now you're talking like a *bodhisattva*."

K'tanu laughed. "I don't know what that is, but Russell is beginning to feel like a shell I was trapped in. When K'tanu was freed, the shell began to dissolve. But I have a lot to thank Russell for. Without him, we wouldn't be having this talk."

"Why not?"

K'tanu laughed. "Because K'tanu doesn't speak English!"

Cate laughed. "We would have found a way to communicate. When I was in Lightland, Antram said that friends' hearts speak the same language—they *know* each other."

"Then your heart will understand that I have to go home. It may sound selfish, but I don't think Cobalt is any of my concern. I wonder if it is any of yours either."

He looked at Cate in silence for a long time.

When Elvin got up to go help Lomax inside the chopper, Chris looked up. Cate and K'tanu were having what looked like an intense conversation high up on the ledge by the bridge. The curve of the arch reminded him of the dream—K'tanu standing by the tree out in the middle of the savanna, carrying his own body. Was it an allegory or a glimpse of the future? The dream elements were undoubtedly coalescing. They were going to Africa. They had the mummy, the heart, and K'tanu. He *would* carry his body across a grassy plain, but why? What was the purpose? Chris dug the heel of his boot into the dirt. Cate believed in K'tanu, so did Lomax, but both of them had personal spiritual reasons. Elvin was willing to help because that's the kind of guy he was.

Chris was the only one without a reason. His desire for Cate had pulled him to Nevada. His outrage at the mummy's theft propelled him toward a confrontation with Cloudburst. His compassion for Russell urged him to help the young man. And the heat of the moment three hours ago precipitated the death of two helicopter crews. And yet he had no real conviction in what they were doing, no matter what he'd said about K'tanu being convincing evidence of life after death. *I'm not a believer*, he thought. *Before all this, I would never have killed anyone, not for the last scrap of bread on earth. But now, in the company of believers, and acting like one myself, I killed. I have blood on my hands.*

A headache began to throb at his temples. The others had their own reasons for being here. He only had one: Cate. But was that grounds for sabotaging the hope of humanity? For murder? All he had to go on was a dream he'd had. And it just wasn't enough.

The helicopter swung low over the canyon. A pall of smoke still hung over the area, a black homing beacon. Below them, they could see the remains of two Comanche helicopters and blackened impact scars on the sheer rock cliff above. "Mid-air?" asked Zuñiga, the pilot.

Cloudburst shrugged, focusing her binoculars. "Whose are they?"

"Can't see the tail numbers, and the transponders are, of course, inoperative," said Zuñiga, swinging around and descending.

"They'd better not be ours," said Cloudburst. As they dropped closer, she saw the final letter on one of the tail sections. "One is from Nellis. They sent two. Any word from the other pilot?"

Zuñiga shook his head. Cloudburst heard him activate the landing gear. "What are you doing?"

"I'm going to land. There might be survivors."

"There are no survivors," said Cloudburst. "Now let's go."

"But, Doctor!"

"Our mission is to recover that boy. Let's go."

Zuñiga cursed under his breath, then pulled back on the stick. The Comanche began to climb.

Twice during the day, they saw jets overhead, heading east, and once they thought they heard a helicopter, but they never saw anything in the admittedly narrow slice of sky above them that the canyon permitted. It was a good hiding place after all.

When darkness came after a most amazingly colorful sunset, in which every rock around them, as well as the sky above, glowed the warmest pink imaginable, Cate's heartbeat finally slowed. They were safe for a few more hours. She glanced at K'tanu, who dozed beside her up on the ledge, the backpack with the stone jar in his arms. His skin was cracked and dry, fading to gray as old black people's skin did, the melanin played out. He was six, going on sixty. Just a few days ago, he'd looked sixteen. A vein throbbed at his temple, his addled pituitary spitting toxic hormones into his blood. His knuckles were white and knobby. She often saw him rubbing them, grimacing in pain. His eyes were distant, remembering another world, wanting to wake up from the nightmare of this one.

In the last few years, Cate had often thought of her own life as a nightmare, but she never thought that mortality in general was one, or even a dream. Life was life, and it was better than death. To be alive was everything, and she had watched millions of people do their best to stay that way. Now, almost all of those people were dead, and those who survived ceaselessly yearned for the good old days before Cobalt. She knew better now. She'd peeked behind the curtain and had discovered that the world was nothing more than a charade, a stage play in front of smoking arc-lamps, the players made up with garish greasepaint, their theatrics a sad farce. They would die and wake up from the nightmare, to the true reality. She looked at K'tanu. Once you'd glimpsed heaven, how could you be happy trapped on earth?

The moon moved slowly across the sky, making her feel like the earth was standing still. The universe was taking people where it wanted, not where they wished. You could only hold on and hope for the best. Cate took K'tanu's hand in hers. He slept on. Squeezing it gently, she closed her eyes and, for the first time in her life, prayed.

EIGHTEEN

FACTOR OF TWO

They set down on the taxiway. Dawn was just beginning to lighten the sky. Cate helped K'tanu out of the chopper. "We've got to get him something to eat," she said, leading him toward the terminal.

"Don't go far!" shouted Chris.

"Where are we?" asked Elvin.

"Durango, Colorado," said Lomax. "I hear you're a whiz at finding fuel." He winked at Chris, not letting the gas tank joke go.

Elvin nodded.

"Then find me some Jet A."

Elvin took a couple of plastic gas cans and trotted toward a couple of corporate jets. Lomax and Chris grabbed more cans and started after him.

"Think they'll catch us?" asked Chris.

"They know we're headed east. I'm surprised we haven't seen them yet."

"You flew two feet off the ground," said Chris. "They probably thought you were a car." He looked over at the terminal. "I'll go hurry them up," he said, trotting off.

Lomax joined Elvin under the wing of a Gulfstream jet. "You're not a part of this," he said. "You can bail anytime you want."

"I might stick with you if you intend to draw fire."

"You a military man, Elvin?"

"Yes, sir," he said. "Corporal, Big Red One. Didn't see combat, though."

"You saw it yesterday, Corporal," said Lomax.

Elvin reached inside his vest and pulled out a Slim Jim. "Got an extra, Captain, if you want."

"Don't mind if I do," said Lomax, taking the jerky stick. Elvin depressed the fuel cock under the jet's wing. A stream of red liquid came out. Lomax smiled. "You fill these up," he said. "I'll crank up the Comanche and bring her closer. It'll go faster." He started trotting toward the helicopter.

"Captain?"

Lomax stopped and turned.

"You're sure we're doing the right thing?" asked Elvin. "What with Cobalt and all?"

"Feels right. I always trust my gut—don't you?"

Elvin went back to filling the cans. "That's what got me into this mess," he said to himself.

"What do you mean, we can't come?" asked Cate.

"It's not safe," said Lomax. He'd gotten almost half a tank out of the Gulfstream. "By now, the word's out. The Comanche's hot. I'm gonna take it far away from you folks."

"But we need your help!" exclaimed Cate.

"That's what I'm trying to do."

"He's right," said Chris. "As soon as he gets in the air, he'll probably be spotted." He turned to Lomax. "Where will you go?"

"We're going southwest, into Arizona," said Elvin.

"You're going with him?" asked Cate.

"You know the drill," said Elvin, ignoring Cate's question, turning to Chris. "You get a diesel. Four-wheel drive. Put a couple of barrels in the back. Fill 'em with Jet A. Red, not blue. Got it?"

Chris nodded, but didn't say anything.

Elvin saw he was scared. "I'll come along if you want."

"No," said Chris. "We'll be all right. We'll stay on the back roads and we'll head for—"

"Don't tell us," said Lomax. "We can't reveal what we don't know."

"You're right," said Chris, holding out his hand. "This has cost you a lot, Captain."

Lomax shook Chris's hand. "There are more important things than staying alive—that's what I believe, at least."

Chris turned to Elvin. "Thanks for all you've done. I owe you."

Elvin produced a Slim Jim. "To remember me by." He tucked it in Chris's shirt pocket.

Lomax walked over to K'tanu. "I guess this is the end of your ride, son."

"I guess I can say I have been on a roller coaster now," said K'tanu. "Thanks."

Lomax grinned. "That's life, kid, if you're doing it right."

They watched the Comanche lift off, swinging low toward the south. "I wish they hadn't gone," said Cate, watching the chopper grow steadily smaller.

"I wish we had another two hours of night," said Chris. "As it is, they might be seen."

"What now?" asked K'tanu.

"Did anybody see you in there?" asked Chris.

"There isn't anybody here yet," said Cate. "A sign says the airport is open only from dawn to dusk. I don't think many people are flying these days."

"Most of the planes have flat tires," said K'tanu. "Only two didn't."

Chris nodded. The eastern sky was pink. The sun was about to peek over the mountains. "The searchers will track us here. We need transportation."

"We'd better wait until dark for that," said Cate, suddenly feeling very exposed.

They shouldered their backpacks and picked up the litter Lomax had given them from the chopper. K'tanu's mummy lay on it, zipped in the olive body bag. Cate was surprised at how light it was. "I'll carry that," said K'tanu, reaching one end.

"I got it," said Cate. "You don't weigh much," she said lightly.

K'tanu nodded and walked on ahead. Cate and Chris followed, heading for a distant row of hangars just starting to glow in the morning light. They jimmied a lock on a hanger at the far end and went inside. It smelled like rat feces, fetid and sour. An old rusty Cherokee single-engine trainer sat on flat tires. Cobwebs on the door indicated no one had been there in years.

Around noon, they heard two jets and poked their heads out the door. One continued south-east, but the other banked, turning back. "He's landing!" said Chris. "You're sure you didn't see anybody when you went into the terminal?"

"I told you," said Cate. "No one."

"That doesn't mean they didn't see you. That chopper makes a lot of noise."

"Maybe they thought we went with them," said Cate.

Chris shrugged. "Okay, Pollyanna."

The F-45 Silver Ghost banked steeply. The engines rotated to vertical, and it settled onto the tarmac not twenty feet from where Lomax had landed the Comanche just a few hours before. "I was hoping he couldn't land here," said Chris, peeking through the door. "The runway isn't very long."

"Technology," said Cate dryly, "is gonna be the end of us."

They were a good hundred yards from the jet, peeking out an inch-wide crack in a door, but Chris still felt exposed. The jet engines cut out and moments later the canopy retracted. The pilot climbed down from the cockpit. "He's got a gun," said Chris, watching through binoculars.

"Someone *must* have seen us!" whispered Cate.

"I thought you said no one did," countered Chris.

"I can't be sure!"

"Wait!" said Chris. "He's stopping. Looking at something." The pilot was bending down, touching the asphalt. He lifted his hand, sniffing it. "He sees the fuel we spilled," said Chris. The pilot stood and looked around. Chris closed the door. They were in total darkness in the hangar.

"What are you gonna do—wait for him to come over and knock?" asked Cate.

Chris reached out for her, found her wrist, and pulled her to him. "Don't panic."

Cate wrenched her arm free. "I'm not panicking. Give me those," she said, taking the glasses.

"Cate!" said Chris, but she had already cracked the door. "I don't see him."

"Good," said Chris.

"Maybe he's checking hangars." She opened the door a little more and poked her head out.

"Cate!" hissed Chris. "No!"

Cate scanned with the glasses. The pilot was nowhere in sight. The row of hangars prevented a clear view of the terminal. She took a step out onto the taxiway. Chris reached for her, but she took another step. "I don't see him."

"Get back in here!" said Chris.

Just then, she saw him. The pilot appeared from behind the hangars. She ducked inside the doorway, leaving it open a crack. The pilot was holstering his firearm, heading resolutely toward his aircraft. "He's leaving," she said.

Chris shut the door, plunging them into darkness again. "We should too."

"What if he just went back to his plane to get a bigger gun?" asked K'tanu.

Just then the jet turbines coughed to life and Chris smiled. "I say we wait until dark, then we get the hell out of here."

They heard a low-flying jet once more that afternoon as they sat inside the dark, sweltering hangar. K'tanu was sitting inside the little low-wing plane, running his hands over the instrument panel. Chris had given him a flashlight so he could see.

"I like flying," said K'tanu. "In the Other World, I often flew."

"In Lightland?" asked Cate, who was leaning against the wing.

"No, in what you call 'dreams.' In that world, I could fly."

"I flew in Lightland, too," said Cate. "I was an eagle, and later a hawk. Then your son threw a stone and killed me. I was feeding my chicks."

"N'kala is a good hunter," said K'tanu. "He often killed birds for dinner."

On his couch in the rear of the hangar, Chris stewed. "I went skydiving once," he said flatly.

"I didn't know that," said Cate.

K'tanu switched off the flashlight and got out of the plane, feeling his way toward Chris. Next thing Chris knew, the flashlight was dropped into his lap, startling him. K'tanu sat down next to him. "What is skydiving?"

"You jump out of a plane with a parachute."

"What's that?"

"It's like a big sheet connected to you with ropes. As you fall, the sheet catches the air, slowing you. You land gently. It's a rush."

K'tanu said, "You live in an amazing world. So different from mine."

"But you fly without wings, and Cate over there doesn't just *fly* like a bird, she *is* one."

Cate walked toward Chris. "You're just jealous," she said. "You want to fly too."

"I've had enough of flying," said Chris. "I like it on the ground. Less can go wrong."

"But Cobalt's down here," said Cate. "Leaving Yucca, we've just multiplied our chances of infection by a factor of, oh, a *hundred*. So in addition to a truck and fuel, we'd better scare up some masks and bleach."

"And food," said K'tanu.

Chris pulled out Elvin's Slim Jim and tapped K'tanu on the arm with it. K'tanu took the jerky and tore open the wrapper as he'd seen Elvin do. He bit it, then spit it out. "What is this?" he asked, handing the stale, plastic-wrapped dried-beef product back to Chris.

"The future," said Chris, putting it back in his pocket.

NINETEEN

ON THE ROAD

The DCI called Cloudburst just before nightfall. "Didn't find them," said Fox. "We searched a five-hundred mile perimeter."

"What do we do now?"

"They're probably still close by. I've got a half-dozen choppers on recon."

"But what if they ditched the chopper like you said?"

"Then I suggest an APB to law enforcement; but if we do, your secret's out. Everybody will know they've escaped and from where."

Cloudburst gritted her teeth. What choice did she have? "We've got to get them back."

There was a long pause. "This boy Russell. He's really immune?"

"Yes."

"And he's the only one?"

"For now," said Cloudburst. She didn't want to reveal that Cate had destroyed all the frozen embryos and stolen the heart. If they didn't get Russell back, they only had the current cell cultures to work with. His disappearance could put them back years, and might kill the project altogether. "We've got to get him back," said Cloudburst. "He's our only hope."

"Then let's pull out the stops," said Fox. "Let everyone know. I'll need physical descriptions for the APB." He paused, thinking. "You know, Doctor, the law-enforcement grid is pretty sketchy these days. Lots of wanna-be cops doing what professionals used to do. We'll have to offer some kind of reward—no one will risk contact with others without some incentive."

"Tell 'em they'll be first in line for the vaccine."

"You have a vaccine?"

"We will if we get that boy back," said Cloudburst. "Tell everyone his safety is of the utmost importance." She paused, then continued in a softer voice, "But between you and me . . ."

"Yes?"

"If he dies and we get him frozen quickly enough, we can clone him again."

"I gather that isn't for public consumption," said Fox. Up until now, he'd thought Cloudburst was just a standard-issue scientist, all hard facts but no hard sense.

"It's a contingency plan."

"I want you on the air tomorrow morning," said Fox. "Oh-seven-hundred. By fifteen after the hour, the whole country will know what's up. We'll get this kid back, one way or another."

Cloudburst said goodbye and hung up. *One way or another.* She put her head in her hands and visualized her life's work destroyed by some Texas "good-old-boy' with a 12-gauge and a pickup who'd always wanted to be a deputy sheriff, but couldn't pass the mental stability test.

Cate Seagram, you will pay for this.

They finally left the hangar after it was fully dark. The rising moon glowed unseen behind the Rockies to the east. "It'll be up in an hour," said Chris. "We'd better find a car by then."

"Won't be easy," said Cate, as they walked down the row of hangars. "It's been six years since most cars have run. Tires are flat; batteries are dead; gas has evaporated. Any ideas?"

Chris trudged ahead, carrying his half of the litter. "I'm open," he sulked.

Cate, carrying the back end of the litter, looked at Chris's back. What was up with him? He'd been moody and distant all day. They hadn't shared any real affection since just after he'd arrived at Yucca. Maybe he regretted getting into this situation: on the run, the military after them, and who knows how many law-enforcement agencies.

The airport was south of town, and it was a good mile's trek along a road that in former times would have been busy, even at this hour. The moon eventually showed itself over the mountains and they hurried on, trying to stay in the shadows. They saw a vehicle coming toward them and ducked behind some trees, but the sedan turned onto a side street before it reached them.

Looking back to the intersection where it turned, they saw red taillights as the vehicle stopped. The driver got out and went inside a building. A light went on in an upstairs window. The car sat idling, its headlights still on.

K'tanu was looking through the binoculars. "Police cars have lights on top, right?"

"And cop cars are MHBs," said Chris. "They run on practically anything: gas, ethanol, solar, batteries, diesel."

"You're not suggesting we steal a police car?" asked Cate.

"Can you think of a better getaway car?" asked Chris, inching forward.

"Fine," said Cate, sighing. "You guys go back around the corner and wait. I'll get the car and come back for you."

Chris shook his head. "No, I'll do it."

"Chris, I appreciate the gallantry, but this litter's pretty heavy for me. That cop will probably be coming out any minute. We don't have time to argue. Go!" She trotted toward the cruiser.

"She's brave," said K'tanu, picking up Cate's end of the litter.

"Yeah? Well, sometimes bravery can look a lot like stupidity," said Chris, watching her approach the vehicle. "Let's get around the corner, like she said."

As Cate moved toward the cruiser, she kept her eyes on the lighted upstairs window. When she was still twenty paces from the car, the light blinked off. She sprinted to the sedan, yanked the door open, and jumped inside. The cop came out the front door with a cup of coffee just as Cate peeled out. He stood on the steps, slack-jawed, his coffee pouring out onto the ground. "Hey!" was all he managed to say as the cruiser squealed around the corner and disappeared.

Chris and K'tanu waited under a large elm the next block over. The cruiser screeched around the corner and skidded to a stop. "Hurry!" said Cate, jumping out.

They bundled the mummy into the back seat, along with K'tanu. Cate headed for the driver's side, but Chris stood in the way. "I'll drive," he said, getting behind the wheel. Cate glared at him, then got in the passenger side. They peeled out. "Man, this thing's powerful," said Chris, gripping the wheel tightly. "Wow!"

"Hey," said Cate, "turn on the radio."

"No music—I'm concentrating," said Chris, heading toward the main road out of town.

"I meant the police band," said Cate. "Here it is," she said, flipping a switch.

"—if you're the one who stole my car, dammit, bring it back!" yelled someone.

"Should we answer?" asked Cate.

Chris shot her a look. "Are you kidding? Did he *see* you?"

"I don't think so."

"Randy? Come on, man, it's not funny," said the cop on the radio. "Bring it back."

"Who's Randy?" asked K'tanu from the back seat.

"Put on your seat belt," said Cate, buckling her own.

They hit the main street at fifty, tires squealing, turning south toward the airport. "Wait!" yelled Cate. "We just came from there!"

"You wanna hang around a small town in a stolen police car?" asked Chris.

"That depends," said Cate. "How much gas do we have?"

"Come on!" came the cop's voice. "I'm supposed to be on patrol! There's a fax here from Homeland Security. I got to get on the road!"

"Shit," said Chris. "Already?"

"Shut up and drive," said Cate, opening a road atlas. "Okay. We're on which highway?"

"Five-fifty," said Chris. "I just saw a sign."

"Okay, look for one-sixty east. That will take us through the Rockies." Cate patted Chris on the shoulder, knowing that for the moment, at least, they were safe. "Oh, honey! It's the scenic route!"

It was two A.M. when they rolled into the outskirts of Taos, New Mexico. They still had a quarter-tank of gas left, but Chris thought they were far enough away now that they could slow down a little and hunt for another car. "First, let's get rid of these lights," he said, and he and Cate got out and pried the light bar off the roof, chucking it into a ditch by the freeway off-ramp.

"We'd better keep our eyes open for a place to hide in case we don't find anything right away," said Cate.

"Where are we?" asked K'tanu.

"New Mexico. We've gone about two hundred miles."

"Oh," he said, leaning back. He looked ashen in the interior dome light.

"Food," whispered Cate to Chris. "First order of business."

Chris nodded, but what Cate had said about cars back at the airport was also true of food. Packaged food was increasingly hard to find and often inedible. Stores had long since been emptied out. No one was making Oreos anymore. Once in a while, you could find a house with food storage, but that was a rarity, and you'd have to search dozens of homes and stumble over hundreds of dried-out, hideous-looking corpses to find them. Most dead people now looked worse than K'tanu's mummy, which was at least wrapped up, not lying in a bed looking like a dried apple.

They rolled through a Taos suburb called Arroyo Seco, which K'tanu translated for them as "Dry Creek." He'd learned a little Spanish from Lieutenant Zuñiga, one of the pilots at Yucca, and as they drove through the darkened streets, she heard him repeating Spanish words quietly to himself: "Rio," "Calle," "Avenida," and so on.

"You should rest," Cate said, turning to him. "We're gonna find food and then another car."

"Food," said K'tanu wistfully, the backpack on his lap.

Arroyo Seco was an upscale retirement community with enormous houses on large horse properties. There was an airport in nearby Taos; there might be fuel there. But first, a new vehicle.

"We've got to go inside one of them," said Cate, watching as they passed several houses.

"Some of those houses have people in them," said Chris. "With guns."

"Is there any way to tell from the outside?"

"Maybe. You know, signs of habitation."

"Like a mowed lawn?"

"Doubtful. Mowers use gas. But a trimmed hedge might indicate inhabitants. We don't want that. Instead, look for a prosperous-looking place that's overgrown—preferably with an R.V. or a big garage. They usually have toys inside, and gas."

Suddenly, he stomped on the brakes, throwing them all forward in their seats. K'tanu bumped his head on the seat in front of him. Cate's head glanced off the side window.

"Chris!" she shouted, rubbing her temple.

Chris stared ahead, eyes burning. "I know where we can get everything we need!"

"I never seen nothing like that before," said Elvin. "I don't care what happens now."

They had set down on the north rim of the Grand Canyon, near the west end, where the canyon crumbled down into desert, leaving the Colorado to wind between low, eroded hills. The sun was setting and the sky was a brilliant orange. Not a cloud could be seen.

"You liked it?" asked Lomax.

Elvin bit off the end of a new jerky stick. "I stood at Angel's Point once," he said. "It's impressive, but it don't beat hauling ass down that river, two feet off the deck!"

"We had to stay under the radar."

"But we got to put our heads up before long, right?" said Elvin. "So they'll see us?"

"Not much choice now." He pointed west. "Canyon ends just a few miles that way. Then the river enters Lake Mead, near Vegas."

"But you said we weren't going to Vegas," said Elvin. "One too many air bases."

Lomax picked a jerky stick out of Elvin's fishing vest and snapped it in half, munching on it. "We'll never make it that far before they see us. We come up out of the canyon more than a couple hundred feet and radar will scan us. Then it will be just a matter of minutes."

They gazed out across the canyon. The south rim was a good ten miles away and much lower in elevation. It was incredibly hot. Late-afternoon haze made the view wavy and surreal. Lomax took a swig from a water bottle and gave it to Elvin, who did likewise. The pungent smell of sage hung in the air. A hawk screeched, skimming along the canyon rim right in front of them.

"He's hunting," said Elvin as the hawk disappeared below the rim.

"And we're the prey," said Lomax.

TWENTY

ALL POINTS

Dr. Cloudburst straightened her white lab coat and took her place
in front of the camera. She wore a black skirt, flats, and a cream
blouse with a thin gold-chain necklace. She'd trimmed her hair and
tucked it behind her ears, leaving short bangs. In the mirror, she'd
assessed her looks as professional yet personable—the right mix to
engender confidence and empathy.

"Fifteen seconds," said the cameraman.

Cloudburst heard the national anthem rising on the speakers,
and the Homeland Security logo faded in on the monitor to one
side. The red camera light stopped blinking, turning a steady red.
"My fellow Americans," she began. "I am Dr. Sally Cloudburst, head
of the Special Pathogens Branch of the Centers for Disease Control.
Since the outbreak, we have made every effort to destroy the Cobalt
virus, which has killed so many of our fellow countrypersons. A few
weeks ago, we broadcast a message of hope. We discovered a young
man named Russell who was immune to the virus, and a complete
study of his DNA genome was under way. At that time, I told you
it was only a matter of time before we unlocked the secrets of the
Cobalt virus and developed a cure." She paused for effect, pursed
her lips thoughtfully, and put on her best I-can't-believe-what-I'm-
about-to-tell-you look. "Since that time, we have had a setback. A

terrible setback." She squared her shoulders and looked at the camera lens so intently that she saw her own reflection. She nodded, and a three-dimensional facsimile of Cate appeared on the holo behind her.

"The CDC has been struck by terrorists. This is Cate Seagram, who once was a trusted researcher. She, along with her accomplice, a man going by the name of Christopher Tempest, kidnapped Russell yesterday."

On the holo, Chris was shown as seen on security cams. Cloudburst had chosen the images herself, intending to make him look wily, ragged, and slightly deranged. She did not entirely fail.

"Russell was living in a secured facility in the Nevada desert. With Seagram's help, Tempest commandeered a military helicopter and fled. As of this afternoon, we believe they are somewhere in the Four Corners area and headed southeast." She shook her head sadly. "Russell is in great danger. These terrorists' motives are unclear, but the success of their plot could mean the end of all human life on earth."

Cloudburst took a deep breath. "We *must* get Russell back safely. He is the key—the *only* key—to ending the pandemic. The Air Force has been searching the skies for the missing Comanche helicopter, but thus far without success. It is likely now that the fugitives have abandoned the helicopter and are now on the ground. We need your help. Law-enforcement agencies have been alerted and are on the lookout for three people: an adult English-American male, an adult Scandinavian-American female, and a teenage African-American male. If you see them, *do not approach*, but contact your local law-enforcement agency."

Tears filled Cloudburst's eyes. "Please help us find Russell. His safety is of the utmost importance. Some people call him the 'Miracle Man,' and that is not too far off. He is our greatest hope. We *must* find him and bring him home safely. On behalf of the United States government, I ask for your help in stopping this insane plot to interfere with our efforts to eradicate Cobalt. The kidnappers must be stopped. Please help us. Be careful, be wise, and be vigilant."

Just before the CDC logo wiped the frame, Cloudburst gave the camera one last heartfelt look. Then the red light went off.

Samuel Fox leaned back in his chair in his office in the West Wing of the White House, inhaled the Cuban, and produced a blue smoke ring. "Helluva show."

"I especially liked the tears at the end," said his assistant, Major Wolfe.

Fox smiled. "I couldn't have pulled that one off. Neither could Madame President." He indicated the holo, on which the pictures of the fugitives continued to cycle. "That Cloudburst is a force of nature, Ben. I believe she'd do anything to get that boy back."

Wolfe nodded. "Think the broadcast will do the trick?"

Fox shrugged. "Who knows? Big country, even bigger now that nobody lives here. Our fly-boys haven't turned up the chopper yet. I believe we've run them to ground. Someone will spot them and we'll pick them up."

Wolfe nodded. He was trim and impeccably tailored, considering the olive uniform he wore was six years old. His head was shaved and he carried a side arm. Now that the Director of Central Intelligence was the ranking official at the White House (the President was still at the "undisclosed location" and had been since the outbreak), Wolfe never left his side, and the safety on his sidearm was never on.

Fox blew another smoke ring. "She says the kid's the key. Don't know if I believe her."

"Why is that, sir?"

"Remember? She said he was kidnaped for 'unknown reasons.' I never could get out of her what those 'unknown reasons' might be. Money?" He laughed. "Hell, anyone who wants money these days can waltz right into any bank and haul out as much as they can carry. Then they can use it to start a fire. There's only one commodity that's worth anything now."

"And what's that, sir?"

Fox considered his cigar. "Being alive. With ninety-nine percent of the country dead, those that are left *know* they won the world's biggest lottery. So who among those people would attempt to prevent a cure?" He shook his head. "They must be nucking futz," he chuckled, taking another puff. "You know what else, Wolfe?"

"What, sir?"

"I sort of hope we don't find 'em. Personally, I don't really care if they find a cure or not. I'm alive and I don't intend to go near another contagious person for the rest of my days—days in which I will smoke one of these beauties every evening." He luxuriated in the blue smoke hanging in the room. "Because if they cure Cobalt, then we'll be right back to square one, worrying about mortgages and politicians and cholesterol. And I won't get to do this." He took a long, savory puff. "Who ever let things get so out of whack that it took three hundred million people dead before I could smoke in my own office?"

"There ought to be a law."

Fox laughed sardonically. "That was the whole damn problem to begin with."

Chris still held the phone book page when they walked through the tall double doors.

"Wow," said Cate, looking around.

"It's big," said K'tanu, holding his backpack.

"I guess that place in Montana really *was* just a little hole in the wall by comparison," said Chris.

That "hole-in-the-wall" could have fit under the arch connecting the mansion and the carriage house. They stood in the marble-floored entry, which was big enough to play basketball in. Overhead, an immense chandelier with a thousand crystals twinkled in the flashlight beam.

"Be morning soon," said Chris. "We'd better get the car inside."

They had left the cruiser under the arch. The private drive from the road was a mile long; Chris had watched the odometer. Hemmed in on both sides by pinion forest, it wound along, then suddenly opened up onto a large man-made lake, a rise of brown, shaggy lawn, and a stone Tudor mansion topping a hill, surrounded by artfully-placed boulders as big as cars.

"Castle Seidel," said Chris as they pulled up the curving brick drive.

There were no signs of forcible entry in any part of the house, which meant, in their experience, that there were probably dead people inside. While he hunted for Charles Seidel's name in the Cimarron phone book, Chris told Cate about the graves on the Flathead River south of Kalispell. He believed the whole family was up there for the summer when Cobalt hit. "Doesn't mean he didn't leave servants or a caretaker here," said Chris as he pulled a crowbar out of the cruiser trunk and strode toward the side door of the carriage house.

"There's a swimming pool," said K'tanu, standing in the breezeway, looking to the west toward the mountains, a hazy blue in the morning light. Beyond the pool, the overgrown lawn rolled up hills for a good mile, then disappeared into the forest, which climbed the Sangre de Cristo mountains beyond, still wreathed in morning mist.

"Did you ever find out what he did for a living?" asked Cate, watching as Chris slid the crowbar between the door and the jamb.

Chris heaved against the door. "Killed things. Lots of 'em." The door gave way with a loud *pop!* and they stood back, holding kerchiefs to their faces, an old habit when opening long-closed houses. Chris lowered his hankie and sniffed. "No dead in here," he said, entering the garage.

Chris played the flashlight around the cavernous interior. His jaw dropped. There were over a hundred autos inside, parked in neat rows on a spotless gray-painted floor. "I didn't know he was a car nut," said Chris. "All he had in Montana was a couple of ATVs and a pickup." They walked past Duesenbergs, an ancient Aston Martin, an even dozen vintage Porsche 911s, three Silver Cloud Rolls-Royces, and a collection of Ford Mustangs, one each year from 1965 to 2015, when Ford-Mitsubishi discontinued it.

"Is there room for our car in here?" asked Cate, almost laughing.

All along one side of the carriage house were twenty roll-top doors with small rectangular windows high up on them. Chris jumped up on the hood of a copper-colored Tucker and tugged the rope pull, releasing the first door. He jumped down and he and Cate raised the door. Chris laughed. "Look!" he said. "There's a car lift at the end." He looked up. "There must be more cars upstairs."

"I hope there's gas downstairs," said Cate, heading outside toward the police cruiser. They pulled it in and rolled the door closed again. At the far end, beyond the car lift, they found what they were looking for: a recent black F-M Excelsior diesel crew-cab four-wheel-drive pickup. They also found a complete mechanic's shop and gas pumps. "If I know old Charlie," said Chris, looking around, "he's got a backup electrical system somewhere. When we find it, we'll be able to get a cold beer out of the fridge, watch satellite TV, and order a pizza."

They went back outside under the breezeway. In the backyard, near the pool, K'tanu was sitting on a lawn chair under a ragged umbrella, holding his backpack to his chest and looking out across the expanse of green-pine and blue-spruce forest. The estate lay at the edge of Carson National Forest, flowing right into it without interruption. To their left was a long row of red stables with white piping, a parade ground, and corrals for training. To the right, a row of guest cottages and various swing sets, monkey bars, and even a rusting Ferris wheel. A stream danced behind the cabins and a cool breeze blew down from the Sangres, carrying with it the scent of fresh earth and forest.

"What a place," said Cate, turning to Chris. "We could stay here. Like forever."

"You can, if you want," said K'tanu.

Cate and Chris exchanged a look. "I just meant," said Cate, "that it's a wonderful place, not that we'd *actually* stay."

K'tanu shrugged. "Okay."

Chris proposed they go inside. K'tanu declined, saying he'd been indoors too much of his life already. Besides, the sun was rising, painting the tops of the Sangres pink.

Chris and Cate crowbarred the kitchen door open and walked inside. The kitchen had ornate Italian tile, blue granite counter tops, and three immense Sub-Zero stainless-steel fridges. "Smell anything?" asked Chris, holding his flashlight like a baton. He was always jumpy in empty houses; he'd stumbled over more than one horrifying scene and been scared half to death.

"How'd you remember he lived here?" asked Cate as they walked into the first of two formal dining rooms boasting ornate, dark tables and chairs, flocked wallpaper, and Dutch-master oils on the walls.

"Seidel had some letterhead in a desk in Kalispell. The address was in Cimarron, like that old movie," said Chris. "Now that I see this place, I'm kind of surprised he was in the phone book. I mean, who would Seidel want to talk to who didn't already know his phone number?"

They passed into a vaulted and paneled music room. There were a pair of Steinways nestled curve to curve, their lids raised, blanketed in dust. A harp sat nearby, the strings sprung, and all along one wall were shelves and shelves of music books. Cate opened a violin case. "I don't know much about violins, but I'll bet this is a Stradivarius. Seidel must have invented something to be this rich," she said, closing the lid.

Chris looked around at the spacious room, one wall draped with tapestries and the other filled with stained-glass windows that looked like they came from some ancient cathedral in Europe. "Maybe he invented being rich," he said, still amazed that this was the same guy who lived so relatively simply in Montana.

It took them three hours to investigate the house, and they never even got to the fourth floor. They quit counting at thirty-three bedrooms and twenty-one baths. There were two kitchens, one at either end of the home. A six-lane bowling alley. A one-hundred-seat stadium movie theater with red velvet curtains and a fifty-foot-wide screen. In the projection room were metal shelves full of ancient thirty-five millimeter prints. Chris had never seen actual film stock. Two giant xenon-bulb projectors had platters of wound film waiting to be projected. "*Gunga Din*," said Chris, picking up an octagonal storage box. "Ever heard of it?"

Cate shook her head.

But the really good stuff was in the basement. There, Chris found what he'd been looking for. Behind several strong metal doors, whose resistance to his crowbar only steeled his resolve to open them, he found an oil-fired power plant and a dipstick, that when raised, said Mr. Charles Seidel of Cimarron, Kalispell, and probably Paris or Monaco, had over thirty thousand gallons of fuel oil storage. In a room that looked like Mission Control, the main breaker had been tripped, and Chris gingerly snapped it back on. Deep within the foundations of Castle Seidel, a rumbling began, and the light fixture overhead began to glow. In the next room, Cate heard water running. She found a bathroom faucet spitting brown water, which soon turned clear.

By then, the lights were glowing fully, and the place shook when the air conditioning kicked on, a bank of green lights glowing. They raced upstairs, turning lights on, then off as they passed, knowing that if there were one running faucet, there might be others, and hoping they hadn't just sent a beam out into space announcing their arrival.

Later, when all was checked and only the fewest lights needed were lit, they found the food storage in the basement—row upon row of dried food and barrels of wheat and grain. Thousands of gallons of drinking water, even though Seidel had a functioning well on the property. When Chris found a case of beef jerky, he stopped, thinking of Elvin. He held up a jerky packet, a crooked smile on his face. Cate hugged him in the cool of the cellar. "I'm sure they're all right," she whispered.

Chris nodded. He reached over and shut off the light, plunging them into humming darkness in the basement of the richest man they'd ever known, surrounded by ten years' worth of food, water, warmth, and comfort.

"Thanks, Chuck," he whispered, feeling Cate's arms around him and real hope for the first time in years.

TWENTY-ONE

INJURIES—REAL AND IMAGINED

Cate held the sledgehammer in both hands. "I don't see why we have to do this."

Chris turned off the garden hose and swirled the muddy water around in the bucket. "Just do it, Cate," he said, exasperated.

"It will get plenty beat up and dirty on the road," said Cate.

"It needs to look like it's been outside for five years, driven by someone who is *not* a fugitive. Swing away."

Cate looked behind her. K'tanu sat on a blue and white Coleman cooler, holding his backpack, watching. He'd said little since they arrived there yesterday. Most of the time he just sat out on the lounge chair next to the pool, watching the sun arc between the house and the mountains, and often knelt with both hands palms-up on the ground, eyes closed, lips moving. She wanted to ask him what he was doing, but of course it was obvious. She'd done it herself just yesterday.

She reared back with the sledge.

"Not the windows," said Chris. "We need good windows." He tossed the bucket of muddy water onto the hood, splashing Cate. She frowned and swung hard, denting the front fender just behind the wheel. "Good girl," said Chris. "Pretend it's me."

She swung again with a lot more force, then said, "Oh, shit."

"What?"

"Come here."

Chris rounded the truck. The good-sized dent she had inflicted was slowly popping itself out. She looked up at Chris. "Self-healing fenders? I never heard of that."

Chris pointed his flashlight at the fender. By now, there was only a slight crease where the iron maul had hit, and even that was disappearing. A piece of paint had chipped off and the surrounding paint was oozing, covering the bare spot. As they watched, the fender made itself as good as new.

"Like the chopper, kind of," said Chris. "I thought this thing looked different. When I pulled it out of the garage, I saw dials on the dash I've never seen before. No idea what half of them do."

Cate ran her hands across the now perfect fender. "So much for looking old." She looked across the dirty hood. "At least it doesn't wash itself."

Chris laughed. "Yeah, we've got that going for us."

They helped K'tanu into the rear seat and shut the door. Chris had emptied two big plastic water-storage barrels in the basement, lashing them behind the cab and filling them with diesel fuel. K'tanu's mummy, now wrapped in one of Nadine Seidel's quilts inside the vinyl body bag, lay in the truck bed on the litter, along with boxes of provisions and bottles of crisp-tasting well water.

Chris pushed the ignition button. The headlights came on. Before them, Charles Seidel's mansion of stone and brick brooded in the darkness. Chris looked at Cate and wanted to say something. She was fiddling with the GPS unit on the dash. He reached over and touched her hand. "I love you," he said.

Cate nodded and continued turning dials, attempting to get the display to make some sense.

"I love you," said Chris again, louder.

"I love you too," said Cate, not looking up. "Ah! There!"

Chris looked at the console between the two front seats. A vivid 3-D red and brown aerial-view holo was suspended over a tiny projector. Cate waved her hand through the holo, pointing. The map zoomed in, and there, sitting in front of an immense building with a curving drive in front of it, in the midst of a deep green forest, was a tiny, black rectangle. Cate looked up, smiling. "That's us!"

She looked back at the display, fascinated. Chris continued looking at her. Her long blonde hair was gathered at her neck, and she wore a black baseball cap and a bulky tan sweater. Her skin, normally pale from working underground, was pink from the day's sun. She was beautiful and she was a million miles away.

"Yeah," sighed Chris, "that's us."

"You're gonna do *what*?" asked Elvin over the rotor scream.

"Crash land," said Lomax, flipping switches.

Elvin tightened his seat belt. "On purpose?"

Lomax nodded. "See those vapor trails?" He pointed out Elvin's window. For the last half hour, the Comanche had been following the Colorado as it lazily wound south of the Grand Canyon. When they popped out into Lake Mead, it wasn't five minutes before radar indicated two aircraft headed their way.

"Can't outrun 'em," said Lomax. "Can't get back to the canyon in time to lose 'em there. "They'll be pissed about their buddies. They'll fire on us, probably just disabling fire, but it will force us down."

"Okay," said Elvin, nodding. "Then let 'em! Why would we do it ourselves?"

The Comanche nose-dropped and the water raced toward them. Lomax tightened his own harness. "Because if they disable us, I may lose control. If I do it, we just might live. Like the odds?"

Elvin shook his head. "Who cares what I think?" He shoved the helmet mike out of the way.

Lomax wheeled the chopper around and headed back up the river between the low, rounded hills. "We passed some rugged territory back there. A good place to get lost in. And it will take them some time to find us."

Elvin didn't answer. He just steeled himself for the crash.

"Hey, Elvin," said Lomax. "Gimme a smoke."

Elvin didn't move. They were racing up the river, following its gentle curves. The tawny land before them was steadily rising, becoming more rugged. On the radar screen, two blips had angled into their wake, twenty miles behind them. When Elvin didn't respond, Lomax reached over for a Slim Jim sticking out of his fishing vest. Elvin batted Lomax's hand away. "After we land, and only if I survive," he yelled over the turbine noise, still staring ahead.

Lomax nodded. "Fair enough."

They passed the Canadian River before seeing anyone, and even then it was just a small sedan going the other way on a side road. The moon, though just a sliver, glowed through the high clouds, illuminating everything with a pale, silver light. Chris drove with the lights off, moving as fast as he dared. There were no pile-ups on the road, but he expected they would encounter some if they went near any big towns. He thought about Elvin and his case of hand grenades. He wished he had a couple with him now, just in case.

Cate discovered another talent the truck had. Radar. After fussing with it for a while, she understood it pretty well. "It has a variable scope, designed for close range mostly," she said, using the arrow keys to delve deeper into the subsystems. "Anything metal that moves, registers. Look." She pointed at the screen. "We're pretty much alone out here tonight."

"This isn't exactly an interstate," said Chris. "What's the range?"

"It looks like about ten miles," said Cate. "That's plenty of time to hide and not be seen." She beamed up at Chris, pleased with herself. She glanced back at K'tanu, who was sleeping on the rear bench seat. She turned back to Chris. "We've got to hurry."

Chris nodded. "I don't dare go over forty, Cate."

"I know, I know," she said. "I meant hurry and figure out exactly what we're doing."

"What do you mean?"

"I mean, what are we doing?"

"Taking him to Africa."

Cate shivered. "It's a dead continent by now. It must be."

"Probably no worse than America," said Chris. "And it's the same risk every time you meet another person, no matter what continent you're on."

Cate looked out at the darkness. They passed a sign that said, Tucumcari 5 Miles. The two-lane road wound between stands of pine and grassy meadows. "It's beautiful," she said, "now that humans are gone."

"Why do you always do that?" asked Chris.

"Do what?"

"Make it sound like mankind is a blight?"

"Humankind, thank you," said Cate.

"Whatever. You of all people."

"What's that supposed to mean?"

"Aren't you trying to save *human*kind? Isn't that your raison d'être?"

"So? That doesn't mean our species deserves to be saved; we've made a mess of everything."

"Everything?" said Chris. "You just saw a fender repair itself. You're looking at a radar screen. We have a GPS that pinpoints our location within three feet."

"That stuff doesn't make life better, it only makes it easier. And I'm not sure easier is better. It may make things worse. What are we doing here?"

"That again? Taking K'tanu—"

"No!" shouted Cate, and they both looked back. K'tanu shifted in his sleep. Cate whispered, "No! I meant why are we here on earth? What is the point?"

"You should know, you've been beyond it. I figured when you were a hawk in Lightland you had the proverbial birds'-eye view." He shook his head. "So tell me, Cate, why *are* we here?"

Cate glared at him. "I don't know. And neither do you."

"I never said I did. But you seem to think mankind is worthless. Emphasis on *man*. You also seem to think you have higher knowledge than I do, so I'm asking, sincerely: Why are we here?"

Cate's anger burned. He just didn't get it. "I said I don't know! That's the point! We're supposed to find out, each of us, for each of us. And all this," she said, indicating the truck around them, "has nothing whatsoever to do with the answer. In fact, I think it gets in the way!"

"For getting in the way, it's taking us down the road at a pretty good clip," said Chris. "You won't appreciate technology until you've lived without it."

"Oh, and you have?" asked Cate. "Hunkered down in a rich man's cabin, eating his food stores and burning his books?"

"They were library books. And I burned them *after* I read them."

"Congratulations. When did *you* ever live without technology?"

"Those few days in the Sudanese desert gave me a pretty good perspective, thank you."

"Well, I've lived without it too," said Cate. "I was out there, just like you were, after the outbreak."

"Right," said Chris. "But at that time, we didn't live without technology, we just used simpler technology. Instead of planes, cars. Instead of cars, motorcycles. Instead of motorcycles, bikes. We raided supermarkets, tipped Coke machines over, crowbarred warehouses. We used technology. I'm just saying that it's a straw man—not a very worthy opponent for you lofty spiritual types."

Cate looked at Chris for a long time. "You're jealous." There was surprise in her voice.

Chris snorted. "Am not."

"Am too. Look, Chris, I didn't ask for what happened to me. When I came back—"

"Would that be from Sinai, Moses?"

She ignored him. "I didn't expect you to understand it. I didn't even know if *I* understood it. All I know is that it changed something inside me, the way I see things. I can't explain it."

"You just know it's real," said Chris flatly.

"Yes."

"And that, ladies and gentlemen, is why science and religion don't mix."

"You're right," she said evenly. "They don't."

"So don't expect too much from me," said Chris.

"Is it too much to hope that you'd *believe* me?"

Chris didn't say anything for awhile. Finally: "I'm taking you there, aren't I?"

"I can't make your journey for you, Chris."

"I didn't ask you to."

Her voice was quiet, barely heard over the hum of the tires on the asphalt. "I love you." She reached out and touched his arm. "You believe *that*, don't you?"

After a long time, Chris nodded. "Sure."

K'tanu lay in the back seat, his eyes shut, listening. It was the most confusing conversation he'd ever heard. Cate and Chris certainly talked a lot about things that couldn't be expressed in words. He thought about his other life, so long ago. He remembered once returning from hunting, an ibex slung over his shoulders. Maya greeted him at the village gate and nestled her head in his neck. When she looked up, he saw the gazelle's blood on her cheek. He wiped it away and looked into her eyes. At that moment, he knew there was nothing in the world she would not do for him, no hardship she would not cheerfully share, no fear she would not battle at his side. Without a word, they entered the village and skinned, cooked, and ate the meat around the central fire pit. After, he watched her hold the baby Anja to her breast and felt warmth in his chest. She was his and he was hers. Together they were unified against a harsh world. They never argued; what was there to argue about when a storm was approaching? What was there to disagree over when food was scarce? What was there to criticize when a child was sick?

As he listened to the wheels on the road, K'tanu opened his eyes looked out the window. Dark shapes whisked past the vehicle. He was moving faster than he ever had outside of the Other World. He was being taken across an immense continent, green and brown, with trees he did not recognize. There were no animals except dogs and mottled cattle. He felt adrift on their journey until just before they left the big house in the mountains. He had been sitting by the swimming pool, looking up at the sky as the stars came out.

He did not expect to see any constellations he recognized, but then he saw her, appearing alongside Mother Moon, near the horizon. She was Hapsati, the daughter of Father Sun and Mother Moon. The tiny, glittering star accompanied her father on his daily journey, remaining visible for a time in the western night sky after he'd died, then appearing on the eastern horizon just before his birth. She had always been with him. K'tanu was delighted beyond words to see that she still loved Father Sun so many thousands of years later.

Until moments ago, K'tanu thought all had changed in the world, but he was wrong. Hapsati still traveled with Father Sun, who still moved across the sky, following his wife, Mother Moon. The sky overhead was still mostly the same. Many of the stars had moved a little, but he could still make out the lion, the hunter, and the eagle constellations. Only the world below the bowl of sky had changed. The permanence of the sky gave K'tanu hope. Maybe this world was not yet over. It had changed, but maybe it was merely a season, and one day everything would return to a familiar cycle. He desperately hoped so.

Sitting on the lounge in the darkness by the pool, listening to Cate and Chris loading the big truck, K'tanu's feet finally touched the ground. He was really here, though he did not know why. He wanted to return to Lightland, but he did not know how. He was traveling with these two lonely and fearful people, but he did not know how to take away their loneliness and fear. The scarab amulet would no longer transport his soul. The jawbone did not whisper to him. He was trapped in the Waking World, but it was not his world, and he was alone.

Now, as they rolled down the ribbon of road in the darkness, he listened to the quiet in the truck cab. Cate and Chris had stopped speaking, each one considering his or her own thoughts. He wished they knew what a gift each was to the other. He thought of Maya, and turned, facing the seat back, feeling hopeless.

TWENTY-TWO

HEARTS ON FIRE

The chopper set down on a peninsula of sand that jutted out into the bend of the brown river. The sun sent shadows slanting across the canyon floor. Cloudburst got out first, following the beeping of the ELT receiver. "It's close," she said, nodding at Ron. He looked around, aware of their exposed position. He pulled out his pistol and chambered a round. Cloudburst turned and glared at him. "I don't care if you shoot yourself," she said, "just don't shoot anybody else."

Ron shoved the pistol back into his pocket. The rotors finally stopped turning and the only sound was the gurgling of the river fifty feet below them and the soft beeping of the receiver. They edged around the curve of the promontory, which was layer upon layer of crumbly, gray shale. Before them was a steep slope of fallen shards, and Ron slipped as he walked across them, sending a cascade of stone down the slope and into the water with a loud splash. In front of him, Cloudburst shook her head at his clumsiness. God, how he hated that woman.

"I see it," she said, walking faster. When Ron turned the corner, he also saw the Comanche. It was canted onto a sandbar, its rotors bent and broken, as were the wheels. The nose had a huge dent in it and the windscreen was shattered. The cargo door was open. Cloudburst slid down the shale slope. Ron thought it would almost be fitting if Tempest or cranky old Lomax popped her one in the forehead right there. But no one fired, and soon she was standing next to the empty Comanche cargo bay. Ron slid down the slope, falling once, grateful no one was watching, and came puffing up behind Cloudburst. "Anybody inside?"

Cloudburst picked something up and handed it to him. He took the slender brown stick and broke it in two, biting off a chunk. "Fresh," he said.

Cloudburst looked around, scanning the shadowed canyon walls. "This has something to do with that truck we found west of Yucca. Wasn't there a case of these inside it?"

"Accomplices!" whispered Ron, pulling his gun and looking around.

Cloudburst switched off the beacon receiver and began climbing up the shale slope. "Let's hope they're as incompetent as mine."

Lomax and Elvin lay on their stomachs, watching through binoculars as Cloudburst and Ashby climbed back up the rock fall. "She's pissed," said Lomax. He handed the glasses to Elvin. "It's always good when the enemy's angry—they make mistakes."

Elvin watched them edge around the shoulder of rock toward the chopper waiting on the sandbar. "We'd better get," he said. "You picked a helluva place to crash. They can't fly up the canyon—it's too narrow. We can't stay in the canyon for the same reason; we'll drown. And we're exposed up here on top."

Lomax got up and moved away, bent over. He climbed down into the narrow canyon crevasse behind them. The Comanche's turbines fired up. Elvin ran to the crevasse, scrunching down. "They think we're long gone," said Lomax. "They'll expect us to go down river."

"So we go upriver?" asked Elvin. He checked his vest; he only had a dozen or so Slim Jims left. He'd have to ration them. But if they stayed near the river, at least they wouldn't die of thirst.

"We go north," said Lomax.

"But that's all desert."

Lomax nodded. The sound of the chopper's rotors increased in pitch. Lomax ventured a peek. The Comanche hovered over the canyon, then swung around toward them. Lomax ducked. In another moment, the sound changed. "They're heading off," said Lomax, looking again.

Elvin hazarded a look. The Comanche was headed west, following the river, moving slowly and deliberately, staying as low as it could. "We hunker down here until nightfall," said Lomax. "Then we cross the canyon and head for Mesquite. It's only forty miles." Elvin hung his head. Forty miles? Lomax slapped him on the back. "Two nights' traveling, tops, Corporal. Easy going."

Elvin lifted his head and saw the chopper in the distance, cruising slowly, turning from side to side. He automatically picked a jerky stick out of his pocket and was about to snap it in two, then reconsidered. He looked at it a moment, then put it back in his pocket. "Sure," he said, "easy going."

"There's nobody out here," said Cate, watching the radar holo as they rolled along.

"Good thing, as flat as it is," said Chris. "How far now?"

"Less than fifty miles," said Cate, consulting the map. They were traveling down a road that was so straight, it seemed to go on forever. On either side of them, the fields were brown and empty.

"Once upon a time," he said, "this was America's breadbasket."

"What's that?" asked Cate, pointing.

In the distance, the horizon glowed. "Looks like a fire," said Chris.

"Lightning," said K'tanu, leaning forward.

"Yep," said Chris, "Lubbock is on fire. So much for stopping there."

"We should check out the airport anyway," said Cate.

"If anyone still lives in town, they'll be trying to put it out. And that means air tankers, maybe. The airport might be busy."

"Let's look anyway," said Cate. "If you're right, we won't be noticed in the commotion."

"If I'm right, there will also be police."

"They're not looking for this truck," said Cate. "Besides, it's still dark. Let's chance it."

Chris nodded. They had little choice anyway. Highway 84 angled southeast, heading directly for Lubbock. They might skirt the town by a few miles, but they had to go by it, no matter what. As they drove, they began passing blackened fields and fire-gutted barns and silos. The eastern horizon was full of red-tinted smoke. Finally, they saw actual flames, and two cars passed them going the opposite way, headlights flashing. The second blared its horn, startling Chris and almost sending them off the road. "There's gonna be cops," he muttered, regretting their decision.

"It smells like bread cooking," said K'tanu.

"This complicates things," said Chris. It looked like the fire had passed that way shortly before. The fields still smoked, and off to their right they saw a farmhouse ablaze. As they passed the dirt lane, they saw a woman staggering down the lane toward the main road.

"She's hurt," said K'tanu, pointing.

"Can't stop," said Chris.

"Chris," said Cate, watching as the woman turned and fell down.

Chris gave her a look and she said no more. Out of the corner of his eye, he saw K'tanu, his nose against the window, watching until both the woman and the farmhouse were out of sight.

"I'm not the bad guy," muttered Chris, focusing on the road.

The airport was abandoned after all. "I guess the fire wouldn't be so out of control if they had tankers," said Chris.

"Or a way to fill them," said Cate. Lubbock had really shaken her up. It was an inferno. The fire had reached the outskirts of town just a few hours before they did, and hot westerly winds had whipped it into immense walls of flame. As they roared down one zigzag road after another, turning east, then south, then east again, they saw entire fields ablaze. Telephone poles were going up like Roman candles, popping as the asphalt in them ignited. One exploded just as they passed, sending a flaming glob of tar onto the Excelsior's windshield. Smoke filled the cab and the flames burned the glass black. Chris had to stop and scrape the smoking goo off the hood. As he did so, a police cruiser raced by, its lights blazing, but not slowing. Chris got back in and jammed the truck into gear.

Now they sat in the Lubbock airport parking lot. The gate to the ramp was closed. Chris pressed the bumper against the gate, popping it off the track. They bumped over it and stopped behind a row of hangars. "We ought to keep going," said Chris plaintively.

"It's almost dawn," said Cate. "We'll be spotted."

"Everyone within a hundred miles will be converging on this town to put the fire out. The military will help. The airport will be crawling with people as soon as it's dawn."

"And if we're seen going the opposite direction, it will raise suspicions," said Cate.

"We've already seen people doing that. It didn't surprise us. It won't surprise them."

"We should stay and help," said K'tanu.

Chris and Cate both turned.

"We can help," repeated K'tanu.

"You're kidding," said Chris.

"K'tanu," said Cate quietly, "we can't risk being seen. You understand that, don't you?"

"We should stay and help."

"*They* might not recognize us," said Chris, "but Cobalt doesn't care who we are. You might be immune, but Cate and I are not. Who knows what fire does to the virus? It might release it into the air. Hell, we might be breathing it right now. No. We're getting the hell out of here." He started the engine.

Cate turned to K'tanu. "He's right. It's too dangerous. For all of us."

K'tanu opened his door.

Chris turned around in his seat. "Oh, for God's sake!"

"Yes," said K'tanu, getting out of the truck. "For God's sake."

Chris glared at Cate. She got out, took K'tanu's hand, and led him over by the hangars. The air hung with acrid smoke. The eastern horizon was glowing red from the fire and the coming sunrise. "We're doing this for you," she said, looking up into K'tanu's face. "We can't help *everyone*, K'tanu, we just can't."

"We could have helped that woman we saw."

"We're trying to help *you*."

"We can do both." He turned away.

Cate noticed that he still clutched his backpack. She yanked it out of his hands.

"Hey!" shouted K'tanu.

"Why is this so important to you?" asked Cate, backing away.

"Give it back!" said K'tanu, reaching for her.

Chris got out of the truck. "Cate, don't!"

"So you *do* care about what happens to you!" shouted Cate. "Just like *we* care what happens to *us*!"

K'tanu stopped, then turned and walked slowly back to the truck.

"Oh! So you *do* care, don't you?" said Cate, holding the backpack out, shaking it.

Chris walked over to Cate. They watched as K'tanu got into the truck, closing the door. Chris took the backpack from Cate and put his arms around her. She dropped her head on his shoulder. "I'm sorry," she said, starting to cry. "I'm sorry."

Chris saw K'tanu's face in the window, lit red by the smoky sunrise. All hope was gone from his eyes.

WISDOM OF SOLOMON

When they landed at Yucca, there was another Comanche sitting on the helipad in front of the main doors. The pilot was still inside and the rotors were still spinning. Obviously, the visit would be short. As Cloudburst and Ron jumped out and walked between the two large doors, someone shouted, "Halt!" and they heard a gun being cocked. They froze. To their left, coming out of the shadows, was Samuel Fox. At his side was Major Wolfe, his weapon drawn. Fox nodded at Wolfe, who holstered his firearm. "Dr. Cloudburst, so nice to finally meet you," said Fox. "You're wondering what prompts this visit." Cloudburst noticed that the man had impossibly white teeth for someone who smoked cigars, which was what he was doing right now.

"There's no smoking here," she said automatically.

Fox laughed and raised the Cuban to his mouth, drawing on it deeply. "Of course not." He exhaled a great cloud of smoke and started toward the main doors. Cloudburst and Ron followed him, Wolfe bringing up the rear. Ron noticed that Wolfe never took his hand off the butt of his sidearm nestled in its holster.

Fox stopped at the entrance and turned, forcing Cloudburst and Ron to blink in the sun, which was low on the western horizon and shining directly into the entrance. "I take it you haven't yet found our fugitives," said Fox. "Or rather, *your* fugitives."

"We found the chopper. It's only a matter of time."

"You said that about a Cobalt vaccine, as I recall," said Fox.

"When we get Russell back, yes," said Cloudburst. Fox was tall and built like a linebacker. Wolfe stood to one side. Better targets, she figured, if it came to that. She noticed that at no time did Fox let her get within ten feet of him. She smiled inwardly and took a step forward. In an unconscious *pas de deux*, Fox took a step back. Wolfe, however, took a step forward. Cloudburst stopped.

"*If* you get Russell back," corrected Fox, apparently unaware he'd asked her to dance.

"They can't get far. Now, if you'll excuse me, I have to arrange a search detail."

"Already done," said Fox. "We heard your transmissions. I ordered one out of Nellis."

"We can handle it ourselves, thank you," said Cloudburst, wishing she could see his eyes, but he was a mere smoke-shrouded silhouette standing before her.

"The President would like to see you," said Fox.

"Me?" asked Cloudburst. "What for?"

Fox shrugged. "Didn't say. But we can guess, can't we?"

Cloudburst nodded. "When?"

Fox exhaled a great cloud of smoke. "Why, now, of course."

After the episode with K'tanu at the Lubbock airport, they drove all day and the next night, no one really caring if they were seen or not. They saw a great number of vehicles heading toward Lubbock, and quite a few going their way as well. It was the most people Chris had seen since the outbreak. The radar screen was so full at one point that Cate counted over fifty individual blips. Two planes flew overhead, headed toward Lubbock. The fire proved to be a literal smokescreen, allowing them to make the seven hundred miles from Lubbock to Brownsville on the Gulf in just a day and a half.

They had a scare north of San Antonio, though, on Interstate 10, when they heard gunshots. It was late evening and Chris brought the Excelsior to a dead stop in the middle of the empty road. They got out and listened. The gunfire continued and then something that sounded like a bomb went off. Cate got back into the truck. "What do you think it is?" asked Cate, remembering her unnerving encounter with the two young attackers so long ago when she was headed for her parents' place in the Shenandoah.

Chris peered through his binoculars. The land was flat, but it rose a little ahead. Whatever was happening was beyond the rise. K'tanu sat in the back. He'd said almost nothing since they left Lubbock. Cate turned to him, then back to Chris. "What should we do?"

"Side road, I guess," said Chris. "And we were making such good time. What was the last turnoff we passed?"

Cate consulted the GPS on the dash.

"Camp Verde," said K'tanu.

"What does that mean?" asked Cate, trying to draw K'tanu out.

"Green camp," said Chris, still looking through the glasses. "I was counting on the San Antonio airport for fuel." He got back into the truck.

"There's an airport in Hondo, west of San Antonio," said Cate, punching buttons. The trip computer holo floated in the air between them.

Chris put the Excelsior into reverse. "John Wayne," he said, turning them around.

"What?" asked Cate.

"We'll find fuel there," said Chris, heading back. "I'm lucky with movie names."

There was no gas at the Hondo airport. They checked the fuel farm; the tanks were emptied long ago by people like Elvin. Cate looked at the map. "Kelly Air Force base in San Antonio."

"No," said Chris. "Absolutely not."

"How much gas do we have?" asked Cate.

"Half a tank. There must be other airports."

"There are," said Cate. "But can we risk running out of gas hunting for one with fuel?"

Chris shook his head and pulled back on the two-lane highway headed east. "Shit."

"No way, no way," muttered Chris.

"No choice," said Cate. So they cut the chain link fence near the river and entered the base grounds, driving down a taxiway, their lights off. On the right were a half-dozen gray transports. Cate pointed out that their tires were inflated; a sign they were in use. "I don't see any fighters."

"They're around," said Chris. "See the tower?" He pointed to their left, across two parallel runways. A red light shone, but no lights could be seen inside.

"They're not on alert," said Cate. "Thank goodness."

"Not yet, at least," said Chris, turning toward the cargo planes. He drove under the wing of an immense gray transport and turned off the engine. Cate was about to get out when Chris grabbed her arm. "Let's see if they've noticed us first."

They waited. When five minutes had passed without a greeting party, they got out. "I only know about the little jets," said Chris, looking around on the belly for a fuel-dump valve. He didn't dare use his flashlight. The moon, nearing a quarter, was hidden behind low, dark clouds, only a weak glow indicating its position overhead.

"I don't see anything," said Cate.

"What about that?" said K'tanu, pointing. Beside an immense hangar was a fuel-tanker truck.

"We couldn't be that lucky," said Chris, trotting toward it.

This time they were. The truck was locked, but the tanker was full. Cate drove the Excelsior over and they found a drain cock on the underside. Using their five-gallon buckets, they filled the two barrels in the truck bed, then the gas tank. They were just finishing up when they heard an engine firing up on the other side of the runway. They'd been working so steadily that they hadn't noticed an F-45 Silver Ghost turning onto a taxiway not far from them. The plane's landing light swept across them. They ducked behind the big black Excelsior and waited, not knowing what else to do.

The fighter taxied out of sight. In a few minutes, it roared past, taking to the sky. They jumped back into the truck and sped down the taxiway, hoping against hope that the Ghosts didn't travel in pairs.

Back on the freeway, south of San Antonio, Cate and Chris finally relaxed. "Our luck is holding out," said Chris.

K'tanu looked out the window. "Can you stop?"

"What for?" asked Chris.

"I want to ride in back, with the mummy."

Chris pulled over. K'tanu got out and climbed into the truck bed, sitting down next to the mummy, his back against the fuel barrels, holding his backpack. Chris went to the rear of the truck. "It will be cold," he said, taking off his coat and handing it to K'tanu. "We're almost there. Brownsville is only a couple hundred miles."

"Okay," said K'tanu, putting the coat on.

"Are you hungry?"

K'tanu shook his head.

"There's water in the cooler. No ice, but, hey."

K'tanu nodded.

"She didn't mean it."

K'tanu nodded again, not meeting Chris's eyes.

"We're all tired."

K'tanu pulled the collar up and closed his eyes. Chris got back into the cab. For a long time nothing was said, then he turned to Cate. "He'll be okay."

Cate nodded. "He's more okay than we are."

Most of the main highways in Texas had been cleared of wrecks, and bandit pileups were rare. They saw lots of cars on the roads, but like everywhere else, cars were like surgical gloves. With the windows rolled up and ULPA masks on, the occupants felt safe. Interstate 35 ran straight for over a hundred miles, dead-ending in Laredo on the Rio Grande. Cate pointed to the river, calling to K'tanu in the back.

"It's the Great River," and K'tanu nodded, but didn't say anything. When Cate rolled her window up, her face was flushed. "He hates me."

"He doesn't hate you," said Chris. "He hates *us*."

"What do you suppose it is that we don't understand?"

"Who knows? He won't talk. Are we supposed to read his mind?"

"I don't know," said Cate. "He seems to be able to read *ours*."

Twenty years before, the flood of illegal immigration had been stanched somewhat along the New Mexico, Arizona, and California borders with the construction of the "Friendship Wall," a great concrete barrier fifty feet tall and over three hundred miles long, stretching from Tijuana to El Paso. The land just beyond the wall was reputed to be mined, not by the Border Patrol, but by local militias. In any case, illegal border crossing virtually ended along the Wall, but where it ended and the Rio Grande flowed out of the Rockies near Las Cruces, it was more difficult to stop. Gunboats patrolled the river, but illegal entry continued. Latinos wanted the work, and Americans didn't want to pay ten dollars for a hamburger.

But now the border towns were empty. The military had pulled back, mostly because no one was crossing the border anymore. No one really knew how badly Cobalt had devastated Mexico, but in any case, the reasons for coming north had vanished. Latinos harvested their own lettuce and oranges in their own gardens and groves in Mexico, and Americans, for the first time since the Great Depression a hundred years earlier, did the same. What governments could not do, Cobalt had done quite effectively. Illegal immigration was no longer a problem. But neither was *legal* immigration.

Their stop in San Antonio ensured they had enough gas for the rest of the trip, which they made in broad daylight. The relative bustle of central Texas gave way to a silent, hot emptiness as they approached the Gulf coast. To their right, the Grande curved lazily between low, sandy bluffs.

They drove through Rio Grande City and did not see a soul or a vehicle on the road. Tumbleweeds blew across the highway, pushed by a hellish wind from the west. Dust-devil funnels moved slowly across dry, empty fields. The land was returning to its natural state, and the only greenbelt was on either side of the wide, muddy river. "It looks like the Nile," said Chris.

Cate wanted a bottle of water out of the back, but was afraid to face K'tanu. She didn't know what to say to him. She wanted him to forgive her, but she couldn't think of why he should.

Brownsville was a flat, empty town of single-story houses, much like its sister city on the other side of the river, Matamoros. They stopped the truck where the river took a lazy curve northward. The Gateway Bridge crossed here, empty and rusting, the asphalt melting in the blazing sun, weeds sprouting between bridge sections.

"I've got to get some sleep," said Chris, turning the truck around.

"There's a church," said Cate, pointing to a ramshackle Catholic church on a side street. The windows were boarded up. The tiny cemetery was overgrown. Trash had collected in drifts against the iron fence surrounding the forlorn-looking sandstone building.

"Perfect," said Chris. "Nobody's been here since before the plague." He steered the Excelsior into the dirt lot behind the church. They helped K'tanu out. He moved with such obvious pain that Cate almost cried. His hair was going white, and his skin was like brittle paper, lined and blotchy. His eyes, so clear and white before, had turned a jaundiced yellow. They guided him to the door, which Chris pried open. They went up three wooden stairs and found themselves standing in the alcove behind the apse. Dust motes floated in the slanting morning light, which streamed through a broken skylight. The pews under the opening were rain-damaged and the hardwood floor had rotted through.

An ornate mahogany altar with a marble top stood in the nave, covered with dust and bird droppings. Behind it, a gilded wooden statue of the Virgin Mary holding the infant Christ child stood atop a pedestal, the dry wood split from crown to foot, the baby Jesus cut in half.

"The wisdom of King Solomon," said Cate, looking up at the ruined sculpture.

"What?" asked Chris, helping K'tanu to sit down on the front row of pews.

"When two women came to him, each claiming a baby as her own, he ordered it cut in two and half given to each woman."

"God, Cate," said Chris.

"But one woman begged him to spare the child and give it instead to the other woman. That's how Solomon knew who the real mother was."

"He took a big chance," said Chris, sitting next to K'tanu. The church was poor; there was no glorious stained glass like Castle Seidel; only dirty, smeared windows high up on the walls. Pigeons had nested in the rafters; he heard their quiet cooing. He looked over. K'tanu was already asleep on the pew, holding his backpack to his chest like a teddy bear.

Cate stepped off the dais and sat by Chris. "Religion. I don't think I'm ready for it."

Chris put his arm around her. "Doesn't make much sense, does it?" he mused, looking around. All along the walls were small alcoves with statues in them and Roman numerals on top. The signs of the cross? Chris knew there were twelve or thirteen of them, reminders of the passion of Jesus. Christians believed he died for them, something Chris never understood. How could someone's death benefit another person? He looked down at K'tanu, sleeping on the pew next to him. *He's going to die, and we're taking him to his grave. Why? A dream? A secret longing that has possessed all mankind? A retrograde desire for a bloody god? An ancient death wish lurking in everyone's heart? A god who dies for man? A man who dies for god? Where did it end?*

And what was his part in it? Bystander? Participant? Believer? Nonbeliever? He glanced at Cate, whose breathing told him she was also asleep. Lover? They were risking everything in the hope that in helping this young, dying man, they would also somehow help themselves. That was the truth of it. They weren't altruistic; they were hoping for some benefit, though Chris hadn't the slightest idea what that benefit could be. They were going to take K'tanu to Africa and he would die there, and for what? Cobalt would still rage across the planet, eventually killing them like it did everyone else. He felt a tickle at the back of his throat and coughed. Had he contracted the virus on their trip? No, it was just the dust in the air. He looked up. Were the pigeons carriers? Carrier pigeons? Weren't they extinct?

Like us?

K'tanu awoke with the sun in his face. It shone down on him like a pillar. He blinked and moved his head, which ached terribly. His neck was stiff. He moved, and the backpack tumbled off the bench onto the floor with a loud *clink!* Terrified, he snatched it up and unzipped it. The alabaster jar was intact and the lid was secure. He'd duct-taped it shut back in New Mexico. Cate and Chris were slumped against each other across the aisle, sleeping, his arm around her.

K'tanu reached into his jeans pocket and pulled out the scarab amulet. He'd rubbed it shiny during his many attempts to return to Lightland. His fingers pressed against it now, repeating the ritual, even as he looked through the shaft of dusty sunlight and the dim altar beyond. He stood and walked up the three creaking dais steps. The stone-altar surface was dirty, but once upon a time it was white, like the heart jar. Using his sleeve, he cleaned off the stone and knelt before it, placing the amulet on the glinting marble and withdrawing his hands, lacing the fingers together as he'd seen Captain Lomax do before he ate his meals. He looked up. There was a statue of a lady dressed in long, flowing robes, a circle behind her head, holding a tiny baby, who also had a golden circle behind his head. Her skin, once white, was now black, like his, and the baby's as well. She was looking down at her child lovingly. K'tanu thought of his mother, Joanna, whom he'd never met. Cate said that Joanna was not really his mother, but just a "surrogate" who only carried him in her womb. He looked at the mother and child again. He was his own child, his own father; his own brother. And yet, he was also M'uano and D'ranja's son. He was Anja's father and she was no bigger than the sculpted baby when she died of the Bleeding Sickness. Maya had looked down at Anja just as this woman looked down at her baby.

The baby was the Christian god. Lieutenant Zuñiga was a Christian. Captain Lomax used to be one, but now he believed in someone called Osiris. He'd shown K'tanu the silver amulet hanging on a chain around is neck.

K'tanu pulled the chain out, holding the ankh gently in his palm. Before they parted, Captain Lomax had given it to him. K'tanu wondered if this symbol would be found in a Christian church. He scanned the ornate carvings surrounding the statue of the woman and child, but he did not see it. Then he looked above the statue and saw the cross. It only lacked a head and it would be exactly like the ankh. Maybe they were the same a long time ago. His eyes rested once again on the baby in the woman's arms. Maybe the head of the ankh detached itself and entered the child and all that was left was the cross that meant so much to people like Lieutenant Zuñiga.

Looking down at the scarab amulet on the stone table before him, K'tanu closed his eyes and repeated the prayer. "N'gala no edila Maya e hamarka ta salu. Ta salu." His fingertips touched the amulet and he steeled himself.

Nothing happened. He whispered the words again, aching to feel Maya's head resting on his shoulder, his son's arms around his legs, tiny Anja in his arms. Instead, he smelled only dust and musty bird droppings. He bowed his head again. *What have I done?* he pled silently. *Why can't I return?*

He opened his eyes. He could not remember his son's name! He looked around, his heart sinking like a stone. What was his name? He could see his face, round and beautiful, his dark eyes flashing, his lips moving, but he could not hear what the boy was saying. What was his name? K'tanu placed his forehead on the cool marble. He had lost his son! Had he been pulled out of Lightland, like K'tanu? Was Maya crying right now, after the boy had disappeared from before her very eyes? Was she calling his name? What was his name?

"Father Sun," whispered K'tanu. "I am selfish, thinking only of myself. Take care of my son; hold him close. If I cannot be there, please let him stay in Lightland to comfort his mother."

He stretched his arms across the marble, the scarab amulet between them, and wept.

TWENTY-FOUR

GESTURE OF FAITH

"Madame President," said Sally Cloudburst, extending her hand.

Lucinda Burrows took a step back, smiling wanly. "Please, have a seat." She indicated a chair on the other side of her desk. Cloudburst sat. Fox and Wolfe stood behind her, near the door. They were in an exact replica of the Oval Office, complete with hologram window views, though she knew they were a good ten stories underground, and in North Dakota to boot.

"Any progress?" asked Burrows. To Cloudburst, she looked ragged and pale, and her furtive looks made Cloudburst suspect a creeping paranoia. Cloudburst looked over her shoulder at Fox, who smiled. It probably didn't help things much that the President was attended by Samuel Fox, aptly named, as was his sidekick, Major Wolfe.

"We found the helicopter on the Colorado River, near Lake Mead."

"I was at Lake Mead," said Burrows dreamily. "They renamed the dam for me."

"Yes, Ma'am," said Cloudburst. "The area around there is rugged; they can't get far."

"It's a marvel of engineering," said Burrows. "One hundred years old this year!"

"Yes, Ma'am," said Cloudburst, resisting the urge to shout, "Now, focus, you ninny!"

"I wish we could hold a centennial," said the President. "It would be nice, don't you think?" Burrows looked at Fox. "Sam, we should plan something, don't you think?"

"Superb idea, Madame President. I'll see to it."

"Good," said Burrows, turning back to Cloudburst. "Now, what were we discussing?"

Cloudburst stood in the upper level of the Undisclosed Location, glaring at Samuel Fox. "You dragged me all the way out here to see . . . *that?*"

Fox lit a cigar. They were waiting for the elevator to take them up to the surface. Ron stood behind Cloudburst, still reeling both from the excitement of almost meeting the President (he'd been kept out in the hallway) and the disappointment at what Cloudburst was revealing about Lucinda Burrows now. "She was lucid when I last saw her," said Fox, winking at Major Wolfe, who stood behind Ron, making Ron very uncomfortable.

"And when was that?" asked Cloudburst. The elevator doors opened and the security detail entered. They followed and the doors closed behind them. The elevator started up. Fox blew a smoke ring. Cloudburst coughed and ostentatiously waved the smoke away.

Fox merely smiled.

"Does she even know what's going on?" asked Cloudburst, suddenly aware that she was the only woman in the car, surrounded by big, beefy soldiers who probably feared and loathed women, especially since the President was such an easy target.

"She is the President," said Fox, "though her eight years were up two years ago." He smiled. "Why? Are you thinking of running?" The men in the car laughed. Cloudburst turned and caught Ron laughing as well. He closed his mouth.

She turned back to Fox, looking up at him with undisguised hatred. "Are you?"

Fox inhaled the cigar deeply. He let the smoke out slowly, his gray eyes never leaving hers. "Why should I?"

Just then, the door opened, and there stood a Marine holding out a sheet of paper to Cloudburst. She reached for it, but Fox was too quick and snatched it away. He scanned it quickly and handed it to Cloudburst. "Your fugitives are in San Antonio, Doctor."

Chris woke. Water was dripping onto the pew near his head. He looked up. It was dark and it was raining. He looked at his watch: 3:27. Beside him, Cate was asleep. He couldn't see much in the darkness. Suddenly, lightning lit the church and Chris jumped up, waking Cate, who looked at him groggily. "K'tanu!" he yelled, running under stream of water coming in the broken skylight, getting drenched. "K'tanu!" he shouted again, snatching up a flashlight, shining it around. "He's not here!"

Cate bolted for the back door, Chris following. Outside, the parking lot was a sea of mud. The Excelsior had not moved. They ran to the truck bed and threw aside the tarp. The mummy was gone, though the litter remained. Rain poured down from a black sky.

K'tanu's back ached from pushing the old wheelbarrow. He'd found it leaning against the rear of the church. It had taken him almost a half hour to reach the bridge, the mummy threatening to fall out with each step. When he was halfway across Gateway Bridge, he stopped and leaned against the rail. It was raining and the sky was black. Mother Moon was hidden by clouds. There were no lights, just the glinting silver of the river lazily flowing under the bridge. From this point, the bridge sloped down toward Mexico; the going would be easier now. His hip popped as he straightened. His sweatshirt hood was sopping wet and he pulled it back, feeling the warm rain on his face. Grabbing the handles, he lifted the wheelbarrow again and trudged forward.

When he stepped off the bridge, K'tanu stopped and turned back. "Goodbye, my friends," he whispered. "Thank you."

"Limosnas?" came a weak voice.

K'tanu turned. In a doorway, barely out of the rain, lay an old brown woman on a bed of sopping rags, her bony hands held out before her. "Caridád? Por favór?"

K'tanu set his backpack on the wheelbarrow and peered into the dark alcove. He bent and stuck his head inside.

She recoiled. "Estóy enferma! No te acercas!"

K'tanu stopped, letting his eyes adjust to the darkness. Her skin was blotched and her eyes were red. Her hands were covered with blood, which also dripped from her nose. "Are you all right?" he asked in Spanish, dredging up Russell's meager memory of the language. The woman hid her face. K'tanu knelt before her. She scrunched back into the rear of the alcove. He pulled a water bottle from his pocket and held it out for her.

She shook her head. "Ya hay bastante agua," she said, gesturing at the street, where water coursed past them in the cobblestone gutter.

"Plenty water," said K'tanu. He felt inside his jacket and found one of the Slim Jims Elvin gave him as a good-bye present. He broke it in two and peeled plastic away. He bit his half and held the other half out to her. She smiled toothlessly up at him, shaking her head. He placed the stick on her lap. When he looked up, she was pointing at him.

"Tu crees," she said. "Tu crees."

I believe? came Russell's voice in his head. *I believe what?*

"Eres discípulo de Osiris."

A chill ran up K'tanu's spine. He looked down. When he'd leaned forward, the chain with the ankh symbol had fallen out of his shirt. "Osiris?" he said, using her pronunciation, "O-see-rees?"

"Sí!" she grinned, touching her narrow chest. "También yo!" She reached out to him and he helped her to her feet. "Sígame," she commanded, shuffling out into the downpour. She headed down the street. K'tanu followed, taking the handles of the wheelbarrow, lifting it. Water poured over the lip. The woman looked back, waving him forward. He followed her down the street.

They made several turns and then came to a cinder block house with a corrugated tin roof, wood-roofed porch, and darkened windows.

"El sacerdote," said the woman, pointing.

"Sacerdote?" repeated K'tanu, peering through the rain. There was a sign on the front door that he could not make out. He set the wheelbarrow down and walked toward the house. At the foot of the steps, he saw the sign clearly. The letters "D.O." appeared below an oval, inside of which was an ankh symbol. "Discípulos de Osiris," he said, turning.

The old woman was gone.

"Señora!" called K'tanu, trotting to the corner. She was far down the street, heading back to her hovel. He turned back to the house just as the front door opened. A thin man in a ratty striped bathrobe stood in the doorway. K'tanu wheeled the barrow over to the house and walked up the steps. He reached inside his shirt and pulled out the chain, showing the ankh.

The man smiled.

Chris hunched over as he ran. "We should have brought the truck."

Cate trotted ahead. "He's on foot; we might miss him!" She ran across the Gateway Bridge, her feet splashing in the puddles left by the rain.

"We don't even know if he came this way!" yelled Chris. He was soaking wet. The Excelsior sat at the bridge terminus, its headlights glancing across the wet pavement, sending his shadow out in front of him. "*The Third Man*," he thought. *I'm Joseph Cotton chasing Orson Welles through Vienna.*

Suddenly, Cate stopped. When Chris reached her, she was stooped, talking to someone in a doorway. Chris looked into the darkness, saw the sick old woman, and yanked Cate back.

"Chris!" said Cate, struggling to get free.

"She's got Cobalt!"

Inside the alcove, the old woman held her hands out. "Caridád?"

"She needs help," said Cate, straining against his grip.

"She's sick!"

Cate whirled around to face him. "I know that!"

"Well?"

"Do you know why K'tanu left?"

"He was mad at us about something."

"And you know why?"

"Because we don't want to contract Cobalt? He's mad at us for *that*?"

"He's mad at us because we're afraid."

"Afraid?" he laughed bitterly. "Would we be doing all this if we were *afraid*?"

"Caridád?" begged the old woman.

"She needs help," said Cate.

"K'tanu needs help," said Chris. "We need help. Hell, everyone needs help."

"One at a time," said Cate, reaching inside her windbreaker, pulling out a breakfast bar. "Here," said Cate, extending it to the woman.

"No, gracias," said the woman, smiling toothlessly.

Chris ran his hands through his hair. Cate was exposing them both to Cobalt. He reached to pull her back, then stopped. The woman was holding out a Slim Jim. Chris reached inside his jacket, and pulled out the jerky stick Elvin had given him, showing it to the old woman.

She nodded, waving the jerky at him. "Sí! Sí!"

FOOLISHNESS AND HOPE

"It's them," said Cloudburst, watching the security feed. They sat in the tower at Kelly Air Force Base overlooking the runway. Ron pulled back from the window, feeling vertigo. He hadn't changed his clothes in two days. He smelled his armpit and grimaced.

"Are you sure?" said Fox, indicating for the traffic controller to play it again. The video went back, then started forward again. It was dark, and even the infrared security cameras yielded only blurry red images of the truck and its occupants.

"Look," said Cloudburst, pointing at the screen. "There are three of them."

"I thought they had an accomplice," interjected Ron. "That makes four."

"Shut up," said Cloudburst. "Lomax couldn't have been with them when they were here the night before last. He was hundreds of miles away, leading us on a wild-goose chase."

"Oh," said Ron.

"But how can you be sure it's them?" asked Fox.

"Who else could it be?"

"Could be anybody," said the flight controller. "We catch people stealing gas all the time."

"Then why didn't you catch them *this* time, asshole?" growled Cloudburst, striding from the room.

"What's her problem?" asked the controller.

"She's running for President," said Fox, leading Ron and Wolfe from the room.

The controller watched them go. "Well, she's not getting *my* vote."

Chris ran up the steps of the old house the woman had been jabbering about and pointing at. He knocked. No answer. He squinted into the dark windows. He knocked again, then saw it: the oval with the ankh symbol.

"She says they're Disciples of Osiris," called Cate at that same moment.

Chris ran back to the truck, hopping in. The rain pounded on the roof.

"El sacerdote!" said the old woman.

"What does that mean?" asked Chris.

The old woman placed her hands together and bowed her head.

"Praying?" asked Cate.

"El sacerdote," repeated the woman.

"Well, whoever she's talking about isn't home," said Chris.

"Break down the door," said Cate.

"Okay." He started to get out, when suddenly, a great rumbling came from the south.

"Sounds like a jet engine," said Cate.

"Ya mismo vuele," said the woman, floating her hand through the air.

Chris slammed his door and shoved the truck into gear.

The Matamoros airport was little more than a narrow runway with an empty tower. As they skidded into the muddy parking lot, Chris saw the jet at the far end of the taxiway, moving slowly out onto the runway. He hit the gas, blasting through the chain-link fence. The truck's rear end fishtailed and clipped an old Piper, whipping the plane around, the wing narrowly missing Cate's door as they roared by. The old woman let out a yelp as she was thrown about in the back seat. Bouncing onto the runway, Chris sent the truck into a slide that nearly rolled it, coming to a stop facing the jet, which was accelerating to take-off speed. Chris jumped out, waving his arms, but the jet did not slow. Cate blinked the headlights. The jet suddenly veered left, brakes squealing. Chris's heart skipped a beat—the jet would never stop in time. Suddenly, the Excelsior lurched forward, narrowly missing him as it bounded off the runway. Cate.

Chris turned back. The jet was bearing down on him. He dove off the runway as it roared by, brakes shrieking, turbines reversed. It finally came to a stop about thirty yards down the runway. Chris got to his feet, his left ankle badly sprained, and limped toward the jet. As he approached, the fuselage door opened and someone fired a gun into the air. Chris dropped to the ground. When he looked up, a silhouette was pointing a gun at him through the falling rain. "I'll be damned," said a man. "Chris, is that you?"

Chris looked up. "Lomax?"

Cate ran over to Chris, helping him to his feet. Lomax extended the retractable steps and holstered his weapon. "I thought you two weren't coming."

"What are you doing here?" asked Chris.

"Come in before you drown," said Lomax, waving them forward.

When they were inside, they saw K'tanu sitting at the rear of the cabin, his head down. Cate ran to him and threw her arms around him. "Why did you leave?"

"I'm sorry," he said.

Chris hobbled over. "Are you okay?"

K'tanu looked up and saw Lomax frowning at him. "I told the Captain you weren't coming."

"Well, you were wrong," said Cate.

"I came alone for a reason."

"Did you two plan this?" asked Cate, looking at Lomax.

"No," said Lomax. "But I knew you were headed for Africa. There are no flights from the states going there, so I knew you'd end up in Mexico, as far from Yucca as you could get. That's here. So I got in last night and talked to the local priest—told him to keep a look out for you folks if you showed up."

"I was lucky Lomax was here," said K'tanu.

"But you don't believe in luck," said Chris. "You believe everything happens for a reason."

"Yes," said K'tanu. "So when the priest told me Captain Lomax had arrived, I knew it was meant to be."

"Fair enough," said Chris. "Then our catching you before you took off was also meant to be."

"Africa is dead," said K'tanu. "You said so yourself. It's too dangerous."

"We can decide what's too dangerous for us," said Chris.

"Oh! I forgot!" said Cate, jumping up and rushing out the hatch.

Lomax and K'tanu exchanged a look.

"Oh, right," said Chris. "We've got someone with us."

"Who?" asked K'tanu.

"The woman who showed us where she took you."

K'tanu blinked. "You know she has Cobalt, don't you?"

Chris shrugged, as if to say it was Cate's idea.

K'tanu stood and embraced Chris tightly. Chris patted his back, embarrassed. Lomax headed back into the cockpit. K'tanu released Chris and they both deplaned, walking toward the black Excelsior sitting just off the runway. The rain had let up; it was now just a drizzle. Cate had the driver's door open and was fussing with the old woman inside.

"Her name is Dolores," said Chris. "I think."

They heard the squealing of tires and looked up. An old pickup roared toward them, skidding to a stop near the jet. Chris reached for his revolver, but K'tanu touched his arm, shaking his head. A moment later, the truck doors opened and two men got out.

Chris squinted. "Is that . . .?"

"Don't shoot, sheriff," said Elvin, striding toward them, his hands raised. The ever-present Slim Jim was in his mouth and his blue corduroy vest was dirtier than ever. Behind him was a dark man in a long overcoat and hat. *The sacerdote*, thought Chris, putting the gun away.

Elvin grabbed Chris's hand. "Good to see you, pal."

Cate came running up. "Elvin! What are you doing here?"

"I thought you were leaving," came Lomax's voice from the hatchway.

"Yes, sir," said Elvin. He nodded at the Excelsior. "But when I saw that truck heading for the airport, I thought something was up."

"That was us, trying to get *up*," said Lomax, "but some fool drove his vehicle onto the runway. Damn near got himself killed."

Elvin smiled at Chris, then gestured at the man standing quietly behind him. "This is Roberto Vasquez, head honcho of the local batch of Osiris disciples."

Vasquez gave them a curt, formal bow. He was very tall and very thin, almost cadaverous.

Cate turned to Vasquez. "Señor? Do you speak English?"

"Certainly," said Vasquez.

Cate grabbed his elbow and steered him toward the Excelsior. "I don't know what she's saying . . ."

Soon they were out of earshot and Chris turned to Lomax. "How did you guys find us?"

"We crashed," said Elvin.

"It was a *controlled descent*," corrected Lomax.

Elvin shrugged. "Ending in a crash."

"Corporal."

"Sorry, sir," said Elvin.

"But how'd you get *here*?" asked Chris.

"After we scuttled the Comanche, we were hiking to Mesquite," said Lomax. "Another chopper came toward us, dipping the nose."

"That means he's a friendly," added Elvin.

"It thought it might be one of my guys," said Lomax. "So I took a chance. There were those present who questioned my decision."

"Coulda got us shot," muttered Elvin.

"Do *you* want to tell this, or can I?"

Elvin looked away, chewing his cheroot.

"We got lucky," said Lomax. "The pilot, Zuñiga, is a good man. When I explained what was going on, he agreed with us, saying Russell had the right to live his own life, even if he *was* a clone. He took us over the border to Juarez, where we hooked up with some Disciples there. One of them was a retired software millionaire." Lomax nodded at the jet. "He loaned me his Hawker."

"But you gotta have it back by ten," laughed Elvin.

Lomax frowned in mock anger. "I will, if you'll let us get the hell out of here." He nodded at Chris and headed back to the jet.

Chris turned to Elvin. "What? You're not coming?"

"Nope," said Elvin. "I haven't even seen most of *this* country, yet."

Chris nodded at the Excelsior. "Then you'll need a ride. And this." He removed Seidel's .357 revolver from his jacket pocket. "Since you're out of grenades, you might want this—it kind of goes with the truck." He placed the gun in Elvin's hand.

"Keep it," said Elvin, giving it back. "You'll need it more than I will."

Chris looked over at Cate, who was talking with Vasquez in front of the open Excelsior driver's door, remembering the look she gave him after his excitement at downing the choppers over the Virgin River. He never wanted to see that look again. "That's what I'm afraid of."

"Love is some kind of virus," said Elvin. "Your heart aches, your eyes water, and finally, you lose your mind. I hope I catch it someday." He turned to the Excelsior. "Who's inside there?"

"A woman with Cobalt," said Chris.

Elvin glowered at Chris, then let out an exasperated sigh. "Okay, but put her in the back. I wanna live to rescue *my* princess."

Chris nodded. "Thanks, Elvin."

While Elvin waited, Chris and Cate put Dolores on the litter in the truck bed, bundling her up with blankets from the plane. Vasquez put his hand on Dolores' forehead. "No quieres ir a Africa?"

"Me muero aqui," said Dolores weakly.

"What did she say?" asked Cate.

"She wants to die here, not in Africa."

Chris nodded. "Me too."

The Hawker was on a steep climb. K'tanu leaned back, feeling the pressure on his chest. When the jet cleared the clouds and leveled off, he finally had the courage to look out the window. The world was gone. All that was left was a sea of gray clouds below and inky darkness above. Mother Moon shone through the window. As he watched, the clouds dissipated and he saw whitecaps on an endless black sea, far below. A map of the Atlantic appeared on the seat back in front of him, a straight red line between Mexico and Egypt. He glanced across the aisle where the mummy had been belted across two seats. In the seat beside him was the backpack holding the alabaster jar. He looked out the window and thought of Maya.

Chris appeared at his side. "May I?" K'tanu picked up the backpack and Chris sat down next to him. "It's a short flight—only fourteen hours."

K'tanu nodded but said nothing.

Chris took a deep breath. "I know you don't want us here, but we promised to help you."

"It was wrong for me to leave you behind. I felt bad, so I left you a present."

"Present?"

"It's in your pocket."

Chris reached into his quilted vest pocket and withdrew the yellowed, brittle jawbone.

"It no longer speaks to me," said K'tanu. "Perhaps it will speak to you."

Chris held the mandible out to K'tanu. "I don't think so."

"But you must *listen*," said K'tanu, ignoring the offer. "And hope." He looked out the dark window. "The way we *hope* Captain Lomax can find Africa."

"We call that a 'leap of faith,'" said Chris. "Forty thousand feet over water, at night. When you think about it, it's not so much faith as foolishness."

"Foolishness is what hope looks like to those who have none."

Chris considered the jawbone in his hand. "I don't know if I have any hope left in me."

"But hope does not come from inside you," said K'tanu. "It is everywhere and in everything. It is the foundation of life. You just draw it in, like a breath, and once it is inside you, it grows." He took a deep breath and held it, closing his eyes.

Chris did the same, feeling his heart beat and the cool bone in his closed hand.

The C-130J Super Hercules set down on the tarmac at George Bush International Airport in Houston and stopped in front of the empty terminal. A cordon of olive-green military vehicles encircled the transport. A man in a biosuit and ULPA mask emerged from a vehicle clutching a manila envelope. At the foot of the gangway, Ron Ashby met him and took the envelope, opening it.

"Ron!" shouted Cloudburst from the top of the stairs. "Bring it up here!" Her voice was muffled by her ULPA mask.

Ron ignored her and read the message, then turned.

"Well?" growled Cloudburst.

Ron took his time climbing the stairs. "They're not here. No flights out in the last seventy-two hours." He handed the message to Cloudburst and shouldered his way past her, sitting down across the aisle from Major Wolfe, whom he almost considered a friend now, the man had shadowed them so closely over the last few days.

Cloudburst scanned the message, then turned to Fox. "How far does radar reach?"

"Surface or long-range?"

"Whatever!"

"Surface is about a hundred miles. Long range is inoperable. Why?"

"Well, we're only certain they didn't leave from here. That leaves about two hundred airports on the Gulf."

"Three hundred, if you count Mexico," added Ron.

Cloudburst turned, but instead of a scowl, a smile was on her face. "Thank you, Ron." She turned to the cockpit, where the pilot and copilot were leaning into the aisle, listening. "What's the closest airport in Mexico?" she asked.

"Matamoros," said the pilot. "Across the stream from Brownsville."

Cloudburst sat down and buckled her seat belt. "Brownsville. Sounds lovely."

TWENTY-SIX

CROSSING THE LINE

The sleek Hawker jet came in low, the early morning sun throwing its shadow across the rushes and swamps. K'tanu was glued to the window. The delta was incredibly lush, but as they flew further south, the desert began to squeeze the Nile into a narrow passage. He looked back. Chris and Cate were sleeping, leaning against each other, two rows behind him. He stood and headed for the cockpit.

Lomax was leaning back in his seat, arms folded, watching the gauges. The autopilot had brought the craft down to just a couple thousand feet above the ground. When K'tanu entered, Lomax gestured toward the empty copilot's seat. "We're about there."

"Where are we going?" asked K'tanu, buckling in and looking out the window. Little villages dotted the delta, and occasionally, he could see a small boat plying the muddy waters.

Lomax flipped a switch, disengaging the autopilot. "Back a ways, we passed Alexandria on the coast. Named after Alexander the Great, a general hardly older than you who conquered the world a couple of thousand years ago. Up ahead is Al Qahira, which means "the victorious," named by the Arabs, who conquered it about a thousand years ago."

"There's been a lot of conquering here," said K'tanu.

"I didn't even mention the Romans, Persians, or Turks," said Lomax. "The Nile is the second-longest river in the world. Your friend Chris back there believes it might also be the cradle of civilization." He looked at K'tanu. "I'm talking about you, son. Your people started it all."

"My people all died."

"Not all of them, or else none of those folks down there would be there." Lomax paused, thinking. "When we were en route, I went back to use the john and you were asleep. I looked into that backpack you never let out of your sight. What's in that taped-up jar that's so important?"

"My heart. I have to return it to my tomb, along with my mummy. Are we close to that place?"

"No. That's in Tanzania, several countries south of here."

K'tanu thought of how big the United States was. "That will take us weeks." He rubbed his swollen knuckles. "I don't think I have that much time."

"Well, most of east-central Africa—where you're from—is shut down. No one goes in or out. Not that anyone wants in, except you guys. But Chris wouldn't let me go there. He said he had a plan and that I should head for Aswan, in southern Egypt."

"How far is that?"

"Another fifty minutes," said Lomax. "We'll head up the river, give you a good look at what your descendants have been up to. Industrious people. Built the pyramids."

"I've seen pyramids in holos."

"Well," said Lomax, "if you look down about now, you'll see the real thing." He banked the jet to the right. K'tanu saw the outskirts of Al Qahira, hazy under a pall of cooking-fire smoke, but out to the west, in a desert of sand dunes, was the Great Pyramid of Khufu, with several smaller pyramids ringing it.

"There's the Sphinx," said Lomax, pointing. "A lion with a man's head."

K'tanu looked, thinking of Talon, the lion he'd killed to obtain its heart, to save his people. But in the end, it came to nothing and they all died anyway. He wondered who had survived to build such an immense statue. "You say they looked like me?"

"There's some controversy about that," said Lomax, resuming their course up the Nile. "There were some black pharaohs from the south about 700 B.C., but most Egyptians were of another race—not white and not black. Probably a mixed race of your people and others."

"What's going on?" came Chris's voice. He was in the cockpit doorway, rubbing his eyes.

"Sightseeing," said Lomax. "We just passed the pyramids."

"How'd they look?"

"Old," said K'tanu, rubbing his knuckles. "Very old."

"Four thousand years old," said Chris, hunkering down between the two seats, "but still younger than you. They were some sort of astronomical device, set in such a way that the stars and the sun aligned at certain times of the year. We still haven't figured that all out."

"The sun? Did they worship Father Sun?"

"In a way, yes. They believed their kings were descendants of Ptah, the sun god. He created the world by imagining it. Then came Atum, who created Shu and Tefnut, air and water. Shu and Tefnut married and bore Geb, the earth, and Nut, the sky. Geb and Nut bore Osiris and his brother Seth and their sisters Isis and Nephtys."

"Not much time for playing cards," laughed Lomax.

"So Osiris isn't really a god?" asked K'tanu.

"He kind of represents God," said Lomax. "He judges the dead to see if they're worthy to enter Lightland—where you were, I guess."

"I don't remember any judgment," said K'tanu.

"Maybe this is it," said Lomax.

K'tanu looked out the window. Al Qahira's smoky haze was gone and the land below was distinct in the slanting morning sun. The brown river moved placidly between narrow green banks, sand dunes literally edging right up to the date palms and empty fields, now gone to seed.

"Up here on the left is Thebes," said Lomax. "The biggest temple complex of all." He dipped the wing so they could see. There were dozens of immense structures, giant pylons and forests of stone columns. "Across the river," said Lomax, pointing west, "is the first pyramid. See it?"

"Ah!" said K'tanu. "That mountain?"

"That's right," said Chris. "Below it is the Valley of the Kings, where many of the ancient pharaohs were buried."

"Time to buckle in," said Lomax. "Daraw is coming up and I've got a checklist to run." Chris turned and went back. "You stay, son," said Lomax, winking at K'tanu. "Might need you to land this if I have a heart attack or something." He saw the alarmed look on K'tanu's face and smiled. "Just kidding. It can land itself. I just wanted the company."

They were skimming a thousand feet above the ground at three hundred miles an hour, so things below were moving very fast. K'tanu tightened his seat belt. "Okay."

"Welcome to Africa," said Lomax, flipping overhead switches. "You're almost home."

"Here's the taxi now," said Lomax, pointing. An ancient, muddy Land Rover was moving slowly across the tarmac toward them. Lomax turned to Cate and Chris. "Take good care of my boy, now." He extended his hand.

Chris took it. "You've been a lifesaver."

"Your turn now," said Lomax, nodding at K'tanu, who stood by the body bag lying on the asphalt, his backpack slung over his shoulder. "You get him home. *All* the way home."

Chris nodded. "Thanks," said Cate, hugging Lomax. "You're one of the best," she whispered, kissing his cheek.

Lomax laughed. "In a world this empty, that isn't much of a compliment!"

The Rover stopped and an Arab got out wearing a turban and a long, striped djalaba, his face hidden behind a dirty white surgical mask. Cate and Chris began loading their things into the truck.

K'tanu came over to Lomax. "Thank you, Captain."

"Listen," said Lomax, "is Lightland really all it's cracked up to be?"

K'tanu smiled. "It was for me."

"My wife and kids are there," said Lomax, eyes glistening with a memory.

"I will look for them," said K'tanu. "Though they may be far way."

"Maybe you can find them," said Lomax. "Tell them I'm doing my best."

"I will tell them you're coming as soon as you are done here."

"I wanna tell you something," said Lomax, lowering his voice. "You didn't just come here to die. There's some other reason . . . I can feel it. You do *that* thing, and then you'll be ready to go home."

"I will try," said K'tanu. "Thank you for everything."

"Thank *you*," said Lomax, turning back to the jet. "It's nice to know I'm not crazy after all."

"Yes, you are!" laughed K'tanu.

Lomax waved and boarded the jet. Chris and Cate waited by the Rover. The mummy was safely stowed in the back. The driver was in his seat. K'tanu hobbled toward the truck.

Cate and K'tanu stood on a dock in a marina behind the Aswan High Dam, which was built to regulate the yearly Nile floods. The boats were mostly dilapidated *feluccas,* with triangular sails and narrow wooden hulls. Across the empty lake, the Philae temple stood on a man-made island, its yellow sandstone walls glistening in the sun. Chris strode down the dock toward them. "This is fine!" He pointed at a flat-bottom boat with a torn canvas awning amidships and black diesel smoke puffing out of the stack.

"It looks like the *African Queen*," said Cate.

"Exactly!"

"But didn't they have all sorts of trouble with that boat in the movie?" asked Cate.

"Salim says it runs fine. No one will notice us in it either."

"They will if we're on fire." Cate turned to K'tanu. "Chris lives through old movies." She started toward the Rover to get their stuff.

Chris followed her, gesturing. "Life's most important lessons are in old movies, you know."

K'tanu turned to the boat. Salim, a small, wiry man with skin almost as black as K'tanu's, stood on the gangway. He was the first black man K'tanu had ever seen up close. He felt an instant kinship with him and smiled, but the man glowered at him and turned away.

Cate and Chris carried the body bag down the rickety dock and followed K'tanu onto the boat. "This is gonna be an adventure!" said Chris.

Colonel Paul Underwood, head of the Border Patrol in Brownsville, Texas, sat behind his desk. He wore his ULPA mask as he always did when strangers showed up, which wasn't very often. He recognized the Indian doctor from the CDC holos and of course, everybody knew Samuel Fox. But that didn't mean they weren't infected. His mask would stay on, thank you, and no offense intended. He studied the pictures Cloudburst gave him. "We pretty much have an open-border policy now," he said, looking over at Fox, "which is good, because I got ten men and the whole Texas border to patrol."

"You can't see much from behind a desk," said Cloudburst, angry at how Underwood was deferring to Fox. He barely looked at her when she spoke. Probably a racist or misogynist or both.

Underwood ignored the jab. "Why Matamoros? There's nothing down there."

"They're on the run," said Fox. He noticed Underwood eyeing the cigars in his shirt pocket.

"Have you seen them or not?" growled Cloudburst.

Underwood leaned back. "Or not," he said. "But we do know a jet landed at Matamoros a couple of days ago, then left shortly after. Is one of your fugitives a pilot?"

"Yes. Our *former* head of security," said Cloudburst. "Captain Lomax."

"Tell me about him."

"What's to tell? He's a grunt."

"I think what the Colonel means," said Fox, "is what was Captain Lomax's motivation to help them? Was it financial or personal?"

"I doubt it was financial. Personal, maybe."

"Was he frustrated with his job?" asked Underwood. "Unhappy with the chain of command?" For the first time he looked directly at Cloudburst, accusation in his eyes.

"He seemed a little touchy sometimes, but—"

"Touchy about what?"

"Oh, he's a religious fanatic. He was always grousing about how the government made religion a crime and all that paranoid nonsense."

"What religion does he follow?" asked Fox.

"Some bizarre sect." She turned to Ron, who had been standing in the corner, trying to be invisible. "What was it, Ron?"

"Egyptian, I think," said Ron.

Underwood leaned forward. "Disciples of Osiris?"

Ron nodded.

"Hmm. There are quite a few Disciples in Matamoros."

"Thank you for your time," said Fox, removing a cigar from his pocket and giving it to Underwood. "Compliments of Rafael Castro." He turned and left the room.

Cloudburst frowned, following Fox into the hallway. "What?"

Fox was lighting a cigar. "Fugitives need help. And what better help than fellow believers?"

A light went on in Cloudburst's eyes. "Let's go to Matamoros."

"Can't, myself," said Fox. "I'm under strict orders to not leave the country. But Major Wolfe will accompany you. I think you will find him indispensable where you're going."

They stood on the porch of the old cinder-block house. "This is it," said Ron. "I recognize this." He pointed at the ankh symbol inside the oval on the door. It was late and there were no lights on inside.

They wore masks and gloves; had worn them since crossing into Mexico an hour before.

"Let's surprise him," said Cloudburst.

Wolfe prepared to kick the door in. "Wait," said Cloudburst, turning the knob and flicking on her flashlight. The door opened. Wolfe drew his weapon. "Hello?" said Cloudburst, stepping inside the small parlor, which contained numerous Egyptian-themed papyrus paintings on the walls. Her light played across one, which showed a man sitting on a throne, two women fanning him with palm fronds and another man kneeling before him. Behind the supplicant was a big scale tended by a jackal-headed man weighing a jar against a feather. "This must be the place," said Cloudburst.

"Quién es?" said someone. A light went on down the narrow hall. Wolfe cocked his weapon.

"Amigos!" said Cloudburst, waving for Wolfe to put the pistol away. "Friends!"

Roberto Vasquez looked up at them through a glaze of blood. He sat limply in the chair, his wrists duct-taped to the arm rests. His head ached, but not as much as the fingers on his left hand, which the American soldier had broken, one by one.

"We will start on the other hand soon," said Cloudburst. "Comprendes?"

Vasquez shook his head.

"He understands," said Wolfe, wiping the blood off his gun. He'd used it to batter the old Mexican and now it was wet and slippery.

"No sé," repeated Vasquez weakly.

Wolfe held up the short length of pipe.

"No!" shouted Ron, turning away in disgust. "He doesn't know!"

Cloudburst turned to Ron. "Of course he does. He's just reluctant. Thinks God will punish him if he tells." She turned back to Vasquez, lifting his chin so their eyes met. His eyes were red and the left one was swelling shut. "But God's punishment comes later. Right now he has to deal with *mine*." She nodded at Wolfe, who slipped the short length of pipe over Vasquez's middle finger, stopping at the first knuckle. He placed his other hand firmly on top of Vasquez's hand, then lifted the pipe slowly. There was an audible *pop!* as the joint broke. Vasquez screamed.

"And still two more knuckles on that finger," said Cloudburst grimly.

Ron turned away. On a nearby couch was the body of an old woman who had obviously died of Cobalt. He grimaced at her, tightening his mask, though he wanted more than anything to pull it off and throw up again, even though there was nothing left in his stomach.

"If you're going to be sick, do it outside this time," said Cloudburst.

"I'm okay," said Ron.

"That's good, because we need you. Ask him again."

Ron did not turn. "Donde se fueron?" he asked the wall.

Vasquez didn't answer, but screamed when Wolfe lifted the pipe sharply.

Ron whirled around. "I tell you, he doesn't know!"

Wolfe looked at Ron blandly. "Ask him again."

Ron glared at Wolfe, then got up and stormed out, slamming the door behind him.

Wolfe turned to Cloudburst, who turned to Vasquez. "Por favór, donde se fueron?"

Vasquez felt the pipe move up to the last knuckle and steeled himself.

Cloudburst walked out onto the porch, followed by Major Wolfe, who closed the door behind them. "Maybe he didn't know after all," said Wolfe.

"Well, we'll never know now, will we?"

Wolfe shrugged. "Guess he had a weak ticker."

Cloudburst sighed and pulled down her mask. "He was infected anyway. You saw the bruises on his neck." She looked across the street. Ron was sitting in the Hummer, sulking. The sky was gray with the coming dawn. She turned to Wolfe, who was pulling off his surgical gloves. "Doesn't matter. The minute I stepped inside the house, I knew where they went."

"Where?"

Cloudburst started down the wooden steps. "Africa."

ANCIENT DREAMS

They chugged up river, the old boat moving surprisingly fast. The lake was immense, still, and empty. There was no vegetation anywhere on shore; tawny desert sand and stone ran right into the blue lake waters.

"Where does all the water come from?" asked K'tanu.

"Two rivers meet at Khartoum, in the Sudan," said Chris. "The Blue Nile comes down from the Ethiopian highlands near the eastern coast of Africa; the White Nile from Uganda, near the center of the continent. That's the branch we'll follow to Tanzania."

"It sounds like a long way," said K'tanu. "Why didn't Captain Lomax take us there?"

"Uganda has been a military dictatorship for decades," said Chris. "They would have shot us down. Besides, we're being followed."

"You don't think Cloudburst is still after us, do you?" asked Cate.

"If they're more than a day or two behind us, I'd be surprised. That's why this detour. She'd never imagine we'd travel up the Nile on a boat."

They sat amidships, under a faded and torn canvas awning. The oily smoke from the engine made it impossible to sit aft. Salim, the sullen, mute captain, sat in the bow, steering with a joystick jutting out of a small aluminum box attached to the engine by a twisted electrical cord. K'tanu's mummy lay at their feet near the keel. K'tanu held his backpack in his lap. "It will take weeks."

"A few days," said Chris. "Salim will take us to Khartoum, where we'll get a faster boat."

"You hope," said Cate. "But you don't know."

"Who knows anything?" said Chris, feeling unappreciated. He gazed across the water, wishing he had sunglasses. The noon sun was incredibly bright. He'd shucked his shirt and K'tanu did likewise. He noticed a muscle in K'tanu's upper arm, hidden until now, that trembled slightly and constantly. He handed a tortilla-like flat bread to K'tanu. "Here."

"Not hungry," said K'tanu, looking out across the lake.

Chris bit into the bread, then stood and shouted at Salim. "Can we fish?"

"No fish," said Salim without turning around. He sat cross-legged, wearing his turban and a heavy robe, even in the wilting heat. He still wore his mask, even out on the lake. Chris figured that after a day or two, if his passengers showed no signs of Cobalt, Salim might take the mask off. Until then, they were under quarantine.

"Look!" said K'tanu, pointing. To the west, reddish clouds hugged the horizon, blocking the setting sun. They watched as shadows crept across the barren land toward them. Soon the entire sky was reddish-gray. Chris pulled his shirt on and nodded at K'tanu to do the same. "Sandstorm."

Chris went forward and spoke to Salim. "Let's get to shore."

Salim jumped up, taking the joystick with him. "We no stop! Haboob!" he shouted, pointing at the storm clouds. The wind had picked up and the boat was rocking furiously.

"Salim, we need to make land," said Chris.

"American shut up!" yelled Salim. Suddenly, the canvas awning was torn off its stanchions and kited away. K'tanu got down on the floor next to the mummy bag, clutching his backpack. Chris looked around. They were in the middle of the lake, a good mile from a shore that was disappearing before his eyes, lost in the coming sandstorm. He went aft and found Cate. They huddled with K'tanu on the deck, the wind howling around them, waves crashing over the sides. Chris looked forward, but he could not longer see Salim sitting on the prow.

Stinging sand filled K'tanu's ears and hair, coating his face. He could no longer hear what Chris was saying. The boat tilted wildly and they all slid across the deck. Then it rocked back and they were hurled against the gunnels again. Chris yelled and K'tanu saw a bloody hand reach toward him. K'tanu grabbed Chris and held him. Chris's face appeared, covered with dirt and sand, a nasty gash above one eye. He was flailing about, yelling. K'tanu found Cate and held on to her. The boat rocked again, sending them sliding. The wind was so loud the diesel engines, a constant throb just minutes before, could not be heard. "We'll capsize!" shouted Chris. "Can you swim?"

K'tanu shook his head.

"What?"

"No!" shouted K'tanu.

"Help us, K'tanu," yelled Cate. He looked down at her, the sand stinging his eyes. "Help us!" she cried again, grabbing his shirt. Her hair swirled, whipping across his face. Chris was bent over next to him, his shirt pulled over his head. K'tanu felt around on the floor for the backpack. It was gone. A terrible fear gripped him. Had it been tossed overboard? It was heavy and would sink. He squinted into the darkness and hoped the black shape he saw against the far gunnel was the mummy.

"Father Sun!" whispered K'tanu. "Mother Moon!"

Cate lifted her head. "Yes! Make them stop the storm!" She had her arms around his waist. K'tanu still held onto Chris's shoulder, keeping him from sliding away as the boat tilted steeply. K'tanu's nose was so full of dirt he found it difficult to breathe. He opened his mouth and his tongue was instantly coated with sand. Water blasted over the gunnels, dousing them. An instant later they were again covered with muddy sand. Then another wave washed over them and the cycle repeated.

"Father, Mother," whispered K'tanu. "Why are you angry?" They were tossed across the deck, smashed against the gunnel, then hurled back. It took all of K'tanu's strength to hold onto Chris and Cate.

"Make it stop!" cried Cate hysterically.

"We're going to die!" yelled Chris.

Suddenly K'tanu opened his eyes and shouted, "Help me see!" He let go of Chris, peeled Cate's arms away, and got to his knees.

Cate looked at Chris. "No!" she shouted. "You'll be thrown overboard!"

K'tanu grabbed one of the awning support stanchions and stood. "Let me go!"

"No!" yelled Chris. "K'tanu! Don't!"

Suddenly, K'tanu was gone. Cate groped for him. Nothing. Chris felt around. There was only blackness as another wave pounded them, hurling them across the deck. They grabbed onto each other. "He fell overboard!" shouted Cate. "K'tanu!" she screamed. Chris held her tightly.

"Salim!" called K'tanu, making his way slowly forward. There was no answer. He was constantly pounded by giant waves breaking across the boat. Then he saw the joystick cord snaking out of the engine hatch and disappearing into the water. He reeled it in. When the joystick box was finally in his hands, he knew Salim was gone. He sat and pushed the red knob forward and heard the distant response of the engine. Squinting into the darkness, he whispered, "Father, give me eyes." Without knowing why, he moved the stick to the left. It was an unlikely direction; when he last saw the shore, it was on his right. The engines groaned. "Your wrath is just," he said, "but please, help me see through the storm." He released the pressure a little, navigating by feel.

After a long while, the darkness lightened to a deep gray. Waves still crashed across the boat, but K'tanu was turned into the wind now and they were less forceful. His eyes still smarted from the grit, but he thought he saw something far ahead. The wind began to die. He looked up. A single star shone through a break in the clouds. He peered ahead and saw a rocky shore about a hundred meters away. He headed for it.

Chris stumbled forward, holding on to Cate. They had both been injured. Chris's brow was dripping blood and Cate's forearm had been gashed. Chris tore off a strip of his shirt and bound Cate's arm, mopping his own forehead with a remnant. "Where's Salim?" he shouted.

K'tanu shook his head. As more clouds shifted, the moon lit the scene with an otherworldly blue light. The water quieted. The storm had passed them, moving east. The shore was close. "I'll get a rope," said Chris, going aft. "To the right," he yelled. "Port!" K'tanu turned the boat and felt a bump as the bow nudged against rock. Chris jumped ashore and K'tanu flipped a switch on the joystick. The engines died and they were enveloped in silence, except for the lapping of the water against the bank. K'tanu helped Cate off the boat and followed her up the rocks.

"What is that?" asked Cate, pointing. They turned. Before them, across a gravelly expanse, rose a flat-topped mountain. They started for it, but before they had gone a dozen paces, the moon slipped out from behind a cloud and Chris inhaled sharply. "Abu Simbel."

"Abu *what*?" asked Cate.

Before them were four giant, seated figures, each over sixty feet tall, sculpted into the side of a mountain. Chris led them forward. "Abu Simbel, built by Rameses the Great, pharaoh of the nineteenth dynasty." The head and torso of one of the figures had fallen to the earth in room-sized chunks. Chris fished his flashlight from his vest pocket and aimed it up at the figures.

"Who are they?" asked K'tanu.

"They are all Rameses."

"What an ego," said Cate.

There was an open, rectangular doorway between the two middle figures. Passing through it, they found themselves in a great columned hall, each column sculpted to look like the pharaoh, his arms crossed over his chest. Chris pointed the flashlight. "He's holding the crook and flail—"

Cate touched Chris's arm. "We'll take the tour in the morning," she said, collapsing against a pillar. "Right now, all I want to do is sleep."

K'tanu sat opposite her, leaning against another column. Chris walked a little further into the temple, noting the small sanctuary at the far end. Abu Simbel had once been one of Egypt's biggest tourist attractions, but no one had been there in years. Garbage littered the floor and cobwebs hung from the pillars. He walked back to Cate, who was already asleep, her chin on her chest. He sat down and put his arm around her, closing his eyes.

"News from New York, Doctor," said Wolfe, handing Cloudburst the sheet of paper. They were once again back at the Houston airport. "Not good," he said, turning away.

Cloudburst looked at the printout and sighed. It had been a long shot. The message detailed how the Army had entered the burned-out hulk of the Metropolitan Museum of Art, searching for the offices of Christopher Tempest. Walls were caved-in and mud a foot thick had hardened like concrete on the floor. Cloudburst was hoping that Tempest's Tanzania trip before the outbreak was detailed in the Met's computer, but the system was completely destroyed in the fire.

She already called Corporal Jennings back at Yucca and had him access the tapped VidPhone conversations back in 2029 between Seagram and Tempest. Unfortunately, Tempest neglected to say exactly *where* in Tanzania they had found the mummy. Jennings did a USGovNet search on Al McFadden, but since he was not a U.S. citizen, she only got records of his research papers. No information about where he had been excavating when he died.

She crumpled the message. Major Wolfe stood by the door, ramrod-straight as usual. Ron was slouched in a chair, looking gloomy as usual. She cleared her throat and both men looked at her. "We're going to Tanzania."

Ron visibly blanched. "But that's Ground Zero," he said. Even Wolfe looked surprised. Cloudburst savored the moment, looking at these two cowards. "I think it's where they're headed, and so are we." She left the room, feeling fully in control for the first time in days.

〜〜

"K'tanu, awake."

K'tanu opened his eyes. A light glowed at the rear of the temple. He stood, rolling his shoulders against the neck ache.

"K'tanu," came the voice again.

His heart leapt. It was Maya's voice. He moved toward the sound and stumbled into a stone altar, banging his knee and falling to the ground. "Maya!" he called, clutching his throbbing knee. "Maya!"

"I am here."

He looked up. Beyond the altar was a short hall. He limped down it. The light got brighter until he had to shield his eyes. He entered a small alcove where four stone figures were seated, facing him. In front of them was a brilliant point of light. "Maya?"

The light expanded, dimmed, and took human form. There stood Maya: tall and beautiful, her skin luminous, a colorful drape around her hips, her full breasts bare, her curly hair falling across her shoulders. He stumbled to her, enveloping her in a tight embrace. She was cold fire in his arms. Her heart beat against his, but it was not skin he felt, it was the stuff eternity was made of.

"My love," she said, touching his chin with her nose.

"I feared I would not see you again."

"You are coming?"

"Yes," he said. "But we are still far away and I am dying."

"Then you must hurry," said Maya. "And you must remember."

"Remember what?"

"Who you *are*," she said, releasing him. He reached, but his hands passed through her. The light grew brighter until she was too luminous to gaze upon. Then the light pulled in on itself, forming a tiny point of brilliance. It winked out.

K'tanu collapsed on the floor. "Maya, Maya, Maya."

TWENTY-EIGHT

HEJIRA

"K'tanu, wake up."

K'tanu blinked. The sun was in his eyes. A bright figure stood before him. His heart leapt, then the figure moved out of the light. It was Chris, who was handing him a bundle. "I thought you might want this."

K'tanu clutched the heavy backpack to his chest. "You found it!"

"It was tangled in the body-bag straps."

K'tanu unzipped the backpack and removed the alabaster jar. It glistened in the light. "It's not broken!" he exulted. "It's okay."

"It *is* stone," said Chris. "Are *you* okay?"

K'tanu replaced the jar, stood, and slung the backpack over his shoulder. He looked down at Chris. "Yes. Let's go." He strode toward the entrance. As he walked, Chris noticed that he did not limp, even though his left knee was swollen and his back was bent.

Cate stood just outside the entrance. "What's this?" she said, pointing at a relief carved into the side of one of the seated statues.

"It's Rameses taking prisoners," said Chris. "Hittites, Syrians, and Nubians."

K'tanu stopped and looked at the relief. The king had three men by the hair, his hand raised high, holding a knife. One of the captives was black. "These were my people?"

"We are entering their land now. We call it Sudan, the Egyptians called it Nubia, but those who lived there called it Kush."

"Then I am almost home," said K'tanu, heading toward the boat. Once on board, he went to the bow and picked up the joystick. Chris pushed them off from shore and hopped on board, coming forward. "I'll steer," he said.

"I can do it," said K'tanu, sitting as he'd seen Salim sit, cross-legged in the bow.

"But you don't know where we're going."

"Upstream, right?"

Behind them, Cate said, "He knows as much about boats as you do." K'tanu and Chris turned to her. "And I know more than you both, but if he wants to steer, let him."

"It's not a matter of *letting* him," said Chris. "I just thought—"

"I will steer well," said K'tanu. "No crashes."

"Okay," said Chris, edging back toward midships.

Cate came forward and sat next to K'tanu, looking out across the lake. The sun was just up, and the clear sky was a rich blue. A warm breeze blew from the north, behind them. "Thank you," said Cate.

"For what?"

"For saving us in the storm."

"I just held on."

"I know. That's what you do, K'tanu. You hold on."

K'tanu nodded. He would hold on, until the last. Up until now, he had been too willing to let others control his destiny—there was too much Russell still left in him. When Maya visited him last night, he'd been given a great gift. He doubted she would be permitted to come again. The hope she rekindled in his heart would have to sustain him for the rest of his journey. For the rest of his life.

"You can't make me go," said Ron. "I'm not in the Army." He glanced at Major Wolfe.

"I'm not sure anybody needs to go," said Samuel Fox.

They were in the White House—the *actual* White House—in the oval office. Fox had set up shop there, and when Cloudburst first entered the historic room, she realized that Fox wasn't just acting like the President, in reality, he *was* the President. "They destroyed everything," she said. "Without Russell, we have nothing."

"But why Africa?" asked Fox. "Seems a little extreme, just to get away from you."

"Some kind of *hejira*," said Cloudburst, ignoring the jibe.

"Hejira?" asked Fox. That was a new one.

"A sacred journey," said Cloudburst. "I think they want to take Russell back to where his forebears lived in Africa six thousand years ago."

"Why?"

"They think the mummy's soul is inside Russell."

Fox leaned back in his chair. "How do you know this?"

"I've been checking up on the Disciples of Osiris."

"You mean they believe that when someone is cloned, the spirit whose body they cloned is yanked out of the afterlife and put into the clone?"

"No, they don't believe that," said Cloudburst flatly.

"But you do."

"No. But Seagram and Tempest do. Maybe even Russell, by now."

Fox opened the humidor on the spacious desk and removed a cigar. Cloudburst sighed and opened a window, sitting on the sill. "I thought you said Russell was kidnapped," said Fox, lighting the cigar. "That's usually against a person's will."

"Stockholm Syndrome. You know what that is, don't you, *Mister President*?"

Fox leaned back in the plush leather chair. "All right. Major Wolfe will accompany you."

"But sir!" said Wolfe, "Is that really necessary?"

"Just get the kid back alive."

"Or not," said Cloudburst.

Ron straightened, suddenly alert.

Fox sighed, nodding. "Or not. Just get him back."

As they traveled up the Nile, the surrounding land did not change much. On either side of the wide and slow-moving river, beyond overgrown fields and date-palm windbreaks, wind-blasted desert rolled away to the white horizon. They saw few people, but occasionally a felucca came from the shore bearing dates and tangerines and flat bread, which they purchased.

"So, am I a Nubian?" asked K'tanu, steering as he ate.

"No, but they're probably you," said Chris. "'Nub' means 'gold' in Egyptian, so you can guess why the pharaohs conquered Kush. But the Kushites got their revenge—they conquered Egypt when it was their turn. They built pyramids at Jebel Barkal, where we'll stop for the night."

"And they looked like me?" asked K'tanu.

"The Greek historian Herodotus said they were the best-looking men in the world."

K'tanu smiled. The stark and severe landscape *did* seem familiar, not so different from what he saw on the security cams at Yucca Mountain, except for the ribbon of river slicing through the hot emptiness.

That evening, when they rounded a wide bend, Chris jumped up. "There it is!" he said, pointing. On the eastern shore, beyond the screen of date palms, was a large mesa, glowing a brilliant red in the setting sun.

Cate stood up. "What is it?"

"Jebel Barkal," said Chris. "I worked here many years ago, excavating a temple and several pyramids."

They docked on the muddy bank and went ashore, walking across narrow dirt causeways between overgrown grain fields. K'tanu carried his backpack, limping behind Chris and Cate. As they passed through the tree windbreak, the eastern desert opened up before them, with the rocky mesa dominating the view. The cloudless pink evening sky formed a spectacular backdrop. At the foot of the mesa were tumbles of stone and wind-eroded lion statues.

"Here it is!" said Chris. "The Blessed Mountain."

"Where are the pyramids?" asked K'tanu.

Chris pointed to the left. There were a half-dozen quite small and very steep pyramids made of rough sandstone blocks, crumbling at the corners.

"It's no Abu Simbel," said Cate. She turned to go back to the boat, K'tanu following her.

"They ruled all of Egypt, right from here!" shouted Chris.

Cate and K'tanu just kept walking. Chris turned back to the mountain. He'd lived in a tent right over there for three months and excavated the pit to the right, which had filled up with sand again. He'd climbed the mesa several times that summer. Tonight he would climb it again.

After the others were asleep, Chris got up quietly and headed for the mesa. It took him over an hour of hard scrabbling, but with one last push, he pulled himself up on top. He had a flashlight, but the quarter moon was so bright he could have read by it. He walked to the southern end of the mesa. Far below, the Nile curved gently, bordered by green foliage. Beyond it, the desert continued for two hundred miles to Khartoum. The land to the north was empty and flat, as it was to the east. Jebel Barkal was the highest promontory for hundreds of miles. No wonder the Kushites chose this place for their temple; it was close to their god, Apedemak.

Chris sat on the mesa edge, his legs dangling. He lay back, stretching his arms out, looking up at the Milky Way, which steamed out of Sagittarius and flowed north through the summer triangle, where Vega twinkled directly overhead. In ten thousand years, the solar system would move far enough along its orbit to make Vega the North Star instead of Polaris.

It's just gas and dust and thermonuclear furnaces, he thought. *Could there really be a god out there, watching us? Maybe even laughing at us?* He shook his head. No, the universe was just too big.

But something that goes on forever has room for everything—even God.

That's what Lomax had said. Chris sat up and pulled the jawbone out of his hunting vest pocket, turning it over in his hands. It had been rubbed to a polished gleam thousands of years ago when K'tanu listened to its whispers. Chris held the mandible up to his ear, wondering.

Yes.

He nearly dropped it in surprise. It was warm from being in his pocket. He looked at it, then put it up to his ear again.

Yes.

"Yes, what?" he whispered, feeling foolish, talking to a piece of bone. Was it like hearing the ocean in a conch shell, but what you really heard was *your* blood pumping in your ears?

No.

A chill coursed up his spine. *Am I that desperate?* he thought, *that I need to believe in God?*

Yes.

"*What* should I believe?" he asked, pushing away his skeptical alter-ego. It had run his life for almost forty years, but not now. Please. Not *now.*

Yes, said the bone. *Just believe.*

Chris nodded and the final, deepest part of him finally surrendered, throwing down his pride and education and hard-earned skepticism. He lay back on the ground, looking up at the starry sky. "I want to," he whispered.

Suddenly, the stars above him began to move in a circular pattern, each one trailing an arc of light, until the sky above him was a million concentric circles slowly rotating around an empty center directly overhead. Then the center began drawing the stars in to it, consuming their light like a black hole, until the entire sky was totally dark, an abyss that momentarily filled Chris with a heart-stopping fear that he would fall into that emptiness and be lost forever.

Then suddenly, there was a great flash and the entire sky became a single star, brighter than any sun. Chris lay on his back, spread-eagled, frozen, impaled by the blinding light. It burned his skin black, vaporized his eyes, melted his bones, leaving nothing of him but a cooked cinder in a shallow depression on the red sandstone.

And then he was standing next to himself, looking down—not at a piece of blackened ash, but at himself, his eyes still staring blindly heavenward, unblinking. The image of K'tanu standing by the gurney, looking down at his own body, flashed across his consciousness. He looked up. The sky was full of stars again, but this time each one shone as brightly as noonday. He turned and looked out across the desert. In the darkness, the Nile glowed like an emerald snake, undulating across the view. Every tree sparkled and every rock glittered like a cut diamond. The torch of the moon moved slowly overhead. Gem-like raindrops fell from the clear sky onto the parched land. Where they struck, radiant trees sprang up, bearing enormous, luminous fruit the color of sapphire, ruby, and aquamarine—the food of gods, not mortals.

Chris looked down at himself lying on the ground. His body stirred and sat up. Their eyes met.

Looking at his revived self, Chris said, "My time is over. I must go."

"Who are you?" asked the new Chris, looking up at him.

"The part of you that cannot believe." He turned and walked away, disappearing into the darkness.

The seated Chris felt something in his hand. The jawbone. He lifted it to his ear and listened.

Welcome.

TWENTY-NINE

CIVIL STRIFE

They sat midships. The sky overhead was full of dark, moody clouds. The brown river had widened and taken on a blue cast. "We're close to Khartoum," said Chris. "Where the rivers meet."

"So the Blue Nile really is blue," said Cate.

"It comes from the Ethiopian highlands. The White comes from the Ruwenzori Mountains."

"He's getting worse," whispered Cate, nodding toward K'tanu, who sat in the bow, hunched over, focused on the river ahead as if willing them to go faster than the ancient, noisy diesel engines would allow.

"I know," said Chris.

"We'll never make it in time."

"I was hoping to get a truck in Khartoum, but now . . ."

Cate nodded. "We'll have to risk flying again."

Khartoum sat in the fork between the two Niles, a small, modern city center with tree-lined streets and desolate slums of flat-roofed hovels stretching off to the south. But they saw more living people there than they had in any other place in Africa. It didn't make sense.

An old rusting bridge spanned the White, and they put ashore nearby. Before getting off the boat, Chris grabbed a couple of masks out of his backpack, handing one to Cate, which she put in her pocket. He hadn't told her about his epiphany on Jebel Barkal the night before last because he wanted to make sure he completely believed it himself before announcing it to the world.

The day after his mesatop revelation, Chris sat on the boat gunnels, thinking. The inner skeptic had indeed left and everything had changed. The river, the shoreline reeds, the empty land beyond the palms—everything was different. Instead of a dead land, it was a vibrant macrocosm bursting with possibilities. He felt as if he'd just stepped onto a mysterious, previously hidden road. He squinted into the distance, trying to see the Great Rift mountains to the south, but they were still too far away. His inner path would also take him to mountains of a sort. He wondered if his new perspective would meet the coming challenges.

Now, as they walked down the muddy streets of the Khartoum, he removed the ULPA mask from his pocket. When they passed an overflowing trash can, he tossed it in. He would take no souvenirs of his old self with him on this new journey. He didn't intend to die, but if he did, he would try to face it without fear. The doorway K'tanu had spoken of had begun to open. He was not ready to pass through it yet, but knowing it was there, that it was *put* there, made it less fearsome. One day he would walk through it, but not today. Today he had business: find transportation.

K'tanu walked ahead, wearing his backpack. Chris followed, pushing an old wooden wheelbarrow containing the mummy in its beaten green vinyl bag. Two women with water jars on their heads were briefly seen down a side street. Cate said, "The people are hiding."

"Scared of foreigners," said Chris.

"I'm not a foreigner," said K'tanu, striding ahead.

Just then, they turned a corner and K'tanu stopped. He bent down and gestured into an open doorway. Chris and Cate came and stood behind him. A child, no more than four, was standing inside the doorway. K'tanu held a Slim Jim out to the boy, whose eyes were bright with curiosity. K'tanu picked him up. "My son N'kala is about this age," he said.

Chris scanned the boy. He didn't seem sick, only underfed. The boy munched the jerky, his arm around K'tanu's neck, who murmured quietly, "N'kala no gara e misna. No gara."

A tall woman appeared in a doorway, momentarily startled, but when she saw how gently K'tanu held her son, she smiled. K'tanu handed the boy to her. He touched his chest, then raised his palm toward her. She didn't understand the gesture, but repeated it.

"Look at them," whispered Cate to Chris. "They could be related."

"His descendants must have traveled south, as I thought."

Cate elbowed Chris. "Look closer, professor! It's the first family K'tanu's ever seen."

In the doorway behind the woman was a man. When she went back inside with the boy, he remained behind, a question in his eyes. K'tanu held his hand up as before, bowing his head. The man nodded and closed the door. K'tanu stood like that for another moment, then turned and walked down the street. Cate took Chris's hand and they followed him.

"I'm looking for Umar," said Chris. They were standing in the airport terminal. The giant plate-glass windows were broken and trash was strewn across the terrazzo floor.

"He dead," said the black man. "Long time."

Chris turned away. It was too much to hope for. Umar was the pilot who'd ferried them south into the Sudd swamp back in '24. He also got them out when the civil war heated up. Umar had been old then, and would probably have died by now anyway of natural causes.

"But he son alive," said the man.

Chris turned back. "Umar had a son?"

The man pointed across the runway to a row of corrugated Quonset hangars. "He fly."

On the other side, they met a man who knew Umar's son Hakim. "He come back tomorrow," said the man, wiping his hands on a rag, turning back toward an ancient twin in the hangar, its engine parts strewn across the greasy concrete floor.

"He's not dead?" said Chris.

The man laughed. "He bad pilot, but he not dead yet!"

Hakim had to be his father's son. He had the same stocky frame and prematurely graying hair. When he was introduced to K'tanu, he pointed at K'tanu's ashen hair. "You gray too. Bad luck, huh?" He was in his late twenties, a muscled and happy man, even though his whole family had died of Cobalt. "Except Papa," he said. "He die in war. Dinka soldiers shoot him over oil fields." They were loading their things into an ancient, sand-blasted Cessna 310 twin.

"The civil war?" asked Chris.

Hakim nodded. He helped Chris put the mummy bag behind the second row of seats, not asking any questions, even though it obviously held a body. "Always war. All my life, all my papa's, all his papa's. Fight over nothing. But I fly everybody and stay in business."

"And business is good?" asked Chris. Though the hangar was old and sky showed through rusty holes in the corrugated tin, Hakim had three planes inside that looked almost airworthy.

"Good today," said Hakim, holding up the keys to Salim's boat. An hour ago they went to the river to see it. The boat was a shambles, but Hakim smiled. "Now I visit cousin in Omdurman, across the river."

Hakim said the civil war had actually slowed Cobalt's advance. The battles between the ruling Arab Muslim army in the north and the black tribal insurgents in the south kept the Sudanese borders impassable. It wasn't until a Ugandan politician flew in late one night in 2027, seeking a hospital, that Cobalt reached Khartoum. Within five months, the plague emptied out the city, then just disappeared. The war raged on, but Cobalt was done reaping lives in Khartoum. Hakim said he didn't know anyone who had it now.

"Really?" asked Cate.

Hakim shrugged. "All things pass. George Harris say that. He a Beatle."

"Harrison. I know," said Chris.

"Who was a beetle?" asked K'tanu, touching the gold-and-serpentine scarab in his pocket.

"Musician. You know, rock and roll?" said Chris.

"Yes!" said Hakim, opening the door and gesturing them inside. "Ready for rock and roll!"

"Needle in a haystack," said Ron, shouting through his ULPA mask. "An infected haystack!"

Cloudburst ignored him, lifting her soaking silk blouse away from her skin. It was incredibly hot in the airplane. They had been on the tarmac at Kenyatta for almost three hours. When the pilot finally opened the door to cool things off, Ron put his respirator on. Cloudburst noted that while Wolfe didn't put his on, he kept it on his lap, next to his Glock pistol.

The pilot was returning to the cockpit. Last night, after they departed from Washington, headed for Nairobi, Cloudburst asked him if he'd make a slight detour to Dar es Salaam in Tanzania. He'd refused then and just now refused again. She undid her seat belt and stood, stretching, looking out the open door. The Nairobi airport seemed abandoned, except for three jeeps facing them full of masked black men with mirrored sunglasses brandishing automatic weapons. "Not taking any chances, are they?"

Wolfe frowned. "Someone from the embassy will be here soon," he said, indicating the satellite telephone on the seat next to him. "In the meantime," he said, looking out the window at the soldiers, "it might be a good idea to sit tight."

"Sit tight?" shouted Ron, his voice muffled by his mask. He unbuckled his belt and went to the door, hauling it shut, then pulled his mask down. "Is that the extent of your *wisdom*, Major?"

"Ron?" said Cloudburst, patting the seat next to her. "Let's talk about what we're going to do when we catch them."

Ron held his ground. "If you're really gonna follow them to Ground Zero," he said, shaking his head, "you're nuts, you know it?"

Cloudburst looked at him. She had a quiet conversation yesterday with Wolfe about what to do if Ron got unmanageable. She glanced back at Wolfe, who squinted at Ron, his expression indicating that he was quickly tiring of Ron's incessant negative bullshit.

Oblivious, Ron looked at the ceiling. "Somebody turn on the air conditioning!"

"But Ron," said Cloudburst, "that's *outside* air."

Ron looked at her fiercely. "The hell with it. I'm hot."

MOUNTAINS OF THE MOON

Hakim took his time gaining altitude. The engines coughed and sputtered, but Hakim just smiled. His stories about armed southern tribesmen concerned Chris, who imagined hard-faced men sitting behind Howitzers, scanning the sky, waiting for them. Hakim said he was flying low so they would recognize his plane.

"But you fly for both sides!" exclaimed Chris as they skimmed across the immense Sudd swamp, almost scraping the tops of the immense mangrove trees.

"But they don't know who I'm flying *today*!" laughed Hakim.

In the back seat, Cate and K'tanu were too engrossed in the countryside to listen in on the conversation. The Sudd was an everglade triangle where the White Nile got lost for a hundred miles on its way down from the Ugandan highlands. Upriver from the Sudd, as the land rose in elevation, Cate saw rapids interrupting the river and the beginnings of jungle. The White Nile forked below them and Hakim banked right. "The Albert Nile," yelled Chris over the engine din. "We'll follow it to the Ruwenzoris."

The land began rising dramatically, and here and there granite outcrops jutted from the dense forest below. Hakim climbed to five thousand feet, and to her right, Cate saw the Zaire rainforest stretching endlessly to the western horizon. They were entering the natural reservoir of mankind's worst nightmare: viral killers like AIDS, Ebola, Marburg, and Cobalt. Just looking down at the steaming jungle made her wish for a Racal suit.

"Look!" said Chris, pointing out the windscreen. "Murchison Falls!"

Hakim did a tight turn above the tall, ribbon-like falls, then headed west again. "Not safe yet. We over Uganda and they don't care *who* I fly today—they shoot us down."

He stayed above the western shore of a long blue lake with forests crowding in on both sides. "Lake Albert," said Chris, pointing. At the southern end was an immense, jagged mountain range that disappeared into fluffy clouds. "The Mountains of the Moon."

"Is that snow?" asked K'tanu, noting glaciers high up on the slopes.

Chris nodded, noting that Hakim did not vary his course. "Are we going above them?"

Hakim shook his head. "Mountains too tall; we go around."

Chris gulped, but turned and gave Cate and K'tanu a thumbs up. It was too loud in the plane to talk much, so he was glad she didn't hear the last exchange.

Soon they were enveloped in clouds, which would have put Chris in a panic, except they were intermittent, and occasionally he saw the land. It was terrifying and beautiful. The Ruwenzoris at this altitude were treeless black-granite spires, cascading down to lush green jungle far below.

"Ah!" shouted Hakim, banking left. "The crowns!" He found a hole in the clouds and headed directly for the mountaintops. The plane bucked, buffeted by updrafts, and Chris was about to say something, when the view opened up before them and they saw the six great peaks of the range, including majestic Mt. Stanley, over sixteen thousand feet tall. As they banked past the mountain, heading south again, its snow caps glittered in the noonday sun.

"K'lii!" shouted K'tanu, pointing. And there, in a narrow pass between two peaks, they could see far to the east, into Tanzania—the blue of Lake Victoria, the yellow Serengeti Plain beyond, and in the hazy distance, Kilimanjaro, smoke rising from its unmistakable, flat-topped cone.

"How far is it, Chris?" asked Cate.

"It's got to be five hundred miles," he said, astonished at the impossibly distinct view.

And then it was gone, clouds blocking out even the Ruwenzoris a few hundred yards away. K'tanu turned to Cate. "This is where Father Sun dies each night. In these mountains." He gestured out the window, but they were inside the clouds again, the view nothing but white-cotton softness.

"Lightland," whispered Cate, touching his hand.

The White Nile skirted the Ruwenzoris to the west. Explorers like Burton, Livingstone, and Stanley thought the Nile began there, but the Mountains of the Moon were just one of the watersheds feeding the four-thousand-mile river. When they suddenly emerged from the clouds at the southern end of the range, Hakim descended quickly, turning southeast, passing over Lake Edward, another shoestring lake on the western Rift rim. K'tanu strained to see K'lii, but clouds filled the eastern horizon. Below them, the Ruwenzoris sloped steeply down to jungle.

"Rwanda," said Chris, pointing. "We're almost there." He'd noticed the low gas gauges, but Hakim just hummed a short, repetitive melody to himself, unconcerned. Instead of the cold, astringent mountain air, a warm mugginess entered the cabin. The black clouds they passed through had just disgorged a torrent of rain. Mist rose from the verdant jungle below.

Hakim called Kigali airport, announcing their arrival, but got no answer. "Hope they have fuel," he said. "I want to go home too." They circled the airfield once. It was empty, except for an old DC-3 on the apron. There were cars in the parking lot, though, and as they circled, Chris saw a number of blue and white taxis. He glanced back at K'tanu, who had fallen asleep. There were deep lines on his face, and his hair was noticeably thinner and grayer. His knuckles were swollen, the fingers cramped almost clawlike, but there was an almost beatific smile on his face. His eyelids fluttered. He was walking in the Other World.

Chris looked out the window. He too was about to enter a dream world, and he too was a different man than he had been the last time he was here. He put his hand back between the seats and touched Cate's knee. She reached forward, taking his hand and holding it tightly.

When they landed in Dar es Salaam, on the Indian Ocean, Cloudburst was fit to be tied. They were farther from their objective than they had been in Kenya. From Nairobi, Tanzania was just a couple hundred miles to the south. Now they were three hundred miles to the east. She figured the fugitives were somewhere between Lake Vic and Kilimanjaro, because that's where all the archeological digs in the country were. They'd wasted a day and a half in Nairobi. Kenyan military pilots refused to fly into Tanzania, which they called the "Death Star," a play on Tanzania's nickname of "Dark Star," so called because of its dim, miserable past and its unrealistic, perennially brightly-forecasted future. It took a hefty bribe of dollars (ironically, still in use in Africa, though not at home) and Major Wolfe pulling his gun to convince the pilot they really needed to go to Tanzania. Cloudburst wanted to land in Arusha, just west of Kilimanjaro, but the pilot braved Wolfe's gun, glaring up at the Major, daring him to shoot him now that they were in the air. So they landed in Dar, which was empty and foul-smelling. Cloudburst put on her ULPA mask. Ron had put his on when they entered Tanzanian airspace. Wolfe only put his on when he saw Cloudburst don hers.

The Dar es Salaam airport looked abandoned, but when they got out of the plane wearing respirators, people began to appear. Ron guessed that if the locals saw visitors wearing masks, they would probably believe the foreigners weren't infected. Nevertheless, the three of them stood by the plane in the wilting humidity for thirty minutes before anyone approached.

"Where's Ground Zero?" asked Wolfe while they were waiting.

Ron laughed. "You're standing in it."

Wolfe almost looked down but stopped himself. He noticed that in addition to the ULPA mask, Ashby had also pulled on surgical gloves. They had blue Racal suits in the plane, but they hadn't yet put them on—which was starting to seem like a bad idea to Wolfe. He glanced back at the open hatch one too many times, and Cloudburst said, "We're not in any danger, you know."

Wolfe looked over at Ron, who shrugged and gave him a mirthless smile. "It's all bloody sludge from here on in."

"Don't pay any attention to him," said Cloudburst. "If you want, put on a suit. But if you think it's hot now . . ."

Wolfe placed his hand on his pistol butt. If Death came for him, he'd take it with him.

They had a difficult time finding an aircraft. Helicopters had always been a luxury in Tanzania, and the only aircraft at Dar were a few old single-engine Cessnas. "But it's thousands of square miles between Kilimanjaro and Lake Victoria," said Cloudburst to the pilot, a fat black man.

"You are too many," he said, indicating Cloudburst, Ashby, and Wolfe.

"And you're too fat," said Ron, failing to notice that he was almost as big as the pilot.

The pilot glowered at them and shook his head. "Two trips."

Cloudburst sighed. At least they'd get to Arusha. Then they could stage air sorties or go overland. The search area was big, but largely empty. Cate and Tempest had to be going someplace where there were archeological digs. She wished she were back in Yucca. She had a feeling there was a clue in her files that only she could find. Corporal Jennings was trying, but he didn't know what to look for. They were so close. Her chest tickled and she coughed. The pilot looked up. Ron gasped. Wolfe had a respirator on, and the blue eyes above the mask became cold and severe.

She lifted her hand. "I'm fine." Then she turned away, hoping that was true.

THIRTY-ONE

OLD SCARS

They stood on the ship deck, looking out across Lake Victoria. No shoreline was visible. The first stars were coming out, even as the sun set behind the Ruwenzoris, turning the sky a brilliant orange. Their trip down the mountain from Kigali had taken only one day, surprising, considering the poor condition of the road.

They had K'tanu to thank for it. He was the one who spied the *matatu*, an ancient, wood-framed bus, and with grunts and hand signals had negotiated passage for them to the lake. Swahili, spoken in most of central Africa, was nothing like his ancient language, but people saw a familiarity in his looks and made assumptions, jabbering away at him as if he could understand. At one point, standing on the pier at Bukoba waiting for the ferry, a man came over to K'tanu, saying, "Salama, achimwene!" When K'tanu didn't respond, he continued, "Maasai? Jina lako nani?" His teeth had been sharpened into points, a fearsome look, but he was smiling, and K'tanu smiled back.

Chris recognized the unique dentistry. "He's Maasai. I think he's asking if you are too."

"Who are they?"

"A tribe living around here. Tall, like you. Respected and feared."

K'tanu turned back and held up his hand, palm out, as he did
to the man in Khartoum. "Um fala K'tanu. Galama e niri se." He
bowed his head respectfully.

The man cocked his head. "Ya kigeni. Unatokea wapi?"

K'tanu shook his head. "K'tanu," he said, touching his chest.

The man smiled. "Hazari," he said, touching his chest.

"Maharaba," said Chris. *Thank you.*

When they got on the ferry, Hazari motioned them toward his
kit, which he quickly spread out in a corner of the deck at midships.
Within minutes he had set up a small charcoal cook stove and shared
with them a meal of *ugali*, a maize and cassava gruel, served with
sweet tea. Cate grimaced at the drink, which was obviously equal
parts sugar and tea, but Chris enjoyed his, remembering John N'garra
serving him tea just before their fateful escape from Sopa Lodge at
Ngorongoro Crater a lifetime ago.

Little was said as they ate, but Hazari studied K'tanu, noting the
silver ankh hanging around his neck, and indicating his own tattoo
around his upper arm. "Maasai," he said proudly, indicating the
woven pattern. "Natokea Mwanza." He pointed at the dark eastern
horizon.

"He's from Mwanza, where we're going," said Chris. K'tanu
didn't understand much of what Hazari said, but he enjoyed listening
to the lilting, melodic tongue. Hazari was near K'tanu's age, but
he kept calling him *mzee*, which K'tanu figured meant "elder" or
"grandfather." When he went to stand, Hazari helped him to his feet
and guided him to a private place where they could urinate over the
side of the boat, then took his elbow, leading him back to Cate and
Chris. When they said good night, Hazari bowed to all of them, then
turned to K'tanu, saying, "Usiku mwema."

K'tanu nodded. "Usiku mwema."

Hazari was delighted at K'tanu's clumsy attempt at Swahili.
"Asante, mzee. Asante." He turned away, rolled up in his blanket,
and went to sleep.

$\wedge\wedge\wedge$

Chris woke. Orion was directly overhead; it must have been well past midnight. The ferry chugged steadily across the seemingly endless lake. He rolled over. K'tanu was gone. Hazari was snoring softly, wrapped in his threadbare gray blanket. Chris got up and went to the rear of the boat. There was no one there, just sleeping people scattered around the deck. He went forward and found K'tanu in the ship's bow, his hands cupped on his lap. As he approached, Chris saw a bloody knife glistening in K'tanu's hands. His cheeks were covered with blood. Chris grabbed the knife away from K'tanu. "What happened?"

"Nothing," said K'tanu, his voice flat and distant.

"Nothing?" said Chris.

"I've wanted to do this for days. I remembered the three lines, like those on the jar." He indicated the backpack at his feet. "When I saw my wife, I was ashamed, for I no longer had my scars. I was a man without a tribe."

"You saw your *wife*?" asked Chris, pulling out his handkerchief and dabbing at the blood on K'tanu's face. *It must hurt like hell*, he thought. *I would have passed out, but he's just sitting here like it's a hangnail.*

"At the temple of the seated statues. She visited me there."

"What did she say?"

K'tanu looked out across the water. "It would be hard for you to believe."

Chris pulled the jawbone out of his pocket, holding it up. "Actually, it wouldn't."

K'tanu smiled, then closed his eyes. "It spoke to you. Good."

"I haven't told anyone until now, but . . ."

"But now you understand why I am here."

Chris nodded and they both looked out across the darkness of Lake Victoria.

〰〰〰

They flew past Kilimanjaro, its crumbled summit wreathed in black smoke, the famous white glaciers long since melted away. The lava on its southern slope glowed a smoky red. Cloudburst brought Ron along with her on this leg, afraid that if she left him behind, he wouldn't come when it was his turn. Wolfe was waiting back in Dar. She knew Wolfe's sense of duty would prevail; Ron was another story.

Ahead, the dome of Mt. Meru jutted up through the clouds. On her lap was her pistol, which she'd taken out of her knapsack, along with the blue ULPA mask. The pilot had not said one word since they left Dar two hours ago, and that was fine. Ron, too, was quiet in the back seat, his mask on, surgical gloves pulled up over a long-sleeved shirt. Even his pant legs were duct-taped to his boots.

I'm coming, Cate, thought Cloudburst, rubbing her finger lightly across the gun's trigger. The land below, visible occasionally through the clouds, was marbled with jungle and empty spaces. Even a campfire would be a beacon. There were no more tourists in Tanzania. The wildebeests migrated to Kenya and back without an audience, except for stalking lions. She smiled, feeling the coolness of the gun in her hand. *I am hunting you, Cate.*

Mwanza sat on a rocky hill rising above the southern lake shore, a city of thousands of dirty brown shacks. The ferry navigated between large tumbles of exposed granite boulders in the bay. When they got off the boat, Cate was again surprised to see that no one wore masks. She was glad; she didn't want to put hers on, and neither did Chris. Perhaps Cobalt had finally gone to ground. She hoped it hadn't mutated, becoming dangerous, even for K'tanu. But she knew he would not wear a mask, regardless.

She had already been warned by Chris when she first saw K'tanu's face this morning. Chris said the mummy had similar scars under his eyes, three rows of wavy lines, more evidence that K'tanu was who he said he was—not just a man who shared the mummy's DNA, but the soul who had lived in both bodies at different times, for neither of them was born with the scars.

Chris wanted to tell Cate about his vision atop Jebel Barkal, but something held him back. Cate would want details, and in the telling, he might lose the mystery of it, which still burned strongly in his heart but at the same time felt delicate and fragile.

K'tanu's friend Hazari returned, indicating that they should follow him. Cate and Chris carried the body bag. K'tanu walked ahead with Hazari gently leading him along by the elbow. Cate noted the physical similarity between the two men. "I just hope he doesn't file his teeth down," she said, grimacing.

Chris shook his head. "He'll do what he'll do. And we won't have a thing to say about it."

Hazari knew a man who would rent them a Land Rover—sell was more like it, when Chris heard the price. But they had money. The priest in Matamoros told Lomax that dollars were still used in Africa, where many Disciples of Osiris went after the American Cobalt outbreak. Vasquez had handed K'tanu several handfuls of bills, which he had used as padding in his backpack around the precious alabaster jar.

They paid the seller and got a tank of diesel and two full gas cans, which they lashed to the rear bumper. They placed the mummy in back, along with food they got at the market: more ugali, flatbread, fruit, and, surprisingly, a stringy, tough meat that looked and tasted a lot like beef jerky. "Pelele," said Hazari, making an eating gesture.

"What is it?" asked Chris, afraid to swallow the mouthful he'd been testing. Hazari stretched his arms out, made flapping motions, then extended one arm out in front, moving it slowly.

"Elephant?" asked Cate.

"Elephant!" said Hazari, then making a small gesture, his hands close together.

Chris laughed. "Hyrax! It's a small animal, actually a cousin to the elephant. And it tastes pretty good."

"Preety good," repeated Hazari.

K'tanu sat on a stack of tires, winded from their walk from the dock. In the bright sunlight, he looked faded and ashen. The bloody cuts under his eyes were black, covered with the dust that blanketed everything in Mwanza. Cate winced at the thought of infection he was risking. However, when Hazari saw the cuts, he pointed at his own armband tattoo, saying, "Ndugu, K'tanu! Masaai ndugu!"

"Yes," said K'tanu, somehow understanding the term. "We are brothers."

T H I R T Y - T W O

SAFARI

Their first glimpse of the Serengeti was lit by the rising sun, which turned the sky from lavender to pink to flame blue. Undulating brown plains rolled toward the Rift uplands far to the east. Serengeti is a translation of *siringet*, a Swahili word that means "endless expanse," and from their vantage point, the name certainly seemed apropos. Thousands of moving beasts shimmered in the distance like a heat mirage. Giant granite outcroppings, or *koppies*, dotted the plain, surrounded by forests of umbrella-like acacia and spindly fever trees.

"Something's different," said Chris. "The elephants are gone."

"How can you tell?" asked Cate.

"Decades ago, elephants were forced into the park by human settlement, and they destroyed the young acacia groves, creating an emptier plain. But now, without people, the elephants have gone back to their old habitat, and woods are growing on the savanna again."

K'tanu had insisted on sitting up front so he could see better. He let out a cry when he saw the first white-tailed bushbuck, or "kudu," as Chris called it. It bounded across a meadow, then disappeared into a forest of stately, broad-leafed croton trees. K'tanu made Chris stop the Rover. He got out, bent down, and smelled some purple flowers sprouting nearby. He even examined a pile of fresh dung. When he got back in, he said, "Wildebeest," and leaned back, smiling.

The road wove between groves of olive, cedar, and cactus-like euphobia trees. When they cleared the trees, and the expanse of plain opened up before them, they saw rising columns of fluffy cumulus clouds, tops flattened by stratospheric winds, creating the familiar anvil shape. Within minutes, a deafening rain was pounding on the uninsulated truck roof. They watched the gossamer curtains of rain move across the distant landscape, and when first shafts of sunlight poked through, producing a double rainbow, tears sprang to K'tanu's eyes.

By that evening, they reached the park headquarters at Seronera, a collection of single-story concrete structures built to resemble cylindrical, conical-roofed native huts. A herd of black-tailed Thomson's gazelles grazed on the long brown grass between the empty buildings. By now, the sun was setting, shrouded in clouds, the sky changing from red to orange to indigo. A giraffe nibbled leaves from a tall acacia tree. The nearby gazelles took no notice when the visitors spread out their blankets and Chris fired up the propane stove for dinner.

"I wish I could hunt," said K'tanu, sharpening a stick, "but I'm too old now."

Cate looked at the gazelles. "You could probably walk right up to one and pet it."

"I wasn't talking about hunting *them*," said K'tanu.

Cate was afraid to ask what he *was* talking about.

Awakened by distant thunder, Cate expected to see clouds, but the night sky was clear. The moon perched on the western horizon. Her watch said it was about five in the morning. They had camped next to the Rover. The air was still very warm. Chris slept next to her. Beyond him she saw K'tanu on his back, his chest rising and falling rhythmically, also asleep.

Then she noticed that the gazelles were gone, and fear tickled her stomach. She scanned the darkness and saw a pair of yellow eyes in a thornbush. She got up on her elbows to see better, and the eyes looked at her. The thicket was only fifty feet away. She realized the thunder that awakened her was gazelle hooves beating a retreat. The golden eyes in the bushes blinked, and then a black shape emerged. It was a lioness, two hundred pounds at least. Cate held her breath, knowing she was probably giving off waves of fear hormones. The lion moved slowly forward, her eyes never leaving Cate. Cate wanted to wake Chris, but she couldn't even swallow, much less move. She looked over where K'tanu was sleeping. He was gone. Cate felt a sudden, warm wetness between her legs. Did the smell of urine draw a predator or chase it away? No one had ever taught her that all-important fact.

Just then she heard a low, throaty growl. The lioness's head swiveled toward some bushes at the clearing's edge. They shook with movement. The lioness froze, intent on the ticket. There was another low grumble, sounding huge and dangerous. The lioness squinted at the bushes for a few moments, then turned away and loped into the darkness.

Cate leaned her head back against the Rover fender, her heart racing. After a few moments, she saw K'tanu come out of the very bushes the growls came from. She jumped up and ran to him. "Did you see it?" she whispered hoarsely. "It must have been huge!"

K'tanu held the sharpened stick, the one he'd been working on over dinner. "She is gone now."

"But there's something over there!" whispered Cate, pointing at the bushes. "It sounded *big*."

K'tanu smiled. "It was supposed to."

"That was you?"

"I was a rhino. *Zangara*." He led her over to the truck, and they sat down a short distance from Chris, who still snored quietly.

Cate looked at K'tanu for a long time. "I'm glad you're here."

He looked off into the darkness, satisfaction in his eyes. "So am I."

〰〰〰

K'tanu told her he would stand guard, but there was no sleep in her, so they watched the dawn arrive together. When the first rays of the sun slanted across the plain, Cate broke camp quickly, insisting on driving. She didn't tell Chris about the lioness until they were several miles down the road.

He shook his head. "I must have been really tired to not have heard that."

"That's what's so amazing," said Cate. "The whole thing was almost silent. The lioness didn't make a sound. I never heard K'tanu get up. And when he grunted, she thought he was a rhino and disappeared without making a sound. I had no idea death was so quiet."

K'tanu sat up in front with Cate, his eyes on the horizon. The road was a faint dirt track across the savanna. They passed tree-tufted koppies where male lions lazed in the sun. An immense, shifting black shape in the distance became a herd of wildebeest. "They are early," said K'tanu. "The rest of the herd trails behind, returning to the south. See the calves?"

Scattered among the wildebeest were zebras and antelope, making the journey in the safety of numbers. A hyena loped across the road, a wildebeest haunch clamped in its jaws. A brace of black and white vultures circled overhead. Soon, even the grass gave out, and the plain became parched and cracked. The track disappeared and they drove down into a shallow gully.

"I recognize this!" exclaimed K'tanu. "There were woods when I lived here, and the animals used to come along this river bottom."

Cate stopped and he got out, looking out across the empty land. "There was a river here. I recognize that," he said, pointing at a nearby koppie. "It is just as it was; the furthest west I'd ever been. I was hunting with my father." He shucked his shirt, fell to his knees and raised his hands, speaking words of a language no one on earth spoke or understood except him.

When they stopped for lunch and the clouds of buzzing blowflies drove Chris and Cate back into the truck, K'tanu simply whisked them away with a wildebeest tail he'd removed from a carcass they had passed. He replaced the silver chain holding the ankh symbol around his neck with a sinew from the same dead wildebeest, and even brought back a piece of bloody meat, reacting in alarm when Chris suggested cooking it. "It is the brains," he said. "You don't cook them."

They passed a suburb of tall, conical termite mounds where snarling jackals had taken up residence. To the east, beyond the veil of late-afternoon clouds, the collapsed volcano of Ngorongoro awaited the arrival of its oldest native son. Lightning lit the clouds, and distant thunder echoed dully across the empty plain.

The SatPhone rang again, and this time she got to it before it stopped ringing. "Cloudburst."

"Dr. Cloudburst?" came a distant, tinny voice. "It's Corporal Jennings. Can you hear me?"

"I hear you. Speak slowly and clearly. What is it?"

"Something that might help. Something in your files."

"What is it?" asked Cloudburst, gripping the phone tightly.

"That name, McFadden. The guy Tempest knew."

"Al McFadden, yes," said Cloudburst. "What about him?"

There was a long, whining shriek. She pulled the phone away from her ear.

". . . he was there," Jennings was saying.

"Was *where*?"

"Where you are, right?"

"Say again!" shouted Cloudburst. "What did McFadden say?"

"He was around there," said Jennings. "Where you are now."

"Say the place! The *place*."

"He did research with Tempest at Olduvai Gorge."

Cloudburst hung up. "I know where they are."

It was nearing sunset when they passed a weathered sign pointing to Lake Ndutu, a dry alkaline salt flat. "We're almost there," said Chris, who had taken over driving. The shadow of the Rover stretched out before them. The light had taken on a dull orange quality, muting all colors. The air was muggy and still. They topped a rise and saw the road angle across a shallow, rock-strewn depression. "Olduvai Gorge," said Chris.

"The Valley of Bones," whispered K'tanu, his eyes wide.

They rumbled down the hill and entered the depression, crossing a trickle of water before going up the far slope. As it ran south, the gorge grew deeper, alternating bands of light volcanic ash and dark sediment slicing across the strata.

They crossed a peninsula of flat land between two tributary canyons. Chris stopped the truck. "This was the Leaky's camp." He got out and walked to the edge of the gorge, now filling up with shadow. "There's a plaque down there where they found the oldest human, *Homo habilis*, two million years old. And further south," he said, pointing beyond the gorge, "Mary Leaky found footprints in petrified ash that were 3½ million years old."

"There are many bones here," said K'tanu.

"Millions of years worth," added Chris.

"The diviners always warned us to stay away from here," said K'tanu. "I only came here once. It wasn't my choice."

Gray clouds formed a wall on the eastern horizon. When the last light had drained from the sky, K'tanu stood. "I will show you," he said, taking his newly-made spear and picking his way down into the gorge. Chris and Cate followed. Little had changed in Olduvai in millennia. Millions of years ago, the earliest hominids had lived along a small river that carved the gorge. Volcanos to the east laid down layers of white ash, sealing the bones of the dead forever in the dry ground.

The moon rose above the clouds, lighting their way. Its full face was brilliant, pock-marked with silent, dry seas, not so different from the land they stood upon. They walked along the sandy gorge bottom, following the sandy course of the seasonal spring, now dry. K'tanu limped ahead, using his spear as a staff. After a half hour, he stopped and sat on a rock. As Cate and Chris approached, they saw he was sweating profusely, even though they'd been walking downhill. He pointed at the gentle slope across from them. "There," he croaked, winded.

"How do you know?" asked Chris.

"That stone." K'tanu pointed at a granite boulder a few yards up the slope. It was mostly hidden by scrub, but quartz crystals glittered on its surface. "It's smaller now, but it's the same stone. I found the mandible next to it."

Chris looked around. He knew the gorge well. Young paleontologists were required to memorize its layout before they were trusted with a shovel. The Leakeys found "George," a *homo habilis* skull, in a side gully a hundred yards further down. They had already passed Bed II, where "Cinderella," a woman's partial cranium, was found. But they never dug in this spot. Chris stepped across the dry riverbed and climbed up to the boulder. The remarkable thing about Olduvai was that some of the most amazing discoveries had been found right out in the open, exposed when a flash flood scoured the gorge. He reached into his pocket and removed the mandible, holding it up in the moonlight. Then he scooped out a bit of dirt by the boulder and tucked the bone into the depression, covering it over.

"What are you doing?" asked Cate.

"I don't need it anymore," said Chris. "It belongs here, with the other bones."

K'tanu nodded in agreement.

"Why? Did it speak to you?" asked Cate. "When?"

"Jebel Barkal." Chris crossed back to them.

"What did it *say*?"

He put his arm around her and whispered, "To believe."

"Believe what?"

"I think that's part of my journey, to find out."

They turned and walked back toward the Rover. Above them, the Milky Way mirrored the path of the gorge, its precious jewels glittering in dark, eternal canyons.

THIRTY-THREE

NGORONGORO CRATER

The Rover followed the narrow dirt road eastward in the darkness, climbing until they were almost a thousand feet above the Serengeti. In front of them, the jagged caldera rim was backlit by the coming dawn. On either side of the caldera, dead volcanos thrust upward into low-lying clouds, a reminder that this whole section of the Rift was volcanic. At one time, Ngorongoro soared to a height of fifteen thousand feet—Kilimanjaro's smaller sister.

When they emerged on the rim, the sun had just broken across the caldera. A fever-tree forest dominated the southern quarter of the crater, the Mandusi swamp the north. In the middle of the crater, the mist on Lake Magadi shifted, its brilliant pink pupil of thousands of flamingo glittering. East of the lake, wildebeest herds moved across grasslands which ran to the foot of the sheer eastern wall, miles away.

They got out of the truck and walked to the rim, which fell off precipitously. K'tanu dropped to his knees, overcome. "Ngoro," he said reverently. He tried to unzip his backpack, but his arthritic fingers would not bend. He turned, his face pinched in frustration. Cate unzipped the pack and handed the alabaster jar to him. He held it up, catching the sun in its polished surface. "Father Sun!" he cried hoarsely. "My sacrifice!"

Something glinted on the far rim, catching Chris's eye. He thought it was probably a reflection off the tall windows of the Sopa Lodge, where McFadden and his men fought off the Maasai. Something else, though. The sun was *behind*—

K'tanu got to his feet and turned. "Thank you," he said, tears in his eyes.

Cate buried her head in his chest, tears spilling onto her cheeks.

Chris, too, was overcome. "Thank you, K'tanu," he said. "We'll never forget—"

"No! No!" said Cate, pulling back and pointing. "Look!"

Emerging from the clouds on the eastern rim was a small aircraft. The reflection! Cate lifted her binoculars. "It's an airplane," she said. "It's turning this way!"

Even without the binoculars, Chris could see the plane change course. "Cloudburst."

"What do we do?" asked Cate.

"Go. Now," said K'tanu.

"But we're not there yet," said Chris. "We were going to take you to the tomb."

"I will cross the caldera myself."

"It's twenty miles!" said Cate. "It's too far!"

"I will make it *if* you lead them away."

Chris looked at K'tanu. He was right. If they continued eastward along the southern rim, the plane would land at the Serena Lodge airstrip and intercept them. If they headed away now, Cloudburst might think they had just stopped at the crater to take a look.

"Chris!" cried Cate. "What do we do?"

"I know a place." He turned to K'tanu. "You can make it by yourself?"

"I must." He took Chris's hand and held it in both of his.

Chris felt K'tanu's bony hands and remembered. "I'll get him." He went to the rear of the Rover.

Cate shook her head. "No, K'tanu. You can't even make it yourself, much less carry . . . *him*."

K'tanu picked up the backpack and put it on. "You are loved," he said to Cate, nodding toward Chris, who was pulling the mummy out of the Rover. "Show him the same."

Cate nodded. "In Lightland, then? Will we see you?"

"Not for many years, I hope."

She hugged him. Chris came over, bearing the mummy, which he'd removed from the body bag. "It's lighter this way." He handed it K'tanu, frowning when he saw how something weighing so little bent K'tanu's back so severely.

"Now go!" commanded K'tanu. Chris had to drag Cate away. K'tanu raised his chin and nodded gravely.

On the far rim they saw a flash of light. "Something moved!" shouted Cloudburst.

"I told you to stay in the clouds," said Wolfe. "Or come down out of the sun. Shit." He started fiddling with his gun.

Ron looked from Wolfe to Cloudburst. "What moved?"

They had banked away from the mist-shrouded rim, and were now were two thousand feet above the crater floor. Mist spilling into the caldera like a waterfall hid the western rim for a moment. Cloudburst raised her binoculars. Another glint of light. A windshield, catching the sun? *Flight is a sure sign of fear*. She nodded at the pilot. "Follow them."

Its engine straining, the plane skimmed across the rim directly over the tree K'tanu was hiding under, so low he could read its tail number. The dust still hung in the air from the fleeing Land Rover. The plane disappeared, following the exterior crater slope.

K'tanu picked up the mummy and slowly got to his feet, his back crying out in pain. A narrow, rocky path led down from the rim, soon swallowed up by the jungle. He started down it, keeping his eye on the far crater wall, knowing if he could make it there, his journey would be over.

⋀⋀⋀

Where the slope leveled out somewhat, Chris jumped the Rover off the road, heading overland. The plane had not yet appeared above the rim. Cate kept a lookout, hoping and yet not hoping to see it.

"There they are!" she shouted.

The plane appeared in the sky where they had parted with K'tanu.

"Do they see us? Are they following?"

"I don't know."

Chris slammed on the brakes, raising a cloud of dust. The plane corrected course, turning in their direction.

"They see us now," said Cate, rubbing her forehead. She had bumped it on the dash when Chris braked.

Chris stomped on the gas, hoping there were no big gullies ahead or they'd be killed, as fast as he was going.

"There's a road down there," said Cate, pointing. "We can make better time!"

Chris shook his head. "We don't *want* to make better time. We want to keep them chasing us as long as possible." A big bump sent them airborne, and they landed so hard Chris slammed his forehead against the steering wheel. Dazed for a moment, the Rover almost rolled but Cate grabbed the wheel, righting them. Chris gripped the steering wheel again.

"I guess we're even," said Cate, noticing that the cut on Chris's forehead had opened and was bleeding. "Where are we going?"

"Believe it or not: Disneyland."

CROSSROADS

"What are they doing?" asked Ron, watching the Land Rover bounding across the caldera flank ahead of them.

"They can't get away," said Wolfe. "We're twice as fast as a car."

Cloudburst looked at her map. "There's nothing this way. The Gorge is back there." She pointed out the pilot's window.

"We can't get to them up here," said Wolfe. "We've got to land. How much fuel do we have?"

"Plenty," said Cloudburst, looking at the gauge. "We can chase them for another hour before we have to turn back."

"That's too long," said Wolfe, driving his elbow into the window, popping it out, sending a blast of wind into the airplane. Cloudburst's map got plastered onto Ron's face. The pilot shouted. Wolfe jammed his gun against the man's neck. "Just fly."

"What are you doing?" said Ron, peeling the map away.

Wolfe poked the gun out the window, steadying it against the prop blast. "My job."

The shot ricocheted off the hood as the plane screamed past them. Chris instinctively ducked. The Cessna banked steeply, turning back.

Chris turned to Cate, a question on his face.

"Yes, I saw *North by Northwest*," she said. "Now drive!"

To their right were the sloping, gullied flanks of several dormant volcanos. To their left was the flat Serengeti plain. They were jouncing across short, dried grass, a fairly level road not fifty yards down the slope to their left. Cate pointed and Chris nodded, jumping a berm at the roadside and landing on its washboard surface with a crash. Cate's seat, loosened early on, broke loose from its moorings. She braced her feet against the firewall. "Here they come!" she shouted.

The aircraft had turned sharply and was diving straight for them. Chris saw an arm sticking out a side window and a muzzle flash. Before he even heard the sound, he veered off the road again, and the plane careened past so close they could smell its exhaust. Chris got back on the road. "He's gonna hit us one of these times." Behind them, the plane was extending its flaps, slowing, and starting to turn back.

"How slow can they go?" shouted Cate.

"To about twice as fast as we're going," said Chris, glancing at the speedometer. "Why?"

"Can they land on us?"

"That's not in the movie," said Chris, dodging a boulder, straightening their path again, the rear end fish-tailing. The road was hardpan and raised little dust. An idea struck him and he turned decisively into the soft shoulder, sending a plume of fine brown dirt high into the air. Suddenly, the plane behind them disappeared and Cate cheered. "Is that in the movie?"

Chris thought about the crop duster diving into the pesticide cloud and crashing into the fuel truck, but when the Cessna emerged unscathed from the cloud, he shook his head angrily. "No."

The gunshots echoed off the caldera walls and K'tanu looked up. It was only a matter of time before Chris and Cate were caught. He tried not to think about the price they would pay. He had to be worthy of it, so he moved ahead as best he could, stumbling down the steep game trail.

When he finally emerged from the undergrowth, scratched and weary, the rolling caldera floor opened up before him. Mist still hovered above the lake. Directly in front of him was a small stand of trees where, if things had not changed, a spring still bubbled. He trudged under the candelabra trees, called *tomvu* by his people, their curved, uplifted arms covered with tiny, waxy green leaves, good for burns. He laid his burden down next to the pool, noticing that coming down the slope, one of the mummy's feet had caught on something and had been nearly torn off. He grimaced. It was his own foot he'd nearly lost.

He pulled out his pocket knife and cut a circle of cloth from his pant leg, wrapping it around the foot to secure it. Suddenly, he was struck in a way he had not been since he first saw the mummy in the Yucca Mountain catacombs. This was *his* body. He sat back on his haunches and pondered it. It gave off a bitter, tangy odor. The Russell part of him, the part that rarely emerged now except to translate, asked him if he was insane. He shook the thought away and gripped the silver ankh at his neck, then bent and drank from the spring. The water was brackish, but still refreshing.

When K'tanu emerged from the trees, he found himself standing on the mud flats surrounding the lake. When he'd last hunted here, during the rainy season before the Bleeding Sickness came, the lake had filled a good portion of the caldera. Now, approaching summer, the lake was half that size. On its southern shore, waterbuck, bushbuck, and eland drank furtively, keeping a lookout for predators. As he trudged across the cracked, muddy flats, he heard crashing in the Lerai forest to the south—elephants uprooting small trees. Out in the middle of the shallow lake, thousands of flamingo basked in the morning sun.

As he took each slow, burdened step, he wondered what he would do if he saw a lion or a jackal, or worse, if they saw him. He could not run. He'd stupidly left his makeshift spear in the Rover. All he had was a pocket knife. So as he trudged along, he kept one eye on the grazing animals. They would see a predator long before he did.

At the lake edge, he knelt, holding the body in his lap, his aching spine popping as he bent. Sweat ran into his eyes. The wrapping on the mummy's foot had loosened and it hung by a sinew thread. He squeezed his eyes shut, almost as disgusted at his dead body as he was with his living one, so old and weak, so ready to quit, to fall face first into the mud and die.

He looked east, where mist still shrouded the crater wall. He knew exactly where the tomb was: left of a great, forested arm that flowed down to the crater floor. When he was last there as a young man, he could have trotted the remaining distance easily. Now he would be lucky if he made it at all. He looked up at Father Sun, who knew the day's outcome already—only K'tanu was in doubt.

"What the hell are you *doing*?" shouted Cloudburst, grabbing Wolfe's arm. He batted her away. She was practically in the pilot's lap, the plane banking steeply left, throwing them all to one side.

"Stop it!" yelled Ron, pressed against Wolfe's shoulder. Wolfe elbowed him sharply. Ron grabbed his nose as blood cascaded down his face.

Wolfe squeezed off another shot. "Aiming for the tires," he shouted, putting a hand in Cloudburst's face and pushing her back.

"You'll hit Russell!" she screamed.

Wolfe pulled the gun inside. They'd passed the car and the pilot was turning back again, lowering the flaps to slow them, suddenly throwing them forward as the plane lost speed. "I thought you didn't care what happened to him," said Wolfe.

"If you have to shoot somebody," spat Cloudburst, "shoot yourself, asshole!"

Wolfe clenched his jaw. He had orders from Samuel Fox. When they had the kid, all bets were off. *Then I'll frag this shrew and get out of this shithole.* But for now, he still needed her. He nodded mildly at Cloudburst. "Sorry."

THIRTY-FIVE

OL DOINYO LENGAI

"Maybe they're out of bullets," said Chris.

"No, they're wondering how far we're going," said Cate. "They don't know how much gas we have. And they can't land just anywhere."

They were a fifteen miles north of the crater by now. They had passed two small collapsed volcanos—calderas like Ngorongoro. Ahead of them, an immense cone filled the horizon, its white, flattened top smoking.

Cate looked at Chris, dismayed. "You are not."

"No choice. We've got to get back to the highlands."

Cate looked at the volcano, its brown slopes eroded with deep gullies, white froth spilling down the western flank like runny cake icing. "What's it called?"

"Ol Doinyo Lengai. Maasai for 'Mountain of God.'"

Cate nodded. "Well, that sounds as good a place to die as any."

K'tanu plodded across the grassland, following a game trail that for thousands of years had run from the river in the north end of the caldera to the Blue-Eyed Sea in the center. The caldera was still full of wildlife, and even though he suffered in the hot sun—his back aching, head pounding, tongue swollen—he smiled through cracked lips. Wildebeest were still abundant, as were buffalo, zebra, rhino, tsesseba, and gazelle. In the distance, grass moved, shielding predators: lions, leopards, jackals, and wild dogs. He hadn't seen any yet because most of them hunted at night. An eagle soared overhead. Ahead, high up in a grizzled thorn tree, two buzzards sat, their beaks white in the sun. It was afternoon, and thunderclouds had begun to gather, raised by the heat and moisture of the crater. Shadows flitted across the waving grass.

As he crested a rise, K'tanu stopped. Not a mile in front of him, standing alone in a sea of yellow oat grass, was the Lightning Tree, its dusty green canopy suspended by spindly limbs, just like the pictures he'd painted from his dreams.

An hour later, he was standing under the acacia. He lay the mummy down, dropping his backpack as well. There was a flash of lightning, and thunder rumbled across the caldera. He could still make out the far crater wall and the green shoulder of land. It was only a few hours away. He limped out under the darkening sky and knelt, touching his forehead to the ground, his arms stretched out before him, palms up. More thunder, and then warm rain splashed on his bare back. Soon the ground around him was puffing dirt as the heavy drops struck the parched earth.

"Shit!" said Cloudburst, looking through the binoculars. "There's a road!"

Wolfe grabbed the glasses and looked for himself. "Where?"

"To the right. It winds around the back." She nudged the pilot. "Circle it."

Sure enough, as they rounded the volcano, they saw a dirt switchback snaking up the steep eastern slope. The Rover was raising clouds of dust as it climbed toward the summit.

"We gotta land," said Cloudburst.

"And do what?" said Ron. "Chase them on foot?"

Cloudburst folded the map. "You need the exercise anyway, fat boy."

ʌʌʌ

Chris lowered the glasses. They'd stopped well up the volcano's slope. "Good. They're landing." He handed the binoculars to Cate, who looked. Below them, on a flat stretch of grassland east of the volcano, the Cessna was touching down.

"So what?" said Cate. "They don't have a car. We've got plenty of food. We can wait them out. They're not going to climb the volcano on foot."

"No, they're not," said Chris. "Look to the left."

Cate raised the glasses again. There was a group of buildings, a farm house, a barn, and an old rusty flatbed truck. "I see the truck, but I'll bet it doesn't run."

"Look in the corral behind the buildings."

Cate squinted. "Damn." She lowered the glasses. "Horses."

"So what is it, a mule or a donkey?" asked Ron.

"Who cares?" said Cloudburst, throwing the ratty blanket over the animal. "It's got four legs and a strong back." She looked up at the volcano. "From the looks of the road up there, they can't go much faster than we can."

Wolfe was standing by the fence with his arms folded. "Hasn't this gone on long enough?"

Cloudburst turned. "We've chased them halfway cross the world. I'm not stopping now."

"Let's get a chopper," said Wolfe. "We could land on the summit and wait for them there."

"And while we're gone, they'll get away," said Cloudburst. "Besides, we don't have time."

"Why not?"

"Because he's dying," said Ron flatly. "The kid. He's dying."

"How do you know?" asked Wolfe.

Cloudburst climbed onto the donkey, adjusting her backpack. "You know about killing things, Wolfe. Let us worry about keeping them alive. Hah!" She struck the donkey's flank and it started off toward the volcano.

The dirt track finally gave out, reduced to a rutted path. Cate got out, looking up. The summit smoked, but she didn't hear any explosions. She'd once stood near the Kilauea magma vent in Hawaii, watching the red sprays arc into the tropical night sky, recoiling from the deafening sound and fierce heat. But this volcano was silent except for the whistle of a warm breeze. There weren't any lava flows either, at least on this side of the volcano. She remembered the white frosting on the western slope. "Chris," she said, "what kind of volcano is this anyway?"

"I was right," said Chris, looking through the binoculars. "They're following us on horseback." He looked at his watch. "It's after three. That's almost eight hours. I wonder where he is."

"He's closer," said Cate. The summit was only a few hundred yards above them. She patted his shoulder. "And so are we."

"Just a sec," said Cloudburst, looking through her binoculars. "The truck's stopped. The road must end there. They're on foot." She paused, still looking.

Ron was impatient. "What?"

Cloudburst handed the glasses to Ron, but Wolfe snatched them away, looking through them. Ron resisted the urge to shove Wolfe off the donkey and instead focused on Cloudburst, who was sitting, her arms folded, eyes downcast, frowning.

"What?" asked Ron.

Cloudburst spurred her mount forward. Wolfe lowered the glasses and handed them to Ron, who lifted them. He found the truck high on the volcano's slope. Beyond it, people were moving on foot. "They're carrying him," said Ron, lowering the binoculars. "Does that mean he's dead?"

Neither Wolfe or Cloudburst said anything; they just continued up the road.

~~~

"This makes no sense," said Chris, lugging the back end of the plastic body bag.

Cate trudged ahead, her back to him. "They have to see three of us, not just two."

"But why'd you put so much stuff in it? It weighs a ton."

"It has to look real. You can't just sling it over your shoulder like a coat from the cleaners."

"I could have *faked* carrying something heavy."

"You can't fake anything, Chris," laughed Cate. "Which is why I love you."

K'tanu stood at the base of the caldera slope. Now the hardest part would begin. He looked over his shoulder. Father Sun was just a few hours away from his own death. K'tanu needed to hurry if he was going to get to the top of the cliff by then. The rain clouds had moved west, toward the plains. He looked up. The defile before him was heavily wooded, but he had found an old game trail. It was narrow and rocky, and thorn bushes and nettles would scratch him bloody, but it went straight up to the rim. He looked back at the mummy lying on the ground. It was too heavy. He'd dropped it many times. The foot was nearly torn off and the entire corpse was covered with mud and dirt and glistened with his own sweat.

Perhaps he could leave it here and take its place nestled behind Maya's mummy. One body was as good as another, wasn't it? But if that were true, why then did his people make such an effort to mummify the dead? He didn't know; he was no diviner. The only way he could be sure he'd done right was if he awakened in Lightland. If he didn't, his soul would sleep forever in a coma and he would never see his beloved Maya again.

No, he would have to carry the heavy body up the steep slope. If he didn't make it—if he fell down and gave up, exhausted—he would never rise again. He bent and picked up his mummy, groaning, and took another step toward his own grave.

THIRTY-SIX

MOUNTAIN OF GOD

When they reached the summit, Cate momentarily forgot their predicament. They were surrounded by a smoking, white fairyland of immense lava sculptures. Eons ago, the volcano's top had blown off, leaving a bulging, white dome dotted with *hornitos*, tall spatter cones resembling the termite mounds they'd seen out on the Serengeti. Bubbling lakes of chocolate-colored magma spotted the landscape, draining into muddy brown rivers that flowed to the edge of the sloping, flattened summit. All around them, steam rose from vents, enveloping everything with a white, sparkling vapor.

"*This* is a volcano?" asked Cate.

"I was here once before," said Chris. "The magma is mostly calcium carbonate."

Cate turned to him. "That's laundry soap."

"Hot laundry soap—half the temperature of basalt lava."

They walked between hornitos and bubbling lava pools. Cate heard a distant, rhythmic *thump! thump! thump!* "What's that?" she asked, peering into the steam cloud.

Chris led her along a path of crumbling, white, rain-eroded lava, soft and crunchy underfoot. Indeed, the whole dome seemed as delicate as spun sugar. They rounded a hornito with a collapsed side.

The thumping was the regular popping of a large magma bubble inside the hornito cone, resonating off the chamber walls.

"And what's this?" asked Cate. An immense sculpture, an arc of what looked like molten silver, rose from a spatter cone, frozen in midair. Cate stared, then reacted when fingertips of lava began breaking off the arc, striking the ground, tinkling like breaking glass.

"Stand back," said Chris, pulling her away.

Just then, the entire fifteen-foot curve of lava shattered, sending shards flying. A piece struck Cate's shin, and she yelped, jumping back. "What *is* this place?"

"It's one of a kind," said Chris. "The lava starts out almost black, then turns gray and white as it cools, all within forty-eight hours."

"Is it safe to walk on?"

"If it's solid. If it isn't, you'll disappear into an eight-hundred-degree milk shake."

Ron had fallen behind. Cloudburst had given him the biggest donkey, since he was the heaviest, but his mount had stopped a half mile back and would not go another step. Ron trudged up the dirt road, head down. Cloudburst turned to Wolfe, who rode next to her, checking his gun. "Put that away," she hissed. "Plenty of time for that, if they're not reasonable."

"And this guarantees they will be," said Wolfe flatly.

The trail gave out when it reached the summit. "What if they're armed?" she asked.

"Then we shoot them, or they shoot us, or we shoot each other. Think happy thoughts."

"Maybe we should wait until dark."

Wolfe looked at the smoke billowing into the sky. A few hundred feet below, clouds had moved in, surrounding the volcano summit in an ocean of white. The sun was just three fingers above the horizon, glimmering redly across the cloud floor. "I don't want to be on top of a volcano in the dark," he said. "Let's finish this and go home."

They reached the summit. Dozens of hornitos cast long shadows across the dome and a thick blanket of steam hung over everything. They heard distant drumming. "It's not too big—maybe a hundred meters across," whispered Cloudburst. "Not many places to hide."

"If they're still up here," said Wolfe, his gun drawn, moving forward.

"Where would they go?" asked Cloudburst.

Their path led across crunchy, dried magma flows. They jumped across a steaming, muddy brown lava river. Cloudburst adjusted her backpack. Her gun was inside, in case she needed it.

From their aerial circuit of the summit, Cloudburst knew their quarry would be crazy to try and descend by any route other than the one by which they came up. They were up here, hiding behind one of those tall, smoking, white anthills. The thumping continued, and here and there, magma erupted from the taller cones, spattering the ground with a sound that made Cloudburst think of wet rags hurled onto cement. At the far end of the sloping plateau, a sheared-off brown hill marked the volcano's highest point.

Wolfe moved forward, holding his pistol with both hands, muzzle down, squinting into the steam that completely surrounded them.

Seeing how quickly Wolfe's shape became vague just a few feet in front of her, Cloudburst knew they'd never surprise Cate and the others. They'd had several hours to get to know the summit. They were probably watching them right now, and if they wanted, they could probably kill them both—if they had the nerve. She stopped and raised her hands to her mouth. "Cate!" she called.

Wolfe whirled around, frowning.

"Cate!" she called, louder. There was no answer.

Wolfe gave her a "what did you expect?" look and started forward again. They picked their way along the edge of a pool of bubbling brown lava. Beyond it, three large hornitos were clustered tightly together. Suddenly, the middle one erupted, spewing lava fifty feet into the air. They quickly retreated to avoid the falling globs of magma. Wolfe brushed a steaming gob off his forearm with his other sleeve, grimacing in pain. Then he froze, pointing at the hornitos.

Near the base of one of them, the body bag lay in a crumpled heap. Wolfe crossed to it, then gestured at two sets of footprints leading around the rear of the hornitos. He raised his gun and moved forward, followed by a wary Cloudburst. A rhythmic, low-frequency pulse came from one of the cones. They peered inside an irregular hole in the cone flank and saw a magma bubble expand and then pop with a rich, throaty *galumph*.

"What do you want?" came a voice.

They turned. Cate stood on the far side of the lava pool, barely visible through pillars of rising steam.

"Where's Russell?" said Cloudburst.

"He's with Chris, who has a gun aimed at your head."

Cloudburst took a step and heard the sound of breaking glass. She looked down. Lava shards crunched underfoot, some sharp enough to cut through a boot. She smiled at Cate. "Oh, I don't think he'll shoot us."

"No?" said Cate. "He wants to get even with you for shooting at *us*."

Wolfe was scanning their surroundings for Chris, but the steam made it hard to see much in the failing light.

Cloudburst let out an exasperated sigh. "Believe me, Cate, no matter what else happens, I'm not leaving here without Russell."

"Dead or alive?" asked Cate flatly.

"I don't want to hurt him—I've known him longer than you have."

"And yet you have no idea who he really is."

"Then educate me." Cloudburst called, "Russell! It's Mama Cloudburst, honey. I've come to take you home! You want to go home, don't you?"

"He *is* home," said Cate.

Cloudburst turned to Wolfe. "I don't think Dr. Tempest has a gun, do you?"

Wolfe took aim at Cate. "Say the word, Doctor."

"Not so fast," came Chris's voice. "I will shoot."

"I doubt you could shoot yourself, much less us," said Cloudburst.

"I'm from Montana," said Chris. "Hunted all my life."

"Russell's not going back with you," said Cate. "Cobalt's over—gone to ground."

"Nonsense," said Cloudburst.

"We came all the way across the continent," said Cate, "and didn't see anyone with Cobalt."

"You're lying," said Cloudburst.

"She's not!" shouted Chris.

Wolfe finally thought he knew where Chris was. He took a step forward, catching Cloudburst's eye, nodding to their right. *Keep him talking*, he mouthed silently.

"What's your proof, Dr. Tempest?" asked Cloudburst, taking off her backpack. She might need her gun after all. Wolfe took another step forward, turning slightly to the right.

"Everywhere!" said Cate. Behind her, a large vent suddenly exploded, sending a spray of steam into the air, startling all of them.

"Russell!" shouted Cloudburst.

There was no answer.

"I just realized something," said Cloudburst, bending and picking up the body bag. "When we passed your truck, the mummy wasn't in it. Where is it? Where's Russell?"

"He's here," said Cate.

"No," said Cloudburst. "I don't think he's anywhere *near* here—he's at the caldera." She turned to Wolfe. "End it, now."

Wolfe swiveled his gun, squinting. The setting sun made it hard to see anything in the steam.

"Shoot!" said Cloudburst.

"Don't rush me," said Wolfe, waiting for movement.

All this time, Chris had been slowly creeping forward from his hiding spot behind a hornito. For a few terrifying moments, Wolfe had looked straight at him, but Chris had his white tee shirt pulled up over his head, and Wolfe's eyes had moved on. Chris was now just a few feet away. It would be easy to—

Suddenly, someone lunged past him, slamming into Wolfe, who stumbled at the edge of the lava pool, arms wheeling, then fell in, screaming. A huge cloud of steam rose as the scream died. When it cleared, Wolfe was gone. The brown surface of the pool churned.

"Ron!" shouted Cate.

Ron stood next to Cloudburst, chest heaving, his hands still out in front of him, as shocked as everyone else at what he'd done. "You all right, Cate?" he asked, squinting through the steam.

Cloudburst fumbled in her backpack. Ron turned, pulling a gun from his waistband "Looking for this?"

"Are you *insane*?" shouted Cloudburst. "Don't tell me *you* want to shoot her?"

"No, not her," said Ron, pointing the gun at Cloudburst.

Cloudburst took a step back. "What the *hell* is wrong with you?"

Ron glanced at Cate.

"You're kidding," said Cloudburst. She turned to Cate. "Seagram, are you seeing this?"

Chris appeared out of the steam, just a few feet from her. "That's enough."

Cloudburst shook her head. "What next? You two gonna arm-wrestle for her?"

"Shut up," said Ron, the gun trembling in his hand, still pointed at Cloudburst.

"Ron," said Chris. "Don't."

"Clear this up, Cate," said Cloudburst. "Are you in love with Ron?"

"I'm not doing this for her," said Ron.

"Well, are you?" shouted Cloudburst.

Cate didn't speak; she didn't know what to say.

"Hear that resounding affirmation, Ron?" said Cloudburst. "How does that make you feel?"

The steam parted and Cate finally saw Ron's face. Crushing agony filled his eyes.

Cloudburst shook her head in dismay. "Ron, you are the most pathetic loser on this entire planet."

Ron turned his attention to Cloudburst. The gun in his hand stopped shaking.

"No!" shouted Chris, lunging.

Ron squeezed the trigger and Cloudburst stumbled back. A red bloom appeared on her chest. She fell to a sitting position, a stunned look on her face. "But I'm the good guy," she said.

The ground rumbled, and the lava pool began to boil, spitting globs of magma into the air. Cate stepped back. Slowly, a great arm of lava arched from the pool, freezing in mid-arc. High on its uppermost curve was Wolfe's smoking body, encased in silver, red eyes like burning ball bearings, clawlike fingers stripped to the bone, clutching at the steaming, empty air.

Cate ran to Chris and buried her face in his shoulder.

THIRTY-SEVEN

THE BEGINNING OF THE WORLD

The red sun perched on the horizon. K'tanu crawled the last half-mile up the steep trail, dragging the mummy behind him. The damaged foot had finally torn loose and been lost. He had no strength to go back and look for it. He felt wetness on his upper lip and idly wondered if it was raining. But it was blood, dripping from his nose. He wiped it away, leaving a red streak on his dusty forearm.

Then he saw it: the gray boulder at the turn of the trail. He let go of the mummy and stumbled to his feet, his hands stretched out before him. The path was overgrown, but he pushed through. The tomb was open, the stone rolled to one side. Tears sprang to his eyes. If it had been sealed, he would not have been able to open it, not in his condition. He had also been worrying about the tomb's contents. In his time, enemies often raided tombs, hacking mummies to pieces, smashing heart jars and feeding the contents to dogs, stealing the scarab amulets, thereby denying the dead passage across the River of Death.

He took off the backpack and knelt, feeling the cave's coolness on his face. The sun's rays angled into the entrance, but his body blocked most of the light. He pulled vines aside and crawled inside, following the cramped passage as it turned to the right. As he made his way along, his hand touched something cold and hard: a rusty digging trowel. He continued forward, gouging his head on the low, uneven ceiling. When he touched the cut, he came away with tufts of brittle, bloody hair in his hand.

Finally, he reached his beloved Maya, whose mummy was spooned up behind N'kala's small one. The diggers had not disturbed them! Grateful tears welled in K'tanu's eyes as he ran his hands along Maya's mummy, feeling the bulge over her breast. Anja was bound tightly in her mother's arms. There was a depression in the earth behind Maya, where his own mummy once rested. He reached and found three stone jars at the head of the mummies. He looked back at the entrance. The sun's rays lit the ceiling with a faint, reddish light. Father Sun was dying in the lands beyond the caldera. He had to hurry.

He crawled out of the tomb and stood, nearly fainting with light-headedness. Everything seemed vague and insubstantial, as if he were already crossing over into Lightland. *Not yet!* he plead silently. *Not yet!*

He slowly made his way back to the mummy and began dragging it back to the tomb. It was incredibly heavy. He had to pull it forward a bit, rest, then pull it forward again. As he labored, the sky went from yellow to orange to blood red. Finally, bathed in sweat, he hauled the mummy the last few feet to the tomb entrance. His hands shook as he opened the backpack and pulled out the stone jar, peeling away the gray tape, removing the stopper, and tilting it down. The plastic bag tumbled onto the ground. He opened it and removed the heart. It was cold but soft, and blood—his blood—slicked his palms.

K'tanu turned to the sun and held his heart out, closing his eyes. "For you, Father," he murmured. As if in response, a distant peal of thunder echoed across the caldera.

He secured the heart in the jar, then rolled it into the cave. By now, the interior was only dimly lit. He crawled along the passageway, pushing the stone jar before him and pulling the mummy behind him.

At last, he hauled his mummy into position. Even in the poor light, he could see how mangled and filthy it was next to Maya's mummy. He dug into his pocket and withdrew the green scarab, tucking it into the wrappings under the crossed hands. He placed the dirty, scarred alabaster jar above the head, next to Maya's jar, then leaned back on his haunches. In the dim light, there were three mummies, his small family together once more, united forever. He bent forward and touched each body in turn. When he reached Maya's, he whispered, "In Lightland, my love."

K'tanu crawled out of the cave and got to his feet. He put his back to the entrance stone and pushed. Surprisingly, it moved. He gritted his teeth and pushed again. Miraculously, it rolled into place with a great *thud*, sealing the tomb. He pulled the vines back across the entrance and hobbled to the trail, beginning his slow, labored ascent to the rim.

He fell twice on the way up but refused to stop. When he finally reached the rim, his legs gave out and he collapsed on the ground. With one final effort, he raised himself to a seated position and looked out across the caldera. The last rays of the sun shone into his cloudy eyes. K'tanu looked over his shoulder. Mother Moon was rising majestically above the trees. Tonight, she would watch over both K'tanu and Father Sun as they died and awaited rebirth tomorrow.

K'tanu thought about Chris and Cate. *If you are still alive, may our next meeting be far in the future. If not, may we see each other today, in Lightland.*

As Father Sun slipped below the horizon, K'tanu held his hands out, palms up, eyes closed.

I am ready.

Epilogue

Blue Ridge Mountains, Virginia

2037 A.D.

MOTHER JANICE

They stood on the cracked asphalt road, facing the old faded clapboard house, barely visible behind the drooping cypress trees. The front yard was row after row of raised green mounds, a simple white cross atop each one. A shovel leaned against the porch, vines winding up the handle. It was May, and the yellow sun shone down on a quiet, green world.

They walked up the gravel drive. Cate carried a plastic bucket containing rubber gloves, bleach, and yard bags. They stopped in front of the porch. Kudzu lianas had woven themselves around the screen door, pulling the top hinge loose. It canted toward them, strangely welcoming.

"You're sure you want to do this?" asked Chris.

"A long time ago, she offered to help me," said Cate. "I want to return the favor."

"And you're not afraid?"

Cate smiled and took his hand in hers. "No. Not anymore."

Acknowledgments

The invaluable insights and gentle criticisms of a number of friends are undoubtedly the reason you have read far enough into this book to find this page. Therefore, their praises should be sung, and properly so, by the one who benefitted most from their help.

Various forms of the manuscript were read by Bonnie and Jeff Sheets, Doug Page, Bill and Lisa Hansen, Bill Conner, and Lissa Buchi. Each offered perfectly good advice on improving the book, some of which I was smart enough to take, all of which I considered carefully.

Reid Later did a masterful job of editing. His ability to correct and clarify without erasing my writing style is remarkable. Therefore, all errors herein are traceable only to me, which is how he likes it.

Bonnie Sheets and I struggled through almost a score of cover designs before we found the right one, and I am indebted to her patience and good cheer throughout the process. Douglas Page found and expertly photographed our model Kenzo, who was as good-hearted as he was good-looking.

Barry Reeder offered his wisdom from concept to marketing. If you picked this book out from among many others, Barry is undoubtedly the reason.

And finally, dear reader, thank you for taking a chance on a story that breaks all the rules of genre writing. I hope you enjoyed visiting *Lightland*. If you did, I am pleased beyond words. Suffice it to say, you are the reason I write.

Kenny Kemp

KENNY KEMP is an award-winning and best-selling author and filmmaker, whose memoir *Dad Was a Carpenter* won the Grand Prize in the 1999 National Self-Published Book Awards sponsored by *Writers' Digest* magazine. Shortly thereafter, he was signed by HarperCollins to write a multi-volume historical fiction series set in Judea at the time of Christ. He also runs his own publishing company and speaks at writers' conferences nationwide, encouraging new writers to find a way to get published. When not writing, he works as a contractor, practices law, and flies his private plane.

Visit him at his website: *www.kennykemp.com*